Just Desserts

Titles by Barbara Bretton

Just Desserts

Barbara Bretton

**Doubleday Large Print
Home Library Edition**

JOVE BOOKS, NEW YORK

THE BERKLEY PUBLISHING GROUP
Published by the Penguin Group
Penguin Group (USA) Inc.
375 Hudson Street, New York, New York 10014, USA
Penguin Group (Canada), 90 Eglinton Avenue East, Suite 700, Toronto, Ontario M4P 2Y3, Canada
(a division of Pearson Penguin Canada Inc.)
Penguin Books Ltd., 80 Strand, London WC2R 0RL, England
Penguin Group Ireland, 25 St. Stephen's Green, Dublin 2, Ireland (a division of Penguin Books Ltd.)
Penguin Group (Australia), 250 Camberwell Road, Camberwell, Victoria 3124, Australia
(a division of Pearson Australia Group Pty. Ltd.)
Penguin Books India Pvt. Ltd., 11 Community Centre, Panchsheel Park, New Delhi—110 017, India
Penguin Group (NZ), 67 Apollo Drive, Rosedale, North Shore 0632, New Zealand
(a division of Pearson New Zealand Ltd.)
Penguin Books (South Africa) (Pty.) Ltd., 24 Sturdee Avenue, Rosebank, Johannesburg 2196, South Africa

Penguin Books Ltd., Registered Offices: 80 Strand, London WC2R 0RL, England

JUST DESSERTS

A Jove Book / published by arrangement with the author

ISBN: 978-0-7394-9225-3

JOVE®
Jove Books are published by The Berkley Publishing Group, a division of Penguin Group (USA) Inc., 375 Hudson Street, New York, New York 10014.

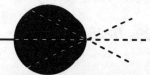

**This Large Print Book carries the
Seal of Approval of N.A.V.H.**

For Kali Amanda Browne
(aka The Food Goddess)
and the wonderful Marie

Watley-Browne: Love and thanks
for friendship, laughter, and
the world's best cookies.
I love you both!

1

Manhattan

The other attorney leaned forward and fixed Finn Rafferty with a look meant to remind him which one of them had Harvard Law on his side.

"Our own report on outstanding paternity claims against your client came in yesterday," Hampton Sloan IV said in the clipped and highly enunciated way of those to the manor born.

Finn, whose own background was more blue collar than blue blood, leaned back in his chair and fixed Sloan with a look meant to tell him that he already knew the answer.

"And—?" he prompted. These Ivy League types had a real jones for making you beg.

"To my surprise, the names on your list are no longer an issue."

Tell me something I don't know, Finn thought. This wasn't the first time (and it probably wouldn't be the last) that he had been down this road. "No surprise to me. Those names have been vetted more than once."

He had to hand it to aging preppies with roman numerals after their names. Being wrong didn't even register on Sloan's patrician features. Finn, however, was having a tough time keeping "told you so" from registering on his.

"Glad it all checked out." He gathered up the signed documents scattered across the top of the cherrywood desk. "Mr. Stiles will countersign and then we can consider the prenup a done deal."

The smile on Sloan's face should have tipped Finn off but he was already planning his escape route from the city. "As I said, Mr. Rafferty, the original list you provided checked out, but our investigators turned up one more name that seems to have escaped notice."

"We didn't withhold any names, if that's what you're implying. The list was complete and current."

"It would seem your investigators didn't go back quite far enough, Mr. Rafferty." Sloan slid a crisp manila folder across the desk. "I think you'll find this very interesting."

Finn, who had been hoping to hit the road before rush hour started, looked down at the folder. " 'Maitland,' " he said, reading the label. "What's this?"

"Read the summary page, counselor." It was never a good sign when the other side's attorney looked that amused.

He flipped open the folder. The summary page was on top of the paper-clipped stack. "Where did this come from?"

"Like I said, our investigators are very thorough."

"We're talking Tommy Stiles, the man who actually wants to know if he has other kids out there."

"Then he should be exceedingly happy if this turns out to be a DNA match."

A graduate of Harvard Law would have tendered an enigmatic smile, slid the folder into his briefcase, then waited until he was safely ensconced in his own cherrywood-

and-leather office before he read the contents.

Finn, however, had graduated SUNY Stony Brook and he read it twice while Sloan watched.

Name: *Hayley Maitland Goldstein*
Dob: *08/17/1969*
Mother: *Jane Maitland*
Father: *Thomas Joseph Stiles*
Place: *Lexington, KY*
Siblings: *n/a*
Marital Status: *Divorced/Michael*
                               Goldstein
                               (February 1999)
Children: *1 daughter (Name: Elizabeth)*
Occupation: *Bakery Owner*
Current Residence: *418 Main Street,*
                                  Lakeside, NJ

He met Sloan's eyes across the wide expanse of antique desktop. "I don't know how in hell we missed this. Our people are relentless when it comes to tracking down paternity claims." Tommy was probably the only superstar on the planet who was actually disappointed each time a claim was found to be without merit.

Sloan leaned back in his chair and for a moment he looked almost human. "It was a fluke," he admitted. "The original birth certificate was amended two weeks after the baby's birth to read *Father: Unknown.*"

"That's not uncommon," Finn said. "Usually the original is destroyed."

"Not this time." According to Sloan's people, the hospital in Kentucky had held on to the original records in a basement storage room where they stayed for years until they ended up being scanned into the county's genealogical database two months ago. "Quite clearly a mistake on their part but an interesting turn of events for our respective clients."

"'An interesting turn of events'?" Finn said, meeting the other lawyer's eyes. "That's one way to put it."

The other way was *holy shit*, but he kept that observation to himself.

Midtown traffic was hellacious as usual. It took Finn almost an hour to make his way from West Fifty-seventh across town to the Queensborough Bridge entrance, but he barely noticed it. The Maitland folder was open on the passenger seat and each time traffic ground to a standstill, he read more of the background information Sloan's people had uncovered about Jane Maitland and her daughter, Hayley.

The more Finn thought about it, the less he believed there was anything to the claim. There was nothing unusual about reverting to *Father: Unknown* status. More than likely Jane Maitland and Tommy had come to some kind of understanding about paternity and the issue was dropped. The only reason it was being addressed now was because some overzealous record keeper had saved the original documents instead of destroying them.

Traffic at the entrance to the bridge was at a literal standstill. Finn dug deeper into the file and found a photo of Dr. Maitland. He couldn't quite match up the fiercely intelligent but plain-looking scientist with nineteen-year-old guitarist Tommy Stiles. Call it sexist on his part, but the whole thing just didn't compute. Not even when you factored in the whole older woman/younger man dynamic.

A dead end, he told himself as he waited for traffic to start moving again. Nothing more than a formality.

And then he saw Jane Maitland's curriculum vitae.

She was an oceanographer.

A world-famous, prizewinning, planet-changing oceanographer.

Suddenly it all started to make sense.

He looked more closely at the paperwork. Hayley might have been born in Kentucky but her mother had been teaching at Princeton during the years before and after. Tommy had grown up right outside Princeton.

And there was the ocean...

Two hours ago he had been certain this new prospect would turn out to be a dead end like all the others. Now, the more miles he racked up, the more certain Finn became that the Stiles family was about to increase by two.

New Jersey...the ocean...the timing.

By the time he rolled past the sign welcoming him to East Hampton, he was reconfiguring Tommy's prenup to include the Goldstein girls as legitimate heirs.

He made the turn onto Greenleaf Path on autopilot. The toughest part would be getting Tommy alone so they could talk. The place was usually bursting at the seams with family, friends, friends of friends. Sometimes the only way they could get any work done was to head down to the beach and talk business while they walked the shoreline.

Tommy's place didn't look like much from the road. Two stories of sprawling sun-bleached shingles set on what passed for a hill in the Hamptons. The house sat so close to the water that it was practically built on beach sand. There were times when it seemed like a stiff breeze would send it hurtling into the Atlantic. It wasn't until you wound your way up the driveway that you got a real sense of the place. Ten bedrooms, twelve full baths, and two guesthouses tended to make an impression.

The first time Finn saw the place, he was a scared sixteen-year-old kid with no family and enough baggage to fill the hold of a 747. Tommy Stiles was his father's best friend, and when Jack and Mary Ann died, it was Tommy who opened up his heart and his home to Finn.

And how did Finn repay him? He had done his level teenage best to throw it all back in the guy's face.

The Hamptons were another planet to the kid from a small town in central New Jersey. The people were aliens who might as well have been sporting antennae and wearing shiny silver jumpsuits. Tommy's kids—and there were a hell of a lot of them—all had one thing in common: they hated the ocean. When the winds kicked up they retreated deeper into the house, hiding beneath headphones and loud music, counting down the minutes until the sun came out again.

Not Finn. The briny smell, the percussive sound of the waves breaking along the shore, the silvery glint of sunlight against the dark, unknowable ocean. It got into his blood fast and hard and before long he loved it the way Tommy did.

It seemed like another lifetime. He could barely remember the angry, lonely kid who had shown up on Tommy's doorstep with his father's Stratocaster, an old leather jacket, and what was left of his heart.

Tommy wasn't like anyone Finn had ever known. You couldn't get a rise out of the guy. You couldn't make him angry. The house had reverberated with enough teenage rebellion and adolescent angst to fuel a thousand TV movies, but during it all Tommy's gut-level goodness carried them through.

Everyone loved Tommy Stiles. Even his exes loved him. The place looked like a Mormon family reunion on holidays and birthdays, what with the former wives and girlfriends and kids who flew in from far and wide to be with him. A man had to be doing something right to be loved like that.

Definitely not the kind of guy who'd cold-bloodedly ignore his firstborn child.

Willow's Porsche was angled at the head of the driveway near the path that led to the front porches. Willow was young but she knew how to mark her territory. As the presumptive next Mrs. Tommy Stiles, Willow was also making sure the others in line to the throne understood exactly how important she was in the hierarchy.

Zach and Winston, Tommy's teenage sons by LeeLee James, a backup singer with a smoky alto and world-class legs, were staying at the house this semester. Their matching black Highlander Hybrids were tucked in behind Willow's sports car. The Toyotas were expensive carrots being dangled in front of their teenage noses by Tommy, who hoped that the prospect of wheels would inspire them to knuckle down and hit the books. They were good kids but academia wasn't their strong suit. Both of them wanted to follow in their father's footsteps and go out on the road as musicians, but Tommy was hanging tough on the subject of college.

There were a few cars Finn couldn't identify parked off to the side and an LIPA repair truck near the garage. A quiet day for once. He claimed his usual spot across from the mailbox.

The entrance foyer was an enormous, light-filled room with marble floors the color of beach sand. The walls had been hand-painted by artisans flown over from Italy who knew how to turn bare plaster into a sunny day. Twin staircases flanked the foyer. One led to the guest wing. The other led to Tommy's nominally private space. The concept of privacy wasn't big on the rocker's list of life's necessities. Left alone in a room, Tommy would make friends with a houseplant.

A hot-pink tricycle lay on its side at the foot of the guest staircase, a naked Barbie under the front wheel. He had learned to expect the unexpected when Gigi, Tommy's youngest, or some of the grandchildren were in residence. It wasn't unusual to find Barbie headfirst in one of the nine full baths or a Darth Vader action figure in the microwave.

He performed his civic duty by plucking

Barbie from danger, then dropping her into the basket suspended from the handlebars. He then righted the trike and pushed it to a safer spot against the wall. Friends who were parents claimed that was like trying to save the *Titanic* by plugging the hole in the ship with your finger, but he didn't have kids so he gave it a shot anyway.

Music blared from the media room. Kids' laughter rang out from one of the game rooms. He heard the *click-click* of high heels along the upstairs hall and the sound of someone practicing on a tenor sax.

Anton was sitting at the table in the sun-filled kitchen, deveining shrimp. Some musicians went into detox before a major tour. Anton, the After Life's drummer, cooked.

"You staying for supper?" Anton greeted him.

Finn grabbed a Coke from the Sub-Zero fridge. "Depends what happens after I drop a bomb on TS." He took a long pull from the soda bottle and waited for the sugar rush to hit his bloodstream.

"You mean like the bomb he dropped on us yesterday?"

"This would be what, his third farewell tour?" Finn took another gulp of Coke. "I don't see him hanging it up before Springsteen or Joel, do you?"

"I don't know," Anton said, popping the tail off a large crustacean. "You've gotta admit there's something in the air around here. Even Willow's thinking about swapping modeling for writing kids' books."

Finn wisely decided to keep his opinion on Willow's literary future to himself.

"Where is he?" he asked.

"With Jilly in the spa. He's getting highlights."

"Better him than me," Finn said, draining the bottle.

"Amen, brother. Why do you think I shave my head?"

Finn was still laughing when he walked into the huge space that served as salon, gym, and occasional day-care center.

Tommy was reclining in an uber-luxurious leather barber chair in front of a wall of perfectly lighted mirrors. Jilly, his stylist of many years, lifted one of her color brushes in greeting when she saw Finn.

His boss greeted him with the lopsided grin that had won him almost as many fans as his records. "Mission accomplished?" Prenups were part of the modern courtship ritual, like the Harry Winston diamond and the Reem Acra gown. They were a fact of life no sane adult who had achieved any measurable degree of success would ignore.

"They agreed that the claims on the list were all unfounded."

"I take care of my own. I wouldn't let a child of mine go unrecognized," Tommy said as Jilly the stylist tilted his head to the left. "A little more color up top, Jilly. I'm seeing a lot of gray these days."

"Any more color and you'll be Donald Trump's long-lost brother."

She and Tommy exchanged friendly banter while Finn tried to be patient.

"Listen," he said finally, shifting the manila folder from his right hand to his left. "We need to talk."

"Go ahead. Jilly knows all my secrets."

"Not all of them," Jilly said, "but I'm willing to learn."

Finn smiled but said nothing. Tommy studied him for a second then met Jilly's eyes in the wall of mirrors. "Can we break for a few?"

Finn followed Tommy out onto the multi-level deck overlooking the ocean.

"It's probably nothing," Finn said without preamble, "but Sloan's people did an additional background check and found someone."

He handed Tommy the folder. "Her name was or is Jane Maitland. You were nineteen. She was forty. Sloan's people found an original birth certificate for a baby girl named Hayley that cites you as the father." He gave him a condensed version of the discovery. "Jane is an oceanographer, a pretty renowned one, with two doctorates. She's teaching a course in Mumbai this year on the impact of climate change on coastlines throughout southeast Asia."

Tommy peered closely at the grainy newspaper clipping photo of an austere, gray-haired academic. The caption read *"Respected oceanographer rings the global warming bell in Mumbai."*

Finn tried to imagine what the good doctor might have looked like almost forty years ago, but the best he could come up with was the image of an austere, brown-haired academic.

"Recognize her?"

Tommy shot him a look. "She's almost eighty."

"She wasn't eighty when you—"

Tommy cut him off midsentence. "Not my type."

The other thing Finn knew about Tommy was that all women were his type.

"What about the daughter? Do you have a photo?"

"If the other side has one, they didn't pass it along. She owns a bakery in South Jersey, halfway between Philly and Atlantic City." She was building a name for herself by providing crazy expensive cakes for weddings, bar mitzvahs, and the occasional gubernatorial inauguration party.

Tommy looked up at him. "They're from New Jersey?"

"Maitland spent fifteen years at Princeton. The daughter was born in Kentucky."

He could see recognition dawning.

"I grew up two miles from Princeton. You'd be surprised how many university types showed up at our gigs."

"My father told me a little about the early days." Jack Rafferty had grown up in the house next door to Tommy. Two working-class kids with big dreams that, except for one of them dying young, had almost all come true.

"We played a lot of small clubs between Princeton and New York. Springsteen owned the shore. We were out to claim the rest of the state. Thousands of people moved in and out of our circle during those years." Tommy turned back toward the ocean. "She told me her name was Jean. I didn't understand half of what she said to me. We spent a weekend together. I never saw her again."

And there it was. He waited a moment before he asked, "Your choice or hers?"

"Hers . . . mine." He shrugged. "Both of ours. I tried to phone her but the number she'd given me was for a diner on Route One."

"So you're saying it's possible."

Another silence, even longer and more uncomfortable than the previous one.

"It's possible."

"Lakeside?" Tommy asked.

"Between A.C. and Philly."

"About a four-hour drive," Tommy said. "If we leave in the morning, we can get there by noon."

"You're kidding, right?"

"The hell I am. You tell me I might have a grown daughter I've never met and expect me to sit on my fat ass and do nothing? You know me better than that."

Unfortunately Finn did. There were no half measures where Tommy was concerned.

"Not a good idea, Tom. You have the rest of your family to consider." He paused. "And there's Willow."

"I'll say I need to check out the venue for the benefit next week in Atlantic City."

"Why don't you let me do my job before you put yourself out there. Let's find out who we're dealing with."

Tommy opened his mouth to argue the case then stopped. "Shit," he said. "I'm doing satellites tomorrow morning for the benefit, print in the afternoon, and a sit-down with *Showbiz Extra* in the evening."

"Okay," Finn said, not quite managing to mask his deep sense of relief. "I'll call in a few favors. We should have a pretty good idea where we stand by the end of the week."

Tommy said nothing.

"Are you going to tell Willow?" Finn asked.

"Not yet." Tommy's fiancée was a twenty-four-year-old supermodel/high school dropout who was three months pregnant with his seventh child.

Or maybe his eighth.

"I need to meet Hayley Goldstein."

"That could get messy, Tom." Which pretty much guaranteed Finn the Best

Understatement of the Millennium award. "She's lived thirty-eight years without you in her life. No guarantee she wants to meet you."

He could see the wheels turning.

"You said she's a caterer. Hire her for the after-party."

Nuclear warnings sounded inside Finn's head. "She's not a caterer, Tommy. She bakes cakes." Fancy, expensive cakes for fancy, expensive people.

"So have her bake a cake for us."

"Listen," he said carefully, "I don't think this is a good idea. Let me run our own back-ground check, see what I can find out, be-fore we take the next step."

"What does she bake, those fancy cakes like you see at weddings, right?"

The warnings reached DEFCON 3. "Right."

"So tell her we want her to bake us a set of drums or a guitar." He waved his hand in the air. "Whatever. The kids would love it and it would add a little something to her bottom line."

"Tom, let's pull it back before we get crazy. She's a stranger. Her bottom line isn't your problem. Why don't you stay focused on next week's show and let me do my job."

Jilly popped out onto the deck. "You have thirty seconds before those highlights seep into your brain, TS! Get in here now!"

"See what you can find out," Tommy said as he headed toward the door. "I want this moving."

It was Tommy's call. Not Finn's. If Tommy wanted to take the private jet and fly down to South Jersey and confront Hayley Maitland Goldstein with news that—assuming it was true—would turn her world upside down, then that was exactly what Tommy would do.

That was the thing about superstars. Even the nicest among them, which definitely included Tommy Stiles, got what they wanted when they wanted it.

2

Goldy's Bakery—Lakeside, New Jersey

Hayley Maitland Goldstein was fighting a losing battle with a sheet of rolled fondant when her daughter thundered down the back stairs and burst into the kitchen.

"You always did know how to make an entrance," she said as Lizzie grabbed for one of the Linzer tortes cooling on a wire rack. "Good thing I don't have cheesecake in the ovens." Her girl was five foot two and one hundred pounds and somehow she managed to sound like a herd of Clydesdales in a beer commercial.

"Cheesecakes are Friday," Lizzie said with

a powdered-sugar grin. "This is Wednesday. I figured it was safe."

"Nice to know that fancy school of yours teaches you the days of the week." She tried hard not to think about how many cookies she had to sell to pay the quarterly tuition bill at Olympia Prep.

Lizzie, who had clearly decided not to worry about the bakery's profit margin at the moment, snagged another cookie. "I'm honor roll again this quarter."

Hayley wanted to let out a whoop of excitement but Lizzie had reached the age where maternal enthusiasm was a source of deep humilation. She feigned a yawn instead. "Old news, kid. You've been honor roll since kindergarten."

"I've spoiled you." Lizzie split open the cookie and began to lick the raspberry jam from the center. "Maybe I should fail physics or throw a chem test so you'll appreciate me."

"I don't recommend it," she said with a stern glance in her daughter's direction. "The competition out there for scholarships is fierce."

Lizzie rolled her eyes.

"I saw that," Hayley said. "You have two and a half more years of high school,

Elizabeth. This isn't the time to lose your focus." Academic achievement was a family tradition, even if it had skipped Hayley's generation.

Lizzie's blue-green eyes twinkled. "I'm on the honor roll, Mom, not probation. Quit worrying."

"I can't. It's what I do best." She was a worrier. Always had been, always would be. She worried about her daughter, her former in-laws, her cousins, their cousins, her daughter's cousins, her daughter's friends, her daughter's friends' friends, her employees, their families, the weather, the state of the world, the state of her checking account. One night last month she even found herself worrying about Katie Couric's ratings, although Katie had yet to return the favor.

She glanced up at the clock. Maybe she'd better start worrying about the time. The Cumberland County Association of Female Realtors expected a fully decorated cake delivered to the Knights of Columbus Hall by seven p.m. and it was already almost three. Given the fact that the president of the association was the daughter of her former mother-in-law's best friend, she needed to get on it or there would be a lot of explaining to do. Connie Goldstein lived in Fort Lauderdale but her network reached far and wide.

"Don't talk," she warned her daughter. "Don't breathe. I'm going to take another shot at this."

"Since when do you have trouble with fondant? I can do fondant. You've been edgy all day. Aunt Fiona said—"

"Lizzie, please! Hang on to the commentary until I drape the cake."

Rolled fondant was like edible vinyl flooring. It required a sure touch and seamless application or you might as well commission the Home Depot to do the job. She had worked a nice pale blue tint into the concoction and kneaded it until it screamed for mercy. All the fondant had to do now was cooperate.

She inhaled deeply, centered herself once more, then draped the sheet over the bottom tier of carrot cake.

"Okay," she said on the exhale. "That's better."

"Um, Mom? It's lumpy."

"I'll pretend I didn't hear that."

"The top," Lizzie said, pointing with a half-eaten cookie. "It's all bubbly."

"That's the bottom tier. Nobody but the baker sees the top of the bottom tier."

"I thought you were a perfectionist."

"A perfectionist on a deadline." She grabbed a pair of clean shears and clipped the excess around the perimeter. "One down, one to go."

"Let me do the next one."

"I'm not paying five thousand a year so you can learn how to ice cakes."

"I like to ice cakes."

"No, you don't. You like to study."

"I like to ice cakes too." There was that sugary grin again. "It's a genetic thing."

"You take after your grandmother, remember?" Hayley carefully lifted a new sheet of rolled fondant and laid it flat on a marble slab. "Go back upstairs and think lofty thoughts. I need to concentrate."

"I'm letting my brain chill."

"I love it when you talk like your grandmother."

Lizzie wiped her sugary hands on her jeans. "Speaking of Grandma, she's coming home."

"I know." There went her concentration again. "Fortunately I still have time to hide my stash of *People* magazines."

"Not really," said Lizzie. "She's coming home next week."

Hayley stopped what she was doing. "But she was supposed to be in India until after New Year's." Her mother lived the higher life of the mind, which, in practical terms, meant lots of travel to lots of faraway places in search of knowledge, enlightenment, and government funding.

"She e-mailed us her new schedule," Lizzie said. "I printed it out and left it on your desk." Lizzie was the family computer expert who not only understood how computers functioned, but knew how to use them to the bakery's best advantage. Hayley was reasonably sure they were the only bakery in New Jersey with a website, a blog, and a mailing list.

"Why is Jane coming home early?" Her mother loved everything about the academic lecture circuit: the intellectual stimulation, the travel, the smells and sights and sounds of strange cities in faraway countries.

The same things that left her daughter stone cold.

Lizzie shrugged. "She didn't say."

A cold blast of fear slammed into Hayley. "Oh God. You don't think—" She couldn't finish the sentence. Her mother's breast cancer had been in remission for seven years this time around, but the shadow of another recurrence was always there.

"She wants to know if she can stay with us until the sublet on her place runs out and she can move back in."

"My mother wants to stay here with us?" It was easier to imagine Jane pole-dancing than living happily above the bakery.

"That's what she said."

"Something's wrong."

"Nothing's wrong, Mom."

"I know your grandmother better than you do. Something's definitely wrong."

"She's just coming home early. I think part of her lecture tour got cancelled."

"If part of her tour got cancelled, she'd book herself a few new speaking gigs. The one thing she wouldn't do is come home early." The concept of home didn't have the same meaning to Jane as it did to her daughter.

"Maybe she misses us."

"Have you met your grandmother? She loves us, but we're not the center of her life." She didn't mean to sound harsh but that was the reality of being the daughter of a renowned scientist. The work took precedence over everything else.

"Aunt Fiona said Meals On Wheels won't be delivering tomorrow so maybe we could bring her some mac and cheese or something."

"We'll do better than that," Hayley said. "I'll put a pot roast in the slow cooker in the morning. We'll bring her a feast with all the trimmings."

Fiona was Jane's younger sister. Hayley had stayed with Fiona and her late husband during junior and senior year of high school. The fact that Aunt Fee deserved the Croix de Guerre wasn't lost on her.

"Ms. Hughes e-mailed the schedule for next month's mentor meetings. She also wants to know if you could take on two more boys from the vo-tech."

"If they don't mind heavy lifting, tell her absolutely."

"Ginger's driving down to Philly next week. She wants to know if you can get away for lunch."

"I'll call her later."

"Aunt Paula wants to know if you're bringing the circular needles to the knit-in at the Friends of the Library party on Friday."

"Good thing you reminded me," Hayley said. "I totally forgot."

"Aunt Karen and Aunt Dianne IM'd. They said Aunt Paula's turned into a knitting nazi and they blame you."

Paula, Karen, and Dianne were Hayley's best friends since high school. They were the backbone of Lakeside's Friends of the Library. The fact that a knit-in attracted more guests than anything book related wasn't lost on any of them.

Hayley laughed. "I'll take care of it later."

"I paid the utility bill," Lizzie said, "the prop tax, and the quarterlies. Do you want to pay the restaurant supply store in full or in two installments?"

"You decide," Hayley said. Nothing like having a fourteen-year-old financial genius in the family.

"In full," Lizzie said with assurance. "We don't need more bills hanging over our heads."

"Amen to that."

"Don't forget I'm having supper at Aunt Michelle's tonight. She wants me to run TurboTax on last year's returns."

Hayley tried not to dwell on the fact that her former sister-in-law still hadn't filed her tax returns. "Stuffed peppers?"

"Aunt Michelle's gone veggie. They're stuffed with tofu."

"I'll have nightmares all night," Hayley said with a shiver. "I want you home by ten. Tell Michie she has to drive you. On second thought, I'll call and tell her myself." She wanted to remind her former sister-in-law that she was scheduled to open the bakery on Saturday while Hayley and Lizzie went on Lakeside High School's mentoring program spring picnic.

"I can walk."

"Not at ten o'clock at night, you can't."

"Lakeside is one of the safest towns in New Jersey. I read the state demographics on safety and—"

"You're not walking home alone. If Michie doesn't want to drive you, call me and I'll pick you up."

"I'm fourteen. I can—"

"No."

Lizzie's jaw stiffened and Hayley had a quick flashback to a stubborn two-year-old pitching a fit on the floor of the produce department of ShopRite. Where had the years gone?

The dark cloud lifted as quickly as it had

appeared and Lizzie promised she wouldn't walk home.

"Now scram," Hayley ordered as her daughter grabbed another cookie, "or I'll have one hundred angry Cumberland County real estate agents screaming for my head tonight."

Lizzie darted back upstairs and Hayley tried to center her thoughts for what seemed like the thousandth time that afternoon. Working with rolled fondant wasn't her favorite thing in the world, but it wasn't exactly making phyllo dough by hand either.

It shouldn't be a big deal but today it was. For some reason, everything had felt like a big deal today.

She had woken up feeling unsettled for no reason that she could figure out, as if something was looming just out of sight, waiting to pounce like a monster in one of the horror movies on late-night TV.

"Maybe Lizzie's right," she mumbled as she manipulated the fondant into position on the next layer. She had turned worry into an Olympic event. Creative types were supposed to drift through life without a care. Where had she gone wrong?

She had a brilliant mother, a budding genius daughter, and a thriving business.

Why not relax and enjoy?

Other people were able to relax and enjoy at the drop of a hat. Her mother had been known to fall into a deep, rejuvenating sleep in the middle of turbulence over the Indian Ocean. Her daughter had an ability to live happily in the moment that would throw the Dalai Lama into a swoon of spiritual envy.

When life was running smoothly, Hayley worried that she wasn't worrying enough, at which point life usually gave her something to worry about.

Funny how it always seemed to work out that way.

It was probably fate's funny little way of paying her back for all the worry she'd caused Aunt Fee and Uncle Bernie when she was a teenager.

Trish and Rachel were up front manning the counter. Lizzie was upstairs thinking great thoughts. The family pets were all accounted for. She could spend a little time worrying about living under the same roof with her mother, her daughter, three cats, a dog, and a parrot, but that seemed excessive even to Hayley.

Murmuring a prayer to Elizabeth of Hungary, patron saint of bakers, she got back to work.

"I don't get it," Anton said as Finn hung a left onto Lakeside's tree-lined Main Street. "Why don't you just ask one of the chefs at the hotel to make a fancy cake for the after-party?"

A four-hour drive to a family bakery in a small South Jersey town for a layer cake was hard to explain.

Not to mention the fact that Finn was a lousy liar. Sins of omission. Plain old evasion. And that old legal standby: obfuscation. He was no damn good at any of them.

"He wants a cake from Goldy's Bakery."

"Why?"

"Why?" Finn parroted. "What are you, four years old? Because he wants it." Superstars wanted what they wanted at the exact moment they wanted it, and as a general rule nobody on the payroll ever asked why.

At least not to the superstar's face.

"You know I'll figure it out sooner or later."

Anton was his closest friend. He would trust the guy with his life, but not with Tommy's secrets.

"When you do, explain it to me," Finn said. "I didn't see this one coming."

He had done everything he could to talk Tommy out of this, with no luck. "What's the problem?" Tommy had asked him during one particularly heated exchange late last night. "I'm not trying to hurt her. No matter which way it plays out, she's in a win-win situation."

Finn didn't believe in win-win situations. Somebody always came out on the short end of the winning stick and normally it was his job to make sure it wasn't Tommy Stiles. In a perfect world, the idea made perfect sense: a business transaction conducted in a public venue with little chance for messy emotions to come into play. Unfortunately Finn knew Tommy too well. The second he saw this woman who might be his daughter, logic and reason would fly out the window and they would all end up screwed.

"That's it?" Anton said. "That's all you're gonna give me?"

"I shouldn't have given you that much."

"This better be some cake," Anton muttered.

"Looking to steal a few trade secrets?"

"I'm an amateur, baby," Anton said with a

laugh, "but I wouldn't mind copping a few riffs from a master baker."

"You're sounding cynical, m'man. She's supposed to be damn good."

"I'll be the judge of that." Anton had taken a few series of classes at the Culinary Institute upstate and periodically threatened to quit the band and cook full time.

"We're looking for Goldy's," Finn said as he rolled to a stop at a traffic light. "Number four eighteen."

A bank. A card shop. A one-hour photo shop with a FOR RENT sign in the window. Blockbuster. Two dentists. One gynecologist. A holistic therapist who sold handmade candles on the side.

East Hamptonites liked to say they moved out to the end of Long Island for the "small-town" atmosphere, but they were kidding themselves. The Hamptons had become Manhattan East, almost as fast-paced, and definitely as competitive as anything you'd find on the little island on the other side of the East River.

Lakeside was the real deal and it would send most of them screaming for their air-conditioned Range Rovers.

"Up there," Anton said, pointing. "Next to the dry cleaners. Somebody just pulled out."

Finn angled Tommy's shiny black Escalade into the parking spot. He was beginning to see the hand of fate at work.

"It's small," Anton said, gesturing toward the storefront with the sign GOLDY'S . . . SINCE 1969 stenciled across the plate-glass window. An old man sat on a lawn chair in front of the dry cleaners next door and watched them the way most men watched the Super Bowl.

"It's Jersey," Finn said with a shrug.

Which pretty much explained everything.

Trish, one of the high school girls Hayley was currently mentoring, burst into the kitchen looking like she had just bumped into Justin Timberlake and then ricocheted off Johnny Depp.

"There's two guys outside who want to see you and they're unbelievably hot!" Trish was seventeen, the age when the arrival of any biped with a Y chromosome rated a breathless announcement. "One of them looks like a rock star from, you know, way back in the eighties."

Ouch. She had been Trish's age in the eighties.

"A rock star?" she asked, lifting a brow. Rock stars were in short supply in Lakeside.

"A rock star," Trish confirmed. "And he's wearing leather."

There was only one reason an aging leather-clad hottie would show up at Goldy's Bakery at three o'clock on a Wednesday afternoon and it had nothing to do with brownies, cheesecake, or bagels.

"Tell him Mr. Goldstein doesn't live here anymore." And that Mrs. Goldstein couldn't be happier about it. Not even sending him his monthly share of the store's profits dimmed her joy.

"But he didn't ask for Mr. Goldstein. He asked for you."

Why did that surprise her? She was the Goldstein with a bank balance, after all. It had been a while since someone had come looking for her ex but the knot in her stomach was painfully familiar. The faint stench of danger still lingered in the air. She wished she had a dollar for every angry enabler who had shown up at Goldy's in search of the reluctant Mr. Goldstein. She'd be able to buy him out once and for all and still have money to spare.

"Then tell him I'm not here."

"But, Mrs. G., I already told him you were."

"Then tell him the truth," she said. "I'm busy working on a cake that should have been finished an hour ago. I can't spare a second." And here she'd thought her life would settle down after Michael moved to Florida to mooch off his mother. The man's problems had the half-life of uranium.

Trish rearranged her pretty features into an even prettier frown. "He really wants to see you, Mrs. G. Maybe—"

Hayley could feel the hot breath of the Cumberland County Association of Female Realtors on the back of her neck. She whipped out The Look, the same look every mother on the planet had down cold, aimed it in Trish's direction, then hoped for the best.

"I'll tell him," Trish mumbled, then pushed through the swinging door to deliver the bad news.

The Look had stopped working on Lizzie when she was seven, but it was nice to know she still had enough maternal fire-power at her command to keep her young staff in line.

She pressed her ear against the swinging door but she couldn't make out Trish's words, just a high apologetic string of female sounds that was followed by a male rumble. Leather Boy had a good voice, baritone, a little smoky. She couldn't make out his words either but Trish's answering giggle conjured up some painful memories of herself at that age.

First a girl giggled, then she sighed, and the next thing you knew she was in Vegas taking her wedding vows in front of a red-haired Elvis with an overbite. You knew you had made a bad choice when Elvis slipped you his divorce lawyer's business card while you were still shaking the rice from your hair.

She listened closer. Trish said something girly. Leather Boy rumbled something manly. This time Rachel, her other counter girl for the week, giggled too, a sound that sent Hayley's maternal early-warning system into overdrive.

Rachel Gomez was a serious straight-A student bound for Princeton next year on full scholarship. She needed the paycheck more than any mentoring Hayley might have provided her. Rachel had probably never giggled before in her life.

If Rachel giggled, then even Lizzie might not be immune. Fourteen was when it started, that fizzy sensation in your veins, the yearning for things you couldn't define, the sudden realization that boys were infinitely more interesting than global warming or the fate of the humpback whale.

Fourteen was also when young girls parted company with their self-confidence and traded in their love of math and science for a date for the prom.

Sometimes she wanted to lock Lizzie away in her room with her computer, her books, and a cell phone (maybe), and not let her out again until she was twenty-one. Thirty sounded better but even fantasies had their limits. The advisor at Olympia Prep had suggested that Lizzie might be better served intellectually by skipping the rest of high school and starting college in the fall but Hayley was dead set against it. Lizzie might be brilliant when it came to science but when it came to life, she was still only fourteen.

The world could be a scary place. A mother did her best to protect her kid from fast cars, drunk drivers, broken bones, flu, the common cold, but there was nothing she could do to protect her kid from growing up. No matter what you did or how well you did it, your little girl wasn't going to stay a little girl. Right before your eyes she was going to grow up on you anyway and all you could do was pray she didn't follow in your foolish footsteps.

Once upon a time, Hayley had believed that a good woman (her) could turn a bad boy (her ex) into a knight in shining armor (pure fantasy). Ten years of marriage to Michael Goldstein had finally drummed the truth into her head. People didn't change with time. They just became more of who they were to begin with.

In the real world bad boys didn't turn into knights in shining armor. Bad boys grew up to be even worse men and the world would be a much happier place if little girls were taught that basic fact along with their ABCs.

Why didn't women teach their young how to cope with the things that were really important instead of how to walk in their first pair of heels? Why didn't they make a point of sitting their girl children down and telling them the truth about men instead of letting some guy in a leather jacket seduce them over a tray of black-and-white cookies?

That was one of the many reasons why she had helped institute the mentoring program at the high school. Lizzie claimed her overflow worrying needed an outlet but it went far deeper. She saw herself in those girls, insecure, struggling, hungry for love, and ready to hand over their futures to the first guy who came along.

Those idiot girls out there were like ripe fruit on a very low-hanging branch. The slightest breeze would be enough to shake them from the tree and into the waiting arms of Leather Boy or someone just like him and their entire lives would be changed forever.

Except it wasn't going to happen on her watch. With apologies to the good real estate agents of Cumberland County, it was time to prepare for battle.

3

"Stay here," Finn said to Anton. "I'm going to make a call."

He smiled at the dark-haired counter girl who was pretending she wasn't listening and ducked out to phone Tommy. The old man was no longer sitting in front of the dry cleaners. He was perched in the window looking out. The wind had kicked up and a light rain was falling. He ducked under the bakery awning but couldn't get cell service on his phone.

He finally managed a connection by climbing into the backseat of the car and leaning against the window.

He dialed Tommy's cell and was flipped immediately to voice mail. He hung up, then dialed again just in case. Same thing.

"Damn," he muttered. He had forgotten all about the daylong string of interviews Tommy was giving in support of next week's hospital benefit.

It was probably a waste of time but he left a message.

"Listen, I'm here in front of the bakery. I'll do it if you feel that strongly about it, but as your attorney and your friend, I thought it was in your best interest to give you one more chance. I'll call you when we're on our way back."

Finn had no compelling argument on his side. No relevant facts or figures to help plead his case. Just a gut-deep instinct that this was the wrong way to go.

He punched in the number for the house and was routed to voice mail there too.

Calling Willow's cell didn't strike him as a good idea. That would make one hell of a voice mail message. *Hey, Willow. I'm trying to find Tom. Tell him I'm parked in front of the bakery owned by his (maybe) thirty-eight-year-old daughter who's the ex-wife of a guy who has more judgments against him than you have* Vogue *covers . . .*

Nope. Not a good idea.

It's not your life, he told himself. Not his family. No matter how close he was to the extended Stiles clan, he was still an outsider. He could advise, he could warn, he could question, but when push came to shove Tommy was the one driving the bus.

All he could do was pray he wouldn't drive that bus right off a cliff.

The last time Hayley had seen that much leather was at a Village People reunion concert in Atlantic City fifteen years ago. This guy was basically wearing a longhorn. Leather pants. Leather vest. He probably chewed leather instead of tobacco. He was built like a wrestler, stocky and muscular with forearms larger than most people's thighs. He sported the requisite tats, diamond studs, and more rings than fingers. His shaved head gleamed under the fluorescent light.

Everything about him screamed trouble.

From the expressions on Trish's and Rachel's faces, Hayley wasn't a minute too soon.

If he so much as crooked one of those bejeweled fingers in their direction, those two idiotic little girls would follow him right out the door and into the biggest mistake of their lives.

Twenty years ago she had done exactly that and it would be nice if somebody finally benefited from her mistakes.

"Trish!" She sounded like a marine drill sergeant on steroids. "Rachel! I need you two in the kitchen."

Rachel stared at her wide-eyed. Trish looked like she was in a trance.

"Now!" Hayley barked, and the two teenagers sprinted past her.

Even Leather Boy straightened up.

She could get used to this.

"I'm Hayley Goldstein," she said as she rounded the counter, "and if this is about Michael, I can't help you."

"Anton Mezvinsky." He looked a whole lot less dangerous when he was puzzled. "Who's Michael?"

"You're not looking for my ex?" If she sounded wary, it was because she was. Process servers and debt collectors could be very sneaky. She had learned that the hard way.

"I'm not looking for anybody." He gestured toward the street where an enormous black SUV had claimed pride of place in front of the shop. "Finn had to take a call. I came along for the ride."

They stared at each other for a full second or two. She was surprised to note that he had very kind eyes. Dark brown, thick lashes. A touch of sweetness where you wouldn't expect it. Not that she was letting down her guard for even a second, but still . . .

"Anton, unless you're looking to buy a lemon meringue pie, I don't think I can help you."

"If your lemon meringue is half as good as that deep-dish apple I tried, I'll take two."

"You tried my deep-dish apple?" He wasn't local. She knew that for sure. They didn't have table service. So where did he get a slice of Goldy's apple pie?

"Trish gave me a sample."

Trish was giving out samples?

"Makes a customer feel welcome. Great idea."

Anton was right. It was a great idea. Too bad it wasn't hers.

"The cardamom was another great idea."

She blinked and zeroed back in on Anton. "You tasted cardamom?"

"A dash," Anton said. "Faint but it rocked."

"Cardamom's my secret ingredient. Nobody's ever identified it."

Anton grinned, a surprisingly charming sight in a muscular, scary, leather-clad, bald guy. "It's not a secret anymore."

"Are you a baker?"

"Baker, chef, short-order cook. In my business you need something to keep you sane. I'm thinking maybe one day I'd like to open a place of my own, but that's a way off."

Part-time baker, part-time loan collector? Her guard went back up. "So what's going on here, Anton? You seem like a nice guy. I mean, you know your cardamom and that has to mean something, but you know and I know that you didn't come here to admire the baked goods. Either tell me what's going on or—"

Anton raised his hand to stop her. "Wait," he said. "Let me get Finn. He'll explain everything."

Fin? Was that one of those mob nicknames like Paulie Walnuts or Vinny the Chin? Her ex didn't exactly run with the Mensa crowd. Visions of a Tony Soprano wannabe with a chip on his shoulder and a score to settle sprang to life and she debated the wisdom of locking the front door and putting up the CLOSED sign while there was still time.

Anton approached the SUV parked at the curb. She watched, fascinated, as the passenger door opened and a suit stepped out. The Suit towered over Anton. His shoulders were as wide as a running back's, something that was either the result of good genetics or an even better tailor. The rest of him was long, lean, and extremely easy on the eyes.

She busied herself wiping imaginary fingerprints from the glass countertop as The Suit said something to Anton, straightened his tie, then strode across the sidewalk to the front door with Anton riding shotgun. He didn't walk like a guy who spent his life in suits. His walk was loose, easy, and (why not admit it?) sexy. Not that how he walked mattered, of course. She was just saying.

"I'm told you're looking for me," she said as soon as the door closed behind them. She had never been good at playing games, which probably explained why she rarely had a second date.

"Finn Rafferty," he said, extending his right hand. "You're Hayley Maitland?"

"Hayley Maitland Goldstein," she corrected him. Like it or not, that was what was on her driver's license.

He looked surprised. "One of the counter girls told me you were divorced."

She needed to have a long talk with Trish. "I am divorced," she said. "I never got around to switching back to my maiden name." Not that it was any of his business. "What about you? Married? Single? Divorced? Gay?" Let him see how it felt.

"Divorced," he said. "Occupational hazard."

Uh-oh.

Their eyes locked and for a moment she almost forgot he was probably there to collect on her ex-husband's debts. He wore a suit but there was definitely a bad boy lurking beneath the fancy tailoring.

"The counter girl also told me you weren't here," he continued.

"I shouldn't be. I should be in the kitchen working on a commission, so if we could get to the point, I'd appreciate it." She had learned the hard way how to handle her ex's cohorts and it wasn't by flirting with them.

"Is this the way you usually treat a potential client?"

"You mean you're not here to—" She caught herself midsentence. No point airing the Goldstein dirty linen if she didn't have to.

"I'll pay double the going rate if you'll finish that sentence." He managed to say it with such good humor that even she had to laugh.

"There's a going rate for family secrets? I could be a very rich woman." She glanced at the clock then back at The Suit.

He got the message. "Then I'll get to the point: I need a cake in the shape of a set of drums and I hear you're the best baker for the job."

"A set of drums? I can do that." *In my sleep with my favorite spatula tied behind my back.* A little fondant, some chocolate paste, a secret stash of foam, and a wave of her magic wand and she could re-create anything from the string section of the philharmonic to Aerosmith in their prime.

"There's more," he said. "We need to feed two hundred."

She quickly did the math. When you had a kid in a fancy private school, you couldn't help seeing things in terms of quarterly payments.

"We did a wedding reception for five hundred last spring. The main cake was in the shape of a pair of swans. I can show you photos if you like."

"I've already seen them."

"Trish again?" That girl was either a natural resource or a world-class yenta.

"I did my homework. In the last year you handled the Citibank reception at McCarter in Princeton, two election-night parties in Harrisburg and Trenton, and private functions for some very well-known families."

"Tell me your name again so I can do my homework too." Google. A woman's best friend.

"Finn Rafferty." He handed her a business card with lots of information printed on it. East Hampton caught her eye.

She looked up at him. "You're a lawyer?"

"You have something against lawyers?"

"And you're from East Hampton?"

"You have something against Long Island?"

"I'm just wondering why a lawyer from the eastern end of Long Island would drive all the way down to South Jersey to buy a cake."

"You look like you think I'm going to slap a subpoena on you."

He was closer than he knew. "What I'm thinking is that I'm pretty sure you have bakeries in the Hamptons."

He grinned. "Maybe you should bring your counter help back up front. Your cakeside manner needs a little work."

"I'm direct. I find it saves a lot of time."

"I represent Tommy Stiles. He's the one in need of your services."

She burst out laughing. "I'm sorry but I thought you said Tommy Stiles."

"I did."

"As in Tommy Stiles and the After Life." As in super-famous rock star who had been around forever.

"You've heard of him."

Heard of him? That was like asking if you had heard of Elvis or the Beatles. She struggled to maintain her composure. "Of course. He's—uh, he's a singer." A singer who had happened to make his bones alongside Springsteen and Joel, Stewart and Clapton.

Rafferty's hazel-gold eyes twinkled with amusement. "He'll be performing at the Borgata in Atlantic City next week and he wants you to handle the cakes for the after-party."

She hated herself for asking the question but the "Why me?" slipped out just the same.

"Because you're the best between here and New York and Tommy only deals with the best."

She had always believed in herself, but the fact that Tommy Stiles even knew she was on the same planet rendered her temporarily speechless.

Not to mention suspicious.

If Finn noticed, he didn't let on. "We'll supply rooms for you and your staff. Naturally you'll have full access to the kitchen's facilities. Whatever you need to get the job done, it's yours."

"I usually bake the cakes here then schlep them to the site in the back of our van." She started to laugh. "I wish you could see the look on your face."

He had the good grace to look a little sheepish. "I'm from Jersey myself. I know these roads. How many casualties have there been?"

"I'll admit it gets a little hairy on the turnpike at rush hour but that's pretty much how it's done."

"We know your going rate and because

this is short notice, we're willing to sweeten the deal."

"I'll—maybe I can—how about I work up a proposal and fax it over to you tonight."

"I have a better idea. Why don't we hammer out the details right now. I didn't come all this way to go home empty-handed."

"I usually like three weeks' notice for a job like this."

"An extra twenty-five percent."

"Listen, I'm not trying to bump up the price. We're a small outfit and that's a lot of work. I don't want to promise something I can't deliver." She gestured toward the kitchen. "Like the carrot cake the Cumberland County real estate agents expect to dig into a few hours from now. I have to get back in there."

"We're talking major exposure," Finn Rafferty said. He was pushing hard. "Photographers from *InStyle* and *People*. *Entertainment Tonight* will be sending over a film crew. It's going to put you on the map."

She was a big fan of the style and entertainment magazines. She devoured the splashy multipage spreads featuring celebrity weddings and showers and bar mitzvahs, searching for details about the cakes and cookies and desserts. Those magazines, and their TV counterparts, had made superstars out of unknown bakers with a single well-timed story or photo.

Hayley Maitland Goldstein, cake decorator to the stars.

It had a nice ring to it.

So why was she standing there dithering like she couldn't make up her mind if the job was worth her time. She was a decisive, ambitious woman. She should have reeled in this commission before Finn Rafferty found somebody else.

"Do it, Mom!"

She turned around and saw Lizzie standing in the doorway, watching them with her big, curious eyes. It figured this was the one time the kid didn't gallop down the steps like a Clydesdale. "How long have you been standing there?"

"Long enough. This is your Cinderella moment! You can't let it slip away."

"This is my daughter, Lizzie," she said to Finn, who for some reason looked like he had seen a ghost. "Clearly I made the mistake of raising her with a mind of her own."

"Do you know how much it costs to advertise in *InStyle*?" her daughter demanded. "More than we make in a month! We could pay off the kitchen supplies account and lay in plenty of fondant and chocolate paste and get the big oven repaired and—"

Hayley raised her hand to stop Lizzie before it got even more embarrassing than it already was. "I thought you were going over to Michie's to do her taxes."

"She cancelled. She said she still can't find her W-2s."

She glanced at Finn Rafferty, who was clearly trying to figure out what was going on. So much for a Cinderella moment. She could see the glass coach turning back into a pumpkin right before her eyes.

Sometimes reality truly was a bitch.

"Like I said, this is my daughter, Lizzie. She's fourteen years old and she knows more about running a business than I do at almost forty. If you give Lizzie the job specs, she'll run up a proposal in less time than it would take you to drink a cup of coffee and split a deep-dish apple pie with your friend Anton. She handles contracts, billing, and balancing the checkbook for everyone in our family." She paused for breath. "Yes, it's unorthodox but that's the way it is. And if any or all of this makes you uncomfortable, you can still have coffee and deep-dish apple and we'll say good-bye."

She looked at Finn.

Finn looked at Lizzie.

Lizzie looked at both of them.

"Draw up a proposal, Lizzie," Finn said, "and let's get this thing moving."

4

"That's the fourth time," Lizzie said as she tapped away at the computer.

"Fourth time what?" Finn asked, swiveling around to face the teenage wunderkind.

"You keep turning around to stare at my mom."

"No, I don't." He hadn't had time to build up to staring. Every time he turned Hayley's way, she had caught him looking at her and he had to pretend he was checking the clock.

"Yes, you do, and now you're staring at me."

"I'm not staring," Finn said. "I'm trying to read over your shoulder."

"I don't think so," Lizzie said. "You'd have to stand behind me to read over my shoulder. You're staring at my face."

"Sorry."

"If you're looking for a family resemblance, you might as well quit now. There isn't one," she said matter-of-factly as she resumed her rapid-fire typing. "That's why you were staring, right? In case you're wondering, I don't look like my father either."

"I think you look a lot like your mother."

"Nope." She peered at the screen, then fiddled with the touchpad. "I don't look much like anyone in the family. I'm a genetic anomaly."

No, you're not, Lizzie. You don't know it yet, but you look just like your grandfather. From the huge, sleepy-lidded blue-green eyes to the stubborn chin to the slightly off-kilter smile, she was a Stiles through and through.

He couldn't remember ever feeling like a bigger bastard than he did right now. There were things you shouldn't know about people. And you definitely shouldn't know those things before the people had the chance to find out for themselves.

Laughter floated toward them from the center of the kitchen where Anton, scrubbed and draped in a white cotton apron and plastic food-service gloves, worked with Hayley at the bench. She really did know how to make magic with cake and frosting: two rectangular layers of carrot cake were turning into a modern-day Colonial house right before his eyes.

Unfortunately, the other thing happening right before his eyes was a whole lot less than magical.

Anton, usually not big on taking direction, had settled happily into the secondary position, doing whatever she told him, the moment she told him to do it.

And Hayley, the same woman who had practically made him take a lie detector test before she agreed to accept the job, was all relaxed and easy with Anton, a bald-headed, leather-wearing, tattooed rocker she had known for less than an hour.

He wouldn't have figured Anton was her type.

Which begged the question: what was her type . . . and why wasn't he on the short list?

Not that it mattered. He wasn't there on a social call. He was there because Tommy asked him to be there.

"That cake's okay," Lizzie said, following his gaze and fortunately misinterpreting the intent. "But you should see the swans she did for a wedding last year." She paused. "Unless you're looking at my mom again."

"That's a great cake," he said, sidestepping the issue. "Where'd your mom learn how to do that?"

Lizzie shrugged. "She's been working here since forever. Grandpa Goldstein pulled her off the counter and into the kitchen when she was a senior in high school." *Tap-tap-tap* on the keyboard. "She took art classes when I was little. The rest she figured out on her own."

"Are you going to follow in her footsteps?"

"I like working in the store but I'm going to be a scientist like my grandmother."

"Which discipline?" Like he didn't have Jane's CV memorized.

"Oceanographer," Lizzie said with obvious pride. "She gives lectures all around the world." She looked up from the screen. "I need your name for the proposal."

"I'm Finn Rafferty, but I'm not your customer. Tommy Stiles is."

"Which one of you is the famous guy?"

He could hear Hayley's horrified gasp

across the room. Apparently Mrs. Goldstein had been listening . . .

"Elizabeth! Tell Mr. Rafferty you're kidding."

Lizzie's brow furrowed. "I'm not kidding. I just wanted to know which one of them is famous."

Anton's laugh rang out. "Good thing Tom's back in the Hamptons."

"Is he an actor?" Lizzie asked, fingers poised on the keyboard.

"Tommy Stiles and the After Life," Hayley said.

Finn could hear the "d'oh!" in her voice.

"Rock and Roll Hall of Fame," Finn offered.

Lizzie shrugged her fourteen-year-old shoulders again.

"Mucho multiplatinum, multigold," Anton volunteered.

Click-click-click. Pause. Click-click-click.

"The old guy with the highlights!" Lizzie crowed. "I thought he was dead."

The bakery kitchen erupted into loud groans.

"Don't look at me," Hayley protested, waving her hands in the air. "Her father loved disco."

He couldn't remember the last time he heard Anton laugh so loud or so long. "The child needs to sit down and listen to what rock is supposed to sound like. Tommy is one of the greats."

"'Break Me,'" Finn said, listing Tommy's greatest hits. "'Your Place or Heaven,' 'Fear of Falling'—"

"'Fire Fight'!" Hayley and Anton said simultaneously, then slapped plastic-wrapped hands in the air over the carrot cake.

Lizzie rolled her eyes. "Okay, okay!" she said in good-natured defeat. "I get it. He's super-amazing and everyone but me knows it. That's cool."

I like this kid, Finn thought as the printer churned out a copy of the proposal. She was smart, funny, easygoing, so much like her grandfather Tommy that it almost made the puzzles of DNA clear to him. Until a few minutes ago, Lizzie Goldstein hadn't known Tommy Stiles existed. She had no frame of reference she could use to model herself after him. She was her own self and that self was a smaller, feminine version of the grandfather she had never met.

He locked eyes across the room with Anton. The drummer saw it too, which meant

Finn would have to do some explaining on the long drive back out to Long Island. He couldn't deny what was right there in front of them. He wasn't sure he wanted to.

"It's our standard form," Lizzie was saying as she pushed the legal-sized page toward him. "Basic stuff about deposits, cancellation penalties, payment options."

"Great," he said. "I'll take a look."

"I mean, I know you're a lawyer and everything, but I do a thorough job. You won't find anything."

"Then you won't mind if I take a look." The kid had self-confidence, that much was certain.

He scanned the paragraphs, ran the numbers in his head, then reread the entire thing slowly, word for word.

"You were right," he said. "This is textbook-perfect stuff. I know paralegals who couldn't get it this right."

She beamed at the praise. "Thanks. I told you it was good."

"Except for one thing."

"But I'm sure—"

He crossed out a price quote and replaced it with another, higher one.

She took a close look at his change.

"You raised the price!? Nobody raises the price!"

"I offered your mother extra for short notice when we were negotiating."

"She didn't tell me that."

She maintained eye contact like a first-class litigator pleading her case in front of the Supremes.

"She forgot," he said, "but I didn't."

"Are you going to sign?" she asked, unable to mask the excitement in her voice. "I mean, like now? Tonight?"

"I'm going to sign."

"You don't have to take it back for the famous guy to countersign?"

"I can sign for him."

She looked like a kid who still believed in Santa Claus and he felt like the Grinch Who Stole Christmas. Would she still look that happy when she found out Tommy was her grandfather and this whole thing had been nothing more than a convenient way to check them all out before breaking the news?

"Yo!" Anton bellowed. "We need a drum roll here." He started pounding out a rolling beat on the marble slab he had been working on.

Lizzie leaped to her feet. "Let me see!"

The mini-mogul morphed back into a skinny fourteen-year-old right before Finn's eyes.

Hayley looked triumphant. Her smile was wide and, Finn suddenly realized, every bit as lopsided as her father's. Except she didn't know that. She didn't know half the things he knew, half the things she would find out as this whole story unfolded.

There was a guarded quality to her that Lizzie didn't share. He had only done a basic LexisNexis search, but he had seen enough about her ex-husband to understand why she had erected fences around herself and the ones she loved.

There were no fences around Tommy's heart. The only reason he cared about protecting his assets was for the sake of his children. Guarding his heart was something he had never learned to do.

In a perfect world, they would meet and the bond would spring to life between them in the space of a heartbeat. Tommy would open his arms to his long-lost daughter and she would fall into them, no questions asked.

A father-and-child reunion that would erase thirty-eight years of questions?

Not a chance in hell.

*   *   *

What was going on? Finn Rafferty wouldn't stop looking at her.

She wouldn't have known that except for the fact that she kept looking over at him and getting caught. She had tried to conceal it by pretending she was keeping an eye on her daughter but the man had radar.

He probably had a few questions and she didn't blame him. Asking a fourteen-year-old to negotiate the deal for you was probably not the way things were done out there in tony East Hampton.

South Jersey must seem like another planet to him.

Which, following that line of thought, made her an alien.

That would explain a lot.

"So what do you think?" she asked when he finally joined them at the work bench. "This is a basic design, per the client's request, but I'll use some of the same techniques on the drum set for your party next week."

"Looks good."

"That's the best you can do?"

"It looks very good."

Even Anton groaned.

If she had been in his shoes, she would

have been watching the process every step of the way, hanging on every shingle and shutter. Now that the deal was all but signed, he acted like the finished product was irrelevant.

"C'mon, man." Anton sounded exasperated. "Open your eyes. This is a work of art."

"Anton set the windows in place," she explained as Rafferty deigned to take a closer look. "We use finely spun sugar baked in the oven for the panes of glass."

Nothing.

Not even a grunt.

Anton, beaming like a proud father, pointed out various details that seemed to float right over his boss's head. Or was he Anton's boss? They seemed more like friends. The whole relationship was muddled to her.

Trish had been right when she said Anton was a rock star. He was the After Life's drummer, a position he'd held for the past fourteen years. Before joining up with Tommy Stiles, he had played backup for a veritable Who's Who of rock royalty. He was currently separated from his first and only wife and living in a guesthouse on Tommy's Long Island property. To hear him tell it, Stiles was a combination of Rod Stewart and Mother Teresa, a generous, warm-hearted free spirit who would give you the Versace off his back if you needed it.

"Nobody's that perfect," she had said as she carefully urged the sugar paste deck into position at the back of the carrot cake house. "Tell me he pulls the wings off flies or likes to lie around in his Jockeys eating pork rinds and watching NASCAR."

"He does like NASCAR," Anton had admitted, laughing, "but, believe it or not, he's one of the good guys."

She didn't believe it. You didn't get to be that famous for that long by being a good guy. Her ex-husband wasn't even famous and he hadn't managed to make it out of his twenties with his good-guy credentials intact.

Not that it was any of her business. She was decorating a cake for the man, not marrying him. Although if she remembered her celebrity gossip correctly, Stiles was a big fan of marriage and had an army of ex-wives and lovers and children scattered on two continents to prove it.

Classic male menopause, she thought. The aging stud who started up a new young family every time he felt his testosterone level getting lower. Not exactly her idea of a great role model.

A man like that spent his twenties and thirties building a career, making a name for himself, forgetting the fact that he had a wife and children back home who made his freedom possible. Sooner or later the marriage (or marriages) broke up, and our hero found himself a new woman, and next thing you knew he had himself a new wife and a new family and a full-color spread in *People* filled with quotes like "I love being a dad" and "You bet I change diapers."

Again, not that it was any of her business. It was just that she knew Trish and Rachel were standing with their ears to the door, hanging on every word, and she wanted to be the voice of reason designed to bring them back down to earth.

Preferably with a thud hard enough to shake some sense into their pretty heads.

They needed to know women could conduct business with a gorgeous (okay, so he wasn't just easy on the eyes, he was downright eye candy) man and not succumb to simpering, eyelash-batting flirtation.

"Any comments, complaints, suggestions?" she prodded Rafferty after he had finished examining the cake house like it was the space shuttle after a flight. "Your boss is going to be paying serious money. You might as well get exactly what you're looking for."

"I'm looking for a drum set," Rafferty said, too sharply for her taste. "Bass, snare—that's what we agreed on."

"We haven't signed anything yet, Mr. Rafferty. If you want to find yourself another baker, that's fine with me."

"Mom!" Lizzie sounded like she was choking on one of her Linzer tortes.

"Quiet, Elizabeth," she said over her shoulder then swung back around on Rafferty. "All day long I've had the feeling something was going to go wrong and maybe this is the something I've been waiting for. I'm sorry but this whole thing feels weird to me. You're going to be throwing a party in a major Atlantic City hotel. I've been to events at those hotels. I know what they can do. You can't tell me that one of their pastry chefs couldn't whip up something big and gorgeous for you on a moment's notice."

He looked genuinely surprised, which, if she hadn't been so annoyed, would have made her laugh out loud. "You're telling me you don't want the job?"

"I want the job more than I want my right kidney, but I still don't get why Tommy Stiles's lawyer drove all the way down to Lakeside, New Jersey, to buy a cake. There's something you're not telling me."

"You're so making a mistake," Lizzie said in a stage whisper.

Rafferty glanced quickly at her daughter and the look of respect in his eyes shifted something inside Hayley. Every time she thought she had him pegged, he threw her a curve. She'd taken a big chance, letting him work out the contract details with Lizzie. Not too many hotshot attorneys would have sat down with her kid, much less treated her with kindness and without condescension.

So why the sudden loss of enthusiasm? She had a lot of experience with men who blew hot and cold with their affections. For most of the years of her marriage she had accepted the shifting floor beneath her feet as part of the bargain she had made when she married Michael.

Well, she wasn't married any longer. She didn't have to accept anything from any man. Especially not from a stranger.

"Listen," she said as the image of herself on *Entertainment Tonight* faded away, "you were real enthusiastic about my work until you saw this cake and now you can barely spit out two complete sentences. If you don't like what you see, then say so. I promise you I'm not going to impale myself on a cake server if you don't like it."

"Mom!" Lizzie sounded like she wanted to lock her in a soundproofed closet and throw away the key. "What are you doing?"

"Your mom's right, Lizzie," Finn Rafferty said. "I've been acting like a horse's ass and I'm sorry."

"I never said you were acting like a horse's ass. I said you were—" She stopped. Maybe horse's ass was the best description after all.

"I like the real estate agents' cake," Rafferty said.

"You don't sound very enthusiastic," Anton said, a wicked gleam in his dark eyes. "I noticed that too, Hayley."

"It's a great cake," Finn said. "A cake among cakes. A cake that will live long in the memory of everyone lucky enough to see it."

"Not funny," Anton said.

"He's right," Hayley agreed. "Not funny at all."

"I like the cake. I didn't think you could pull it off but you did. You'll probably do a great job on the after-party. Your daughter drew up a perfect contract. The sun is shining. The birds are singing. I still have all of my hair. If I'm missing something, I'll be damned if I know what it is."

She stood there, pen poised, and still didn't sign. What was her problem? All she had to do was bake a cake, not hand over the keys to the bakery. If the goddesses of sugar, flour, and pure creamery butter didn't rain blessings (and contracts) down on her head after the party in Atlantic City, her world wouldn't come to an end. But something continued to hold her back.

"I've been on the payroll almost fifteen years, if that's what's worrying you," Anton offered. "They haven't bounced a check yet."

Bless the bald-headed drummer for breaking the tension. The laughter came as a welcome relief.

"You're right," Rafferty said to Lizzie. "She is a worrier."

"Told you," Lizzie said. "She even worries about Katie Couric's ratings."

"Elizabeth!" she said through the new burst of laughter. "I explained that to you last week. I'm not worried about her ratings, I'm just . . . concerned."

"You worry about news anchors?" Rafferty asked.

"Worry is good," Anton said, still laughing. "When it comes to his kids, even Tommy's a worrier."

She pointed toward Rafferty. "What was that look?"

"What look?"

"You shot Anton a look when he said, 'even Tommy's a worrier.' What's that about?"

"Yeah," said Anton, "what's up with that?"

"Remember that confidentiality agreement you signed last year? Personal observations are off-limits."

"Too late," Anton said cheerfully. "I already spilled everything I know."

"He's joking," Hayley said, amused by the look of intense horror on the attorney's handsome face. "I tried to get him to spill everything he knows but he refused."

"I owe you," Anton stage-whispered as he mopped his brow with the back of his hand.

Rafferty laughed with them but the uneasy look in his eyes lingered. Something was definitely off. She didn't know what it was exactly but her instincts were rarely wrong and she couldn't let go.

He wore an Armani suit, but once upon a time he had also worn an earring. The faint dot left from the piercing caught and held her attention. There was definitely more here than she knew.

"Here's the thing," she said. "I'm not a glass-half-full kind of woman. My glass isn't just half empty, it has a hairline crack and it's about to shatter. This whole thing seems too good to be true and it probably is, and I wish I could figure out exactly what's bothering me about it but I can't, so maybe you could help me out here."

They were all staring at her like she had lost her mind.

"Too much information," she said. "I always do that. I get started talking and I can't stop."

Lizzie groaned and buried her face in her hands.

"This is like winning the lottery, Mom," her daughter pleaded. "Who cares why they picked you? They picked you! Work it!"

"You have a recommendation from the governors of two states," Rafferty said. "Unless you've been passing off Entenmann's as your own, you're damn good and you're the one we want for the job."

"You're right. I'm a culinary genius, the Van Gogh of baked goods, who would be decorating cakes for Charles and Camilla if I didn't live in New Jersey."

They continued to stare at her.

"That was a joke," she said. "Yes, it's true but I meant it as a joke."

"Don't make jokes, Mom," Lizzie said from behind her hands. "I'm begging you! Just sign the contract, pleeeeease!"

She looked at Finn Rafferty. She wouldn't be at all surprised if he went the Entenmann's route after all. "I'll sign it if you will."

To her amazement, he reached for a pen.

Despite her misgivings, her heart leaped with excitement. He was actually willing to go the distance.

"We're leaving in five," she said to Lizzie. "Tell Rachel and Trish they can go home. We'll close up. Don't dawdle!"

Lizzie was out of there in a flash.

Anton, whose cell phone had been beeping, stepped outside.

Rafferty signed both copies of the contract, then pushed them toward her.

"Your turn," he said.

"Well, at least I'll be able to pay next month's mortgage without hitting the credit cards," she said, quickly scanning the contract. "Fifty percent deposit, payable within forty-eight hours. That's a good thing."

"Lizzie gave me the account number. It will be deposited in the morning and you should have access to it by the end of the business day." He was watching her closely. Maybe a little too closely, as if he saw the same shadows gathering overhead that she saw.

"Would you tell me if I was right?" she asked as she signed her name twice. "Would you tell me if there was more going on here than baking a cake for a rock star?"

"No," he said, "but I wouldn't tell you that you were wrong."

5

"Are you going to tell me what the hell was going on in there?" Anton asked Finn fifteen minutes later as they headed toward the highway.

"How much have you figured out?"

"We didn't drive down here just to buy a cake."

"Good guess," Finn said.

"The girl has Tom's eyes."

"She does."

"And his smile."

Finn nodded.

"The mother has his eyes too."

"I noticed." Beautifully expressive eyes that held more than a touch of wariness.

"Does Tommy know?"

"He sent me down here to check things out."

They were silent as Finn rolled up to the tollbooth and grabbed a ticket.

"Damn," Anton said as they merged with northbound traffic. "She was right, wasn't she. She thought there was something else going on and there is."

"Mrs. Goldstein is a smart woman." Finn shouldn't have told her even as little as he had back there but when she looked at him with those wary and beautiful eyes, he couldn't lie.

"And funny."

"That too."

"And not bad to look at."

He'd tried hard not to notice.

"Admit it, friend," Anton said. "You couldn't take your eyes off her."

"I couldn't take my eyes off the kid either. It was like looking at Tom."

"Agreed, but that's not why you were looking at the mother."

"You've been reading too many romance novels, Anton."

Anton actually flinched. "You're never going to let me live that down, are you?"

"Probably not," Finn agreed. "It was a memorable sight." Anton sprawled out in the back of a private jet, lost in something called *The Flame and the Flower.*

"Gotta get your happy endings somewhere."

When the man was right, he was right. "Things not going well with Lyssa?"

"Not going at all," Anton said, gazing out the window. "She says she's filing for divorce."

He didn't have to ask why. Life on the road with a rock band was great when you were twenty-two and single but when you were pushing forty-five and married, it was a whole other animal. It was hard to build a marriage when you were on the road eight months of the year.

"You should ask her out," Anton said, circling back.

"What is this, high school? I'm not asking her out."

"She's your type: tall, skinny, not likely to put up with your shit."

"Not funny," he said, although he was laughing. He wasn't about to get into the wisdom of dating a woman who would probably turn out to be Tommy's daughter. "Want to pick up some burgers? There's a McDonald's at the next rest stop."

"If you want to change the subject, that's cool."

"I don't want to change the subject. I just don't want you running with the wrong idea."

"That you thought she was hot?"

"Is this going somewhere," Finn asked, "or are you just trying to break my balls?"

"She asked me about you when we were working on the cake."

"Yeah?" He slid a glance in his friend's direction. "What did she want to know?"

"If you were married."

"What?"

Anton started to laugh. "Gotcha."

"You're a real son of a bitch. You know that, don't you?"

"I've heard that a few times before."

"That's all she asked?" Could he sound any more like a sixteen-year-old kid without a date for the big dance?

"She tried to get some on Tommy but I stuck to what's been in *People*."

"Smart move. That way we won't have to sue your ass from here to L.A. for breach of contract."

The thought of Tommy suing one of his own made them both laugh out loud.

"When's he going to tell her?"

"I don't know but I almost told her the whole story when she was signing the contract." Only loyalty to Tommy had stopped him but it had been close.

"Some people would be real happy to find out their father is a famous rocker. Everyone knows Tommy takes care of his own. She won't have to worry about paying her bills anymore, that's for damn sure."

"I don't think she'll be one of them." The woman he'd met had something to prove.

"She drives a twelve-year-old Buick," Anton pointed out. "She cuts her own hair. Her life is going to do a one-eighty when she finds out about Tommy."

The thought depressed the hell out of him and, once again, he didn't know why.

Usually he rolled with things the same way Tommy did. The Stiles clan grew larger, the family tree more complicated, and the updates and codicils to Tommy's will more frequent. It was what it was and the emotional fallout washed right over him and away.

Tommy wasn't an absentee father with a

checkbook and a guilty conscience. He was the real deal, a hands-on parent who didn't just want the best for his kids, he tried to help them achieve it. Okay, so maybe he had a few tats, some random piercings, and an addiction to highlights and supermodels, but when it came to family nobody did it better.

If Hayley Maitland Goldstein turned out to be Tommy's daughter, the sky would be the limit. That dented Buick would be history. Her Target days would be over. Tommy, in his benevolent way, would roll over her like a gift-wrapped tank.

Finn tried to imagine what it would feel like if someone walked into his life right now and claimed to be his father. He couldn't wrap his brain around the concept. By the time you reached your thirties, you had a pretty good idea who you were and where you came from. You knew why you were the way you were and if you didn't, it was only because you weren't paying attention.

That wasn't the case with Hayley Maitland Goldstein and her daughter, Lizzie. There was no way they could see this coming and as far as Finn could tell, they had Jane

Maitland, Ph.D., to thank. The good doctor knew how to keep a secret. How she had managed to keep that particular secret for thirty-eight years was one of the things he hoped to find out someday.

In the meantime Hayley was living over a bakery in South Jersey with a beautiful young daughter whose IQ was higher than Finn could count. She had an ex-husband who was down in Florida looking for trouble and probably finding it on a regular basis. She worked hard, took care of her kid, and maybe dreamed about winning the Pick-6 so she could upgrade her kitchen.

Discovering she was the daughter of a multimillionaire rock star could be the best thing that ever happened to her. Tommy would wave his magic checkbook and wipe away her debt. He would see to it that her bakery had the newest and best of everything. Her daughter had talked about Cinderella moments and maybe it would be once the dust had settled.

One thing he knew for sure: the truth was going to slam into the two of them like a runaway train, and no matter how much he wished he could soften the blow, there wasn't a damn thing he could do to stop it.

Back in New Jersey

Hayley pulled into the parking lot then looked over at her daughter. "Do you think we should do this?"

"I think we should," Lizzie said. "I think we earned it."

"It's a major splurge."

"I think we'd be seriously deranged if we didn't do it."

"No complaining at the end of the month when you balance the books."

"Promise." Hayley could see her daughter's wide smile even in the darkened car. "Besides, this time next week we'll be rich and famous."

She didn't want to dim Lizzie's enthusiasm with a standard-issue lecture on counting unhatched chickens but she was a mother. She had to do what she had to do.

"It hasn't happened yet," she said as they followed the Olive Garden hostess to a tiny table next to a huge display of Tuscan wines. "A lot can go wrong between now and next week."

The hostess, who wasn't all that much older than Lizzie, quickly distributed the menus, ran through her spiel of specials, then went back to her post in the lobby.

Hayley had been running on autopilot since signing the contract with Finn Rafferty. Correction, she caught herself. Finn Rafferty negotiated the contract, but it was Tommy Stiles who had set the whole thing in motion and she still couldn't figure out why. Rafferty had admitted there was more to this than cake and that admission still had her unnerved hours later.

"I know what I want." Lizzie turned her menu facedown on the table top.

Hayley couldn't help but laugh. "I know what you want too: salad with lots of red onion, no black olives, lasagna with extra sauce and grated cheese, and everything chocolate for dessert."

"I know what I like," Lizzie said.

"You've known what you liked since you were six months old and decided it was time to stop nursing."

Lizzie's cheeks flamed. "Do we have to talk about that in public?"

She kept forgetting that they were sailing into dangerous waters these days, a place where every maternal utterance could stir up a tsunami of embarrassment and hurt feelings.

"Grandma Jane used to talk about placentas at the playground," Hayley said as she scanned her menu. "I'd be sitting in the sandbox, wishing I could dig my way to China and disappear."

"Mom! Could we not?"

"I'm just telling you that I understand."

"If you understood, you wouldn't talk about stuff like that."

"When you're a scientist, you'll be talking about things like that all the time."

"Not in Olive Garden," Lizzie said, rolling her eyes. "There's a big difference."

They ate their way through the salad bowl, then threw caution to the wind and asked for a refill.

"Is this the life or what?" Hayley said as she reached for her glass of iced tea. "A bottomless salad bowl, all the breadsticks you can eat, and no dirty dishes to wash when it's over."

"Maybe we can do this again next week after we deliver the cake to Atlantic City."

"I was going to have Dominic deliver it."

"What!?" Lizzie looked downright horrified.

"You have to deliver it yourself! This is your chance to get noticed."

"It's going to be huge, Lizzie. We'll need the van."

"You've driven the van."

"And it will be heavy. I'll need help."

"I can help."

"Help with muscles," Hayley said. What she didn't say was that an after-party for a famous rocker probably wasn't the place for an overly articulate, highly impressionable fourteen-year-old girl. Especially not one with huge blue-green eyes and long blond hair.

"Then let me go along for the ride."

"Not happening."

"Why not?"

"Where do I start? How about this: I'm not going and neither are you."

"But you have to go."

"I don't recall seeing that spelled out in the contract."

"Mom! This is your big chance. You have to go so you can bask in the glory."

"We'll let the cake bask in the glory. I'd be happy basking in a flood of new commissions."

"What about *Entertainment Tonight* and

all of the local news guys? The place will be jammed with promo ops."

She shrugged. "Word will get out."

Lizzie narrowed her eyes and leaned across the empty salad bowl. "You're afraid!"

"I am not."

"You are! You shouldn't be but you so are."

It would be nice to keep at least one emotion secret from her daughter. She gestured toward her basic uniform of T-shirt and jeans. "Look at me. I'm not exactly red-carpet worthy. I'd need a whole new wardrobe."

"Wear your whites like they do on the Food Network."

"I haven't had my hair cut since Christmas."

"Wear it in a ballerina bun."

"All I have are sneakers and clogs."

"Clogs are way cool. The interns on *Grey's Anatomy* wear clogs."

"They wear running shoes."

Lizzie was adamant. "Some of them wear clogs."

"You think I should wear my red clogs?"

"Mario on the Food Network wears orange ones and he's famous."

"How much television are you watching lately anyway?"

Lizzie ignored the question. "You'll stand out from the crowd. You need to work this, Mom. I mean, what are the chances something like this will happen again?"

"I'm still trying to figure out why it happened in the first place."

Lizzie fell silent for a moment. "It's not like you aren't great at what you do."

"Lots of people are great at what they do," she reminded her daughter, "and they live their entire lives without a single Cinderella moment."

"Karma?" Lizzie asked. "Like maybe you did something wonderful in another life and now you're being rewarded."

"I'm Catholic," she reminded her daughter. "I don't get rewarded until I die."

Lizzie, who was forging a more ecumenical path between her Catholic mother and Jewish father, sighed. "Does there have to be a reason?"

"You're the logical, scientific one. I thought you believed everything that happens, happens for a reason."

"Luck is luck," her daughter said. "Luck doesn't need a reason. It just is."

That was what Hayley used to say about love and look where that had gotten her.

She tried to push the negative thought from her mind for her daughter's sake.

"Your dad and I used to eat at Olive Garden all the time," she said after Margo dropped off their entrees. "We went to the one near Aunt Fiona's old house the day I found out I was pregnant with you."

She rarely spoke about Michael and when she did, it usually wasn't complimentary. The man had come close to ruining her life and Lizzie's with his gambling and risk-taking. It wasn't an easy thing to forget. She tried to be careful around Lizzie but unfortunately she was only human. Like it or not, the man was still her daughter's father and always would be. She needed to remember that for Lizzie's sake if not her own.

"That's when you two were happy together, right?"

"We were trying, honey." How young Lizzie looked, how innocent and hungry for bits and pieces of her family's past. "Sometimes we were very happy. The day you were born was probably the happiest day of our lives."

Lizzie fell quiet, directing her attention to the plate of lasagna in front of her while Hayley picked at her grilled chicken and pretended it was shrimp scampi drowning in butter and garlic. The silence between them could be a brief one or it could last for hours. The last few months had been a roller-coaster ride of emotions where Lizzie was concerned and there were times when Hayley hadn't a clue what to say or do.

"Hormones," Michelle, her former sister-in-law had said. Michie was the mother of four teenagers and an expert on the subject. "There's nothing you can say or do to make her hear you until she's ready. Just sit back, strap yourself in, and wait for the storm to pass."

Hayley couldn't shake the feeling that there was something more than hormones going on. Lizzie had planned to visit her father in Florida over the Christmas/ Chanukah holidays but Michael had begged off, saying he had some business to take care of in the Bahamas. He said winter break wasn't good for him and then a month later he cancelled their plans for spring break. Easter and Passover raced by without acknowledgment. Eleven times he had promised his daughter—the daughter who adored him—that they would spend some time together and eleven times he had broken her heart.

Lizzie had tried to put a brave face on it, but Hayley knew she was hurting badly. Given the chance, she could happily kill Michael with her bare hands and not feel one single second of regret.

"Did you miss having a dad when you were growing up?"

The question brought Hayley up short. "You can't miss what you never had." She aimed for bright and breezy honesty.

Lizzie didn't smile. "I mean, didn't you ever wish you could have had a dad you could talk to?"

"What makes you ask?"

"I was thinking about Grandma Jane and how she's coming home soon and I started wondering. That's all."

"Is something wrong?"

Lizzie shrugged and looked away. Hayley followed her gaze to the table by the window where a middle-aged father and his teenage daughter were talking earnestly over plates of spaghetti and meatballs. A small event in the scheme of things but one neither of them had ever experienced.

"You're missing your dad, aren't you?"

"Not so much," Lizzie said with a vigorous shake of her head. She looked down at her lasagna. "Maybe a little."

"I know he e-mails you. Has he been in touch?"

"You know." Amazing how inarticulate her straight-A child could become when it benefited her. "Sometimes he leaves comments on my blog."

"Anything I should know about?"

She shrugged. "Just regular stuff."

Whatever that meant. Hayley was constantly torn between wanting to keep close tabs on her daughter's creative outlet and understanding the girl's need for breathing room. It was a difficult and dangerous balancing act. She visited Lizzie's blog every few weeks just to keep an eye on things but she knew that what she saw wasn't necessarily all there was. The rest she had to take on faith.

That wasn't an easy thing for a worrier to do.

"School will be over before you know it. Grandma Connie got a great deal on tickets. She can't wait to see you in July."

"Will Dad be there?"

"I think he's there now," Hayley said, treading carefully. Michael wasn't known as the escape artist for nothing. "Why don't you e-mail him and ask about his plans?" If she had her way, she would hog-tie the son of a bitch to his mother's lanai until Lizzie got there, but the authorities might not take kindly to the idea.

"If you want to talk . . ." She said it gently, letting the words drift across the table and into her daughter's ear. These days there seemed to be dozens of invisible barriers dancing around her daughter. She never knew which of her approaches would succeed and which would be deflected. No topic was more fraught with peril than Michael Goldstein.

Lizzie broke off a piece of lasagna with the edge of her fork. "Did Grandma Jane date a lot?"

"Define 'a lot.'"

"At all."

"Not so you'd notice," Hayley said. "A dinner here and there. The occasional black-tie thing." Professional engagements for the most part. Or at least that was what Hayley had always believed.

"Didn't she ever fall in love?"

"If she did, she didn't tell me."

"Is she gay?"

"Not that I know of."

"So why didn't she have a baby with one of her professor friends instead of going to a sperm bank when she decided she wanted a kid?"

Why indeed. She had only asked herself the same question every day for the first eighteen years of her life.

"You know your grandmother," she said finally. "She's a scientist. She doesn't believe in leaving anything to chance. She wanted a genius child who would be guided by logic, intellect, and the life of the higher mind and the sperm bank promised they could deliver one." She lifted her glass of iced tea in salute. "Instead she got me." A former wild child who loved tattoos, piercings, and boys with double-digit IQs who thought the life of the mind was something you got around to when you were too old for anything else. "I'm surprised she didn't sue the sperm bank for false advertising."

Lizzie giggled, a sound Hayley hadn't heard in a long while.

"And you wonder why I'm a worrier," she said, laughing along with her kid. "If your grandmother couldn't control her destiny, what chance do I have?"

Mumbai, India

John Roman Lassiter IV, professor of antiquities and dean emeritus of the Colchester School for Applied Studies, had the voice of a 1940s radio announcer: a vibrant, rich baritone that made a woman's spine tingle.

The first time Jane Maitland heard him speak she had been enduring a dinner party, engaged in conversation with Arnold Rosenblatt, the man responsible for isolating the effects of noise on indigenous populations of hualanim fish off the coast of Indonesia. A thoroughly fascinating topic and one that usually would have commanded all of her attention and intellect, but this voice, a truly mellifluous, wonderful voice, rose up from the din and ensorcelled her.

How strange to think that after a life lived in happy solitude and singular independence, the sound of a man's voice could change the landscape with the ferocity of a tsunami.

Nothing, not even motherhood, had ever swayed her from her course. She loved Hayley deeply but her inadequacies as a mother had manifested themselves early on. She had watched younger parents with their children and envied the easy intimacy they shared with their offspring. For a brief moment in time she had wondered if she had done the right thing, if her decision to raise the child alone hadn't been the ultimate manifestation of selfishness and not the gesture of deep generosity she had intended it to be.

Those early years were an experiment doomed to failure. Hayley had traveled with her to South America on a research grant, endured an endless expedition in the Bering Strait, and somehow managed to survive a harrowing storm off the coast of Cape Hatteras where Jane had been monitoring the effects of an oil spill on various marine migratory patterns.

It became abundantly clear to everyone that she couldn't mother a child alone and pursue her vocation simultaneously. Certainly not with any degree of success in either field. By the time Hayley started high school, it was obvious that the girl needed a stable, traditional school environment and Jane had turned to her sister Fiona for help.

She chose to believe her decisions had been wise and nurturing and that her willful, scattered, loving daughter had benefited from the presence of two strong women in her life rather than the absence of one man, but as the years wore on, she grew less certain.

Had she done the right thing? She wasn't sure she would ever know. So many decisions made in times of stress and uncertainty, decisions made with a kind heart and generous spirit, decisions that could never be undone. Who could say what was right and what was wrong?

She had been thinking a great deal lately about her professional legacy as well, the lifetime of knowledge that she would leave behind as a foundation for future generations. In the shadow of her eightieth year, she had expected many things to come her way: more acclaim, greater responsibility, the gathering awareness that as her time grew shorter, the decisions she made would grow in importance.

She had never expected love to be part of the equation.

But there he was, seated across from her at the breakfast table in her rented flat, reading his copy of the *Times* with his glasses perched on the end of his regal, aquiline nose, humming something soft and Mozartian while she sipped her coffee and sifted through the documents involved in their return to the States.

The swiftness of it all still had her feeling dazed. After the funding for her tour was cut off, she had been bombarded with lecture opportunities from every major university and oceanographic lab on the planet. She had settled on a four-month lecture/study appointment with a research group in southwestern Australia when a prolonged bout of indigestion sent her to see Dr. Athalye at University Hospital and the landscape of her life was thrown into sharp, uncompromising focus one last time.

She didn't want some attorney on retainer telling Hayley the things her mother should have told her a long time ago.

In a strange way there was comfort to be found in knowing her time was limited. Each minute, every hour, became more precious. You strove harder, cared more deeply, loved with an intensity that the young and healthy couldn't possibly understand.

John cried when she told him and, to her surprise, his tears unlocked her own sorrow and she cried with him. She cried for the first time in almost forty years and a feeling of deep joy washed over and around her, lifting her up higher and higher to a place a scientist would tell you couldn't possibly exist.

When he asked her to marry him, she said yes without hesitation.

He looked at her over the top of his paper and smiled. She felt like she had been smiling back at him all her life.

"Everything in order?" That voice! That mellow, dark-coffee-with-cream voice!

"For the most part. I need to confirm our flight plans but everything else is as it should be."

"Will your daughter meet us at the airport?"

Ah, the lone cloud on the bright horizon finally appeared. "I'm having a car service pick us up, John. Lakeside is a fair distance from Newark Liberty."

He considered her with steady gray eyes set in a tanned and lined face few women would consider handsome. His skin was rough and leathery. His eyes were surrounded by a network of lines and wrinkles that were testament to every one of his seventy-something years on this battered and aching planet. There were times when she believed, foolishly, romantically, that he could see into her soul. The thesis, of course, was wrong on many levels. Not the least of which involved the existence (or nonexistence) of a soul. But somehow she continued to believe.

"Our engagement must have come as a considerable surprise to her."

That tangled and terrible web . . .

"John, that's an announcement I feel better making in person."

He nodded. "I understand." Even though he had told his own children by phone. Their excited shrieks of delight still echoed in her head. "You'll present me as a fait accompli."

"I shall." She inhaled a deep breath. "I think it best if I met with Hayley alone when I did so."

Some of the joy in his gray eyes dimmed. Her heart ached but there was no hope for it. "I would be lying if I said I wasn't disappointed. I had looked forward to taking this first step with you toward building an extended family."

"And we will do precisely that, John, but first there's something I need to tell my daughter."

"About us?"

"There is that."

His eyes saddened. "About your health."

She leaned across the table and took his hand in hers. "No," she said with all the love in her heart, "about her father."

East Hampton

Everyone said Tommy Stiles gave great interviews. He could be funny, irreverent, sincere, bawdy, and painfully honest in a way that made for juicy sound bites and lots of fun for the reporter sitting opposite him.

But not today.

"Cut!" Angela Deming gestured toward her television crew with a sharp wave of her hand. "Take five, guys."

"There's a load of stuff in the kitchen," Tommy said. "Tell Greta to make whatever you want."

"If you can't give 'em a good interview, give 'em food," Angela said as soon as the crew left the room.

"Works for me," Tommy said.

"What's wrong? I've been lobbing softballs and you're not even managing to hit a single."

"Maybe I'm in a slump," he said, struggling with his signature affable grin. "I thought I was hitting doubles at least."

"No," Angela said with a rueful smile. "Trust me, not even close to hitting doubles."

"It's been a long day, Angie. I'm pushing sixty. A single doesn't sound half bad."

"So what's going on? You should be able to do twenty minutes on your benefit concert in your sleep."

"What time is it?" he asked. "Nine, ten o'clock? I've been doing this since eleven this morning. I've spoken to a hundred and fourteen reporters and bullshitted my way through eight satellite interviews with morning-show hosts and lunch-hour talking heads. I'm sorry, Angie, but I've got nothing left."

"Okay, so enough with the benefit." She considered him across the room. "So when's the wedding?"

His signature smile faltered but he recovered before even a pro like Angie could notice. Every now and then practice really did make perfect. "Sooner the better. Willow's about to start the second trimester so we need to move it forward."

"Just an old-fashioned kind of guy, Tommy?"

She meant it in a gentle, teasing kind of way but for some reason the words hit him hard.

"I love her. She's carrying my child. We plan to get married." He leaned forward, dropping all pretense of the affable smile. "Something wrong with that?"

"Coming from anyone else, I'd say it was the biggest con job this side of Milli Vanilli." She nodded as the crew reclaimed their positions at camera, lighting, and sound. "But it's you, so . . ." She spread her hands wide in a gesture meant to convey bewildered understanding.

It was the wrong day for bewildered understanding. Right now Finn was down in South Jersey talking to a thirty-eight-year-old single mother who could very well be his firstborn child. So much time wasted . . .

"When did family become a joke?" he said

out loud, as much to himself as to her. "When I was thirteen, a girl showed up at my door. She was maybe twenty or twenty-one, a college student. She was looking for my old man. Turned out she was his first kid by an ex-girlfriend and she wanted to see the son of a bitch who didn't want her in his life.

"I'm fifty-nine years old. I've made some mistakes along the way but mostly I've been damn lucky. The women I loved still love me even if they don't want to live with me. My kids don't have to deal with anger or custody fights or divided loyalties. We're all in this together. In what twisted universe is that a joke?"

Angie's dark eyes were glittering with excitement. Amusement was okay. Laughter was even better. You never wanted a reporter's eyes to glitter with anything even close to excitement.

"Your children keep a relatively low profile as far as rock star offspring are concerned. I know Beryl is a successful jewelry designer, but we don't really know much about the others." She gave a small gesture toward her crew to start filming again.

She had touched a nerve, a big one. His children were his Achilles' heel. Not fame. Not fortune. Family.

They were each terrific in his or her own way. Maybe it was time to talk about them, to tell them publicly how proud he was.

The bases were loaded, the ball was in the strike zone, and he was going to hit it out of the park one more time.

6

Rhoda, their eighty-pound rescue dog, was waiting for Hayley and Lizzie at the front door.

The Labrador mix leaped up, put her paws on Hayley's shoulders, and gazed at her with the kind of adoration usually found on Hallmark cards circa 1957.

"I know, I know," Hayley said, ducking an enthusiastic dog kiss. "You want to go out, don't you, girl?" She grabbed the industrial-strength leash from the peg near the door and hooked it to Rhoda's collar.

"Want me to walk her?" Lizzie, stifling a yawn, asked.

"Not at this hour," Hayley said. "I'll walk Rhoda. You feed Murray, Ted, and Mary, and make sure the litter boxes are in good shape." The littermates had been found in a discarded cardboard box behind the bakery three years ago and instantly adopted into the family.

"Ugh." Lizzie looked less than pleased. "We should get one of those self-cleaning litter boxes like you see on television."

"Win the lottery and we'll talk," Hayley said as Rhoda danced around in a state of urgent excitement. "And make sure Mr. G has clean water."

Mr. G was a thirty-two-year-old Amazon parrot that had once belonged to her late father-in-law. Named after the famous Lou Grant character on *The Mary Tyler Moore Show*, the parrot had the same irascible demeanor and salty vocabulary of both his former owner and his namesake.

"Don't look so put upon, Lizzie. Following an eighty-pound dog with a Ziploc bag isn't fun either."

Twenty minutes later all of the pets had been tended to, the house was locked up for the night, and Lizzie was racing for the back stairs.

"Lights off by eleven," Hayley called out as her daughter whizzed by. "Not a second later!"

"I know, I know," Lizzie tossed over her shoulder. "You say the same thing every night."

"Because you push it past midnight every night. Tomorrow's a school day. You need your sleep."

She had to admit there was something painfully ironic about a C+ mother advising her A+ daughter on anything to do with school.

Hayley had gone AWOL more times than she could count and her grades had reflected that. If the sun shone brightly in Cincinnati, she had taken the day off to celebrate. Her daughter actually liked going to school and sought out summer classes.

She swung open the door to the family fridge and found a place for their leftovers and Aunt Fiona's care package amid the Tupperware UFOs.

She started a pot of decaf, then sat down at the kitchen table to sort through the mail. Tonight had been special in so many ways that she hated to see it end. The real estate agents had loved the cake—far more than she herself had loved it, to be honest—and the association had mentioned wanting her to handle two more gigs for them before the month was over.

And, of course, there was the whole Tommy Stiles thing, which by itself was enough to fry her brain cells. She would forget all about it for ten or fifteen minutes and then the whole improbable, deliriously wonderful thing would come back to her and she would be overwhelmed with excitement all over again.

She might never be able to rationalize why a world-class rocker would hire a single mother from South Jersey to bake a cake for him, but she had a signed contract in her hands and the promise of money in the bank by this time tomorrow.

Even a world-class worrier had to admit it was looking good.

But the best thing of all was spending an evening with Lizzie. Away from home, away from the bakery, away from all the distractions that went hand in hand with everyday life, Lizzie had opened up a little about how much she missed her father and that insight had moved Hayley deeply.

You don't miss what you never had.

That was what she had told Lizzie and for Hayley it was true. She had never known what it was like to have a father figure, a man who towered above the rest and made you feel safe and secure. The Michael Goldstein that Hayley knew was terribly flawed, but the Michael that Lizzie loved was the father who made the monsters in the closet disappear and she missed him.

Lizzie had been the reason she had stayed with Michael as long as she had and, strangely enough, Lizzie was the reason she ultimately left. Michael had chosen to live a risky life and sooner or later the danger he thrived on would have crept into their home and threatened their daughter's safety.

How did you explain to a fourteen-year-old who was missing her father that sometimes being alone was the better choice? The gray areas of life were invisible when you were fourteen. Your world was cast in black and white. The people you loved were good and true and would keep you safe from harm. How did you explain to that fourteen-year-old that sometimes the people you loved made terrible, selfish decisions and the only way you could protect yourself was to walk away before it was too late?

She remembered how it felt to be four-teen. Any day now Lizzie would wake up, take a look around her, and discover she was living with a slacker cake-baking mom whose math skills were limited to the num-ber of tablespoons of flour it took to fill a measuring cup and the Great Adolescent Rebellion would begin. They probably wouldn't speak again until Lizzie was old enough to vote.

She was glad she had let herself be talked into stopping for dinner at Olive Garden. Over the years she had grown so good at saying no, at being sensible and responsible and cautious, that sometimes she did it without even thinking.

She stood in the hallway, listening to the faint *click-click* of the keyboard coming from Lizzie's room. That noise was the sound track to their lives. Blogging. E-mailing. Creating websites. Doing whatever else your average wunderkind did.

Maybe Hayley worked her too hard. It was so easy to sit back and let Lizzie take care of the contracts, the billing, the website. Right now she was probably uploading the photos of the cake they had just delivered to the Cumberland County real estate agents.

A great kid, a great job, and now a great chance at hitting the big time.

Now if she could just shake the feeling that there was a giant shoe suspended overhead, waiting to drop.

Welcome, Liz. You have 1 NEW message.

TO: rainbowgirl@goldysbakery.biz
FROM: mkg329302@stealthmail.biz
SUBJECT: asap

IM as soon as you get home.

RAINBOWGIRL: I'm here. Where r u?
MKG329302:   u were out late. Everything ok?
RAINBOWGIRL: I delivered a cake w my mom then had pasta at olive garden
MKG329302:   listen I hate to do this but I've got a real problem. Need ur help
RAINBOWGIRL: what?
MKG329302:   need some $ asap.
MKG329302:   r u still there?
RAINBOWGIRL: sorry. How much?
MKG329302:   same as last time

RAINBOWGIRL: I can't do that.

MKG329302:   this is serious. I'm in real trouble.

RAINBOWGIRL: it's almost the end of the month

MKG329302:   that's too long. I need it now

RAINBOWGIRL: I can't. I shouldn't have done it last time. It was wrong.

MKG329302:   you were helping me. That's a good thing

RAINBOWGIRL: why don't you ask your mother?

MKG329302:   she's tapped out. So's everyone else

RAINBOWGIRL: I can't take from the store again. I got it paid back but it was really hard. I had to go into my college $

MKG329302:   you're a smart girl. You won't need that college $. You'll get a scholarship

MKG329302:   ur quiet tonight.

RAINBOWGIRL: don't know what to say

MKG329302:   say you'll help me, lizzie.

RAINBOWGIRL: you have to pay me back by may 15

MKG329302:   ur a good kid lizzie. Ur the only one I can count on.

RAINBOWGIRL: gotta go . . . goodnight dad

**The session has ended
Time: 12:03 a.m.
Duration: 4 mins 37 secs**

East Hampton—After Midnight

Tommy was waiting for them on the front porch. Three empty glasses balanced on the railing and a cloud of cigarette smoke hovered over his head in the dark.

"I thought you quit," Finn said as he climbed the steps.

"I started again."

"That stuff'll kill you." Anton, a reformed smoker, waved his arms in the air between them.

"I want to hear everything," Tommy said as he led them through the sleeping house and into his office.

Taking the bar exam had been easier than answering the man's questions. He wanted to know everything about Hayley. Was she happy? Was she smart? Did she like music? Was she talented? Was she a good mother?

"This is the Hamptons, not Gitmo," Anton said at one point. "Give us a break, will ya?"

If Finn hadn't been so tired, he would have laughed. "We've been at it almost three hours. There's nothing left to tell you."

"Is she pretty?"

"Tall and skinny," Anton said. "One of those big smiles that make you feel good."

"Long, light brown hair with blond lights," Finn said. "She wears it in a ponytail." *She's beautiful, Tommy. Not magazine-cover beautiful like Willow. The kind that lasts.*

"There's gotta be more," Tommy said, drumming the tabletop with his long, bony fingers. "Think harder."

"We were there ninety minutes, Tom. We didn't exactly exchange life stories." Finn leaned back in his chair and stifled a yawn. "That's all we got."

Tommy turned toward Anton, who was nursing his second Red Bull. "Anything he forgot?"

Anton shot a look in Finn's direction. "Did you get her shoe size?"

Finn slapped his forehead with the heel of his right hand. "Damn! Totally forgot."

"You find a daughter I didn't know I had and you're surprised I have questions?"

Finn downed his third espresso and prayed for a reprieve from the governor. "Think how many questions she'll have when she finds out." Not exactly what he'd meant to say but he was tired and his internal censor fell asleep over an hour ago.

"I've been thinking about that." Tommy leaned forward, his blue-green eyes alive with excitement. "Why wait? If we leave now we can get a jump on rush hour and be down in South Jersey before nine."

"Not going to happen," Finn said. "Seriously bad idea."

"Count me out too," Anton said, pushing away from the table. "I'm going to crash."

"Come on," Tommy urged. "We'll split the driving. We're all Jersey boys, right? I haven't had a good diner breakfast in years."

"Later," Anton said. "I'm wasted."

"Don't look at me," Finn said after Anton closed the back door behind him. "The only place I'm driving is home."

"So I'll drive," Tommy said. "You can sleep in the backseat."

"Not if you're driving, I won't. You haven't driven on a highway since nineteen eighty-seven. Let it go for now, Tom. You have a week. Let's see what we can find out between now and then."

"You saw her. You talked to her. I know you. You think this is the real thing. What more proof do I need that she's mine?"

"Blood tests, for starters. Corroboration from the mother."

"There's plenty of time for that. I want to see her with my own eyes."

"Next week." He stifled another yawn. "And I'm not exactly crazy about that idea either."

"Why the hell not?"

"Where do I start?" Finn shot back. "There are legal precedents for handling this type of thing."

"Is this the friend or the lawyer talking?"

"Both. She doesn't have a clue what's going on. The woman has a kid, a business to run. You're going to blow her the hell out of the water when you drop this bomb on her."

He was making progress. He could see it in Tommy's eyes.

"And what about Willow? What about your other kids? Their mothers? Hell, your mother down in Boca is going to jump out of her Lilly Pulitzer when she finds out. Think it through,

Tom. Hayley's been out there for thirty-eight years. You can wait another week to meet her."

Tommy said nothing but Finn could feel his friend's resistance softening.

"I'm asking you to think about the repercussions before you do anything. This isn't just about you, Tom. It's about that woman and her daughter too, and they deserve better."

The silence was long and it wasn't friendly. Tommy was a genuinely good man but superstardom had conditioned him to expect easy acquiescence whenever he exerted his will.

Finn stood up. "I'm heading home. We can talk later."

Or not.

It was up to Tommy.

He drove back to his house in Montauk on autopilot. Great washes of early morning light spilled across the empty roadway. This was the best part of living out on the East End. Not the celebrity sightings or the four-star restaurants with Manhattan menus. The sun-bleached road. Gulls wheeling overhead. The briny, life-giving sea air.

Nothing else came close.

"Damn." The word filled the car. He hadn't handled it right back there. His focus was supposed to be the care and feeding of Tommy Stiles, but the second he laid eyes on Hayley Maitland Goldstein and her daughter, something inside him had shifted. An allegiance he hadn't realized was his to give away had taken a sharp turn toward two total strangers.

Maybe he should bail out on the whole thing. How long had it been since he'd scheduled a vacation that didn't include Tommy and the extended Stiles clan? He had enough frequent flyer miles to take him to Mars and back. Why not spin a globe, pick a spot, and take off for a few weeks?

Or at least until this mess straightened itself out.

He shouldn't have agreed to the whole ridiculous scheme in the first place. He should have tried harder to talk Tommy out of hiring her to supply cakes for the after-party and pushed for proceeding through legal channels. You could say what you wanted about the law and the way it was practiced, but sometimes you needed the cold-blooded distance it provided.

She had known something was going on.

That look of cynical hope in her eyes had made him feel like a shit.

This was the age of celebrity journalism. Paparazzi haunted Main Street in East Hampton like it was the lobby of the Chateau Marmont the day Belushi died. At the first hint of news, they would jump into their SUVs and descend on Lakeside, New Jersey, like a horde of hungry vultures. The Goldstein girls wouldn't stand a chance.

Tommy's kids knew the drill. They had grown up in and around the chaos that came with fame. Their lives were an ongoing reality show that they had been starring in since birth.

For that matter, so had he. His earliest childhood memories were of arenas packed with crazed After Life fans waving light sticks overhead while Tommy and his father made magic onstage. Onstage was where it all happened. Onstage was their reality. The rest was filler.

He remembered the long bus trips before they could afford to lease a jet to take them from city to city. The endless rumble of the road beneath the wheels, the engine's growl, laughter, the faint chords of a guitar rising above the clamor. Everyone he loved all safe and together in the big green bus.

Sometimes he dozed with his head in his mother's lap, listening while she stroked his hair and chatted softly with his father who sat across from them, tuning his guitar while he listened to her dreams for the future.

One day we'll get off the road and—

The sentence remained as unfinished as their lives.

Would they have pulled away one day and settled down somewhere far from the spotlight? Not many people turned away while the spotlight was still shining down on them. Leaving the band would have been like abandoning family. His father and Tommy had been best buds, closer than brothers. Creative, mercurial, deeply decent men whose genius sometimes made them seem scattered and distracted when it came to the stuff of real life.

Real life was the kitchen of Goldy's Bakery where a fourteen-year-old kid negotiated contracts while her mom iced a cake for a group of overweight real estate agents. Real life was a van with a bad transmission, an aging Buick, the look of wariness and hope in her eyes when he signed his name on the dotted line.

He wasn't sure if any of the people in Tommy's extended family, including himself, would handle real life with as much grace and competence as Hayley Maitland Goldstein and her daughter, Lizzie.

7

Goldy's—Around seven a.m.

"You look awful!" Michie announced from the doorway between the shop and the kitchen. She worked the seven-to-noon shift two days a week. "Don't tell me you've been up all night."

"I've been up all night," Hayley said, hiding a yawn with the back of her hand, "and I have nothing but garbage to show for it."

Frank and Maureen, the married couple who had been coming in at four to bake bread for Goldy's for more than thirty years, waved good morning to Michie from across the room.

"She was here when we came in," Frank

called out. "We thought maybe she had a hot date last night and just got home."

Maureen elbowed him in his well-padded ribs. "Less gossip, more bread," she ordered and drew him back to the task at hand.

"Let me see what you've got," Michie said.

Hayley pushed the rough sketch toward her former sister-in-law. "Tell me this isn't as awful as I think it is."

Michie glanced at the sheet of paper then met Hayley's eyes. "It's worse."

"Oh God!" Hayley buried her face in her hands. "I knew it! I never should have taken on this project. I can't make a bass drum out of cake. There isn't a pan big enough on the planet."

"Calm down. You've seen that guy on Food Network. If he doesn't have a big enough pan, he builds one."

"He knows how to weld, Michie! He practically has a machine shop attached to his bakery." Hayley felt herself move another giant step closer to total meltdown. "What am I going to do? I promised I'd fax an idea to them today and I've got nothing!"

"It's only seven in the morning," Michie reminded her. "You have time."

"I have the dentist at nine, my annual at

the gyno at ten thirty, and a retirement cake I need to finish this afternoon for Mrs. Ostrowsky at the bank. Not to mention the fact that the van broke down last night and needs a new transmission."

"Don't forget Lois is taking over for me at noon today."

She groaned. "Which means I'd better make sure her prune Danish is our featured pastry."

"I can't believe anyone still eats prune Danish."

"Goldy's tradition," Hayley said. "Prune Danish on Thursdays, baklava on Fridays, and blackout cake on Saturdays. Some things never change."

"Better you than me," Michie muttered. "I don't know how you stand it."

"Right now my biggest problem is the fact that I need a cake pan the size of a VW."

"I've seen you think your way out of worse messes than this one. Remember the swans? Nobody makes a pan in the shape of a giant swan. You—"

Hayley leaped to her feet and swept Michie into a hug. "That's it!"

The idea was so simple, so perfect, she wondered why it took her so long to see it.

She grabbed a fresh sheet of paper and her marking pens and laughed out loud as the design sprang to life on the page as if by magic.

Monster-sized decorated cookies mounted on padded wire frames, then covered with tinted rolled fondant would serve as the set of drums while ten perfectly matched triple-layer cakes gilded with gold and silver leaf would represent some of the gold and platinum records Tommy Stiles and the After Life had amassed during their long career.

"I'll get there extra early," Hayley said, her mind racing. "I'll need to talk to the hotel's union rep and see if I can get the waitstaff to work up a flashy presentation for the cakes." A darkened ballroom. Some After Life blaring from the speakers. The waitstaff entering from the back, cakes held high, sparklers shooting gold and silver in every direction.

First there would be a long, awestruck silence that would be followed by cheers and stomping of feet and cries of "Baker! Baker!"

Okay, maybe that was going a tad too far, but they would know her name before the evening was out. That much she was sure of.

Michie, however, seemed uncertain. "The contract specifies a cake in the shape of a bass drum. They didn't ask for a giant cookie."

"Michie, come on! They're getting their cakes. The cookies are a bonus."

"But they didn't ask for cookies," Michelle persisted. "They're not expecting cookies. You can't just whip out surprise cookies and expect them to be happy about it."

"Aren't you listening to me? They'll get their cake and cookies too."

"Maybe you'd better fax them the new design and have them sign off on it."

"You're starting to sound like Lizzie."

Michie laughed out loud. "I wish! If I sounded like Lizzie, I'd be running my own company, not working part time in the family bakery for bingo money."

"Okay," Hayley relented. "You might be right. I'll scribble a quick note explaining the changes and fax over the plan. I think they'll be okay with it, don't you? I mean, they must like my work or they wouldn't have driven all the way down to Lakeside."

"I guess." Michie didn't sound quite as positive of that as Hayley would have liked.

"Oh God," she groaned. "You think it's

weird too, don't you? I mean, that Tommy Stiles wants me to do his after-party."

"Hey, what do I know? I think you're a freaking genius with cake but I don't think I'd drive here from the Hamptons for it." Michie shrugged her shoulders. "Maybe the guy's cheap and he figured he'd get a better deal down here."

"He's a rock star, Michie. A millionaire!"

"You read *InStyle*. The richer you are, the less you pay for everything. We save three years to go to Disney World while movie stars vacation every two minutes," Michie said. "You wanna know why? Because somebody else is footing the bill! It's like a law of nature or something."

"I don't think that's what's going on with Tommy Stiles," Hayley said. "He's actually paying me for the cake." Paying her a lot, in point of fact.

Michelle was undeterred. "Okay, then maybe it's some weird kind of money-laundering scheme."

"That involves cake?"

They locked eyes and broke into raucous laughter.

"I didn't say it had to make sense," Michie protested, a tad defensively.

The truth was it didn't make sense and it probably never would. Maybe this really was one of those random acts of good fortune that defied rhyme or reason but showed up in your life just the same.

If only she could believe that.

"Trish is alone up front," Hayley said when they finally stopped laughing about money-laundering baked goods. "You go out there and spell her and I'll fax over the revised plans."

"His lawyer's office opens this early?"

"Probably not but this way it'll be waiting for him when he gets there."

With a little more luck, when the other shoe finally dropped, she wouldn't be there to hear it.

Montauk

Who the hell would be faxing him at seven thirty in the morning?

Finn, fully clothed, had just dropped off into a deep sleep on his living room sofa when the high-pitched whine of the fax machine down the hall erupted. He slammed the sofa pillow over his head and buried his face deeper into the seat cushion but he couldn't block out the sound.

Every time he thought the damn thing was finished it started over again, that ear-piercing shriek arrowing straight into his tired brain.

He could either lie there trying to ignore it or he could get his lazy ass up, stumble down the hall, and rip the phone cord out of the wall.

This had better be one of the overseas promoters with a poor grasp of time zones faxing over an agreement for countersignature and not some moron from one of the contiguous forty-eight.

"What the—?" he muttered as he surveyed the litter of pages scattered across the hardwood floor. The fax shrieked again and began to pump out more pages at a rapid clip.

Time for action. He bent down and peered behind the fax machine, located the phone jack, and detached the cord. Then he yanked the plug from the electrical socket. He considered taking the machine itself and tossing it out the window but decided against it.

He kicked aside a pile of pages and was halfway out the door when something caught his eye and he stopped. He bent down and retrieved a sketch of a drum set and a scribbled note.

Attn: Finn Rafferty
From: Hayley G.—Goldy's Bakery

I'm faxing two pages of sketches for the Stiles project. Instead of creating one giant cake (bass drum), I propose an entire drum set composed of oversized decorated cookies (built up on suitably decorated supports) and ten individual double-layer cakes gilded w/gold & silver leaf to rep After Life's platinum & gold record sales. All at agreed upon price.
Let me know what you think ASAP.

Hayley

He yawned, hooked everything back up again, and scribbled a response on the cover sheet. The woman was clearly one of those morning types. Probably took after her mother.

"Hayley!" Maureen's voice rang out across the bakery kitchen. "Incoming!"

Hayley made a dash for the machine. Talk about a dedicated employee. Clearly working for a superstar wasn't a walk in the park.

She grabbed the page the second the machine spat it out onto the tray.

No problem. 10 cakes idea is great.

FR

Finn was messing in the kitchen fiddling with the wonky cord on his coffeemaker when he heard the fax machine shriek again.

He hadn't moved that fast since his days on the college track team.

Glad you like it but what about your boss?

Hayley

"Again with the fax machine." Frank's knowing grin merited another sock in the ribs from his wife, Maureen. "Hot deal in the works?"

"Hotter than you know," Hayley said with

an answering grin. "There's something big in the wind, Frankie!"

She grabbed the latest fax.

He'll be fine w/it. You have the go-ahead.

FR

I need that in writing.

Hayley

You just got it in writing.

FR

I mean, an amended contract.

Hayley

She jumped when her cell rang.

"You're serious?" a male voice said.

An idiotic smile broke across her face and she turned away from Frank's and Maureen's curious stares.

"I'm very serious."

"You want the contract amended."

"Don't you?"

"I'm the lawyer and I'm not worried."

"That's why I am worried."

It popped out. She hadn't meant to say it but there it was. Good-bye to the ten cakes, the deposit, the whole deal.

But he surprised her by laughing. And not just one of those you'll-pay-for-that-crack kind of laughs. A real one.

Despite herself, her smile widened.

"I didn't mean that the way it sounded," she said.

"Sure you did. I don't trust lawyers either."

It was her turn to laugh. "Now I'm sure I want an amended contract."

Rafferty didn't miss a beat. "If you want one, I'll fax you one."

She listened for subtext but there didn't seem to be any. If she had stepped on his male ego, he didn't let on. The guy was either a darn good actor or remarkably secure.

Now was the time to match his goodwill with a matching display of equal goodwill but she couldn't seem to make that leap.

"The amended contract?" he prodded. "Yes or no?"

"Yes," she said.

She could hear the surprise in the silence between them.

"Okay," he said. "I'll fax it to you later this morning."

"It's nothing personal. I just believe in crossing all the *t*'s and dotting all the *i*'s."

"Check your account later this afternoon," he reminded her. "The deposit should be available by two p.m."

"I know I sound paranoid. I mean, your faxed okay is probably enough but—"

"You're not paranoid. I'd advise a client to do exactly what you're doing."

Which caught her attention. "You didn't advise Tommy Stiles to get the contract amended. You were okay with just the fax. Why is that?"

"I trust you."

"No, really."

He said it again. "I trust you."

"You don't know me. How can you trust me?"

"You own a bakery. You have a kid. You probably have pets."

"Five of them."

"See? You're not a flight risk, are you?"

"Not quite."

"You'll either show up with those cakes or

you won't and if you don't, we'll ask for our deposit back."

"You make it sound very matter-of-fact."

"It's not brain surgery," he said. "We'd be out some money for a while but we'd get it back eventually."

"How?" she asked. "By sending some big strong men with small vocabularies to make me see reason?"

"What goes on down there in Mayberry anyway? You sound like you've been watching too much of *The Sopranos.*"

"My ex had a few enemies," she said, because in the long run the truth was always easier to remember. "We've been divorced a long time but the random aftershock still pops up."

If awkward silences were tax deductible, she would have the biggest refund check in the history of the state of New Jersey.

"Too much information again," she said. "I talk first, think second. You think I'd learn, wouldn't you? I mean it's not like goons were showing up on our doorstep every day looking for him—" Shut up! Shut up! Shut up! "No, wait. That sounds terrible. Let's just say you wouldn't invite his friends to brunch."

Insert really long and awkward silence here.

She plunged forward. "Okay. I told you I talk too much, right? It's a good thing Lizzie isn't here. She hates it when I do this." She paused for breath. "I'm starting to feel really stupid, Rafferty. Now would be a good time to say something."

She waited. She listened.

She heard the sound of . . . snoring?

"Rafferty!" she practically shouted into the phone. "Are you sleeping!?"

8

❦

It was like a bomb blast went off inside the earpiece.

Finn jumped, hit his shin against the filing cabinet, then dropped the cell phone. The cell bounced against the printer stand and rolled under the desk chair near the window.

By the time he retrieved it, Hayley had hung up.

He pressed redial. It rang once, twice, six times.

"Yes," he said when she picked up. "I fell asleep."

"And this information is supposed to make me feel good?"

"I was asleep when you first called. By the time we got back out here last night and talked to Tommy, the night was shot."

"You sleep in your office?"

"My office is in my house," he explained. "The fax woke me up."

A strangled sound emanated from New Jersey. "I thought I was faxing an empty office."

"You're not the first person to think that."

"I didn't mean to wake you up."

"I didn't mean to fall asleep while you were talking."

"Without going into embarrassing detail," she said, "you wouldn't be the first."

He laughed and suddenly he wasn't that tired anymore. "My ex-wife fell asleep one night during sex."

He grinned at the sound of her laughter. "You're making that up."

"Wish I was," he said. "During some of my best moves too."

"That's terrible!"

"If I remember right, that's what my ex said."

Laughing with a woman was a seriously underrated pastime. He wasn't willing to commit to the idea, but laughing with the right woman might even be better than sex with the wrong one.

"I forgot you have an ex."

"I forget sometimes too," he said. "It was a long time ago."

"What happened?"

Simple, direct, no nonsense. More proof, if he needed any, that Tommy's blood ran through Hayley Goldstein's veins. "Nothing very dramatic. We wanted different things."

"Like you wanted to continue seeing other women and she didn't want you to?" She said it lightly but he caught the underlying edge.

"Like she wanted to set down roots somewhere and my life was on the road with Tommy."

"You can't work for a rocker and still set down roots?"

"I don't know," he said honestly. "I was twenty-two and it didn't occur to me to try."

"And you never married again?"

"No."

Under normal circumstances the awkward pause would have been filled with the next question, "How about you?" But he already knew the answer. He should have asked it anyway.

"Well," she said after a few moments had passed, "you must have made the right decision then."

"I thought so in my twenties, but lately I'm not that sure."

"I'm like your ex: I wanted to put down roots."

"Looks like you succeeded," he observed. "You have Goldy's, the cake business, the incredible Lizzie."

"Not to mention the three cats, one dog, and an angry parrot."

"You have a parrot?"

"Angry parrot," she corrected him. "That's an important part of Mr. G's personality."

"How did you end up with a parrot?"

"Pretty much the same way I ended up with the others: soft heart, no willpower."

She gave him a rundown on the menagerie and how they came to live over Goldy's Bakery.

"The noise level must be intense."

"I live with a teenager," she reminded him. "I'm used to it."

"I've been thinking about—"

"Oh my God! It's twenty after eight. I have a nine o'clock at the dentist and I—"

"Go," he said, wishing he had the guts to

ask her to stay. "I'll amend the contract you drew up, sign it, and fax it back to you this afternoon for your signature."

"Sounds great," she said and she was gone.

He was still smiling when he finally fell back to sleep.

Hayley shut down her cell and turned around to find four pairs of eyes staring at her.

"What?" she demanded, aware of the color rising to her cheeks. "Why are you all looking at me like that?"

"So who is he?" Frank asked. This time there was no warning nudge from his wife. "Any guy who can put that look on your face needs to come by so we can check him out."

"He's right this time," Maureen said, brushing back a lock of silvery-white hair from her forehead. "I don't think I've ever seen you glow like that."

"I'm not glowing," Hayley protested. "I'm standing three feet away from a five-hundred-degree oven."

But they weren't buying it. Michie, standing in the doorway to the store, arched a Mr. Spock brow in her direction while a very curious Rachel grinned.

"He okayed the change of plans," she said, pretending that wasn't one of the top ten best phone conversations of her life. Even the hanging up part and the awkward silences. "He'll be faxing over the amended contract."

"Shouldn't you be the one amending the contract?" Michie asked. "You're the one who drew it up."

She groaned. "Lizzie's going to be horrified. What a stupid, stupid mistake."

"Sounds like he's making the same stupid mistake," Michie said. "Just make sure he doesn't make another bigger one in his favor."

Hayley leaped to his defense. "Oh, he's not like that at all."

"No offense," Maureen tossed over her shoulder as she threw a round of bread dough onto the pastry board, "but how do you know what he's like? You met the guy once."

Michie lowered her voice so only Hayley could hear her. "Mo is right. Aren't you the same woman who said he was keeping something from you and you didn't know what it was?"

"I'm late for the dentist," Hayley said, gathering up her purse and car keys. "If the fax comes in while I'm out, just leave it on my desk." She stopped near the back door. "And if Aunt Fiona calls, tell her I'll bring over the chicken Parm at lunchtime."

"Your wallet," Maureen called out. "You left it on the table over there."

She darted over and scooped it up. "You're looking at me again," she said. "I've been up twenty-four hours straight. See how on top of things you are with no sleep."

Which, of course, was both the truth and a big fat lie. It wasn't lack of sleep that had her feeling frazzled, giddy, and self-conscious, and everyone in Goldy's kitchen knew it.

Funny how a little conversation, a little laughter with a man could turn a woman inside out. Let your guard down just once and anything could happen.

Welcome to Lakeside Community Bank—one-stop banking at its best

What can we do for you today?
To transfer money to another account, click here.

ACCOUNT ID: rainbowgirl

ACCOUNT OWNER: Elizabeth Goldstein
PASSWORD: ********
AMOUNT REQUESTED: 1500.00
TRANSFERRED TO: 82073***289393
ACCOUNT OWNER: Michael K.
Goldstein
TRANSACTION CODE: 7

Hit return if correct
Transmission succeeded
Is there anything else we can do for
you today?
To log out, click here
You are now logged out
Have a nice day

Tommy was waiting for Finn on the deck when he got back to the house around noon.

"You look like hell," Tommy observed. "You should ask Jilly to give you one of those oxygen facials. Willow turned me on to them and—"

"What I need is caffeine," he broke in. "Preferably mainlined."

"I'm not doing caffeine anymore. Willow says—"

Maybe it was the fact that he was running

on less than three hours' sleep but Finn wasn't in the mood for the Gospel According to a Supermodel.

"So what's up? I thought you were taking Zach and Winston up to see Russell about new guitars."

Tommy looked out toward the ocean. "LeeLee called from Japan. She wants the whole school thing settled first."

"I thought it was settled." Both boys were engaged in an epic struggle to get through high school.

"One of the dancers she's on tour with broke her leg in a car crash and probably won't dance again. The kid's twenty, a dropout, no other skills. It shook LeeLee up." He glanced over at Finn. "Shook me up too."

"I can see how it would." Right now the only thing Zach and Winston had going for them was their famous father. "How pissed are they?"

Tommy gave a short laugh. "It's gonna be a long day."

"Is there something you want me to do for the boys?" He wasn't sure how his legal training played into the situation.

On the beach a golden retriever chased a

seagull along the shore while its owner, a spot of dark blue against the pale sand, trailed behind.

"I called her."

It took a few seconds for the words to form themselves into something he understood.

"You called Hayley?" He felt like he had been kicked in the gut. He couldn't imagine how she felt.

Tommy nodded. "I got the number for the bakery from Information." He shot Finn a look. "Don't worry. She wasn't there."

"I know," Finn said, breathing easier. "She's at the dentist."

"You talked to her again?"

"Early this morning." He explained about the fax and the design change.

"She's conscientious," Tommy said with a wry smile. "Where'd she get that from?"

"She's talented, creative, a major force, but she's not much of a businesswoman."

"She's kept that place afloat for what— almost ten years now?"

"You did your homework."

"That's why you left the folder with me, right?"

Finn nodded. "She's a total right-brain type

with a strong practical streak that doesn't extend all the way to things like contracts."

"So Lizzie really does keep her eye on the bottom line."

"Seems like."

"Not a great situation."

"So far it's working." But for how much longer was anybody's guess. Kids grew up, left home, started their own lives. Hayley was going to have to either take over the business side of the business or find someone else to handle the job.

"What about that ex-husband of hers? Is he still a problem?"

"Not so much. He's staying down in Florida with his mother and hanging with the South Beach crowd. The investigator we hired did some poking around. It wasn't pretty."

The expression on Tommy's face was priceless. "And she sends him a check every month?"

Finn shrugged. It was what it was and it had all been settled long before any of them came on the scene. "The bakery belonged to his family. His father left Hayley the sixty percent share and gave the rest to the son." Props to the late Stan Goldstein for divising a plan that allowed her full control of the bakery and prevented her ex from selling his share out from under her.

"She should buy the son of a bitch out."

"She and the kid live over the shop," Finn reminded him. "I doubt she can afford to buy anyone out."

Tommy turned to face him and Finn raised his hand between them.

"You're moving way too fast, Tom. Nothing's been proven yet. Nothing's even close to being settled. Take it a step at a time."

"I didn't say anything."

"You don't have to. I've known you my whole life. I think I know how you feel about family."

"I knew it!" Tommy said, a look of triumph on his face. "You believe she's my daughter too."

Finn made a sharp right turn into lawyer mode. "Yes, I think it's the likeliest outcome, but that doesn't mean you throw yourself into this before some careful thought. We went down this road last night. Weren't you listening?"

"I'm going to drive down there."

"Jesus, Tom, what does it take to get

through to you? You'll meet her next week at the after-party. We should have a good idea where we stand at that point and we'll take it from there."

"Why wait?"

"Because this whole after-party thing was your idea. We've committed to it. Let's go through with the plan."

Tommy was an easygoing, hang-loose kind of guy, but when he got serious, he had a way of commanding your attention that was second to none. "You were right before when you said the after-party idea was ridiculous. Let's cancel the contract and tell her what's going on."

"Have you tried to contact her mother yet?"

Tommy looked at him blankly. "No."

"Anybody show up to draw blood or take a DNA sample?"

"I see where this is going."

"First things first. You want to meet her? You'll meet her next week at the party. We should know more by then, have a game plan in place. Once you've seen her and talked to her, we can decide on the next step."

"Why the change of heart?" Tommy asked, looking at him with open curiosity. "Two days ago you thought I was an asshole for pushing the party; now you think it's a great idea."

"Because she needs it." Shit. He hadn't meant to say that. "What I'm saying is, this is important to her, to the bakery. To Lizzie. Whatever happens or doesn't happen between the two of you, she'll have the afterparty and the publicity and maybe a chance to really build that business and buy out her son of a bitch ex-husband and find a place to live that isn't over a bakery that starts cranking out rye bread at four in the morning."

Tommy studied him for a moment. "Sounds like I'm not the only one who read through the folder."

He tried to brush it off. "You wanted me to go down there and scope things out and I did. That's what you pay me for."

"A word of advice," Tommy said as he turned back toward the ocean. "Next week when we're down in Atlantic City, don't play poker."

9

❦

"This is Finn Rafferty. Leave a message."

"Hi, Finn. This is Hayley Goldstein. I—uh, well, it's almost nine p.m. and the fax still isn't here and I was wondering if maybe there's a problem. Give me a call on my cell when you can."

She glanced over at Lizzie, who was munching on a PB and J and hanging on every word.

"Too needy?"

Lizzie nodded. "A little."

"I was trying for nonchalant."

"Maybe the famous guy changed his mind."

"Tommy Stiles," she reminded her daughter, "and wouldn't you think Finn would call and let us know?"

"Maybe he's embarrassed."

"He's a lawyer," Hayley retorted. "Lawyers don't get embarrassed."

"They signed the contract," Lizzie said, wiping her hands on a square of paper towel. "At least we can keep the deposit."

"That's not right."

"It's in the contract, Mom. It's perfectly legal."

"If they back out, we return the money."

"Sometimes you scare me," Lizzie said. "I'm fourteen and even I know that's not the way you do business."

Hayley bent down and kissed the top of her daughter's golden blond head. "Then I'm very lucky to have you around to keep things running smoothly."

"What about when I'm not here anymore? You're going to have to think ahead. Maybe take a business course or two at the Y or something."

Hayley was working on a suitable retort when her cell phone rang.

"You didn't get the fax?"

It's Finn, she mouthed to Lizzie. "No, I

didn't," she said. "I was wondering if you changed your mind."

"Why would I change my mind?"

"What I mean is, I was wondering if your boss didn't like the new design and he decided to back out."

"I would have called you."

She felt like a two-ton rock had just been lifted from her shoulders. "So he liked the new design."

"Everything's fine," Finn said.

"But did he like the new design?"

Lizzie groaned and Hayley shot her a quelling look.

"What was that noise?" Finn asked.

"That was my daughter. She thinks I talk too much."

"Mom!"

"Say hi to Lizzie for me. Tell her Tommy was impressed by that contract."

"I'm glad he liked the contract, but how about my cakes?" She wasn't feeling the love and it was making her nervous.

Silence.

By now she was accustomed to their awkward pauses and she waited it out.

"I didn't show the design to him."

"You're kidding!" She started pacing the kitchen. "How could you not show it to him?"

"Tommy's not a detail kind of guy," Finn explained. "He knows your rep. He saw some of your other work. He trusts you."

"The president of the Cumberland County Association of Female Realtors has known me practically since I was in utero and even she didn't trust me that much. What's with you people anyway?"

"Rock stars are different."

"You're not a rock star. You're a lawyer."

"Hey, what's the problem? We're not backing out. The deal is still on. I sent you the fax."

"I didn't get it."

"But I sent it. We're debating a problem that doesn't exist."

"We're not debating anything. I just wanted to know why you didn't show your boss the new design sketches."

Poor Lizzie was pretending to bang her head against the kitchen table. She aimed a fierce look in her daughter's direction.

"Why don't I fax it to you again and— sorry, hold on a second."

She heard the muffled sounds of conversation in the background.

"Hello, Hayley." A different voice, more tenor than baritone, with a touch of New Jersey thrown in for good measure. "This is Tom."

She tried to speak but nothing came out. She leaned back against the refrigerator and tried to remember how to breathe.

"Mom?" Lizzie jumped up and ran to her. "Are you okay?"

Oh my God! she mouthed to Lizzie. *It's Tommy Stiles!* She was sharing an awkward silence with a rock star!

Lizzie nudged her in the ribs. "Say something!" she hissed.

"Hello?" Tommy Stiles said into the phone. "Did we lose the connection?"

She couldn't just stand there breathing into the mouthpiece. That wasn't how an almost-forty-year-old adult businesswoman was supposed to act.

"S-sorry," she managed as Mr. G the parrot flew down the hallway toward the back bedroom. "A parrot just flew by."

"A parrot?"

"Mr. G," she said. "A yellow-naped Amazon we adopted after his first owner died. Actually his first owner was my late father-in-law, Stan. He was a great guy. He had trouble adjusting the first two years—not Stan, I'm talking about Mr G. Stan was already dead. I—" She stifled a groan and Lizzie giggled. "Sorry. I talk too much. Next thing you know I'll be telling you about pilling the cats."

Tommy Stiles started to laugh. "Mr. G? Did you name him after that Philly weatherman from the eighties?"

"You remember Mr. G?" she said, laughing with him. "I didn't know you kept up with South Jersey television."

"I'm a Jersey boy," he said. "Some things never change."

Lizzie was hanging on to Hayley's arm, trying to hear the other half of the conversation. "Actually I'm a TV Land fan. Mr. G was named for Lou Grant from the old *Mary Tyler Moore Show*—"

"Tell him about Murray and—"

"Lizzie!"

"Is that your daughter?" Tommy asked.

"Yes," Hayley said. "My very nosy fourteen-year-old-daughter."

"Put her on. Finn says she's an incredibly impressive young woman. I want to congratulate her on that contract."

She waited, fully expecting the maternal worry vibe to kick in, but to her surprise it didn't. "Hold on." She covered the mouthpiece. "He wants to talk to you."

Her gregarious, self-confident daughter went a whiter shade of pale and looked like she wanted to bolt for anywhere but there. Hayley was about to make her apologies to Tommy Stiles when Lizzie drew in a breath and reached for the cell.

"Hello?... Yes... Thanks... I used a vetted contract as a prototype... Fourteen... No, not really... Okay... Yeah... Wow, thanks... Here's my mom."

Wide-eyed, she handed the phone back to Hayley, who by now was reasonably sure the powdered sugar on the two doughnuts she ate for supper was having an hallucinatory effect on her. "He's sending us backstage passes to see the concert!" Lizzie stage-whispered.

Clearly this wasn't the moment to inform her daughter that there was no way on the face of God's green earth that she would ever let her go. Setting a beautiful fourteen-year-old girl loose in a sea of leather and testosterone was like setting a match to gasoline. It wasn't about to happen while she still had breath in her body.

"This is Hayley again," she said into the

receiver, wondering how she would strike a balance between the protective mother and ambitious businesswoman without alienating the man who held her future in his guitar-plucking hands.

"I'm back," Finn said. "Tommy had to take another call."

"I wish I'd had a little warning," she said. "It isn't every day you talk to a rock-and-roll legend."

"I'm sorry," Finn said. "He realized I was talking to you and he grabbed my cell."

It was hard to imagine a skinny, sixty-something musician muscling in on a guy with a linebacker's build. "Did you tell him to say those things?"

"You don't tell rock stars to say anything. He likes your work. I told you he did."

He sounded uncomfortable. Maybe a little bit guilty? She didn't want to think about it. Maybe it was time to try focusing on the fact that professionally this was the biggest thing that would probably ever happen to her.

"You know what?" Hayley said. "I'm not going to take us down that long, dark road again. You didn't back out on the deal. That's good enough for me."

"Still waiting for that other shoe to drop?"

"Sooner or later the other shoe always drops," she said as he laughed. "It's just a matter of time."

You're right, Finn thought as they said good-bye.

It was just a matter of time.

Three weeks short of his thirtieth birthday, Tommy's girlfriend Sherri told him she was pregnant. Up until that moment he had managed to dodge the reproductive bullet. Marriage, kids, the whole family thing had been back-burnered throughout his twenties and he had pretty much assumed it would be back-burnered throughout his thirties too.

Fame didn't leave a whole lot of room for anything else.

When Sherri gave him the news the only thing he could remember was the rush of white noise that filled his head with sound. Everything he knew about family, about being a good father, he had learned from the Raffertys. He and Jack had grown up together, next-door neighbors who became best friends.

Best friends who had managed to become famous before they turned twenty-one.

Finn was sixteen when it happened. A happy, good-natured kid who worshipped the ground his old man walked on. Who could blame him? Jack was Tommy's best friend but he was his role model as well. The guy was a great rocker but an even better father. The kid was lucky to have him there to guide him to adulthood.

"I'm not asking anything from you," Sherri had said to him, her voice low, her words measured. "I'm going to keep the baby and I'm not going to ask anything from you. It's my decision and if you want to walk right now, that's okay. But if you want to stick around and be a father to him, then—"

That was when he kissed her.

Forty-eight hours later they were married in the Little Chapel of Dreams on the Vegas Strip. Amber was born eight months later. The next year Beryl joined the family. Four years later Topaz arrived but by then it was too late.

Sherri filed for divorce a few weeks before Topaz's first birthday.

When a marriage breaks up it takes a family down with it. Once the smoke clears and the hearts start to mend, alliances shift, and when it's over a man can find himself on the outside looking in. And the ugly truth was you could only stay out there with your nose pressed up against the window just so long before it got old and you turned and walked away.

Except that he didn't. He stayed where he was, he stayed plugged in, he stayed there at the center of his family and somehow what was bad between Sherri and him wasn't bad any longer. She still didn't want to be married to him but she wanted him in her life, in their children's lives, and he was glad to be there.

It had been the same with LeeLee, who gave him Zach and Winston, and then again with Margaux and the unexpected baby of the group, Gigi.

And now there was Willow. He knew the odds were against them. *Won't make it past the first anniversary . . . She's too young . . . he's too old . . . another kid . . . What the hell is he thinking?*

He had heard it all. He even agreed with some of it. But he loved her and he believed she loved him and they had made a baby together and maybe, just maybe, this time it would all work out the way it was supposed to.

This time last week he didn't know Hayley Goldstein and her daughter, Lizzie, existed. Now they had claimed a piece of his heart. Hayley was warm and funny and charming. Lizzie was an outspoken delight. They were his blood. He didn't need any fancy blood work or DNA tests to prove what he knew in his gut.

They were family.

His family.

The circle was about to widen yet again.

"There you are." Willow's breath tickled the side of his neck. "I've been looking all over for you."

He slipped an arm around her waist and drew her closer. "You knew where to find me."

"The beach," she said, resting her head against his shoulder. "Where else?"

They had been together over a year but her beauty still had the power to take his breath away. The moonlight slid along the planes of her perfect face like a caress.

It wasn't that she made him feel young; she made him feel whole.

"Did your nap help?" he asked.

"Pretty much." She stifled a yawn. "Everyone warned me all I'd want to do is sleep the first three months. I thought they were kidding."

"A few more weeks," he reminded her, "then it will pass. You'll have more energy than ever before."

She ducked her head, then looked out toward the ocean. "I hate that you've done this before. I wish this were your first time too."

"You wouldn't if you had seen me when Sherri was expecting. I was clueless."

"Don't make a joke, Tommy. I'm serious."

"I know." He held her closer. "I'm older than you are, Wil. We can't change that." He didn't want to change it.

"Sometimes—" She stopped then shook her head.

"Sometimes what?"

She aimed the full force of her beauty in his direction. A younger man would've been knocked flat. He was only temporarily staggered. "Sometimes I wish it could be just the two of us." She placed her hands on her still-flat belly. "And the baby."

"It is what it is, Wil. I have children."

"Lots of children," she corrected him. "And they all hate me."

Shit. Anything but this.

"They don't hate you, Wil. They don't even know you."

"They hate me. They think I'm going to take away all their money."

"They don't think like that. They've seen a lot of women come and go. They worry. That's all."

"I don't want your money," she said fiercely. "Do they know my hourly rate? Do they know how many covers I did last year? I can make my own money."

The best thing to do was keep his mouth shut. He nodded sympathetically and waited for the other shoe to drop.

"I don't know why you're making this so hard, Tommy. We should sign the prenup and put it all behind us. Maybe then your family will believe you're serious."

"That's why we have lawyers," he said in an attempt at tension-busting humor. "Let them do their thing."

Tears welled in her enormous cornflower-blue eyes. "Wait until our baby is born," she said. "We'll have our own family. Things will be different when it's just the three of us."

Except it would never be just the three of

them. Like it or not, Tommy Stiles was a package deal.

Lakeside, New Jersey—the Next Day

Hayley was working on the framework for the drum set the following afternoon when Lakeisha, another one of her high school interns, popped into the kitchen. "Mrs. G., there's a courier out front with a package. He says you have to sign for it."

"It's probably the fondant shipment. You can sign, Keish."

"No," the young girl said with a shake of her head. "He says it has to be you."

Hayley groaned out loud and put down her soldering iron. "Is he UPS or FedEx?"

"Nope."

"Airborne? DHL?"

"Uh-uh."

"What's he wearing?"

Lakeisha thought for a second. "I don't know. Dark pants and a shirt?"

Exactly the kind of sneaky outfit a process server would wear.

She brushed her hands off and led the way up front. Sometimes it seemed like her ex was the gift that kept on giving. He had been in Florida now for over two years. Shouldn't he be South Beach's problem?

A handsome young man in black trousers and a freshly-pressed white shirt stepped forward from the knot of middle-schoolers in line for their daily cookie fix.

"I have a delivery for Hayley Maitland Goldstein."

Uh-oh. One of those brightly colored cardboard envelopes perfect for delivering legal documents was tucked under his arm.

"I need to sign something?"

He handed her one of those handheld electronic thingies and a stylus.

She scribbled her name on the screen, then went back into the kitchen and dropped the envelope onto the counter near the phone.

"What's that?" Lizzie was leaning against the sink, eating the heel from a loaf of day-old rye bread.

"I thought you had debate team practice today."

"At four," Lizzie said. "We're out of milk upstairs."

"Then run down to the corner and get some. I have to work on the drum set."

Lizzie gestured toward the envelope with her piece of bread. "Aren't you going to open it?"

"Not right now."

"Maybe he sent an autographed photo," Lizzie said. "I checked on eBay. We could put it up for one hundred fifty dollars to start. The last one sold for two hundred seventy-five dollars. Of course, it was framed and matted, but still . . ."

She picked up her soldering iron. "What on earth are you talking about, Lizzie?"

"Tommy Stiles. He said he was going to send us backstage passes for his concert next week."

She'd completely forgotten. That was the thing about waiting for the other shoe to drop. You were so busy listening for the sound that you missed everything else going on around you.

"Don't look at me that way," she said as she pulled opened the envelope and pulled out two passes marked ALL ACCESS. "That's a school night. You can't go out on a school night."

"You don't mind if I go to Aunt Michie's for dinner and taxes on a school night."

"That's different."

"How?"

"You're six blocks away and with family, that's how."

"But it's still a school night."

She slipped the passes back into the envelope and tossed the entire package onto the counter. "I'm not having this discussion, Elizabeth."

"I'm glad I'm not all right-brained like you are," Lizzie observed. "I believe in a logical progression of ideas."

"You're fourteen. There is no logical progression of ideas when you're fourteen."

"I'm all about logic!" Lizzie burst into unexpected tears. "I can't believe you don't know that about me!"

With that her very logical daughter raced back upstairs and slammed her bedroom door so hard the house rocked.

Her heart sank. Poor Lizzie was about to see her beloved logic go head-to-head with her hormones and there was nothing Hayley could do to prevent the collision.

These passionate outbursts were happening more and more often lately. One second she was the Lizzie of old and then in the blink of an eye she turned into a stranger Hayley didn't recognize, much less know how to deal with.

It happened to the best of them and the only thing a parent could do was be there to catch them when they fall.

If only Stiles had sent her all-access passes to a convent school . . .

MKG329302 is online
RAINBOWGIRL is online

MKG329302: u came thru for me honey—thanx
RAINBOWGIRL: the deposit's in your acct?
MKG329302: it was
RAINBOWGIRL: so now you're not in trouble anymore
MKG329302: well u helped ur old man get a little breathing room
RAINBOWGIRL: where are u
MKG329302: fl
RAINBOWGIRL: aunt michie said you were in the Bahamas
RAINBOWGIRL: dad r u still there?
MKG329302: gotta go honey—c u later

MKG329302 has ended the session

*   *   *

Lizzie still wasn't speaking to Hayley the next morning. Even if it was nothing more than an apple and a glass of milk, they sat down together at the kitchen table every day for breakfast. Illness was the only acceptable excuse. Aunt Fiona had done that for her when she was growing up and even though Hayley had done her share of grumbling about it, she realized now the value of family time even if the family in question didn't fit the TV Land model.

She could put up with the silent treatment as long as they were together.

"Do you have band practice this afternoon?" she asked as her daughter gathered up her books.

"Yes."

"The usual time?"

"Yes."

So it was going to be Monosyllabic Friday. She could handle that too. "I'll pick you up at the side door at six sharp."

"I can walk home."

"We're having supper with Aunt Fiona tonight."

Lizzie nodded and headed for the back stairs.

"Not so fast," Hayley said. "You don't have to like me right now, but we don't leave without saying good-bye."

Lizzie brushed an air kiss in the vicinity of her cheek. An odd feeling of time passing washed over Hayley and she pulled her moody young daughter into a hug.

"I don't know why we can't use those passes next week," Lizzie said when Hayley finally let go. "I mean, this is a once-in-a-lifetime thing."

"I'm afraid it's going to stay a once-in-a-lifetime thing."

"You always tell me how experience is more important than money. Being backstage at a rock concert is a major experience, Mom. I don't see how we can not take advantage of the opportunity."

Overnight the levelheaded budding scientist who took after her grandmother was showing definite signs of being her mother's daughter.

Hayley laughed despite herself. "You didn't even know who Tommy Stiles was until this whole thing started."

"I used Google. He's old but really major."

"I told you that."

"I mean, one day I could tell your grandchildren about it. It would become a family legend."

"My grandchildren?"

"This could be huge. It's like seeing the Beatles in person."

"The Beatles broke up before I was born."

"You know what I mean."

"The answer is still no. You're not going to the concert." She took a good long look at her daughter. "You don't care one bit about seeing Tommy Stiles perform, do you?"

"Sure I do."

"Out with it," Hayley demanded. "Why are you really so interested in going?"

"I need a reason?"

"Lizzie."

Resentment poured off her sweet-natured daughter in almost visible waves. "Amanda's father said he'd pay me five hundred dollars if I could get Tommy Stiles to sign an album for him."

"Meaning a real-life record album, not a CD."

"I know what an album is, Mom."

"You would actually charge Phil Morasco five hundred dollars for a signature on his own record album?"

"It was his idea."

"Just because he's foolish enough to offer doesn't mean we have to be greedy enough to take him up on it." *Please, God, don't let her start thinking like her father.* How many times had she prayed that only the best of Michael Goldstein showed up in his only child and left her innocence and generosity intact?

"I still think we should go backstage."

"We don't know these people, honey, and we don't know who knows them. You've done setups with me before. You know what it's like. I'd love to watch a rock concert from backstage but I can't, and if I can't be there to make sure you're safe, then you're not going to be there either. Case closed."

Lizzie got it. She didn't want to get it, but Hayley could see the beginnings of acceptance in her daughter's big blue-green eyes.

"I've gotta go," Lizzie said. "I hear the bus."

"Six o'clock," Hayley reminded her once more as she darted out the door. "Don't forget!"

But Lizzie wasn't listening. She was already gone.

10

"Wow!" Michie circled the workbench a few hours later and nodded her head. "I don't know how you managed but you nailed it!"

"The balance is a little off on the snare drum but I'm on the right track." Hayley had raided her stash of foam core and foam, then used her handy-dandy utility knife to cut them into the proportions she needed for the drum set. A layer of fondant, some basic decorating, and the prototype was born.

"What kind of cookies are you thinking?"

"Spice," she said. "Somewhere between chewy and crisp. They travel better."

"You don't think they'll break on the way to A.C.?"

"I'm going to back them with fondant-wrapped supports."

"So why not just make the drum set from foam and foam core and decorate it?"

"Because I promised an edible drum set and an edible drum set I'm going to deliver."

"What about the cakes?"

"Five yellow with raspberry filling, three lemon with lemon filling, two chocolate with almond butter cream."

Michie sighed loudly. "I can't believe you're not going to use those passes."

"I'll be busy setting up for the after-party, Mich."

"That's why you have people. Let them do the setting up."

"This is too important."

"At least you're going to show up for the party," Michie said. "You had me worried there for a while."

"I guess I'd be crazy not to."

"Good thinking."

"Lizzie says I should wear the white baker's jacket and pull my hair back."

"Minimalist in a sea of excess. A professional woman in a sea of groupies and su-

permodels." Michie nodded. "Our girl has good instincts." She cast a critical eye over Hayley.

"What's with that look?"

"Minimalism has its place but when you're over thirty-five you can't take it too far. I'm thinking liner, shadow, and maybe a few individual lashes."

"I'll be working," she reminded her former sister-in-law. "Schlepping cakes. Sweating over the installation."

"So you'll do some touch-ups before the party."

"I'll be touching up the cakes."

"Don't fight me on this," Michie warned. "You know cakes, but I know cosmetics and this is one battle I'm going to win."

"This whole thing is getting way out of hand. The cakes are the star of this show, not the cake baker."

"Who cares about the cakes! We're doing this for the guy."

"Stiles?" Hayley was horrified. "He's old enough to be my father."

"Not Stiles, the lawyer."

"Not my type." She should have thought for a second before she answered. Michie's antennae were practically doing the conga.

"Since when is tall, dark, and gorgeous not a woman's type?"

"I don't recall saying anything about him being tall or dark or gorgeous."

"Lizzie told me." Michie grinned. "So did Trish and Rachel. Even Lou next door said he was pretty cute."

"He's a lawyer, Mich. He wears a suit and lace-up shoes."

"Last I heard that's not a criminal offense."

"It should be."

"You know there's nothing wrong with liking a guy in a suit. Maybe it could work with this one."

"And I suppose you heard that from Lizzie too?"

Michie's smile widened. "She said there were sparks."

"Trust me. There were no sparks. He's a nice guy. He's fun to talk to. That's it." Okay, so it was a bit of a lie but this was nobody's business but hers.

"Even better," Michie said. "If there's nothing at stake, you can consider him a refresher course."

"Okay, now you're starting to scare me."

"When was the last time you flirted with a guy?"

"I don't know." Hayley pondered. "Around 1993?"

"Then you're overdue. Think about it: you drop off the cakes, see a rock concert from backstage, and flirt with the kind of guy we don't usually see down here in Lakeside. And just when you think it can't get any better, he pays you for it! I mean, how great is that?"

"You make me sound like a hooker."

"Don't twist my words. You know exactly what I'm talking about."

The sad part was Hayley actually did. Before she married Michael she had been a world-class flirt. She loved that fizzy, frothy feeling when the chemistry between a man and woman was right. The repartee. The laughter. The champagne bubble of joy when everything was possible and nothing seemed beyond reach.

Kind of like the way she had felt every single time she spoke to Finn Rafferty.

"What's wrong?" Michie peered closely at her face. "You look weird."

She felt weird. Light-headed, giddy, younger than she had felt in a very long time. Could this possibly have anything to do with Rafferty? She wasn't a stupid woman and she was far from naïve. How could she have missed the signs when it seemed everyone around her had seen them glowing like neon over the Vegas Strip.

"Sorry," she said, lying through her teeth. "I was thinking about Lizzie."

God bless old friends for understanding.

"Actually I wanted to talk to you about her," Michie said, looking suddenly uncomfortable. "I talked to Ma and she said Lizzie's been calling and e-mailing every day, trying to find Michael."

"I thought he was staying down there with Connie." At least that was what her ex-mother-in-law had been telling her.

"Yes and no. He comes by when he needs money and to pick up his mail. Mostly I think he's doing something we don't want to know about in the Bahamas. Somebody showed up looking for him last week and almost scared Ma into intensive care."

"If I had my way, I'd—" Hayley stopped. "Sorry. I keep forgetting he's your brother."

"Listen, I don't know how you stayed with him as long as you did. I would've kicked him to the curb a whole lot sooner."

So would Hayley if it hadn't been for her beloved daughter. "She misses him so much, Michie, and there isn't anything I can do to help her."

"She's spending part of July with Ma, isn't she?"

"And she's counting on Michael being there too."

"Better she knows the truth. That's probably not going to happen. Besides, do you really want Lizzie in the middle of whatever he's up to? I'm not a worrier like you are, but even I'd think twice."

Hayley had already thought about that same thing two, three, and more times than she could count. The terms of the settlement were clear. Michael had the right to spend time with Lizzie. The fact that he rarely exercised that right didn't change that, even if it did make her feel downright homicidal. Neither did the fact that his circle of acquaintances made the hairs on the back of her neck stand up.

"I can't keep her from her grandmother, Michie. That's not fair."

"Postpone until August when Johnny and I drive down. She can go with us."

"Connie's sending tickets. She said she has all kinds of plans."

Michie sighed. "Well, the good news is

those plans probably won't include my brother."

"The bad news is that Lizzie will be heartbroken." Again.

"She's a smart girl," Michie reminded her. "I'm sure she knows the score."

"Not when it comes to Michael she doesn't. No matter how hard I try to prepare her, Lizzie's going to be heartbroken."

Michie's response was unprintable. "He didn't deserve you and he doesn't deserve Lizzie."

"I was old enough to know better," Hayley said. "Lizzie isn't."

"Don't be so hard on yourself. You were in love."

"Was I?" Hayley countered. "I'm not so sure."

"I was there. I remember how it was."

"Sometimes I think I was more in love with your family than I ever was with Michael." After years of following Jane around the globe, she had craved the stability the Goldstein clan offered her. The fact that Michael was sexy, cute, and more than a little dangerous had only been icing on a very delicious cake.

"What I'm saying is that Michael had nothing to do with the way she turned out. It's you, Hayley. We all know that." She paused for effect. "Even Ma knows it."

She brushed away the compliment. "I try to understand how Lizzie feels, but I grew up without a father and never felt the loss. It's hard to really grasp what's going on inside her head."

"You know Daddy loved you like a daughter, don't you?"

She smiled at Michie. "I know and I loved him too. It's just this connection Lizzie has with her dad is something I'll never fully get and it makes it hard to know what to say."

"She told Ma that she can't wait until she's old enough to get her license. Then she can drive down there anytime she wants."

Hayley shivered. "Something new to add to the worry list. Thanks, pal."

"I'm just saying."

"I know." And she did. "I've tried to be both mother and father to her, but I'm not even sure what a father is supposed to do." Her father-in-law Stan had served as her role model but even his good example lost something in the translation. "All I know is that Michael has to be in Florida when she visits, Michie. He *will* be there."

"Don't bet on it," Michie said. "And if you're smart, you'll make sure our Lizzie doesn't bet on it either."

"This is Finn Rafferty. Leave a message."

"Your machine didn't beep. Oh, wait! This isn't a machine, is it? This is your cell number so it's probably voice mail. I'm rambling, aren't I? Sorry. Anyway, this is Hayley Goldstein. It's Friday afternoon around four. I wanted to thank Mr. Stiles for the backstage passes but I don't have a number for him so if you could tell him that—see? I'm rambling again. The thing is, I'd love to watch the show backstage but I'm going to be busy setting up for the after-party, so I was wondering if it would be okay if Lizzie and her aunt Michelle use them instead. No offense meant to Mr. Stiles because, trust me, I'd love the chance to be there myself but—"

She didn't run out of breath. She ran out of time.

"This is Finn Rafferty. Leave a message."

"Sorry. I know I'm starting to sound like a phone stalker but I got cut off. Well, I didn't really get cut off, not in the disconnected sense of getting cut off, the machine—Anyway, I'd really love to be there and see the concert

from backstage but there's a lot of work surrounding the setup for the party so I really
need to concentrate on that. Let me know if
Lizzie and Michelle can use the passes and
please, please tell Mr. Stiles how much I appreciate that he thought of us and—"

She was single-handedly filling up his
voice mailbox.

Call Finn Rafferty a third time in as many
minutes? Absolutely, positively not. Not even
for her beloved daughter. She would send
him a telegram first.

"This is Finn Rafferty. Leave a message."

"Okay. It's Hayley. I promise you this is my
last phone call. No matter what. Really.
Thanks again to Tommy. I mean, Mr. Stiles.
Call me and let me know about the passes.
I'm going to lose your number now."

That should do it.

**Long Island—Near the Queens/Nassau
County Border**

"What's with that phone?" Zach asked as
they climbed back into the Escalade in front
of the Great Neck police station. "It never
stops ringing."

"It's not ringing, stupid," his brother Winston pointed out. "It's vibrating."

The bigger question, Finn thought, was why the mention of words like "vibrate" turned them into snickering blobs of testosterone.

"I'm letting the calls roll straight into voice mail," he said pointedly, more to Tommy than to the boys. Sloan, Willow's lawyer, had been phoning on the hour for an update on the Hayley Goldstein situation, which wasn't a topic he wanted to discuss in front of Zach and Winston.

"Finn's an attorney," Tommy reminded his errant sons, who were looking a little suspicious. "He gets a lot of calls." His voice lowered into the pissed-off-father register. "Like the call he got earlier about your dumb-ass stunt."

The snickers and smirks disappeared, replaced by that blank mask of put-upon teen angst.

"We borrowed the car," Winston mumbled. "What's the big deal."

Tommy began listing the transgressions starting with taking the car without permission and ending with driving without license or registration. "I expect better from you. I'm disappointed."

He had seen Tommy yell at his kids, ground them, take away their allowances. He had witnessed time-outs, serious negotiations, and flat-out warfare and every single time he had come away thinking he had wasted his time at law school. Want to learn the fine art of successful negotiation? Spend five minutes with the parent of teenagers and you'd learn all you would ever need to know.

Watching Tommy switch into parental mode always took him by surprise. He knew the rocker, the client, the musician, the friend, the husband, the ex-husband, the boyfriend, the laid-back easygoing superstar, but out of all of them he liked the parent best.

It was after dark when they reached the house. Tommy and the boys disappeared into the office for what Finn assumed would be the punishment heard 'round the world. Tommy didn't play the spin-control game. When his kids screwed up, they paid the price. And if they had to pay that price with the light of public attention shining down on them, then that was how it had to be. He didn't abandon them. But he didn't coddle them either. He guided them and when they made a wrong turn, he stood next to them as they worked their way back to where they were supposed to be.

For a change the house was quiet. Gigi's tricycle was stashed under the table in the entryway. Canned television laughter floated down from one of the upstairs bedrooms, but for the most part the house was dark and still.

He let himself out the front door, set the alarm, then drove home feeling lonelier than he had in a very long time.

For the first time he envied Tommy. He envied him his kids (even Zach and Winston), his ex-wives, his mistresses, the people who loved him. He even envied him Willow, who had the intellectual capacity of an amoeba. The fame, the money, the big house on the water—none of those things had ever made him wish he could trade places with the guy.

Watching Tommy with his sons today had.

Zach and Winston pulled a boneheaded stunt, screwed up, and got busted in Great Neck of all places and suddenly he found himself finally getting what the whole thing was all about. He had always viewed family life from an outsider's perspective. He was the godson who came to stay. Big brother to the Stiles kids . . . but not really. Sounding board, legal counsel, friend.

Maybe it was time to get a dog, he thought as he unlocked his front door and stepped into the silence. Or a cat. A goldfish even. Someone to share the oxygen with. A living, breathing entity that would be happy to hear his car pull into the driveway.

Hayley didn't have a fraction of Tommy's fame or fortune but her home teemed with energy and life the same as his. Finn had watched the way her employees treated her, seen the affection and respect in their eyes. Her daughter adored her, even if that adoration was tempered by the requisite teenage indifference.

She gathered people into her circle with effortless grace. In the blink of an eye Anton had become her staunchest defender. He could still see the two of them laughing and talking over the real estate agents' cake. She might be expecting the other shoe to drop any minute, but she was still managing to enjoy life while she waited.

He tossed his keys on top of the table in the entryway and headed for the kitchen, unbuttoning his shirt as he went. He was starting to think his whole life was out of whack. He was part of Tommy's family but not really. No matter how important the Stiles clan made him feel, in his heart he knew that he would always be that sixteen-year-old kid who showed up on the doorstep. The kid with no place else to go.

He liked to think things had changed in the twenty-something years since that day but he wasn't entirely sure.

Even the contents of his refrigerator looked like something you would find in a really bad frat house. Pizza. Cartons of half-eaten Chinese and Thai food. Three bottles of Coors and some microbrew.

The pizza looked like it was skidding toward its end date. He quickly shoved two slices into the microwave and pressed the reheat button. He was about to pop the top on a bottle of Coors when his phone vibrated again.

Might as well get it over with. Sloan, Willow's attorney, had left four urgent messages that afternoon and that was before Finn started rolling calls directly into voice mail. His inbox had probably exploded by now.

"Hampton Sloan for Mr. Rafferty at nine twenty a.m. on Friday. Please return the call at your earliest convenience."

"Hampton Sloan for Mr. Rafferty. It's ten thirty on Friday morning. We await your call at your earliest."

"Sloan again, Rafferty. It's noon. I'll be at my desk all afternoon. We need to talk."

"Sloan here. It's two p.m. and it's imperative you return my call. My client is beginning to question this delay and that is something neither of us wants to see happen."

Delete.

Delete.

Delete.

Sloan had every right to be seriously pissed. On a normal day he would have returned the first call immediately. He hadn't expected to spend most of it in Nassau County unraveling the mess Tommy's sons had made of things.

"Three fifteen. Sloan here. This is unacceptable."

Delete.

"Three forty-five. Sloan here."

Delete.

"Your machine didn't beep. Oh, wait! This isn't a machine, is it? This is your cell number so it's probably—"

Hayley.

A big, stupid smile, the kind you were glad nobody was around to see, spread across his face.

"Sorry. I know I'm starting to sound like a phone stalker but—"

His smile grew bigger and stupider, if there was such a word.

"Okay. It's Hayley. I promise you this is my last phone call—"

Not the last phone call, he hoped. Not even close.

"Sloan here at five-oh-one p.m. in the vain hope that you—"

Delete.

"This is Paula at Michalski Brothers. We completed the background check and are sending the results via both encrypted e-mail and courier. Oh—it's Friday at six-oh-seven p.m., your time."

Delete

"Okay. It's after eight. I said I wouldn't call again but now I'm thinking maybe something's wrong and you're trying to figure out how to let me down easy. It's okay if I can't give my pass to Michie. Really. We'll live. Wait—that sounds terrible, doesn't it? I mean, we'll be disap-

pointed but we're not going to— Maybe I'd better stop now before I get myself into a deeper mess. I'm kidding. You know that, right? My e-mail is cakes at goldysbakery dot biz if that's easier."

She answered on the first ring.

"Four messages," he said. "I just got them."

"Only four?" He heard the laughter in her voice and the sound of voices behind her. "I left at least seventeen of them."

"Hang up," he said. "I'll listen to them and call you back."

God, he loved her laugh. You would think her life was nothing but roses and hand-dipped chocolates.

"Just a second," she said. "Lizzie, nuke the chicken and turn the flame down on the potatoes and make sure there's enough iced tea." Then to him, "Sorry. My aunt Fiona's here for dinner."

"Nuked chicken?"

"Sounds great, doesn't it?" She laughed again. "I'm compensating with chocolate cheesecake."

"I can be there in four hours if I break the speed limits."

She laughed but she didn't issue an invitation. Not that he had expected she would. But he suddenly realized how much he wished she had.

He heard the bustle of family life all around her and, just like Tommy, she was at the center of it all.

"Your sister-in-law can use your pass. I'll need her full name—"

"Michelle Goldstein Rivera."

"—and she'll have to bring her driver's license or some form of picture ID with her to the venue."

"What about Lizzie? She doesn't have a driver's license."

"Photo ID?"

"A school identification card. It has her photo."

"That'll do it. Why don't I send you a third pass, just in case."

"I'd love it but, trust me, there's no way I'll be able to take advantage of it. I intend to keep a sharp eye on things until the party starts."

"Are there a lot of cake saboteurs on the loose?"

"You'd be surprised."

He was. Every single time she spoke, he

found himself surprised and delighted and intrigued by her words, her laughter, her history.

"Did you check your account yet?"

"Lizzie did. Thanks for transferring the money so quickly." That wonderful laugh. "Actually my creditors thank you since it'll fly out as quickly as it flew in."

No self-pity. No bitterness. Just life.

"Well," she said, "I guess I'd better—"

"You have pets, right?"

If she was surprised by his clumsy attempt at prolonging the conversation, she didn't let on. "Five," she said, then named them all. "How come?"

"I'm thinking about adopting a dog."

"That's a big responsibility." A beat pause. "A dog might not be such a great idea."

"Dogs love me," he protested. "I'm a dog's best friend."

"I'm sure they hang your photo over kennels from here to California," she said, "but that's not what I'm talking about. Dogs are social creatures. They need company and I'll bet you're never home."

"Okay, then how about a cat? Cats are independent, right?"

"Depends on the cat."

"I'm not going the hamster route," he said. "I draw the line at rodents."

"You need to do your homework," she told him. "I could send you some links to animal rescue sites. There are some great articles on how to match your lifestyle to the right pet."

"Mom!" Lizzie called out from somewhere nearby. "The chicken's nuked, the veggies are ready, Aunt Fee says hurry up or she's taking the cheesecake hostage!"

"I should—"

"You should—"

They both laughed.

"Watch your e-mail," she said and she was gone before he had a chance to say good night.

"I like you, Hayley Goldstein," he said to the empty room. A New Jersey cake decorator with three cats, one dog, a parrot, and a genius daughter.

Who just might be his boss's long-lost child.

Now what in hell was he supposed to do with that?

"Mom?" Lizzie stood in the doorway between living room and kitchen. "Are you okay?"

Aunt Fiona placed a hand on the girl's shoulder. "She's just fine, honey," she said with a wink in Hayley's direction. "Let's go eat."

I like him, Hayley thought as she followed them into the kitchen. A divorced East Hampton lawyer on retainer to a rock super-star.

A guy who wore a suit to work and lace-up shoes and carried file folders around with him.

Now what on earth was she supposed to do with that?

11

Mumbai, India

Jane was exhausted.

The farewell visits, the parties, the impromptu gatherings of colleagues and former students had taken their toll on her dwindling resources of energy and she spent her last day in Mumbai resting.

She used to thrive on the rigors of travel. There was no place on the planet too remote, too rugged, too dangerous for her and her staff. She was one of those human oddities who thrived on poor conditions and four hours of sleep.

She had sailed through her sixties and most of her seventies with the same boundless energy and unquenchable curiosity as she had enjoyed as a much younger woman and she no doubt would have continued to do so had illness not taken hold.

Jane was a scientist. She understood the part genetics sometimes played in illness but she also understood that fate could be both random and cruel and not even the keenest intellect could find order in the chaos.

Her beloved John had altered their travel plans, making allowances for her increased need for rest. They would leave for home late Sunday, spend a night (or was it two?) in London, then embark on the last leg of their return home.

I am afraid, she thought as she glanced about the hotel room that had been her home for months. The emotion was new and untried. She and her daughter Hayley were cut from different bolts of cloth but there had always been respect between them, if not total understanding. There was honest warmth between them, as well, and deep love that had carried them over the rough waters of the early years.

Her daughter embodied both rebel and worrier. Over time the worrier had stepped to the forefront but just beneath the surface Jane feared a rebellious soul waited.

"More tea?" John appeared in the doorway to her bedroom.

"I would love some." She straightened her spine and beamed a smile in his direction. "I'll miss the wonderful teas here."

"We'll make sure you have your fill both here and in London," he said.

Perhaps there was something to the notion of reincarnation, she thought, as the man she loved went off to prepare a pot of Earl Grey. Somewhere, in some other distant life, she must have pleased the gods and was now reaping the unexpected reward.

Not even the reality of her illness could destroy the joy she felt each time she looked into his eyes.

Only one thing held enough power over her to cast a shadow across her sun-drenched landscape and that was the prospect of telling Hayley the truth.

She had intended to take the secret with her to the grave and would have if the grave hadn't beckoned to her sooner than expected. There were genetic components at play in her disease that could have an impact on her daughter and granddaughter. That reality opened her mind to the fact that there was another side to her daughter's genetic cocktail, a side that might contain markers Hayley needed to be aware of.

Hayley had a father and that father had a name. And she deserved better than to hear the news in the cold sanctuary of an attorney's office after Jane was gone. What her daughter did with the knowledge was her business, but without that knowledge she would never be her whole, best self.

It seemed so clear now that Jane wondered why she had waited so long. She had spent her life untangling the genetic histories of marine life, determined to shed light on the secrets of the world's oceans, but she had never once addressed the irony of leaving her daughter swimming in the dark.

Lakeside—around noon on Sunday

TO: cakes@goldysbakery.biz
CC: lizzie@goldysbakery.biz
FROM: maitland.jane@sci-pri.com
SUBJECT: itinerary

My itinerary is in flux. I will be laying over in London for one or two nights. Still unsure how many. I will let you know as soon as we decide. Love to you both and see you soon.

"We?" Hayley stared at the computer screen, then over at her daughter. "She's royalty now?"

"She is pretty major, Mom."

"Not major enough for the royal we. I'm glad you told me to read my e-mail. I wouldn't have believed it if I hadn't seen it with my own eyes."

Lizzie nudged her. "I have to send out some invoices."

"You really are just like Jane."

"Thank you." Lizzie's grin ran from right ear to left ear.

She stifled a yawn. "What day is this? I've been working so hard I've lost track of time."

"Sunday," Lizzie said, fingers dancing across the keyboard. "Almost noon." She scanned the screen. "I sent you the tracking numbers for the gold and silver leaf from Autry Foods and the big drum of fondant from Non Pareil. Both shipments should arrive tomorrow morning but you never know."

"It's Sunday?" Hayley asked. "Shouldn't you be at Tracy's party?"

"It doesn't start until two."

"Is Tracy's father picking you up?"

"I'm walking over with Amanda."

"Will Tracy's father drive you home?"

"I'm spending the night, remember?"

"You know the rules."

"Don't walk home. Call you for a ride if I decide to leave."

"Mr. G can repeat the words," Hayley said, gesturing toward the gorgeous green parrot watching them from his favorite perch. "Do you understand the importance?"

Lizzie rolled her eyes. "The world can be a dangerous place, blah blah blah." She pushed her chair back from the desk. "I'm gonna go get ready."

There must be something in the air, Hayley thought, as she settled down again in front of the computer. Some strange transit of Venus or Mercury gone retrograde, an odd astral occurrence that would explain the bad moods, hurt feelings, and misunderstandings that had been breaking out from one end of the bakery to the other the past few days.

Or maybe it was too much work for too many people in way too small a work space.

Convincing Mercury to quit that retrograde nonsense would be easier than figuring out a way to pay for a larger building. She and Lizzie were still trying to figure out where the money for upgraded ovens was going to come from. Her dream of running the bakery operation separate from the cake-decorating side of the business was still a long way off.

Thank God the orders had been pouring in at a fairly rapid clip. She had three designs that needed to be finalized before she could submit them. Usually she managed a twenty-four-hour turnaround time, but she had been so busy working on the cakes for the after-party that she'd let things slip. She thanked God on a regular basis for Frank and Maureen and Michie and everyone else at the bakery. If they ever tired of picking up her slack, her cake-decorating enterprise would come screeching to a halt.

The bakery was Lizzie's future. Stan had left it in her hands for a reason and that reason was her little girl. He knew his son's faults better than anyone and he was determined to give his granddaughter the security his son would never provide.

Stan hadn't seen a future in fancy decorated cakes. His clientele was perfectly happy with buttercream rosebuds and "Happy Birthday, Tiffany" scrawled across the top layer with a pastry bag. The cake-decorating part of the business was Hayley's baby and, unless she missed her guess, her future. One day she hoped to separate Goldy's from the special-order-cake side of the business, but that was still a long way off. She wasn't about to rock the boat until Lizzie was out of college and the tuition bills had been paid.

Until then she had to continue to find a way to keep Goldy's running smoothly while she poured her creative energies into her creations.

She had worked out a production schedule that would bring her right up to the morning of the concert. Barring unexpected calamities, of course. One of Lizzie's teachers had approached her about designing a cake for an engagement party three weeks out. A flaming red VW bug that would feed one hundred and not rack up more than three Weight Watchers points per serving.

Of course, that meant she had to figure out what constituted a Weight Watchers point before she could promise anybody anything at all.

Not that a new commission was a calamity, but it was time-consuming and right now time was the one thing she needed above everything else.

She brought up the official Weight Watchers site and started reading about core plans and flex plans and points and was deeply immersed in figuring out how she could incorporate a hot fudge sundae into a weight-loss plan when her e-mail alert chimed.

Not another royal missive from Jane, she prayed as she clicked over to her e-mail screen. She hoped her mother got the royal we out of her system before she showed up in Lakeside. This was South Jersey, the place where girls wore rhinestone tiaras with their swimsuits.

TO: cakes@goldysbakery.biz
FROM: finnrafferty@tommystiles.com
SUBJECT: cats and dogs

I took the "who's the right dog for you" quiz on the animal rescue site and it said I'm a Chihuahua. As you can imagine, that's a lethal blow to my self-image.

TO: finnrafferty@tommystiles.com
FROM: cakes@goldysbakery.biz
SUBJECT: re: cats and dogs

Thanks for my first laugh of the day!! There's a lot to be said for being a Chihuahua. The first time I took the test it said I was a Rottweiler.

TO: cakes@goldysbakery.biz
FROM: finnrafferty@tommystiles.com
SUBJECT: re: cats and dogs

Sounds like we both have issues. So how did a Rottweiler end up a Lab mix?

TO: finnrafferty@tommystiles.com
FROM: cakes@goldysbakery.biz
SUBJECT: re: cats and dogs

I went in looking for a small, older, non-shedding dog. I ended up with a giant six-month-old Lab who sheds for a hobby.

TO: cakes@goldysbakery.biz
FROM: finnrafferty@tommystiles.com
SUBJECT: re: cats and dogs

I'm thinking maybe a cat.

TO:　finnrafferty@tommystiles.com
FROM:　cakes@goldysbakery.biz
SUBJECT:　re: cats and dogs

Do you like cats?

Her cell phone rang. Somehow she wasn't surprised.

"I don't know any cats," Rafferty said. "But what's not to like?"

"The litter box, for one thing," she said with a smile so wide her face hurt. "If you're looking for tail-wagging devotion, you might want to stick with canines."

"I'm definitely looking for devotion." She could hear the answering smile in his voice. "I want someone waiting at the door for me with my slippers in her mouth."

"Her mouth?"

"Or his mouth."

"Much better."

"So cats don't do that?"

"Not quite." She started to laugh out loud. "Most cats expect you to be waiting at the door when they get home."

"That's one of the problems," he said. "The cat would have a long wait. I'm not home that much."

"How much is not much?"

"We're on the road six or seven months out of the year. And that's a slow year."

"That's horrible!" She grimaced. "I'm sorry. I shouldn't have said that. I mean, I really do think it's horrible, but I still should have kept that thought to myself. Not that I keep many thoughts to myself, but this might have been a good place to start."

"It's not for everyone," he admitted, "but it has its good points."

"I'm sure it does."

"What does that mean?"

"It means what it means. I'm sure being on the road half of every year has some wonderful benefits."

"You're talking groupies."

"I didn't say that."

"You thought it."

"You don't know what I thought."

"Lawyers don't have groupies. We have accountants."

She didn't even try to hold back the laughter. "Do you like being on the road so much?"

"I used to," he admitted, "but it's gotten old. Or maybe I have."

"You're a lawyer. Why can't you do your lawyering from East Hampton?"

"Because I'm not just Tommy's lawyer. I fill in on rhythm guitar."

"You play rhythm guitar?"

"You sound surprised."

"No, I'm shocked. What are you, one of those Blues Brothers types?"

He groaned. "Can't get past the suit, huh?"

"You have to admit your tailoring doesn't exactly scream rock star."

"Come to the concert Thursday night and I'll show you what else I can do."

A delicious shiver moved up her spine. Now it all made sense. He was a bona fide bad boy in good-guy camouflage. She switched the phone to her other ear to give herself a moment to regroup. This flirting business was unsettling.

"Listen, I should have thanked you right up front for that extra backstage pass but I really won't be able to use it."

"You don't know what you're missing."

"Actually I do," she said, "and that's why this is killing me. Give me your address and I'll send it back so somebody else can use it."

"Keep it," he said. "Maybe you'll change your mind."

"I wish I could."

"You can always press it in Lizzie's scrapbook if you don't use it."

As if on cue, her darling daughter appeared in the doorway.

"Just a second," she said to Finn, and then to her daughter, "You're wearing that?"

Lizzie glanced down at her faded jeans and favorite sweater. "Yeah."

"To Tracy's party?"

"It's the twenty-first century, Mom. This is what you wear to a party."

She could hear Finn laughing on the other end of the line. "How about putting on the skirt you bought at Target last week?"

"I'm late," Lizzie announced. "Amanda's waiting downstairs. I've gotta go."

"Don't forget what I said: call me if you change your mind about spending the night. Do not walk home alone."

"Whatever." Lizzie leaned in to peck Hayley on the cheek.

"Not 'whatever,'" Hayley retorted. "Just do it." She softened a little. "Where's her gift? Do you need any money?"

"I got her an iTunes gift card and no, I'm okay."

With that her beautiful little Clydesdale

thundered down the back stairs and out the door.

"This time I wouldn't blame you if you fell asleep," she said to Finn. "Family business."

"Now I believe she's really only fourteen."

"It gets confusing," Hayley admitted. "One second I'm talking to Alan Greenspan's long-lost granddaughter and the next second she's Hilary Duff's little sister."

"You handle it well."

"So far, so good, but if she takes after her mother, I'm in for a rough ride between here and her eighteenth birthday."

"You seem pretty levelheaded and goal-oriented to me."

"You should have seen me when I was her age," she said, laughing. "I dyed my hair black, rimmed my eyes with kohl, and declared myself Queen of the Goth. It wasn't pretty."

"Bad poetry and existential pain."

"Of course. And that lasted until I found out the really cute guys were the rockers and I turned all hippie chick."

"You still have a hippie chick vibe going for you."

"Did you just say 'vibe'?"

"I told you I wasn't just a lawyer."

"Now I'm starting to believe you."

He was flirting with her. (Wasn't he?) The teasing. The laughter. The underlying buzz of something more. And she was flirting back. (Okay, she was trying to.)

"All things considered, I'd say you're a dog person living a cat person's life."

"Run that by me again."

"You want the devotion a dog gives you but your absentee lifestyle would work better for a cat. And not all cats, just the very independent ones."

"I thought all cats were independent."

"Not mine. They're lap cats."

"What you're saying is either I get off the road or settle for a houseplant."

"I'm not so sure about the houseplant."

"You don't mince words."

"You asked," she reminded him. "You wouldn't want me to lie to you, would you?"

"Give it a shot," he said. "I'll let you know."

They were back on familiar footing again, bantering back and forth, keeping that shimmering bubble of champagne dancing in the air between them.

He was going to ask her out. She might have been out of the romance loop for a while but some things a woman knew without being told. This was goal-oriented flirting and any second he'd take it to the next level.

She waited. He talked. She waited some more.

They talked about cats. They talked about dogs. They ventured into birds, reptiles, and fish. God help them if they started on primates because after that it was a hop, skip, and a jump to ferrets.

She couldn't have been that wrong about the electricity between them. You could almost see the sparks leaping from her cell phone. She was sending out receptive signals. At least she thought she was. Flirting hadn't been part of her skill set for a long time, but short of shrieking, "Ask me out, Rafferty!" into her cell phone, she had made it clear she was wide open to the possibility of breaking bread together.

She babbled on about her menagerie. He responded with stories about Tommy Stiles's considerable menagerie. She was a half step away from discussing the pros and cons of nonclumping litter.

This wasn't going well at all.

"Here's an idea," she said. "Why can't you bring your dog or cat with you to Mr. Stiles's house during the day?" She took his silence as encouragement and pushed forward. "Your pet could board with his pets when you're on the road."

"Fido won't want to come home to Montauk after seeing the Hamptons."

"Fido will cope," she assured him. "Anyway, it's something to think about."

"What I've been thinking about is checking out one of the shelters."

"That's a great idea. We have a wonderful shelter a few miles from the bakery. I volunteer there once a week and it takes every ounce of my self-control to keep from bringing them all home with me."

In the movies this would be the moment when the guy cleared his throat and asked the girl out on a South Jersey/Long Island shelter crawl, but Rafferty let the opportunity slip between his fingers.

"So don't be a stranger," she said as the conversation wound down to a whisper. "Keep in touch."

She waited for the laugh.

"That was a joke," she explained quickly. "I was trying to give you an exit line."

"Maybe I don't want an exit line."

Her heart stopped. This time she didn't mind getting it wrong. If one of the *Grey's*

Anatomy interns saw her now, they'd slap paddles on her chest and prepare to call it.

"Oh." It was hard to say more when you were fibrillating.

"Hayley, I—"

He stopped. She waited. He remained at a full stop.

"That's it?" she asked. " 'Hayley, I—' then nothing?"

Awkward silence number 522.

"You know what?" she said. "I'm all for letting a good silence run its natural course but you're starting to drive me crazy. You called me, remember? The least you can do is finish your sentences."

Nothing. Not even heavy breathing.

"That's it. I'm going to hang up now."

"What are you doing for dinner?" He sounded almost as surprised as she was by his question.

"Leftover pizza and whatever else I find in the fridge. Why?" Don't jump to conclusions. Maybe he just wants to inventory your pantry.

"How do you feel about take-out Chinese?"

"Pretty much the same way I feel about dark chocolate and winning lottery tickets."

"Spicy or mild?"

"Spicy. Is there any other way?" Was this going some-place or was he just taking a survey for the Food Network?

"There's a great place here in town. Best Hunan chicken you've ever had."

Thanks for sharing, Rafferty. "Too bad they don't deliver to South Jersey."

"They might."

"Yes, but that two-hundred-dollar sur-charge is a killer."

"No surcharge," he said. "But tips are ap-preciated."

"What exactly are you saying?"

"If I break a few speed limits I can be there by four."

"You're going to drive four hours to deliver Chinese food?"

"That's the plan."

She couldn't help it. The word popped out: "Why?"

"Because it's the best take-out Chinese on the planet."

Not bad as far as reasons go.

"And," he said, "because I want to see you again."

But that was even better.

* * *

Finn hung up the phone and wondered what in hell he had just done.

Only a total head case would drive four hours on the freaking Jersey Turnpike to deliver Chinese take-out. The thing to do was call her back and cancel. He must have gone temporarily insane.

Only a total head case or a man in—

He wasn't going there.

He liked her. That was all. She made him laugh. Even better, he made her laugh. He liked her unpredictable turn of mind. He liked the fact that the woman got his jokes. Not even people who had known him since childhood got his jokes, but she did.

She was unpretentious, down-to-earth, about as grounded in reality as anyone could be. She didn't play games. If she wanted to say something, she said it. She asked questions. Sometimes painfully direct questions.

Maybe this time those questions would get an honest answer.

12

By 2:30 Hayley had showered, washed and blow-dried her hair, applied then reapplied her makeup three times, tried on six different outfits, settled on jeans and a sweater, changed into a short black skirt and blouse, decided that was too date-y, changed back into the jeans and sweater, then suddenly realized her entire place was covered in a fine layer of cat fur, dog hair, parrot feathers, and the type of clutter usually associated with people who ended up on the local news after the township condemned their house.

How two people had accumulated such a towering pile of junk and managed to distribute that junk throughout every room of their small home defied understanding.

Books, magazines, half-finished crafts projects, science experiments, shoes (lots of shoes), catnip mice, chew toys for dogs, chew toys for parrots, newspapers—you name it, if you looked hard enough you would find it somewhere in the mountain of stuff.

"I can't let him in here," she said to the three cats, one dog, and one laughing parrot who were watching her, wide-eyed, from various hiding places.

He's driving all the way from East Hampton. He's going to need to use the john.

The same john that was currently littered with blow dryers, hair products, skin cream, acne medication, mascara, shadow, blush, enough lipsticks to supply the crew of *America's Next Top Model* for the next three seasons, two bras drying over the shower rod, and some unmentionables she would die if he even knew she possessed.

There was no hope for it. She stripped off her outfit, slipped back into her oldest jeans and worst T-shirt, and got down to work.

This is why God made bathtubs, she thought as she tossed piles of junk behind the magic curtain. If it weren't for bathtubs, big closets, and that dusty space under the bed, nobody would ever have people over.

She glanced at the clock. She had thirty-five minutes to mop the kitchen floor, hide the mop, hide the kitchen (if only), then change back into clothes that didn't make her look like Cinderella before the fairy godmother came to town.

The house phone rang as she slipped out of her scullery maid clothes.

"Aunt Fee, this isn't a good time . . . Yes, I understand . . . Sure, I'd be happy to . . . Not right now . . . Somebody's coming over . . . Yes, the lawyer, but it's not a date . . . No, I don't know what it is . . . He's bringing Chinese food . . . From Montauk . . . Okay, so maybe it does sound a little like a date . . . I'll let you know . . . I promise."

So Fiona thought it was a date. What did she know? Fiona had married her first boyfriend and stayed married to him for over fifty years. The last time Fiona had obsessed over some guy Eisenhower was president. Times had changed. Dating wasn't dinner and a movie anymore. Sometimes you couldn't tell where friendship ended and dating began.

If it began at all.

For all she knew the Chinese food was a cover and Rafferty was stopping by to make sure the small-town baker could handle the uptown job he had commissioned.

She could handle that. She even understood that.

But the fact that a great-looking, funny, decent man was willing to drive almost the entire length of Long Island and New Jersey to see her was enough to make her consider the witness protection program.

Worrying she was good at.

Dating was another story.

Finn sailed across the Verrazano and through Staten Island in a haze of guilt and expectation.

Either that or he was high on fumes from the three shopping bags filled with Chinese food on the backseat.

A full blast of irony smacked him in the face as he rolled down the New Jersey Turnpike. He was the one who had reamed Tommy for crossing the line before they had the facts to back him up. He was the one who had wanted to keep everything strictly contained within a legal framework.

And now he was the one following his heart down to South Jersey at the speed of light.

Exit 8A.

Exit 8.

Exit 7.

The township names whizzed by in a blur as he got closer to Lakeside.

He could still turn around and head back to Montauk. All he had to do was call her and say something had come up, some rock star emergency that required legal assistance on a Sunday afternoon.

Everyone knew celebrities were needy. That was a given. Celebrities required toadies and handlers and lawyers to walk ten steps behind them and clean up the mess. Even the good ones like Tommy created a wake that knocked smaller boats off course, sometimes permanently.

Exit 6.

He had never been good at keeping the personal separate from the professional. Ask his ex-wife. The endless phone calls, the months spent on the road, the temptations. She wanted a real home, a family of her own, and it quickly became clear Finn's skill set came up short.

When they lost the baby they lost the last thread binding them together.

Maybe if he had been older, he would have understood what was happening, but he had been as caught up in his grief as his ex was. Unable to look beyond his own pain. He wanted everything to go back to the way it had been before the pregnancy but that was impossible. She wanted more at a time when he was able to give even less.

She was happy now. She had a husband and home, the kids she had always longed for. Every now and then he ran into somebody who knew her and the news was always good. He was glad. She deserved better than the man he used to be.

Tommy was his boss, his family, the guy who took him in when he needed a home. The boundaries shifted with the circumstances and after a while they disappeared entirely.

"I'm your family too," his wife had said to him during one of their last arguments. "Why can't you understand that?"

His loyalties had belonged to Tommy Stiles. Everyone else ran a distant second.

This was the first time he could remember being conflicted about where loyalty to

Tommy began and ended. The fact that he had driven almost two hundred miles to deliver some noodles and a container of hot-and-sour soup meant something but he wasn't sure he was ready to find out what.

He liked the way she looked, the way she laughed, the things she said, the way she said them. He liked the way she took care of Lizzie, the connection between them. She had inherited a down-on-its-luck bakery and brought it back to life and somehow found time to grow another business decorating upscale cakes.

He wanted to see her again. He wanted to hear her laugh. He wanted to watch the way she tucked her hair behind her right ear when she was concentrating.

He hadn't known how much he wanted it until he heard her voice a few hours ago. He missed her. He barely knew her but he missed her in a way that was so primal, so life-shaking, that on another day he might have run as far and as fast as he could from the feeling.

This time he was running straight into it.

He hit Lakeside at quarter to four and was standing at her door at ten to the hour. Was early better than late? He wasn't sure. Early had to be better. Nobody liked to be kept waiting. Waiting was for doctor's offices and planes, not a first date.

But was this a date? Driving over two hundred miles to deliver Chinese food to a terrific woman had to mean something, but for all he knew she saw him as an overeducated delivery boy.

"She's not there."

He turned at the sound of an old man's voice behind him. It was the dry-cleaner sentinel he remembered from last time. "What was that?"

The guy was short, bald, and easily pushing ninety but he had the presence of a linebacker. "I said, she's not there. She told me to tell you she tried calling but your cell is turned off."

"Who are you?"

"I'm Lou. I live next door. I've known that kid since she was in high school."

He nodded. Lou had a proprietary interest in Hayley's welfare. He got it. "So where is she?"

"Beats hell out of me. When that dog takes off it's anybody's guess." He pointed down toward the lake. "She went that way."

He put down the three shopping bags of

Chinese food. "Would you watch these for me, Lou?"

"What's in it for me?"

"How does an egg roll and a bowl of hot-and-sour soup sound?"

"Like twelve hours of heartburn."

He reached into his back pocket and pulled out a ten. "Feeling better?"

"That'll get you thirty minutes."

"And what happens after thirty minutes?"

"We renegotiate."

So that was where Lizzie got her deal-making skills. It wasn't genetic after all. It was in Lakeside's water supply.

He took off toward the stand of trees at the far end of the block. A pair of teenage girls stopped to watch and giggle as he darted around them. At the corner a middle-aged guy in a pale green minivan leaned on the horn when he should have leaned on the brakes, and Finn thanked high school football for his broken-field running skills. Small towns could be deadly.

The air was rich with the smell of a rainy spring and a few other country aromas he didn't want to dwell on. The grass was wet and muddy and he sank deep into the muck with every step.

"Rhoda!" Hayley's voice sounded from a distance. "Rho-*da*!"

He cupped his hands around his mouth and yelled, "Hay-leeeey!"

There was a beat of silence, then a loud "Rafferty?"

Followed immediately by thundering hoofbeats and an even louder "Woof!" as a dog the size of a humpback whale hurled itself at his chest.

Hayley popped through the thicket to find Rafferty lying flat on his back in the mud, trying to fend off slobbery kisses from an uberfriendly Rhoda.

"Do something," he said, ducking another onslaught. "I think Cujo's in love."

"Don't let go," she said as he hung on to Rhoda's collar to keep her from bolting. "Rhoda has a slight problem with authority."

"Don't we all," he muttered. Then, "What do you feed this dog anyway?"

"She stole some cat food this morning," she said, trying hard not to laugh. "That's Fancy Feast on her breath."

"She's sitting on my lungs. Do you think you could—"

"Sorry! I was taking out the garbage and

she blew past and out the door before I could grab her." She wrapped her hand around Rhoda's collar. "Come on, Rhoda. Let's—"

She hadn't been kidding when she said Rhoda had a problem with authority. Hayley struggled to hang on to the collar but Rhoda had the moves. Rhoda went left as Hayley went right and it was all over.

She fell hard across him, breasts flattened against his thighs, her breath moist and warm against his chest. Her hair smelled like the ocean even though they were miles from the shore. She was softer than he had expected. Rounder. More yielding.

Sometimes the gods managed to get it right.

"Are you okay?" he asked.

"I had the breath knocked out of me. How about you?"

He couldn't stop smiling. "Couldn't be better."

She shifted position against him and his reaction was instantaneous and very rewarding. Her cheeks reddened and she ducked her head. She wondered if he knew she was smiling too.

They were lying in cold mud in broad daylight in a public park while a giant dog nudged them with a very wet muzzle. It was the most fun either one of them had had in a long time.

She made no effort to get up.

He wondered if she noticed that was fine with him.

He liked the weight of her body on his. He liked her peppermint breath, her full mouth. He liked the fact that if he leaned forward he could taste that mouth—

"Mary Jane Esposito is watching us," she said.

"I don't see anyone."

"She's behind that blue spruce over there."

"Does Mary Jane Esposito spend a lot of time spying on you from behind a blue spruce?"

"It's been a long time since I gave her anything to spy on."

Her huge blue-green eyes crinkled when she smiled. He added it to the list of things he liked.

"I'm willing to aid the cause."

"I think we've given her enough to keep her busy."

There it was: the right moment. Their mouths were inches apart. He wanted to kiss her. She wanted to be kissed. All he had to do was lean forward and do it.

"It's cold out here," she said. "We should get back to the house."

She scrabbled for purchase but fell back against his chest.

"You're not much help," she said to him, half laughing, half serious.

"Try again," he invited. "I've got all day."

For an instant she melted against him, pliant and yielding, and then something clicked and she shook her head. "I have a daughter," she said softly. "That changes everything."

If possible, he liked her even more.

He steadied her as she got her footing then managed to get to his own feet, dripping mud and primordial ooze.

Apparently it was a good look in the dog world because Rhoda wagged her tail and nuzzled his hand like they were long-lost friends. For every step backward he took, Rhoda took two forward.

"For what it's worth," she said, obviously trying not to laugh, "she doesn't like just anyone."

"What does she do to people she doesn't like?"

"Pretty much ignores them." Her eyes

were practically dancing with amusement. "It's a kind of good news, bad news thing."

Rhoda, sensing her moment, rose up on her hind legs and placed her two massive front paws against his chest. Her brown eyes were aglow with doggie adoration.

He had to admit there was something to be said for unconditional love.

He looked over at Hayley. "You said she likes Chinese."

"Egg rolls rock her world."

"I brought four of them. If that guy Lou didn't eat his way through the order, she can have one."

"Don't worry. Lou won't eat the egg rolls." She seemed highly amused by the whole thing. "How much did he soak you for?"

"Ten bucks for thirty minutes. He said we can negotiate beyond that."

"Lou is an institution around here. You'll be lucky if you get your bags back for less than twenty."

"He's worse than a three-card monte hustler."

"Don't give him any ideas. He'll set up a table at the corner of Main and Watch Your Wallet."

"Just in case, what else does Cujo here like?"

"Lo mein, hot-and-sour soup—"

"She's not getting the soup."

"She's flexible. Half an egg roll and she'll be your friend for life."

"And another dream comes true."

The laughter she had been holding back broke free. "I'm sorry," she said, wiping tears from her eyes, "but if this is a date, we're in big trouble."

"So you think this is a date?"

"Actually I'm not sure." Her smile down-shifted. "Are you?"

"I debated it all the way down the turnpike. The jury's out."

"I was counting on you to come up with the answer."

"We're both single and there's Chinese food involved. Where I come from that usu-ally means something."

"Maybe it just means we like Chinese food," she suggested.

He glanced down at himself. "And mud."

"We could hose you down in the back-yard."

"Or run me through the car wash." He took

a close look at her. "Maybe we can get a two-for-one deal."

"You can use my shower. Well, you can use it after I re-hide the junk I hid behind the shower curtain before you got here. And, to be perfectly honest, I should tell you the shower curtain has seen better days. If I didn't look like the loser in a mud-wrestling contest, I'd run over to Target and buy a new one."

He started to laugh. "The point of hiding stuff behind the shower curtain is to keep people from knowing you hide stuff behind your shower curtain."

"You sound like you have some shower curtain experience of your own."

"Ovens work too. Great for dirty dishes."

"I'm a baker. I use my oven."

"You use your shower too."

"I keep forgetting you're a lawyer. Everything I say can and will be held against me."

"Don't worry. I don't think this rises to Miranda standards."

She whistled for Rhoda, who had wandered off to inspect an azalea bush, then turned back to Finn. "Come on. I can wash and dry your clothes in the time it takes us to stand here and talk about it."

"It's too much trouble."

"It's not like I'll be scrubbing them against a rock. You can't drive home in a mud suit."

She had a point there.

"It's really simple, Rafferty, I promise. You take your clothes off. I wash them and dry them. You put them back on." She flashed him a grin. "And don't worry. I promise I won't peek."

A date, he thought, as they followed Rhoda back to the bakery.

No doubt about it.

13

Lou next door liked to sit in front of his son's dry-cleaning establishment and watch the world go by. Weather permitting, Lou set up a lawn chair on the sidewalk every afternoon, poured himself a cold one, and waited for something to happen. Unfortunately for Lou, Lakeside was a very small town, which meant that on a given day nothing much did.

Hayley knew that the sight of the three of them—Finn, Rhoda, and herself—all covered in mud and gunk would be a gossip bonanza.

"Don't say anything more than you have

to," she warned Finn as they approached. "Mary Jane Espo already has enough information. And don't let him talk you out of more than twenty bucks. He may look old and innocent but he's an operator."

An operator with the second-biggest mouth in town. News of the tall, dark, and handsome stranger bearing bags of Chinese food had probably spread from one side of town to the other.

"Forty-two minutes," the old man greeted them as he protected the bags of food at his feet from her inquisitive dog. "That's thirty-five dollars."

"Lou!" Hayley shot him her most quelling look. "He is so not paying you thirty-five dollars for watching our food. We'll give you fifteen and even that's highway robbery."

Lou could scowl with the best of them. In his day he had inspired terror in the local kids. "Thirty."

Rafferty stepped forward. "Our agreement was ten dollars for thirty minutes, right?"

Lou took a long drag on his cigar and nodded. "Yep."

"Hayley's right. At that rate, forty-two minutes comes out to fifteen bucks." He paused for effect. "If you round it up."

"What are you," Lou demanded, "some kind of lawyer?"

"He is," Hayley said. "And a good one too."

Lou didn't miss a beat. "Twenty-five. That's with the professional discount."

"Twenty," Rafferty countered, "and I'll toss in an egg roll." He grinned at the old con artist. "That's a professional courtesy."

Rafferty pulled a soggy twenty from his back pocket and handed it to Lou. Lou held it up to the sun, inspected it front and back, then stuffed it into his shirt pocket.

He pushed the bags toward Rafferty.

"I already ate one of the egg rolls," he admitted. "My blood sugar . . ."

She met Finn's eyes over the old man's head and saw a mixture of compassion, amazement, and laughter ready to break free any second. The compassion alone was enough to do her in.

Hayley led him around the side of the building to the back door. "You managed to ransom back our Chinese food with only minor financial damage and Lou still thinks he came out on top. Very impressive."

She wiped Rhoda's massive paws with a rag dipped in the pail of water she kept near the door for that purpose.

"He's tough," Finn said as he pulled off his muddy shoes and left them on the doormat. "I'd rather go up against a hungry divorce lawyer than that guy."

Rhoda shook herself then bounded up the back stairs.

She kicked off her shoes on the mat beside his. "You didn't have to give him anything."

"Tell that to Lou."

"You were kind to him. Not everybody is."

"Maybe I was trying to impress his neighbor."

"I don't think that's the only reason."

"What can I tell you?" he said as he followed her upstairs. "He reminds me of my uncle Paddy."

"Your uncle Paddy extorts neighbors for bingo money?" she asked over her shoulder.

"He instituted a Christmas gift surcharge that put his two daughters through college."

"You lie!"

"He died at ninety-three with six thousand dollars in singles under his mattress."

She laughed out loud. "He would've loved my aunt Fee. She works from home as a seamstress. I think she has every dollar she ever earned tucked away in her hall closets."

Two nosy cats scattered when she and Finn reached the second-floor landing.

"Georgette and Phyllis," he said.

"Mary and Ted, but nice try." Where was Murray? She started down the hall. "The washer and dryer are on this floor. Give me five minutes to grab the stuff I hid in the bathtub and hide it somewhere else, then it's all yours."

"Okay," he said. "Sounds like a plan."

Two huge armfuls of junk later she handed him a stack of brand-new bath towels and a fresh bar of Dial, and pointed him down the hallway.

"Pink?" he said, staring at the fluffy pile of colorful terry cloth.

"Hot pink," she corrected him. "They were final sale at Target. We stocked up."

"Do you have something in white or a manly navy?"

"Hot pink," she repeated. "Good luck."

She told him to leave his dirty clothes outside the bathroom door and she would start a wash before she went upstairs.

"Still think it's a date?" she asked as he disappeared into the bathroom.

Fortunately his answer was muffled by the sound of her phone ringing.

"Is it the lawyer?" Aunt Fiona demanded the second Hayley said hello.

"Lou outdid himself this time. I figured it would take him until after supper to cover your side of town."

"Not Lou. Mary Jane Esposito called to tell me she saw you rolling in the mud by the lake with some strange man."

"He's not a strange man. Yes, he's the lawyer who commissioned the cake I'm doing next week and no, we weren't rolling in the mud. Rhoda ran away. He found her. She knocked him down. I slipped. We both ended up in the mud. And I thought I told you he was driving down when you called earlier."

"You did and I'm disappointed," Aunt Fee said. "I was hoping for something a lot juicier."

"Go back to watching your *Melrose Place* reruns, Fee. I'll call you later."

She heard the squeak as the bathroom door opened and then closed, followed by the sound of running water. One of the benefits to living above the shop was the fact that she had an industrial-strength water heater at the ready whenever they needed it. When you shared close quarters with a teenage girl this was no small thing.

She grabbed his muddy jeans and T-shirt and tried not to dwell on the fact that there was no underwear in the mix. The Suit she met last week wouldn't go commando but the man in the mud with her just might.

Either way she wasn't going to think about it. His underwear (or lack thereof) wasn't any of her business. It never would be her business.

Even if she was doing his laundry.

Finn was fiddling with the wonky shower nozzle when he saw the cat. The huge white feline was balanced precariously on the shower rod, watching him like he was an open can of Fancy Feast.

"Hey, kitty," he said in what he hoped was a neutral, nonthreatening tone of voice. "How about you get down and sit over by the door."

It seemed like a perfectly reasonable request, but the cat arched its back like a circus high-wire walker and took a step closer to him.

Naked in the shower with a pissed-off fifty-pound voyeuristic cat.

Not good.

"Okay, kitty, time to back off."

The cat laughed in his face, clear proof he wouldn't be taking home a stray feline anytime soon. A cat would wipe the floor with him.

"Didn't anyone tell you cats hate water?" he said as he made another pass at turning off the faucet. A fine spray was shooting everywhere and the cat didn't seem to notice.

Old Fluffy made another Flying Wallenda move on the shower rod deeper into Finn's naked comfort zone, close enough that he could smell the catnip on his breath.

How the hell had the cat gotten in there in the first place? The room was small. There was no way he would have missed the king-sized furball, no matter how preoccupied he had been.

He heard loud snuffling outside the door. Just what he needed. A giant cat on steroids on one side of the door and a dog the size of a runaway moose on the other.

The cat watched as he stepped out of the tub and reached for the hot-pink towel. A layer of terry cloth wasn't much in the way of protection but it was a step up from naked.

The snuffling stopped, replaced by a quick double knock. Either Rhoda had shaved her knuckles or Hayley was on the other side.

"Finn, is Murray in there with you?"

Now there was a question he had never heard before.

"If Murray is fat, white, and furry, the answer is yes."

"Thank God! I've been tearing the house apart looking for him."

"He's balanced on top of the shower rod glaring down at me."

The silence went on longer than he liked.

"I can handle it," he said. "Is he homicidal?"

"He's not homicidal." A long pause. "Finn, I don't know how to tell you this, but he needs the litter box."

The door swung open before the words "litter box" faded and Hayley found herself staring straight into the sun.

Okay, so maybe she wasn't staring into the sun but it felt like it. She was staring at Finn Rafferty's splendid, nearly naked body. The same body she had been happily sprawled across less than thirty minutes ago, the interesting contours of which were branded against her hip and thigh. The only thing keeping her from a full-on swoon was the hot pink towel wrapped around his midsection. If it slipped, she couldn't be held accountable.

During her marriage to Michael Goldstein, she had perfected a cool seen-it-all expression that had served her well. Never let them see you sweat. How well that philosophy would hold up against this full frontal peep show had yet to be determined.

"The litter box?" Rafferty didn't look at all his cool and confident self.

She really didn't want to be having the litter box conversation.

"His box is inside the vanity," she explained. "He must have been in there when you closed the bathroom door."

"So he just popped out to say hello."

"He popped out to tell you he wants privacy."

Rafferty poked his head back into the bathroom. "Knock yourself out, Murray," he said and closed the door.

And things had been going so well up until then.

Runaway dogs. Mud wrestling. Litter boxes. What on earth had she done wrong to piss off the fates?

"At the risk of sounding like one of those cat ladies, Murray really doesn't like having the door closed on him."

"Whatever Murray wants." He opened the door an inch. "Maybe he—" The dazed and confused expression he had been sporting suddenly morphed into something a little wicked and a whole lot warmer.

"What's your problem?" she asked. "Animals have preferences same as we do. I have to tell you, Rafferty, I don't think you're ready to—"

She followed his gaze and looked down at herself. Skin, skin, and more skin. Not to mention a small puddle of water at her feet. Rafferty wasn't the only one clad in nothing but a towel. Wet, pin-straight, truly bad hair spilled over her naked shoulders. Naked arms. Naked legs. Naked thighs complete with cellulite and three nasty little spider veins. She took small comfort in the fact that she had shaved her legs last night. Except for the stretch marks she now officially had no secrets.

Where was the earth-destroying meteor when you needed it?

"Your clothes should be dry in fifteen," she told him as casually as she could manage given the circumstances. "We have some T-shirts and yoga pants downstairs in the pantry if you don't want to wait." And a hypnotist who'll erase my thighs from your memory banks. She started backing down the hallway, praying for dim lighting and poor eyesight.

Murray stood in the doorway looking up at Finn.

"Yeah, I know," he said, bending down to scratch the woolly mammoth behind the ear. "You're wondering why I didn't make a move."

Murray purred and leaned into his hand.

"It's complicated, Murr. Be glad you're a cat."

Sometimes being a red-blooded male of the human species wasn't all it was cracked up to be. The heat between them had been palpable. The chemistry had been there from the first moment they met.

So would somebody please explain what he was doing standing there talking to a cat?

14

"What's the point?" Hayley asked her mirror as she tugged on a pair of jeans. Once a man saw your cellulite and spider veins, it was all over. She could go downstairs in a giant onesie and it wouldn't make the slightest bit of difference. The chemistry was dead. Their fantasy romance was over before it even began.

The crackling jolt of pure electricity she had felt lying in the mud with Finn Rafferty had been fleeting and very much one-sided. Whatever she thought he had felt had been a product of her overheated imagination.

And even if there had been the slightest flicker of interest on his part, it was gone now. The sad truth of the matter was that not every adult looked great wrapped in a towel. Finn might have been camera ready in his mucho macho hot-pink bath sheet, but the sight of a grown woman (who had borne a child, thank you very much) in a Scooby-Doo towel wasn't likely to inspire romantic fantasies.

And clearly it hadn't. When two healthy, unattached adults found themselves in an enclosed and private space with only a few layers of terry cloth between them, it was reasonable to think that one or both of them might seize the moment. Not that she had been seizing any moments lately, but still it hurt to bump up against the fact that she wasn't young enough, blond enough, sexy enough, fill-in-the-blank enough for him to consider making a move.

She knew what she must seem like to him. A single mother from South Jersey who smelled of flour and vanilla instead of perfume. A woman whose puff pastry had more cleavage than she did. A woman whose thighs alone were enough to guarantee her celibacy until the next millennium.

She got it. She really did. She wouldn't have made a move either.

But she couldn't help wishing he had tried.

"What're you looking at?" Finn asked Murray, Ted, Mary, and Rhoda as they watched him pace the kitchen. Hadn't they ever seen a man plan his escape before?

He had made a mistake. A big one. One of those colossal, could-have-been-fatal mistakes a man made once or twice in his life and, if he was lucky, lived to tell the tale. He could handle his emotions from a distance but here, in her house, he was veering out of control.

This time last week he hadn't known Hayley Maitland Goldstein existed. Now she was all he could think about.

Maybe it was loneliness that had propelled him. Maybe it was the sound of her voice or her unguarded laughter. Maybe it was the fact that he never knew what she was going to say or how she would say it or when. Maybe it was the strange sensation of having come home to a place he had never been before.

Whatever it was, it was wrong. The timing.

The cast of characters. The inevitable not-very-happy ending.

The thing to do was get up, say good-bye, and walk out the door before he did something he would regret. His car was parked out front. His keys jangled in his pocket. She was upstairs getting dressed. He would leave a note, phone her from the car. Things happen. He didn't live an ordinary life. She would understand.

"Finn?"

He turned to see her standing in the entrance to the kitchen.

"Is something wrong?" Her voice was light, her tone a little uncertain.

Her wet hair was scraped back into a sleek ponytail. She had replaced the muddy T-shirt and jeans with clean clothes. Her feet were bare. Her toenails were painted a pale icy pink. Her only jewelry was a pair of gold hoop earrings that danced with every step she took.

Sunlight streamed through the open window, igniting gold and red flames in her light brown hair. An aura of something so wonderful it didn't even have a name.

And that was when everything suddenly spun out of focus like a kaleidoscope. Colors brightened. Shapes shifted then rearranged themselves into brand-new patterns, each one more beautiful, more amazing than the one before.

Sound flew at him from all around the room, random words thrown his way in random combinations, Scrabble letters forming Scrabble words that made no sense at all. His heart made a quarter turn inside his chest and the sound of its rapid beating drowned out everything else.

The world around him snapped back into focus and all he saw was Hayley.

She was a grown woman. She knew how these things worked. She should have seen the kiss coming but it surprised her just the same. He had been looking at her with a crazy kind of unfocused intensity and she had been about to ask him if he was having a stroke or something when she suddenly realized she was about to be kissed by a man she actually wanted to kiss back.

Every now and then life handed you a perfect moment and this was one of them.

The knowing was almost enough.

That one perfect moment of certainty, of

sweet anticipation—a woman could live off that memory for a very long time.

She hadn't known how much she wanted to feel his mouth on hers until it happened, how she wanted that kiss more than she wanted her next breath of air.

He kissed her mouth, her chin, the tip of her nose, her lower lip, her upper lip, her right temple, her left, her mouth again . . . oh God, her mouth. Long, hot, slow, deep, luscious kisses that made her feel like a candle with a quick-burning flame.

"Is this why you drove down here?" she whispered against his lips.

He kissed her again. Deeper, hotter, slower. A sigh of almost unbearable pleasure escaped her lips.

"You ask too many questions," he said and then he kissed her again.

"You're right." She sighed. "I do."

Her back was against the fridge. She could feel the handle pressing against her spine. Nothing mattered but the heat from his body, the moist warmth of his mouth, the insistent pressure against her hip. She was burning with hunger, melting. If he let go of her, she would sink into a puddle right there at his feet.

"Rhoda," she said when she could catch her breath.

He looked at her like she had started reciting the Gettysburg Address from memory. "You're thinking about the dog?"

"She's never seen me with a man before. I don't think she's enjoying it."

He looked across the room to where Rhoda guarded the doorway.

"Is her fur supposed to stand straight up like that?"

"I don't think—"

"Maybe we—"

Seconds later they closed the bedroom door behind them.

Jeans, sweaters, bras, panties, shoes, clean sheets, paperback books, and a major assortment of blow dryers were scattered from one end of the room to the other.

"Oh God," she said, pressing her face against his shoulder. "That's the stuff I hid behind the shower curtain."

"I don't see anything."

He brushed her hair off the right side of her neck and pressed his mouth against her skin.

Pleasure ran straight from his lips to the molten center of her body.

She moved against him and laughed softly at his unmistakable response.

His mouth moved down the length of her throat. He pushed the neckline of her sweater aside and trailed his tongue along her collarbone.

It had been a long time...a very long time...so long that she couldn't remember exactly when she had felt this open and deliciously exposed...He was gorgeous...he liked Chinese food...he knew how to kiss... A fling...Why not...One juicy secret...Don't stop...don't stop...

"You stopped," she said. "Why did you stop?" She could have kissed him for at least another week or two before she even considered stopping.

"I didn't plan this."

"You stopped to tell me that?"

"I'm talking about protection."

It was hard to think when you were on fire from the inside out. "I thought men always had something with them."

"It's been a while."

"Don't look at me," she said. "I've been living like a nun."

"I saw a drugstore down the street. I could—"

"No!" She grabbed his arm. "Mary Jane Espo's brother owns the drugstore. I'd have to join a convent."

"Sister Goldstein? I like it."

She wasn't about to be mollified. "What are we going to do?"

"You mean besides stripping each other naked?"

"Besides that."

He lowered her to the mattress and slid her panties down her legs. "I can think of a few things."

The bed was soft beneath her back. He wasn't soft anywhere. His arms. His chest. His thighs. The rock-hard erection burning against her belly. She reached for him but he shifted position and began tonguing his way down the center of her body, the valley between her breasts, her navel, her belly, her—

Her cry of pleasure pierced the silent room and on its heels came an almost paralyzing moment of self-awareness. What was she doing . . . She barely knew him . . . No secrets . . . no secrets . . .

His tongue slid deep inside her and she arched against him, taking him deeper, wrapping herself around him, sailing over the edge of the earth. She loved the feel of his big hands on her hips, the way his breath tickled, the parry and thrust of his tongue, his lips tugging gently on her clitoris. His sounds. His smell. His touch. His broad, muscular shoulders and powerful chest. The small tattoo of an intertwined cross and flower on the inside of his right forearm.

He was doing something magical, mystical, with his hands and his mouth, something amazing, something so unbearably wonderful that she came hard against him and would have climaxed again if he hadn't shifted position, trailing his mouth back up her body in a way that made conscious thought all but impossible.

His eyes widened in surprise, then excitement, as she pushed him over onto his back and straddled him. She took his erection in her hands, sliding the length of the shaft, teasing the head until it throbbed visibly. He groaned and gripped her by the waist.

"Don't start something we can't finish." He wanted to bury himself inside her silky wetness as she took him deep and hard.

She leaned forward and flicked her tongue against him. "Wait," she said and slipped from the bed. "I just thought of something."

He watched as she crossed the room. Her body was long and slim, her breasts surprisingly full and round. Her nipples were hard. He saw faint red marks on her thighs where his teeth had grazed her tender flesh. Her sweet taste lingered in his mouth and made him want more.

She opened the top drawer of her dresser, rummaged for a second, then pulled out a small white plastic bag.

The words *Introduction to Sex—Grade 8* were emblazoned in bright red letters.

She slid back into bed next to him and spilled the contents between them. A booklet. A DVD. One lone condom.

"It's been a while," she said with a rueful laugh. "Do these things have expiration dates?"

He held it up to the light. "Tomorrow."

They locked eyes.

"It's fate," she said.

"Definitely."

"You open it. I'm out of practice."

"Been a while for me too," he said, tearing open the package with his teeth.

"Really?"

"You sound surprised."

"I am." Glad, but surprised.

He fumbled with the condom. His fingers felt huge, clumsy. Her breasts brushed against his arm as she reached for the condom.

"Let me."

He loved the feel of her fingers as they worked the condom over his shaft. The sight of her naked body bent to the task, damp hair falling across one shoulder. The fact that they were both there, in that bed, at that moment.

The fact that he was falling in love.

Later

"Where are you going?" Finn leaned up on one elbow and peered through the gathering dusk as Hayley darted for the door.

"Sorry," she said. "I didn't mean to wake you."

"Is everything okay?" Most women liked the cuddling afterward as much as the main event, but once again Hayley was proving herself to be not like other women. She was already halfway out the door.

"We left the Chinese food on the kitchen table. I hope Rhoda and the cats didn't help themselves."

They had just had inventive, incendiary sex right there in that still-warm bed and she was thinking about lo mein? "I'll be down in a minute."

"Take your time," she said over her shoulder. "No problem."

"Are you sure everything's okay? You seem a little distracted."

"I'm fine. Why wouldn't I be fine? I'll start warming things up. You want beer or iced tea or soda? Actually you don't have to tell me. I've got all three. You come down whenever you're ready."

He wrapped the sheet around his waist and swung his legs from the bed. "Are you sure nothing's wrong?"

Even her laugh sounded false. "Why would anything be wrong?"

"This was great," he said, gesturing toward the bed. "You know that, right? You were amazing."

She looked like she wanted to fling herself out the window. "So were you," she said. "I'll see you downstairs."

Of all the stupid, reckless, idiotic things to do, sleeping with an almost stranger in the middle of the day with her daughter just six blocks away had to be at the top of the list.

Hayley sagged onto the bottom step and buried her face in her hands.

What were you thinking, Goldstein? Were you thinking at all?

The thought of just how close she had come to total disaster had her struggling to take a deep breath. Finn was wonderful. Everything about him was wonderful. If she didn't have Lizzie to consider, she would run back upstairs and fling herself at him another ten or twenty times and even that wouldn't be enough.

All these years of being careful, of worrying about how her actions would affect her daughter, and she almost threw it all away with one thoughtless, crazy act.

Lizzie could have popped through the door any second. She could have forgotten a book, a CD, anything. If Lizzie had found her in bed with Finn—

She couldn't finish the thought. How did you explain the importance of choosing a partner carefully, getting to know someone before you decide to have sex, when you leaped into the sack with a guy five days after you met him?

Clearly somebody had been watching out for her this afternoon, some benevolent goddess of stupid, stupid women who let themselves be knocked off track by a man.

It's more than that, Goldstein. At least have the guts to admit it.

The sex had been the best of her life. There wasn't a woman alive who wouldn't sacrifice an IQ point or two for the kind of pleasure she had found with Finn. But the scary truth of it all was the fact that it wasn't just great sex that had her feeling like somebody had turned her world inside out while she wasn't looking.

It was Finn himself. The man who drove four hours to deliver Chinese food. The lawyer who had treated her daughter with respect. The guy who gave Lou an egg roll and a fistful of cash and did it with a friendly shrug of the shoulders.

Finn.

The man she absolutely, positively had no intention of falling for.

"I heated up the soup," Hayley greeted him when he entered the kitchen fifteen minutes later. "Do you want me to slice some extra scallions?"

He shook his head. "Don't go to any extra trouble." Basically he wanted to eat and get the hell out of Dodge.

"Sesame oil?"

"No, thanks."

"I have the hot oil if you—"

"It's fine," he said. "Really. I like it straight out of the container."

"I put the egg rolls in the oven. The microwave turns them all soggy."

"I'm going to skip the egg rolls."

"The shrimp in garlic sauce is ready to pop in the mike. Just say when."

He met her eyes. "The soup's good enough. I think I probably should hit the road before it gets too much later."

"But you brought all this stuff."

"Never order Chinese when you're hungry," he said with a small laugh. "I always forget."

"I'm sorry," she blurted out.

"For what? I'm the one who ordered too much food."

"I hurt your feelings. I can see it in your eyes."

He looked down at his soup. "I don't know what you're talking about."

"I shouldn't have run out like that. I guess I panicked."

He put down his spoon. "I'm not following."

"Upstairs. After we made love. Don't tell me you didn't notice that I ran out like I was escaping a bank robbery."

"Was that you?" He tried to make a joke but he was still feeling a little raw after her escape. "You moved so fast I wasn't sure."

"It's Lizzie," she said. "I wasn't thinking clearly." She met his eyes. "I couldn't think once we started kissing."

He didn't say anything.

"She's fourteen. It's a difficult, dangerous world. That's not the message I want to give her. Lizzie could have walked through that door anytime. How would I explain the fact that you were in my bed?"

There was nothing like reality to bring a man's libido into check.

"I didn't think of that at all."

"Why should you? She's my daughter. This is my house. I should have been the one doing the thinking but I wasn't and I'm sorry."

"You don't have anything to apologize for."

"I should have told you this upstairs. I would have but—" She shook her head. "Like I said, I'm out of practice."

"So am I."

The corners of her mouth began to curve in a smile. "I beg to differ, Mr. Rafferty."

"Muscle memory," he said with his own answering smile. "It comes in handy."

"Stay," she said, brushing a soft kiss against his mouth. "I'm not ready to say good-bye."

He pulled her down onto his lap and nuzzled the side of her neck. "Neither am I."

"We can't—"

"We won't."

"But you're—"

"Yeah," he confirmed. "How do you like that?"

"Very much," she murmured. "Very, very much."

"We could—"

"We shouldn't."

"You could lock the doors."

"Lizzie has a key."

"Call her. Make sure she's still at her friend's house."

"She'd think I was checking up on her."

"Isn't that what parents do?"

"You have a point." She flipped open her cell and pressed 1 and waited. "Hi, Lizzie . . . No, nothing's wrong . . . I can't find Aunt Fee's extra set of keys . . . Oh, we did . . . I

forgot . . . Are you having fun . . . Great . . .
No, that's it . . . Enjoy the movie." She flipped
her cell closed. "They're watching *Grease*. It
just started."

He slipped his hand under the hem of her
shirt and cupped her breast. "So have we."

15

"What time is it?" Hayley murmured into the side of Finn's neck after they both drifted back down to earth.

"Around seven thirty."

"We're safe," she said. "Danny and Cha Cha DiGregorio just won the dance contest at Rydell High. There won't be any surprise visits."

"You wore me out." His laugh was a low rumble. "There won't be any more surprise visits from me either."

They hadn't made it out of the kitchen this time. Their coupling had been fierce, sensual, and inventive. An erotic play of hands and mouths that sprang from the powerful, amazing chemistry between them.

Their return to reality should have been difficult but it wasn't. They settled back down at the table like they had been sharing meals forever. The cats watched from the top of the fridge. Rhoda patrolled the perimeter in search of discards. The parrot observed everything from his perch on the curtain rod.

Except for the phones it was perfect.

"I'm sorry," Hayley said as her cell rang for what seemed like the tenth time in an hour. "This is crazy even for me."

This time it was Michie pretending she wanted to discuss possible hairstyles for the after-party.

"Michie, I can't talk right now...The Chinese food is getting cold...Delicious, thanks..." She turned slightly away from Finn. "Yes, he is...Yes, he is...Yes, I will... Absolutely not...Good-bye, Michie."

"That Mary Jane Esposito really gets the word out," Finn said after she hung up. "I think half the town has called you."

"Seems like it, doesn't it? We take our gossip where we can find it." She gestured toward his cell phone on the table. "You're no slouch in the phone call department either, mister."

"You'd think I was waiting for a transplant."

"Did you ever think of turning it off?"

"I will if you will."

"Can't do it. I'm a mother. It's in the contract they give you right after you deliver."

Right on cue, his phone rang. He picked up his chopsticks and attacked his plate of shrimp with garlic sauce.

"You're not going to answer that?" she asked.

"Nope."

It rang again.

"Don't you want to see who it is?"

"Everyone I know has already checked in today. I'm not expecting an emergency."

"Nobody expects an emergency, Rafferty. They just happen."

"Eat your chicken," he suggested. "It's getting cold."

"You really should answer that phone," she urged. "It could be something important."

"You're a worrier," he responded. "I forgot that."

"A worrier and a mother. I can't sit here and let a ringing phone go unanswered. At least see who it is."

He turned his phone over and looked at the display. "Damn," he muttered, then looked over at Hayley. He flipped it open. "What's up, Tom?"

She tried to appear nonchalant but she was listening every bit as hard as Mary Jane Esposito listened to gossip at Jeannie's Hair Emporium.

"...I can't do that, Tom...She's your fiancée...so tell Willow that...Another few days...Tom, you'd better— Hey, Willow... It's Finn...We're working things out...Not much longer...Sloan and I have been playing phone tag...Tom's right...Absolutely... I'll see you tomorrow."

He powered down and picked up his fork. "That was Tommy."

"I figured that out."

"And his fiancée."

"I read about her in *People* last week."

He looked like he wanted to say something.

"I'm a good listener," she said. "Nosy but discreet."

"Sorry."

"You do realize it's killing me not to ask for details, don't you? The only thing keeping me from bombarding you with questions is the fact that between now and the after-party he's a customer."

"The Code of the Baker?"

"Don't mock what you don't understand, counselor. It's a time-honored tradition. We don't gossip about our customers until the last bite of cake has been eaten."

"And then?"

"Let's just say Mary Jane Esposito and our friend Lou have nothing on me."

He told her a few stories about lawyers and their love of gossip. She told him a few about bakers.

"But when it comes to gossip, nobody beats academics. My mother may live the life of the higher mind, but it's dish that recharges her batteries."

"She's an oceanographer, right? A pretty major one."

"Probably one of the most major," Hayley said and not without a note of pride. "The thing about Jane is that she never went commercial. She's all about the work, which means she pretty much lives on a shoestring."

"You never thought about following in her footsteps?"

"I'm afraid of the water."

"You're afraid of the water?"

"Why are you looking at me that way? Lots of people are afraid of the water."

"Tommy's kids hate the water."

"See? I told you I have plenty of company." She pointed toward his food with her chopsticks. "Want me to nuke it again for you?"

"Who am I kidding?" He tossed his chopsticks down and reached for a fork. "Am I less of a man because I use a fork?"

"You survived the hot-pink towel," she said with a grin. "I think you can probably survive just about anything."

They fell into an easy banter. She ate some of his shrimp. He sampled her kung pao. They made inroads on the veggie lo mein and shared the egg rolls with the menagerie.

"Should we save some for Lizzie?" Finn asked.

"Just a little. I can't believe I'm saying this, but my daughter doesn't fully appreciate the wonders of Chinese cuisine." She polished off the last of the shrimp in garlic sauce. "You were right. This really is the best take-out food on the planet." She looked across the table at Finn. "Why are you sniffing your

sleeve?" Please, God, don't let him start flying the freak flag now . . .

"It smells like flowers."

"That's your imagination."

"No, I smell roses and something else sweet and girly."

"I don't perfume my laundry, if that's what you're worried about."

"Soap should smell like soap," he said, "not a bottle of Chanel Number Five."

"You're smelling plain-old garden-variety Tide."

"This isn't Tide."

"Yes, it is." She pushed back from the table.

"Where are you going?"

"I'm going to prove it to you."

One of the few good things about living in a place with limited square footage was convenience. Her stackable washer-dryer combination was hidden away in her hall closet off the kitchen.

"Bad news," she said as she sat back down at the table. "Spring Meadow."

He actually blanched. "Tell me you're kidding."

"Am I under oath?" A grin twitched at the corners of her mouth. "I meant to use Tide."

"Like walking around in a hot-pink bath towel wasn't bad enough."

"You looked very masculine in that hot-pink towel. Not many men could pull it off." Perfect. For once in her life she didn't say more than she should.

Amused embarrassment suited him. "Hey, what guy doesn't think pink when he's got a date."

"I thought we agreed this isn't a date. We're having too much fun. I don't know about you, but I never have fun on dates."

"Maybe you haven't been dating the right men."

"Actually I haven't been dating much at all." She sighed and leaned back in her chair. "I'm sorry but life's too short to spend it wearing heels and makeup for some guy who can't even make you laugh."

"So you like to laugh."

"Laughing is high up on the list. How about you?"

"Laughing is good." He put down his fork. "You're not looking to get married again?"

"Lizzie and I have been on our own a long time now. I don't know how adaptable I am. Besides, I'm not sure marriage is good enough compensation for giving up my independence."

"There must be something to marriage or it wouldn't be so popular."

"You told me you were married once," she said. "What do you think?"

"I think I did it wrong."

"Wrong partner? Wrong time?"

"A little of everything." He told her about his early marriage, the months spent out on the road, the baby they had lost.

"I'm sorry," she said, reaching for his hand. "I miscarried a baby boy before I got pregnant with Lizzie. I know how much it hurts."

"We didn't handle it well," he admitted. "Once we lost the baby, we drifted so far apart there was no putting the marriage back together."

"Did you love her?"

"As much as I was capable of loving someone then." He met her eyes. "Did you love your ex?"

"I loved his family," she replied. "Sometimes I think that was why I married him in the first place."

"Any close calls since?" he asked.

She shook her head. "I have Lizzie, the bakery, and the cake business to keep me busy. My ex was—" She stopped and shook her head again. "My ex isn't a model citizen, Finn. It wasn't a happy marriage. I wish I could say he's managed to be a good father to Lizzie despite his other shortcomings but he hasn't. A man would have to be very special for me to let him into our family circle."

"I've met Lizzie," he reminded her. "A man would be lucky to be allowed in."

"Do you ever think about marrying again?"

"Believe it or not, I'd like to try again with the right person."

"You should ask your boss for advice," she joked. "He's done it often enough."

"Three times and a fourth in the works."

"What's up with that anyway? Doesn't he learn from experience?"

"No," he said. "That's why Tommy needs live-in counsel."

"No, seriously. How many times can you say 'I do' before you realize maybe you don't?"

"The thing about Tommy is that each time he believes it's going to last forever."

"That's not possible."

"Yeah, it is," Rafferty said. "I've known the guy my whole life and I can tell you that when he falls in love, he falls all the way. Nobody's more surprised than he is when it doesn't work out."

"So the fact that he walks out on these women hasn't registered with him yet."

"He doesn't walk, Hayley. They do."

"You're kidding."

"Every time," Rafferty stated. "The thing is, once you're in the fishbowl, you start trying to find a way back out. The spotlight gets old after a while and they end up walking."

"I saw an item about Tommy in Page Six yesterday. He was buying some big diamond for his latest fiancée."

"Willow."

"Willow." She shook her head. "When did girls start being named after trees anyway?"

"He's a romantic," Rafferty said with a shrug. "Actually he's a romantic optimist."

"Does he have reason to be this time around?"

"Probably not."

"So you're saying Willow will probably walk out on him one day too."

"Odds are she'll be gone before the kid's second birthday."

"So I take it you're not a romantic optimist."

"I'm his lawyer."

"You're a cynic."

"A realist. I believe marriage is possible. I believe it can last a lifetime. I just don't believe it's going to happen for Tommy and Willow."

"I can't believe I'm saying this about a multimillionaire rock star, but I almost feel sorry for him."

"Don't," Finn said. "He's pretty much bulletproof when it comes to romance. He'll fall in love again, marry again, and the crowd at Christmas will get bigger because somehow they all stay friends."

She tried to imagine a convivial gathering of the extended Maitland-Goldstein family, but every time she inserted Michael into the picture, the fantasy came crashing down.

"It's terrific that all of the exes think he hung the moon, but the only thing worse than my marriage was my divorce. It really took a toll on Lizzie. How in the world do Tommy Stiles's kids handle it over and over again?"

"They handle it very well," he said after a moment. "He's a good father."

"Probably as good as mine and I never knew the man."

His expression shifted. He looked downright uncomfortable.

"I'm sorry. A little sperm donor humor. He's your friend and my next paycheck. I stepped over the line."

"You didn't step over the line. You expressed an opinion."

"Unsolicited."

"Most opinions are."

"I guess the whole father thing is a hot-button issue for me."

He nodded but he didn't say anything. She wasn't sure if that was a sign of disinterest or discretion.

"In case you're wondering, I did say sperm donor before. It's kind of like the elephant in the room, isn't it?"

"Your mother went the sperm donor route?"

"She's a scientist. She was forty. There was no man in her life. She wanted a guaranteed brilliant child so she found herself a high IQ sperm donor and proved the entire thesis wrong when she had me."

"I think she did pretty well for herself."

"I'm not a Rhodes scholar, Rafferty."

"You're an artist."

"A baker."

"An artist. I saw your paintings on the walls. I saw the work you've done on the cakes. You're the real deal."

"I'm happy," she admitted, "but there's no getting around the fact that I'm not exactly the brain trust she was hoping for."

Rhoda barked twice, circled the kitchen table, then barked again.

She stood up. "Rhoda needs some out time."

He pushed back his chair but she motioned for him to stop.

"Stay," she said. "Nobody but family should ever have to walk behind Rhoda."

In the end it was always about the timing.

He had been a half step away from telling her everything when the ubiquitous Rhoda decided it was time to hit the street.

He wasn't sure if the dog had saved him from making a terrible mistake or screwed him out of his one chance to find out where this could go.

He checked his phone for messages. Two more from Tommy, both about Willow and the negotiations. One from a friend putting together a charity softball game scheduled for August in Sagaponack. Nothing that couldn't wait.

He gathered up the dirty dishes, scraped them, then loaded them into her dishwasher.

He chucked the empty cartons into the trash while the three cats watched him from the doorway.

"How's it hangin', Murray?"

The humongous white cat, tail held high like the mast of a clipper ship, loped toward him. Was a high-flying cat tail a good thing? It beat the hell out of him.

Clearly he had a lot to learn.

For example, how long did it take to walk a dog? She had been gone twenty minutes at least. He was wondering if the length of the walk was in any way proportional to the size of the dog when the kitchen phone rang.

"Hello! Hello!" Mr. G called out from his living room perch. "Helloooooo!"

By the fourth ring he realized voice mail wasn't going to kick in. Hayley didn't believe in unanswered phones. Lizzie wasn't home. It was up to him or Mr. G.

Opposable thumbs ruled.

"Hello."

Long silence.

"Hello?"

"Sorry." A girl's voice. "I must've dialed wrong."

"Lizzie?"

"Yes." She was definitely her mother's daughter. The slightly wary tone was a dead giveaway. "Who's this?"

"Finn Rafferty. Your mom is out walking Rhoda."

"The famous guy's lawyer? What are you doing there?"

Those Goldstein girls didn't mince words. "Your mom and I were talking on the phone about great Chinese food. I told her we had the best take-out place on the planet in Montauk and ten minutes later I was in the car on the way down here to prove it."

"That's crazy!" Lizzie was laughing as she said it.

"Eight hours round trip," he said. "I think crazy pretty much covers it."

"You can tell me the truth. You were worried about the cakes and that's why you really drove down."

"Sorry, Lizzie. It was all about Chinese food."

"You're not even a little worried?"

"On a scale of one to ten, I'd rank it a zero."

"I'll bet she showed you anyway."

He started to laugh. "You're right," he said, "and it was incredible."

"I told you it would be." He could hear her smile right through the phone.

You had to love the kid. Fourteen years old and filled with confidence and enthusiasm. He knew who was responsible.

Thundering hooves sounded on the staircase followed by a lighter, syncopated step.

"Hang on, Lizzie. Your mom just walked in."

The cats scattered as Rhoda exploded into the room.

"Hey, guys! You don't have to knock me down." Hayley pretended to stagger into the kitchen as Ted, Mary, and Murray tore past her. Her brows lifted when she noticed he was holding the phone.

"It's Lizzie," he said.

Everything he needed to know about her was reflected in her eyes as she took the receiver from him. Love, fear, concern, joy. He knew that look. He had seen it many times in Tommy's eyes when he looked at his brood.

"What's up . . . Yes, I found the keys . . . The food was great . . ." She glanced over at Finn and winked. "It just might be the best . . . She's your friend . . . You know she didn't mean that . . . Yes, I know . . . Lizzie!" She made a quarter turn toward the window.

"Of course I'll come get you . . . Stay put . . . One egg roll, a little soup, and some shrimp in garlic sauce . . . I'll be there soon."

She hung up the phone then turned back to him. He had never seen a lovelier face or a more expressive one.

"Lizzie had a fight with her best friend and now she wants to come home. I have to go get her." Was that regret mixed in with the other emotions?

He hoped so.

"I'm sorry," she said. "She's fourteen. They're very dramatic at that age. Everything's a soap opera."

He said all the right things. It was late. He had a long drive ahead of him. She shouldn't keep Lizzie waiting. He didn't mean any of them. He wanted to stay. He wanted her to stay. He wanted reality to stay away a little longer.

They made their way downstairs, through the bakery, past the workroom with the prototypes of the drum set and the gold records and a shitload of guilt, and out the back door. Her aging Buick was tucked in the driveway, a few feet away.

"Where are you parked?" she asked.

"In front of the dry cleaners." He aimed a

smile at her in the darkness. "I figured Lou might want to keep an eye on me."

"Lou and everyone else in town," she said with a rueful but affectionate laugh. "By the way, I didn't forget that I owe you twenty."

"You don't owe me anything."

"I had a great time today, Finn." She paused. "Even if you do smell like a spring garden."

"You were right before when you said this wasn't a date."

Her voice went softer. "What gave it away?"

"The fact that I'd like to do it all over again."

He heard the hopeful uncertainty in her voice. "No changes?"

"No changes."

"I'd change one thing."

"Okay," he said, thinking of their lack of a condom. "I'd change that too."

She ducked her head. "Not that." A long pause. "I'd change Lizzie's timing."

Her mouth was soft beneath his in the welcoming darkness. The sweet night air dancing in the charged space between them. Rhoda barked from somewhere inside the house. Bits of conversation floated toward them from the street. A radio, set to the Phillies station, alternately blared then drifted away.

The charged space between them vanished as they melted into each other. She was slender, gently curved in ways that surprised and delighted him. He knew her body now, knew it intimately. He knew how she tasted, how she smelled, how she sounded when she came.

But that wariness, that reserve, was still there.

It killed him to know that she was right to be wary. Nothing was exactly as it seemed to be. Nothing but the moment.

"Finn, I—"

"Shh."

He cupped her face with his hands, kissed her hard and fast, then stepped away.

"Go," he said. "Lizzie's waiting."

She nodded, her blue-green eyes searching him for something he couldn't give.

"You know that other shoe I keep waiting for?" she asked.

He nodded.

"I think it just dropped."

16

"The soup at Szechuan Dan's is better than this." Lizzie pushed her bowl away from her and reached for the carton of kung pao.

Hayley plucked a noodle from the half-empty bowl and dipped it in some mustard. "I thought the soup was amazing."

Lizzie fussed with her chopsticks for a moment then abandoned them for a fork. "This isn't bad," she said, spearing a piece of chicken.

"Come on, Lizzie. Give credit where it's due."

Lizzie favored her with a grin. "Okay, so it's great."

"Told you so." It wasn't often the mother of a teenage girl got to say that with impunity.

She divided the egg roll into two and popped a half on her daughter's plate. "So tell me what went wrong over at Tracy's house. I thought you two were best buds."

Lizzie embarked on a long story about science lab and some project she had been working on with Amanda. Hayley tried very hard to keep her attention on her daughter but she kept replaying her day with Finn.

"Mom! You're not listening."

"Sorry. Just repeat the last part and I'll catch up."

"I don't want to talk about that anymore." She brightened. "Grandma Jane called me on my cell while I was at Tracy's. She'll be in London tomorrow. She said she'll stay a day or two then fly the rest of the way home before the end of the week."

"How did she sound?"

"Tired," Lizzie said.

"She's jet-lagged."

"From what? She hasn't even left Mumbai yet."

Good point. Was it possible age was finally making inroads on her superhuman mother? The thought of Jane showing signs of human

frailty sent a shiver up her spine and the worrying apparatus into motion.

"We're going to have to shovel out the guest room," Hayley said. "And make sure the bathroom is up to her standards." The woman had made do on tramp steamers and garbage scows in her search to discover all there was to know about the world's oceans. She had availed herself of strange sanitary apparatus that would make a Navy SEAL go weak at the knees. But once Jane was on dry land, all bets were off.

"No bathroom is up to Grandma's standards," Lizzie said, laughing. "She told me only an operating room is clean enough."

"Well, she's going to have to lower her standards while she's living Chez Us." Hayley laid out the schedule for the next few days. "I'm going to need a lot of help from you this week, Lizzie. Everything's happening at once and we're going to have to pull together to get it all done."

"Aunt Fee wants to know why Grandma isn't staying with her. She's insulted."

"I was wondering the same thing," Hayley admitted. "The last time she stayed with us you hadn't even started school yet."

"She's not a big fan of cats."

"Or dogs."

"Or parrots."

"Or my cooking." Hayley rolled her eyes.

"Or my music."

"Your grandmother's a moocher," Hayley said. "She sends all her money to that save-the-whales foundation of hers and mooches off indigent relatives instead."

Lizzie was laughing so hard she couldn't talk and Hayley wasn't far behind. When your mother was a combination of Einstein and Mother Teresa, sometimes the only thing a dropout daughter could do was laugh, and if she made her own daughter laugh too, so much the better.

Jane could be imperious, demanding, and difficult to live with on a daily basis. She craved logic, quiet, and harmony, three things found only in Lizzie's room and then in random combinations.

Despite her proclaimed lack of regard for material pleasures, Jane preferred Egyptian cotton sheets, organic vegetables, and French milled soaps. Hayley's sheets were Kmart blue-light specials. Her vegetables came straight from ShopRite and her soap was Dial or Irish Spring, depending which brand was on sale.

Aunt Fiona was a bit of a snob too when it came to domestic pleasures. She also lived alone and had a beautifully decorated guest room at the ready. Why Jane hadn't opted to stay with her sister was a mystery to everyone.

Then again, that wasn't the only mystery she had bumped into lately.

"I told you Finn Rafferty liked you."

"Of course he likes me," Hayley said. "I'm a likable person."

"You know what I mean. He *likes* likes you."

"Don't go reading anything into Chinese food, Lizzie." She tucked away the memory of his lovemaking to savor later in private. "At first I thought he came down here to back out of the deal."

"No way."

"I had the feeling all afternoon that there was something he wanted to tell me but every time I thought he was about to spill it, he changed the subject."

"So why didn't he?"

"I don't know. At first he didn't want to go downstairs and see how things were going on the job but I pushed—better to catch problems now than later—and he spent a long time inspecting the prelim drawings."

"They're way cool," Lizzie said around a mouthful of food. "You're an artist, Mom. You could hang those drawings in a gallery."

Hayley had no false modesty about her artistic ability. Her talent was what had propelled her through school, not her academic achievements. "I don't think he was really seeing any of it. It was like he was looking past them and thinking of a way to let me down gently."

"Well, he didn't."

"No," Hayley said as the memory of her rumpled bed blossomed before her eyes. "He certainly didn't."

Like spontaneous combustion, the heat had flared between them, burning away everything but the feel of his mouth against hers, the rough, sweet touch of his hands on her body.

But as much as she would love to believe he had driven four hours for the pleasure of her company, she was a realist and she knew there had been something else going on. The chemistry between them was just a bonus, one that neither of them had expected.

She had spent the last few years maintaining a sharp focus and she couldn't afford to lose it now when it was finally starting to pay off.

No more Chinese food deliveries. No more naked men in hot-pink towels. No flirty e-mails, IMs, or phone calls. And definitely no long, deep kisses that made a woman forget her name.

For the next couple of days she was going to be all about the work, but once that after-party was over . . .

RAINBOWGIRL is online

RAINBOWGIRL: Dad, r u here?
RAINBOWGIRL: Dad? u didn't answer my last email I'm getting worried

RAINBOWGIRL timed out

East Hampton—the Next Morning

It was only nine o'clock and already the day was out of control.

Finn had fielded a skirmish between Tommy and his sons, renegotiated the insurance contract with the airport, and participated in a major slugfest with the musician's

union rep in Atlantic City. At least it wasn't a
regular tour date, which involved a minimum
of fifteen tour buses to haul the set, the musicians, and the roadies. The contracts surrounding that endeavor were enough to
make a lawyer long for the days of the hand-
shake deal.

Tommy's manager usually handled the
special dressing-room requests part of the
package but that nasty job had fallen to Finn
this time around. There was something hum-
bling about requesting twenty bottles of
Poland Spring, two bowls of Cheez-Its, and
a fridge stocked with Grey Goose and Yoo-
hoo for a grown man.

He had been on his way to the kitchen
for caffeine reinforcements when Amber,
Tommy's eldest by his first wife, waylaid him
five feet from the coffee machine.

Like her father, Amber had married young
but so far her marriage seemed to be rock
solid.

"She's horrible!" She griped to Finn as he
poured himself a cup of coffee. "Somebody's
got to talk some sense into Dad before it's
too late. The thought of that walking boob job
as my stepmother makes me want to secede
from the family."

"Willow is high-strung," Finn said, marveling at his own mastery of understatement. Maybe it had something to do with not getting any sleep. "You remember what the first trimester was like. Add a wedding to that and you get—"

"A first-class bitch. Don't go making excuses for her, Finn. All she does is talk about that ridiculous prenup she's so worried about. If she loved Dad, she wouldn't be working it so hard, would she? I mean, everyone on the planet knows he's a pushover when it comes to his family. It's not like he wouldn't be fair."

He caught sight of Jilly, Anton, and three of the backup dancers walking up from the beach.

"We went over this before." He led her into Tommy's office at the back of the house and out of the line of fire. "The prenup is in your father's best interests." He let that sink in for maybe the fiftieth time. "We need to protect his assets, Amber, and sometimes the process can take a while."

"I don't see why." She flopped down onto the huge leather couch by the window and for a second Finn was reminded of the little girl who had followed him around the mansion like a shadow when he first moved in years ago. "It's not like this is his first time."

He sat on the edge of Tommy's glass-and-bleached-oak desk. "Every situation is different. Willow's pregnant with Tom's child. That complicates everything." It was all about his kids, he explained to Amber. Tommy wanted to make sure their share of his assets would remain protected.

Amber rolled her huge blue-green eyes. "Isn't it about time somebody spoke to him about family planning? I love my sibs but this is getting ridiculous!"

She smiled when she said it and Finn smiled back at her. "You know what I'm not saying, right?"

"Yes, and I'm going out of the baby business as soon as number three is born," she said, cradling her barely visible bump. "I mean, is he going to be seeding the crops when he's in his eighties?"

All of Tommy's kids shared his quick temper and even quicker willingness to forgive and forget. It was one of the things he liked best about the Stiles family.

"Why are you looking at me that way? It's

the new haircut, isn't it? I told Jilly I wanted something different but—"

He shook his head. "Sorry. I was just thinking how much like Tommy you are."

And how much like Hayley. After spending a day with her yesterday, he saw more similarities now than before. A way of speaking, of moving, those beautiful blue-green eyes that all of his children shared.

"I'm worried," she said, leaning back into the squashy sofa. "The way Willow's dragging her feet . . . I just know she's up to something."

"She's not up to anything. Blame it on her lawyer and me. We're ironing a few things out, that's all. Give it another week or two and everything will be clear." Probably too clear once they found out about Hayley and Lizzie, but they would deal with that problem when they got to it.

"I don't know why you just don't hand her a settlement and be done with it. Is there anyone who actually believes this marriage has a chance in hell of lasting longer than it takes for the baby to be christened?"

"Your father believes."

Amber sighed loudly. "The man's sixty—"

"Fifty-nine."

She rolled her eyes. "Fifty-nine and counting. Shouldn't he have learned something about old men and the young women who pretend to love them by now?"

"Somebody else made that same observation to me recently and I'll tell you what I told her: he's an optimist. He keeps on believing no matter what."

"'... What I told her?'" Amber's eyebrows were practically on the ceiling. "You're seeing someone! Since when?"

"I'm not seeing anyone." He hesitated. He hated these gray areas of half-truth. Especially with someone who was like family to him. "I saw her once. Yesterday. I don't know where it's going."

"So that's why you weren't answering your phone yesterday!"

"I answered the phone. Ask your father. He called often enough."

"I phoned around six thirty and it went straight to voice mail."

"You didn't leave a message."

"Who is she?"

"Nobody you know."

"Is she from around here?"

"Nope."

"Oh." She looked disappointed. "I was hoping you were interested in Susan Endicott from the bank."

"Who the hell is that?"

"The short redhead in mortgages."

He couldn't put a face to the name or the description. "Why would you think I was interested in her?"

"I don't know." Amber shrugged. "She's good-looking, funny, and she asked about you." She aimed a look in his direction. "I guess I was hoping."

"You don't have anything better to do than try to hook me up with a banker?"

"We've already tried to hook you up with a real estate agent, a dancer, a nurse, and enough freelance writers to start a women's basketball team. What are you looking for, a stripper with a Ph.D. in nuclear physics?"

"She lives in New Jersey," he offered. "She owns her own business. She has a kid." And wit, ambition, a sense of humor, great legs . . .

"That's it?"

"No, but that's all you're getting."

Amber's younger sister Beryl, known to the family as the human whirlwind, burst into the room. Beryl was a jewelry designer who believed there was no part of the human body that couldn't benefit from adornment, a belief system that had led to some strange situations at airport security checkpoints.

"Damn it, Am! Thanks for leaving me with five car seats to cram into the limo. Do you know how long it takes to get five—not two or three, we're talking five—of those things secured? I had to rope poor Anton into helping me corral the kids. Your two actually made the poor man break into a sweat. It wasn't a pretty sight."

Finn laughed out loud. "I would've paid to see that."

Beryl wagged a finger in his direction. "Just you wait, Finn Rafferty! One day you'll be wrestling with a car seat and we'll be the ones laughing."

"Only if I'm setting it up for one of your brood."

"Finn's seeing someone," Amber interrupted. "I think he really likes her."

"Since when?" Beryl asked him.

"Go ahead." He tossed it to Amber. "You seem to have all the answers."

"She's not from around here," Amber said, ignoring him, "and she has a kid."

Beryl's eyes were alight with curiosity. "When are we going to meet her?"

"Don't you two have five kids in restraints waiting for you?"

"He's trying to change the subject," Amber said.

"You think?" Beryl turned back to Finn. "You're lucky we're on the limo clock, faux brother, otherwise we'd get the truth out of you."

"Not a chance," he said.

"Nothing I like better than a challenge." Beryl planted a sisterly kiss on his cheek. "Your secrets aren't safe from me!" She was out the door before he could think up a retort.

Amber tugged his hair in her familiar good-bye gesture then whispered in his ear, "Please, I beg you, do something about Willow before she asks us to call her Mom!"

"I don't think you have to worry," Finn said. "Just be patient. This will all get sorted out."

He watched from the window in Tommy's office as the two women dashed across the crushed shell driveway and climbed into the limo that had been transformed for the occasion into an oversized minivan crowded with kids, toys, suitcases, juice bottles, diaper bags.

The driver beeped the horn twice and he

saw Beryl waving from the open window as they rolled down the driveway. Topaz, the youngest of Tommy's three daughters from his first marriage, was driving up from Virginia where she was studying for a master's in music therapy.

Winston and Zach had wanted to ride down on the bus with the band and the roadies but Tommy wasn't having any of it. They had been ordered to take the jet down to A.C. with their father. Only the teenage sons of a rock star would deem that cruel and inhuman punishment. Little Gigi and her mother, Margaux, were in Philadelphia visiting Margaux's parents. They would join the party Thursday morning at the hotel.

Willow was threatening to boycott the benefit concert and sulk alone at Tommy's Manhattan loft but Finn knew that the prospect of major press coverage rendered her threat moot.

Once a supermodel, always a supermodel.

If there was a camera within fifty yards, her face would be in the viewfinder. She would be working her pregnancy to its best advantage, angling for her own Demi Moore series of covers, while Hayley, who deserved the attention, worked fifteen-hour days and crossed her fingers that her Cinderella moment would last long enough to pay next month's rent and keep Lizzie in private school.

She hadn't a clue that in a few days her worries would be over.

He just wished he could feel happier about that fact.

17

Goldy's Bakery—Tuesday Morning

"You don't have to bite my head off!" Maureen glared at Hayley across the kitchen. "All I did was ask if the new bricks of yeast are in yet."

"This is the third time you've asked today," Hayley said, feeling both peevish and repentant. "I'm not holding the yeast hostage, Mo. You'll be the first to know when it gets here. I promise."

"They don't have this kind of trouble at Abruzzo's in High Point."

It was all Hayley could do to keep from lobbing a ball of fondant at the woman. "Mo, you've been threatening to leave us for

Abruzzo's since Daddy Stan was alive. If you want to go, go. We'll miss you but I don't want you to be unhappy."

"Who said I was unhappy?" Maureen snapped. "All I said was where's the yeast."

If it wasn't the yeast, it was the starter for the sourdough or the vanilla extract imported from Madagascar. Maureen was a gifted baker whose pronounced diva tendencies sometimes turned the kitchen inside out. Her husband Frank coped with it by kneading bread dough with the kind of passion usually reserved for a heavyweight prizefight. The bread was great and so was his blood pressure.

Which was more than could be said for Hayley's that morning.

She put down her whisk and walked over to where Maureen was glaring at an innocent carton of eggs.

"I'm sorry, Mo. I'm a cranky bitch today. I shouldn't have taken it out on you."

"Well, I didn't want to be the one to point it out but you're definitely bitchy today. I told Frank you were probably PMSing."

She told herself not to dwell on the fact that her employees were discussing her menstrual cycle over their coffee break.

"I'm not PMSing," she said with the most nonhormonal smile she could muster. "Michie called in sick, Abbie is on a scheduled personal day, I forgot I was scheduled to speak at Career Day this afternoon at St. Barnabas, and if the rolled fondant doesn't arrive by one o'clock, I just might be forced to drive up to Whippany and kick some serious supplier butt. I am not PMSing." She paused for breath. "What I am is freaking out."

"Okay," Maureen said in an uncharacteristically meek tone of voice. "That's fine."

Frank gave the mound of dough in front of him on the workbench an extra hard punch with the heel of his hand.

"Go ahead," she said to Frank. "You can look at your wife. I know I sound like a crazy woman but I'm not dangerous and it isn't personal. You can even roll your eyes if you won't. I don't mind."

"I wasn't going to roll my eyes," Frank denied.

"Yes, you were." Maureen was all about contradicting her husband. As far as Hayley could see it was one of the cornerstones of their forty-plus-year marriage.

They were so busy bickering they didn't

notice when Hayley stepped away. Escaped was probably a better word for it. What was with everyone? From the moment she flipped the CLOSED sign to OPEN yesterday morning, the questions and looks and whispers had been flying thick and fast. Let one nosy neighbor find you rolling around in the mud with a handsome stranger from New York and watch all hell break loose.

Patsy Coletti wanted to know if he was one of Michael's creditors who played a little rough.

Frank O'Donnell told Jerry Weinstein that Marie DiFranco heard Hayley tell Finn she would see him Thursday in Atlantic City, which started a line of conjecture that reached all the way into Lizzie's high school classroom.

What could she do but tell the truth?

Now the whole town knew she was making some special cakes for Tommy Stiles's after-party and the clamor for tickets was almost deafening. "I'm baking for Tommy Stiles," she told her neighbors, "not hanging with him. If you want a world-class chocolate mousse cake with a ganache to die for, call me. If you want tickets for the show, you'd better call the box office."

"Listen to Miss High and Mighty," Joe Whetstone had said loud enough for her to hear. "She probably has a fistful of free passes. Remember the night her aunt Fiona found her in the backseat with Mikey G? She wasn't such a big shot then."

And I remember the time your check for six dollars bounced and you refused to pay the bank charges on it, Joe Whetstone. One more Miss High and Mighty remark and I'm going to blow your cover.

She didn't remember anyone banging down her door for tickets to the Governor's Reception last year or for the Moonlight Benefit Gala for the Medical Center at Princeton.

But bring out a rock star and suddenly everyone's your friend. Or at least they were your friend until you said no. Half the people in town were angry with her and the other half were disappointed. Even Mrs. Lonergan from church, a woman who had waved good-bye to seventy-five a long time ago, had muttered something unprintable when Hayley tried to explain the situation.

She and Finn had exchanged a flurry of late-night e-mails the last two days. What had started as a lighthearted commentary on the quirks of her Lakeside neighbors had quickly become the highlight of her day. He was funny, self-deprecating, razor sharp yet kind. His wit had an edge to it but was never hurtful. He was the kind of man you could let down your guard around and not live to regret it.

She had typed up the story of the septuagenarian Stiles groupie but then decided at the last minute against sending it. Tommy's Lakeside demographics might not seem so comical to a man whose income was dependent on his client not outliving his fan base.

One good thing about the outbreak of Stiles mania in town was that it had diffused some of the curiosity about Finn's impromptu visit on Sunday. There were only so many gossip-worthy hours in the day and rock star trumped bakery owner's love life every time.

She had to admit, at least to herself, that she had been the tiniest bit dismayed when everyone eagerly accepted her explanation that Finn had driven down to see her on business. You would think at least one of her incredibly nosy and imaginative neighbors might have held out a little longer in favor of a romantic assignation.

But no. They were perfectly content with her story about prototypes and last-minute details.

Which should have made it easy for her to concentrate on the task on hand, but it didn't.

Under normal circumstances she had no trouble zeroing in on what she was doing and working toward her goal. Nothing ever knocked her off course. Not family troubles or financial woes, not even the time she slipped on a broken egg and broke her right hand.

She had never once missed a deadline, never kept a customer waiting. She delivered what she promised when she promised to deliver it, and she had little doubt that the reliability factor was every bit as important in her growing success as the beauty and general deliciousness of her baked creations.

So why now, on the brink of a major career breakthrough, did she feel as scattered and distracted and giddy as a teenager? Okay, so maybe it wasn't every day she spent a long, laugh-drenched afternoon in the arms of a gorgeous man who somehow managed to mingle the bad-boy vibe with a good heart that was visible even on short acquaintance, but that was hardly an excuse for staring off into space with a silly smile plastered across her face.

Or was it?

When a woman hadn't kissed a man in a while, she tended to forget the power of that simple act. When a man came along who actually knew how to kiss (and seemed to enjoy it), what woman wouldn't be knocked sideways with feelings she thought she had left behind in high school? Was it any wonder they ended up in bed?

Who would have guessed sensuality and easy familiarity could be such a powerful combination? In the past, sexual chemistry had been equal parts uneasiness and desire. Laughter had been shadowed with self-consciousness and a touch of fear. Throughout the years of her marriage, she had managed to keep her true self so under wraps that she had forgotten who the real Hayley Maitland Goldstein was. Before long she couldn't tell where that emotional high-wire act ended and where real sexual desire began.

She had been herself with Finn, her muddy, unkempt, wet-haired, cellulite-rippled self, and he hadn't even blinked. In fact, if you judged by their lovemaking, he actually liked that rumpled self. Was it possible that the whole man/woman thing could be this easy, this much fun?

An e-mail had been waiting for her when she logged on that morning. A sexy, silly message shot through the ether at three in the morning while she slept, designed to make her laugh softly as something close to delight rippled along her spine.

No wonder she was having trouble concentrating on work.

"Get a grip," she ordered herself, then wished she hadn't when she caught the looks being sent her way by her employees. "Not you," she said. "I was talking to myself."

Maureen shot a look at Frank, who shot a look across the kitchen to Terri, one of their interns, who pretended she was engaged in an epic battle with a tray of doughnuts in desperate need of glazing.

Hayley had never been so glad to hear her cell phone warble in her entire life.

"You sound terrible, Michie," Hayley said in greeting. "What are you doing on the phone?"

"Tommy Stiles is on the E! channel talking about the benefit concert. Put on the TV now!"

Hayley raced for the back stairs. "Which one is E!?"

"You know . . . *True Hollywood Story . . . 101 Fashion Mistakes . . . When Good Actors Make Bad Movies*—" Michie stopped to cough up a lung.

Hayley winced. "Don't talk, please! I feel like I should be calling nine-one-one for you."

"I hope I didn't give it to Lizzie. She stopped here yesterday on her way to her party."

"I didn't hear that," Hayley said, mentally putting her fingers in her ears. "We definitely don't have time for a sick kid around here."

She leaped over a pod of sleeping cats, dodged an enthusiastic Rhoda, then switched on the television in the living room.

"Discovery . . . A and E . . . Food Network . . . okay, there it is."

"You're out of breath," Michie said between bouts of coughing. "You need cardio."

What she needed was oxygen but she wasn't about to admit that even to Michelle.

Stiles was talking to one of the station's interchangeable hot chick reporters who was probably old enough to be his next fiancée but too young to have any idea who he was.

"He looks pretty hot for a guy in his sixties," Michie said.

"Come on, Michie," she said with a groan. "He's been nipped, tucked, and lifted."

"You don't know that for a fact."

"They all do it," she said. "Famous people can't grow old in this country. It's against the law."

"I like his hair," Michie said around a sneeze. "I wonder who does his highlights."

Nice eyes, she thought as she raised the sound. Some crow's-feet and laugh lines but they were a beautiful shade of blue-green that reminded her of Lizzie's.

". . . Always a Jersey boy . . ." he was saying to the clearly smitten reporter. "We believe in giving back and the South Jersey Children's Hospital Network is a cause worth supporting."

He looked like an old rocker with a bad-boy vibe but he sounded like somebody's suburban dad, which made Hayley laugh just a little.

"He seems like a nice guy," Michie said.

"That's what Finn says."

"Finn's the lawyer, right?"

"Yes, and Anton's the drummer."

Michie launched into an almost operatic

bout of coughing that made Hayley's throat hurt in sympathy.

"We could double date," Michie said. "I get the drummer. You get the lawyer. Wouldn't that be amazing?"

"You're married," Hayley reminded her. "I think Charlie might frown on extramarital dating."

"I told him I'd give him a pass if Angelina Jolie ever comes to town. The least he can do is let me go out for dinner with Tommy Stiles."

"I thought you were talking about Anton."

"I dream big," Michie said, laughing. "It's Stiles or nothing."

"Forget it," she said dryly. "I think you're too old for him."

They cut to a short clip of hospital footage meant to inspire then jumped into a discussion of Tommy's upcoming marriage.

"Have they mentioned the concert?" she asked Michie.

"I missed the very beginning but I haven't heard anything yet."

"I don't think he'll mention the after-party, do you?"

"Honey, he's a grown man. He's not going to talk about cake."

But he was going to talk about his latest woman.

"Willow is successful in her own right," Stiles was saying. Yadda, yadda, yadda. She wanted to hear more about the concert, which might inspire him to talk about the after-party and the fantastically wonderful cake decorator who was going to rock the guests with her creations.

The camera zoomed in for a close-up of the perky young reporter.

"Look at her!" Michie croaked. "She's actually flirting with him!"

"He's famous," Hayley said. "When he's famous it doesn't matter if he's old enough to be your grandfather."

"Think she'd be working it quite so hard if Stiles managed the produce department at ShopRite?"

"Or worked with Lou at the dry cleaner?"

"I can see it now," Michie said. "Old man Dennison from the gas station thinking he had a chance with Trish or Keisha."

"Wash your mouth out," Hayley said through her laughter. "That's downright obscene!"

On screen the perky reporter was wrapping things up. "Tommy Stiles and the After

Life will be appearing Thursday in Atlantic City. There are still a few tickets available but you'd better hurry! Tommy's newest CD, *Best of the Best*, is available now—"

Click.

"So much for free publicity." Hayley sighed. "I'd better get back to work."

Michie sneezed three times in a row. "I'd better get back to writing my will."

"Put me down for your Coach shoulder bag."

"Not funny," Michie said, laughing through her coughing/sneezing fit. "You'll be sorry when I leave you my kids instead."

"Speaking of your kids, I'll pick Jackie up after school and get him to the allergist," she said as she raced back downstairs to the kitchen.

"Bring him back when he's twenty-one and I'll toss in my vintage collection of Tupperware lids."

Talk about an incentive.

Manhattan—Upper East Side

"I'm going downstairs in search of the *Times* and a cup of tea," John said as Jane settled into the narrow bed. "If I can find a cup of your favorite Earl Grey—"

Jane shook her head. "Water only, love. The tests . . ."

He nodded his great leonine head. "But there must be something that would help pass the time more quickly for you."

"Just hurry back," she said in a rush of love and longing that would fell a younger woman. "Your company is all I want."

She meant it. His presence in her life was sustenance for body and soul.

This three-day visit to Memorial Sloan-Kettering had been John's idea. She already had her diagnosis. She understood that the only measures available to her were palliative in nature, not curative. She had accepted the fact that her time was limited.

John, however, had not. He had called in a favor from a colleague here at MSK who had scheduled two full days of tests followed by an interdisciplinary evaluation and treatment recommendation.

She envied John his ability to transcend facts and cleave to hope but she was a realist. She had seen the preliminary reports on her condition and the outcome seemed inevitable and relatively imminent. Two years, the doctors had agreed. Two years could be enough if you lived them an hour at a time.

John would come to accept this on his own terms. Sooner than later, she hoped, but acceptance would provide its own comfort.

She wasn't a fanciful woman. Interpersonal relationships were terra incognita to her. She believed in what could be calibrated, analyzed, dissected into its component parts so the structure could be understood.

People defied her scientific training. They ignored what was there right in front of them and chose to believe what they saw only with their heart.

For the first time in her life she wished she could be one of them.

"Dr. Maitland." One of the residents appeared in her doorway. She wore her stethoscope like a diamond necklace. "I'm Dr. Tomarchio. I wanted to let you know they'll be doing some preliminary blood work later so you might want to stay close by."

"I didn't realize I had a choice in the matter." She said it lightly but the hint of irony was unavoidable.

The young doctor smiled. "You're a patient, not a prisoner. You're more than free to roam."

"I'll keep that in mind."

They chatted a few moments longer, then Dr. Tomarchio moved on to her next patient.

She glanced around the spacious, airy room but saw nothing beyond the fact that John wasn't there. Every minute with him was precious beyond reason. Every minute without him felt like an eternity.

A large flat-screen television hung from the wall. She reached for the remote control device on the bedside table and pressed the power button.

". . . This is Channel Seven Eyewitness News with . . . The News4 chopper is over the scene . . . Watch CBS for Katie Couric's interview tonight with the president of Venezuela . . . Bravo brings you . . . This is CNN . . . Tommy Stiles and the After Life will be appearing Thursday in Atlantic City. There are still a few tickets available but you'd better hurry! Tommy's newest CD, *Best of the Best*, is available now . . ."

He was older, of course. There were lines on his face that hadn't been there that long-ago night, but he still had the same smile.

How strange that across the years it was his smile that she remembered. Not the eyes, although they were mirrored in both her daughter's and her granddaughter's faces, but that wide and guileless smile that had touched her heart for a weekend all those years ago.

Princeton, New Jersey—Early Spring, 1970

The phone rang at three minutes after noon.

Jane had just settled behind her desk to eat a cup of yogurt while she prepared for her lecture. Earth Day was on the horizon, a new concept that was being met with much cynical comment among her peers, and she had been dismayed by the lack of enthusiasm and information among the general population. Granted, the horrific images from places like the Mekong Delta and Da Nang that filled the news each night created an urgency that the supporters of Earth Day had been unable to match, but she hoped to at least capture a few hearts and minds in the weeks ahead for their cause.

Unfortunately, until Hallmark acknowledged Earth Day with a series of greeting cards, universal acceptance was unlikely.

"Dr. Maitland, this is Dr. Woodruff's office

calling. We have the results of your pregnancy test."

She had forgotten. That seemed impossible even to Jane but she had been so busy that the test had slipped her mind.

"Negative, of course," she said. She was a forty-year-old woman. Early menopause ran in her family.

The long silence should have told her something, but she lived her life among academics and sailors, neither of whom were known for a facility with emotional nuance. Long silences were lost on her.

"The test was positive," Dr. Woodruff's nurse said. "You'll need to make an appointment to see the doctor for a prenatal workup as soon as possible."

The nurse continued to talk but Jane couldn't hear the words through the roar of the ocean inside her head. She must have made the necessary noises because the next thing she knew she was out from behind her desk, running flat out down the musty hallway, past her astonished colleagues, her equally astonished students, out the front door, down the stairs, and up Nassau Street until she couldn't run anymore.

Everywhere she turned she saw a familiar

face, someone who knew her or knew of her. Someone who would judge her in ways she wasn't willing to be judged. She needed clarity. She needed distance.

The world was changing. In the not-too-distant future an unmarried professional woman would be able to have a child without facing the censure of a critical world, but not yet. Her life, her future, hung in the balance.

She drove down the shore that afternoon. Proximity to the ocean made it easier to think.

She knew it was ridiculous, the sort of thing a much younger and less experienced woman would do, but she stayed in the same beachfront motel where she had stayed with the young man who was the father of her child. She had met him in a pub near the university. A group of her colleagues had thrown a bash to celebrate someone's marriage or baby or dissertation and Tommy Stiles and three other young men were the bar band that night.

The professor/student dynamic was a classic one. How many of her friends had stumbled into relationships with students young enough to be their children. It had always struck Jane as an abuse of privilege and she kept the lines clearly drawn and inviolable. Besides, she preferred to socialize with people whose frames of reference included Eisenhower, Truman, and FDR.

But this young man was not a student. He was a musician. The world of academe meant nothing to him. Her doctorates, her research grants, her published works, were all but invisible. When he took the stage the world around her stopped spinning. The clamor and conversation in the room ceased.

"I hear they've signed a contract with Epic," one of her colleagues said during a break. "We'll be able to say we saw them when."

For all that she was a scientist who believed only in that which was quantifiable, there was no denying the stardust that surrounded those local kids.

Especially Tom Stiles. The blue-collar high school dropout was on the verge of something wonderful. One of those once-in-a-lifetime opportunities that change a person's life forever.

She told him how transcendent his music was. He told her he wanted to live by the ocean one day. The conversation extended past last call, into the parking lot, then all the way down the shore in the first light of morning.

But this time there were no long walks on the beach listening as he spun his dreams out for her to admire, no interludes of pleasure as she taught him things he would one day thank her for.

That weekend she slept and she cried. Her entire life had been turned upside down with the words *you're pregnant.* Her direction. Her plans. Her future. Everything had changed. For two long days and nights she searched for answers that only the years would provide.

"Nice weekend?" her TA asked when she returned to her office Monday morning.

"Informative," she said with a quick smile. After all the tears and all the hours spent trying to see through the fog of surprise and wonder, she realized that there was only one thing she knew for sure.

She was going to have this baby.

Everything else would simply have to fall into place behind that.

Now

And for a little while it had.

Jane leaned back against her hospital pillows and closed her eyes.

She wasn't one to indulge in looking back. Nostalgia was history bathed in sentiment and sentiment tended to soften edges, to cast flattering light into the places where darkness lived.

He was barely twenty years old. He had his whole life ahead of him. He was standing on the cusp of something huge, the type of fame most people only dreamed about, and even Jane could see he had the talent to back up the promise. They had shared a weekend together and she had been old enough and wise enough to understand that was enough.

Jane wasn't known for her insight into the human condition but she knew at a visceral level that, young as he was, Tom Stiles would do what he perceived as the "right thing" for her and the baby and that choice might cost him his future. She was an established professional woman whose position in the world was secure. She had money enough to sustain herself and her child. She would let Tom Stiles follow his destiny and wish him Godspeed.

And so she never told him.

She had misgivings on the day of Hayley's birth and filled in his name on the birth certificate but soon changed it back to *Father:*

Unknown. The world had continued to change around her and by the time Hayley was a toddler, nobody in her world batted an eye at the middle-aged professor with the baby girl with the beautiful blue-green eyes.

Except for a brief burst of adolescent anger, Hayley had accepted the story that she was the result of AI via an anonymous sperm donor. Everyone did. The story fit right in with Jane's ascetic lifestyle and her commitment to the pursuit of science. There was no reason to question what sounded so right.

For over thirty years Jane had believed she was home free until a doctor in Mumbai discovered that she had metastatic stage IV breast cancer and the genetic component suddenly took on great significance. Hayley and Lizzie deserved to know their complete genetic profile. The options in medical care were changing almost on a daily basis. The amount of family medical history a person brought to the table made a huge difference in both diagnosis and course of treatment. She could no longer deny those two beloved women half of their history.

"I found the *Atlantic Monthly, Time, Newsweek,* and *U.S. News and World Report.*" Her beloved John strode into the room with all the confidence and hope of a man who had always believed happiness was his birthright. "I intend to sneak back down later for a fresh copy of *People*. We can pretend the last patient left it behind."

She wanted to laugh but she couldn't. Emotions, powerful and unexpected, lay waste to her power of speech.

"Are you in pain?" He was at her side in a heartbeat. "Jane, tell me."

She shook her head. She was in pain but it wasn't from her cancer.

"I wish—" She stopped. I wish . . . If only . . . Why didn't I . . ."

He knew. He always knew. He had from the first moment.

He lay down on the bed next to her and she settled into the shelter of his arms as if she had been there her entire life.

"I wish I had met you a long time ago," she whispered.

"So do I," he said, holding her close. "So do I."

18

Atlantic City—the Night Before the Concert

Zach and Winston were sitting in front of the big multicolored fountain in the lobby. Finn was surprised how forlorn two teenage boys with access to a private jet and room service could look.

"What's up?" he asked as he approached.

"He's busting our chops," Zach said about his father. "He won't let us into the casino."

"The State of New Jersey won't let you into the casino either," Finn said, trying hard not to laugh. "You're not twenty-one."

"We could pass," Winston said. "We went to—" He shut up when his brother applied a sharp elbow to the ribs.

Finn decided to opt out of the requisite *why you shouldn't use fake ID* lecture that every underage kid in America had heard a thousand times. Besides, that was Tommy's territory.

"You know it's been a while since your dad performed live. He's probably wound pretty tight right about now."

"He blew during rehearsal," Zach said. "Pitched a fit right in the middle of a song."

"Yeah," agreed Winston, "it was pretty intense but it didn't have anything to do with the music."

The two boys exchanged looks.

"What was it?" Finn asked and then it hit him. "It's Willow, right?"

"She dumped him," Zach said. "She showed up at the airport just before we boarded the jet and they had a major fight on the tarmac. Everybody heard them."

"She didn't dump him, you asshole," Winston sneered. "She said she wasn't going to go to the concert unless he signed something."

"The prenup," Zach said. "That's gotta be it. She probably wants all our money."

"Pretty cynical," Finn observed. "Maybe she's worried about the baby she's carrying."

"Why?" Zach countered. "She's got plenty of money. She's a supermodel."

Which sent Zach and Winston dissolving into laughter.

"Damn good thing your father takes these things seriously," Finn shot back. "Otherwise you two would be in vocational school some place, not flying around in private jets and trying to get into casino VIP rooms."

"What's his problem?" he heard Winston ask as he walked away. "You'd think he was her lawyer or something."

He finally tracked Tommy down backstage at the showroom.

"Where the hell have you been?" Tommy roared when he saw him. "I thought you were coming down with the band."

"So did I," Finn said, trying to rein in his own temper. "I had to wait for some faxes to come through."

Today Tommy looked every bit his age. "Anything I need to know about?"

"A copy of Hayley's original birth certificate with your name on it."

He could almost see the fight seep from Tommy's bones.

"I have a knot in my gut the size of Kansas," Tommy admitted. "A few days ago I couldn't wait to meet her." He dragged a hand through his perfectly cut and colored hair. "I'm not so sure anymore."

"This has to be resolved soon, Tom. That birth certificate is pretty strong proof that she's your child."

"I want it resolved," Tommy said. "Don't get me wrong about that. If she's my child, I'm going to do right by her. It's just Willow . . . the other kids . . . Shit, I don't know how to handle this."

"I don't think Sloan is going to wait beyond Monday morning. Either we take matters into our own hands or he will."

"You mean he'll tell Willow?"

"I mean he'll tell Willow and the press and anybody else who'll listen."

"Willow's not coming to the concert to-morrow."

"I heard."

"Maybe that's not such a bad thing."

"It only buys us one night, Tom. I thought we could take our time on this but I was wrong. I advise you to tell Willow what's go-ing on as soon as possible."

Tommy met his eyes. "And what about Hayley and Lizzie?"

"They need to know what's going on too."

"I'll talk to her at the after-party."

"I don't think that's such a great idea."

"She'll be there, right?"

"Yes, but—"

"You know me better than almost anyone, Finn. I'm not going to be able to be in the same room with her and not tell her everything. You knew that before I did. She's my kid. You know it. I know it. And now she needs to know it too."

"Not tomorrow," Finn warned. "There'll be wall-to-wall press. You don't want this story leaking until you've told the family."

"What would I do without you?" Tommy said with a shake of his head. "You're like one of my own. Always looking after me."

But not this time, Finn realized. This time he hadn't been looking out for his old friend Tommy.

He was looking out for Tommy's daughter.

Goldy's Bakery

She had put out an SOS for help and her friends and staff had answered the call.

"You'll get time and a half for this, guys," Hayley said as she gathered up the empty pizza boxes and tossed them into the trash. "And a bonus as soon as we get paid. Even if you don't work for me."

"Just get us tickets to the show next time," Maureen said.

"And his autograph," Sarah, one of her former protégées, chimed in.

"The hell with his autograph," Dianne said with a laugh. "He hasn't married that supermodel yet. There's still hope for me."

"You're too old," Hayley reminded her old friend. "You can't be a trophy wife if you're over thirty."

"Who said anything about being a trophy wife?" Dianne shot back. "I want him to be my trophy husband."

Laughter rocked the room.

"Shh!" Hayley said, pointing upstairs. "Lizzie's asleep."

"Asleep?" Dianne checked her watch. "It's not even nine o'clock yet."

"She might have caught Michie's flu bug."

Paula pretended to cross herself. "Thank God for flu shots," she said. "That should keep the damage to a minimum."

If you didn't consider not being able to use the backstage passes part of the damage. Actually Lizzie had taken it better than her aunt Michie had. Michie had wailed about the inequities of life and how nothing wonderful ever happened to her while Lizzie had sneezed, popped some vitamin C, then said, "I saw him on VH1. He's really pretty old, isn't he?"

"We have a lot to do," Hayley reminded them, "and not a lot of time to do it. I don't expect any of you to stay here all night. Whatever time you can give me is appreciated."

"I'm splitting the shift with Frank," Maureen said. "He'll take over around one."

"I'll stay until my head hits the counter," Paula said. "John's mother is living with us this month so anywhere is better than there."

Sarah, who was barely twenty-one, smiled one of her Zen-like smiles and said, "Whatever," which Hayley took to mean she would be there as long as needed.

Or something like that. It was hard to tell.

"I start my shift at the hospital at two," Dianne said, "so I can stay until about twelve thirty."

"Mo and I baked the cakes and cookies today. They're on the racks along the far wall. Sarah will make the ganache for the filling and Maureen will show you how to apply it. After the ganache sets up, Sarah and Mo will prep the cakes for the assembly line. Mo and I will handle the rolled fondant. We still don't have the silver and gold leaf so that's going to have to wait until tomorrow."

"What if it doesn't arrive tomorrow?" Sarah asked.

"I didn't hear that," Hayley said, clapping her hands over her ears. "I really didn't hear that."

She was flying blind. If the shipment of gold and silver leaf didn't show up, those platinum and gold record cakes were going to have to morph into something else equally fabulous but she hadn't a clue what that might be. Sometimes you had to shut your eyes, cross your fingers, and jump in feetfirst and hope for the best.

"You're hovering," Mo pointed out as Hayley peered over her shoulder. "We don't need to be hovered over."

"I'm not hovering," Hayley protested. "I'm supervising."

"She's worrying," Dianne said as the silky ganache slid down the sides of the cake. "She hovers when she worries."

"She's always worrying," Paula said.

"Lizzie told my Dana that Hayley thinks Katie Couric should—"

"We're talking cakes only tonight, ladies," Hayley said over their hoots of laughter. "Let's leave the psychoanalysis at home, thanks."

Frank took over for Maureen at one o'clock. Mo promised to return at four to start the breads, bagels, and muffins for the morning crowd. The sixty-something baker could be difficult (and that was putting it mildly) but for all of her threats about moving over to Abruzzo's, Mo was as loyal as they came.

Every so often she heard the jingle of incoming e-mail and forced herself to ignore the temptation. Except for various Nigerian entrepreneurs, there was only one person on the planet who would be e-mailing her at this hour.

She couldn't just stop what she was doing and check her e-mail. That was all this group would need. They would flock around her and try to read over her shoulder and she would face serious teasing for the rest of her natural life.

Of course, she could always slip upstairs ostensibly to see if Lizzie was okay and check her e-mail on Lizzie's computer but then she would be sucked into that whole flirty back-and-forth thing. She would look up and realize two hours had gone by and she had nothing to show for it except a great big smile.

"You're smiling," Paula said. "Anyone who can smile at three a.m. deserves a medal."

"I'm not smiling," she said, smiling wider. "It's a facial tic. Pay no attention."

"She's probably thinking about the lawyer," Frank the Big Mouth piped up. "Every time he e-mails she gets that big smile on her face."

"How do you know who's e-mailing me?" she asked him from across the room. "My e-mail is private."

"You don't have to be Sherlock Holmes to figure it out," Frank said. "Every time you sit down and start e-mailing, you start smiling, and then just like clockwork your cell phone rings, you say 'Hi, Finn!' and you disappear into the pantry." He winked at Paula and Sarah, who were laughing along with him.

"You need a hobby, Frank," she said. "Clearly you have too much time on your hands."

Or else she had to learn to be more discreet.

The hours passed quickly. Too quickly. She was working on the lettering for the bass drum when Maureen returned and fired up the ovens for the morning rush.

Sarah appeared at her side. "We did all we can do on the cakes, Mrs. G. Without the leaf, our hands are tied."

"You did a great job," she told the young woman. "I don't know what I would have done without you."

"You would have managed," Sarah said with a big smile. "You always do."

She sent everyone but Mo and Frank home. They were hard at work filling the ovens with fragrant yeasty breads, sweet blueberry and tart cranberry-orange muffins, tray after tray of soft, warm bagels yearning for mountains of cream cheese. All the wonderful things that made Goldy's the institution it was.

There was something to be said for tradition. People knew what to expect when they showed up at Goldy's and they were never disappointed. If you wanted to be a success in Lakeside, you stuck to the tried and true and that was what she had done. Goldy's didn't belong to her. Not really. It was a Goldstein family institution.

Although it pained her to think about it, Michael still owned 40 percent of Goldy's. If she came into a windfall of cash, the first thing she would do was buy him out. Then every improvement she made, all of the hard work, would be for Lizzie's future and not to pay her ex-husband's bills. The fact that it would also free her to pour her energies into building the cake-decorating part of the business was another incentive.

Her daughter might not end up baking cakes for a living but with a little luck the bakery would provide a financial safety net to see her through the inevitable tough times.

With a little more luck, the bakery would run itself while Hayley secured her position as the undisputed Queen of Fancy Cakes. Examples of her work would be installed in museums from coast to coast. The Food Network would beg her to participate in one of their challenges and she would become a cultural icon on a level with Martha, Rachael, and Emeril while the man in her life looked on proudly.

And if that man happened to be Finn Rafferty, she wouldn't complain.

Atlantic City—Around three a.m.

"You're drunk," Anton said as he flopped down on the sofa opposite Finn.

"Not yet," Finn said, "but give me another hour."

"Where'd you get the Glenfiddich?"

Finn gestured behind him. "There's a bar back there. Help yourself."

Anton grabbed himself a sports bottle of still water and settled back down across from Finn. "You're going to have one hell of a hangover tomorrow, old friend."

"That's the plan."

Anton took a pull of water. "Not bad but it's not Grey Goose."

"How long's it been? Ten years? Twelve?"

"Eleven years, eight months, fourteen days." He took a long look at Finn. "You're not a drinker, friend. Take it from someone with experience: whatever you're getting from the booze tonight won't be worth the way you're going to feel in the morning."

"I'm in love with Tommy's daughter."

Anton paled visibly. "Tell me you're kidding."

"Wish I could. It hit me about two hours ago."

"Amber and Beryl are married. Topaz is a half step up from jailbait." He met Finn's eyes. "You're talking about the cake baker?"

Finn nodded. "The cake baker."

"Not good."

"Tell me about it."

"I mean she's great. Don't get me wrong. She's about as terrific as they come but, dude! There are some complications here even my therapist couldn't figure out."

Finn looked at him over his glass of Scotch. "You're seeing a therapist?"

"Couples therapy. It was Lyssa's idea." Anton looked embarrassed. "Forget I said anything."

"If I wasn't halfway through this Scotch I'd make your life a living hell." He took another gulp of booze. "Lucky for you my own life is a living hell."

"So what are you going to do?"

He refilled his glass. "Finish the single malt, for starters."

Anton reached for the bottle and put it on the side table out of reach.

"You know what's gonna happen at the party, don't you?" Finn asked his best friend. "The same thing I predicted when he came up with this idea. He'll take one look at Hayley and it'll be all over. He'll spill everything right there in front of the press and there won't be a single thing I can do to make it easier for her."

"Nothing new, my friend. You knew that from the start."

"Yeah, but now I'm not worrying about how it'll affect Tom. I'm worried about what it'll do to Hayley."

"I have news for you: you've been worrying about what it'll do to her from the first minute you met."

Anton was right. He had tried to look around it, over it, through it, but the truth was undeniable.

"There's more," he said. "Her mother's coming back from India any day."

Anton whistled. "Now that's not good news."

"When worlds collide," Finn said. "It feels like a bad science-fiction movie."

"Tommy and the Professor," Anton said. "Sounds more like a sitcom to me."

"Tommy, the professor, and the supermodel." Finn started to laugh. "Now there's a three-way from hell."

"I want to be there to see Willow's face when she meets her predecessor," Anton said between guffaws.

"Willow's not that bad," Finn said. "Mostly she's insecure." Her biggest problem was that in many ways she was still a kid looking for approval.

"Let me do the math," Anton said. "Unless I'm wrong, the professor could be Willow's grandmother."

"She's old enough to be Tom's mother."

"Which means Hayley could be Zach and Winston's mom."

"You're right," Finn said. "There isn't a therapist on the planet who could sort this mess out."

"So when did you finally figure out what was going on with you?"

Thinking was getting harder by the minute. "I was—" He cleared his throat and wished it was half as easy to clear his brain. "I was at the laptop working out Sy's retirement package when I opened an e-mail from her. Nothing special. Just a see-you-tomorrow kind of thing and suddenly I wasn't just seeing tomorrow, I was seeing five, ten years down the road and she was right there at the heart of it all."

"Shit," Anton said. "You really are in love." He thought for a moment. "Here's what you have to do: take her out after the party. Get her out of there and away from Tommy. Better yet, get her out of there before it ends. Drive her home. Take her to supper."

"And then what?"

"And then you tell her everything."

He would be doing both of them a favor. Tommy wouldn't have to drop the bomb on Hayley and she wouldn't have to hear the news in a roomful of strangers with cameras and tape recorders.

It was what he had wanted to do from the night they met. Maybe then he could stop feeling like a bastard every time he looked at her.

19

*

Atlantic City—Late Afternoon

"We had you down for a morning arrival, ma'am," the young man with the electronic clipboard said.

Hayley tried hard not to wince. *Ma'am* was a tough one to get used to. She bet it wouldn't have happened if Michie had been well enough to work her magic with hair and makeup.

"I'm late," she said with a controlled smile. "Okay, so I'm very late. I had to wait for a delivery from the guys up in East Brunswick, prep the cakes to a certain point, then I had to wait until Paula finished driving car pool, and I'm not even going to tell you about the really hellacious traffic on the A.C. Expressway." She widened the smile. "But I'm here now!"

He wasn't impressed. He scribbled something with a stylus, clicked a time or two, then looked over at her. "You're cleared to use level two. Show your pass to the guard and you'll be directed to the unloading area. The union rep will send some people to help you."

"Does Homeland Security know about you?" she asked. "Seems like you're wasted here in Atlantic City."

He was efficient and without humor. A deadly combination.

She climbed back behind the wheel of the borrowed minivan and headed for level two. So far the day was turning out to be a total disaster. Dominic called a little after six in the morning to tell her that the van wouldn't be repaired until the following Monday. The town's lone rental car outfit was out of vans and SUVs and there was no way she could load the partially assembled drum kit into the back of a Buick Regal. Paula volunteered her minivan but Hayley had to wait until afternoon car-pool duty was over, which meant she didn't hit the road until three thirty.

Lizzie was teetering on the brink of something nasty, which Hayley *really* hoped wasn't Michie's flu. She wasn't running a fever but there was no denying she wasn't feeling like herself. Bless Aunt Fee for being willing to come over and keep an eye on things until Hayley got home.

And as if all of that wasn't bad enough, just before Hayley left for Atlantic City, she discovered a message from her mother languishing on the house phone. "See you Thursday evening," Jane said in such a cheery, upbeat tone of voice that Hayley was instantly suspicious.

"Are you sure she hasn't told you anything?" she prodded Fee as her aunt settled in to watch over Lizzie and await Jane's arrival. "Something doesn't feel right about this."

"Honey, you know my sister tells me as little as possible," Fee said with a good-natured laugh, "and I return the favor. That's why we get along."

She gave Fee explicit instructions to call her on the cell the second Jane arrived. "I want info," she told her aunt. "Specifics. If she's eavesdropping, text me. Something's wrong and I need to know what it is."

"Stop worrying about your mother," Fee had advised, "and start worrying about those fancy cakes of yours. That's where your future lies."

Fee was right. But the worry lingered just the same.

A hotel employee directed her toward the loading dock on level two where she once again ran the gauntlet of security checks. She parked ten feet from the huge double doors marked THEATER and waited for the union cake-toting workers to show up.

So far the glamour quotient was negligible. The parking garage smelled of exhaust fumes, cigarettes, and sweat. Hardly the stuff dreams were made of. She waited, trying hard not to count down the number of minutes she had left to pull this whole thing together.

Finally three tired-looking employees shoved through the doors and approached the minivan.

"That's a cake?" one of them asked, pointing toward the skeleton of the set of drums.

"Big cookies, actually," she said. "And they're fragile. Please be careful."

"So where are the cakes?" another one asked. "I'm supposed to carry cakes."

"The cakes are in those big white boxes," she said, pointing to the carefully secured stacks of boxes deeper inside Paula's mini-van.

They muttered among themselves, then the third worker disappeared through the doors only to reappear with one of those huge flat carts like the ones she used to buy fifty-pound bags of sugar at Costco.

It was clear they felt the job was beneath their collective dignity but a few minutes later Hayley followed her baked goods into what could only be described as a wonderland in progress. The vaulted ceiling of the huge ballroom was draped with black and twinkled with a thousand stars. Electricians hung from scaffoldings and balanced precariously on ladders as they positioned the lights that would bring the whole thing to life. Chunky crystal candleholders graced every table, sharing space with arrangements of white jasmine and gardenias floating in silky pools of water. The floor of the ballroom had been polished until it gleamed like a skating rink. When the work lights dimmed and the key lights took over, the reflection would be daz-zling.

Somehow the effect managed to be both

over the top and understated, an amazing accomplishment in perennially over-the-top Atlantic City.

The hotel catering staff, clad in black, were busily occupied setting up the various buffet stations while the bar staff laughed and joked in the corner. Waist-high insulated buckets of ice, crates of champagne, focaccia fresh from the oven—everywhere she looked she saw something wonderful or something on its way toward being wonderful.

"Wow!" she said as they rolled to a stop near a table covered with black velvet shot through with faint silver and gold threads. "This is fantastic!"

The union worker gave her a look over his shoulder as if to say, "Gimme a break," but she ignored it. The high-profile events she had supplied cakes for in the past had all been serious celebrations held for serious people. There hadn't been a sequin on the premises at the two inaugural parties.

"Is there any glitter left in South Jersey?" she asked no one in particular.

One of the hotel catering staff, a woman around her own age, stopped to laugh. "If there is then we didn't do our job!"

She pointed to where she wanted the

framework for the drums then waited, barely breathing, while they opened up each of the ten boxes and placed the cakes in the arrangement she showed them on her work-sheet.

She wasn't sure if the union workers expected a tip but since she only had a ten-dollar bill on her, the point was moot.

Focus, she told herself as she took out the fragile sheets of gold leaf. She had to get it right the first time or kiss her dreams of fame and fortune good-bye. The prep work had been completed. More than once during the process, she had been intensely grateful for her art training. Mixing a perfect black that didn't veer toward purple or slump toward brown was never easy. To complicate matters further, she needed color with dimension, not a flat expanse of tint but something with vibrancy and depth. All in all, it was a lot to ask of rolled fondant, gum paste, and royal icing.

Clearly her prayers to Elizabeth of Hungary, patron saint of bakers, hadn't gone unanswered, because she settled immediately into the zone. One by one the cakes were transformed into glittering gold and platinum records celebrating Tommy Stiles and his accomplishments. More than a few jaded hotel workers stopped to admire the intricacies of the design.

A pretty young member of the hotel wait-staff stopped to admire the drums. "I've seen a lot of cool stuff around here but that's probably the coolest thing yet."

"Thanks," Hayley said, feeling more than a little jolt of artistic pride. "I'm very happy with the way it turned out."

"You should be," the woman said. "If I could do something that terrific I sure as hell wouldn't be working the ballroom, serving coffee to obnoxious assholes with comb-overs."

Hayley laughed as she continued to apply gold leaf to the last cake. "I don't think you'll see too many comb-overs with this group, do you?"

"You're new here, aren't you," the woman said. "Honey, trust me, there's always a comb-over lurking. Rock stars have accountants, don't they? Lawyers—" She stopped midsentence. "I'm a married woman. I could burn in hell for what I'm thinking right now."

Hayley turned to see what had captured the woman's attention. Finn, in a tight black T-shirt, even tighter jeans, and a leather strap around his wrist, met her eyes across the ballroom and everything else melted away.

"I know him," she said.

The woman looked from Finn to Hayley. "You know him?" She sounded dubious.

"He's a lawyer," Hayley said, not taking her eyes off Finn's approach.

"Yeah, right." The woman was almost salivating. Who could blame her? Finn looked like a magic hot fudge sundae that not only didn't make you fat, it banished cellulite and gave you bigger boobs.

She had been right that first day when she had noticed he didn't walk like any lawyer she had ever known. He walked like a full-color two-page ad for sex.

"I'm glad I found you," he said with a nod to the nosy woman next to Hayley.

"Glad to be found," she said.

So this was how it felt to be the prom queen. She had waited twenty years to find out and it was every bit as good as she had imagined it would be.

Her new best friend nudged Hayley in the ribs. "You didn't tell me you were with the band."

Hayley, smiling widely, met Finn's eyes. "Am I with the band?"

"Tonight you are."

Suddenly she regretted her decision to guard the cakes instead of rocking out backstage. She was with the band!

"I could still get you backstage," he said, reading her mind.

"I wish I could but I'd better stick around." *I'm a business owner . . . I'm a mother . . . I'm a business owner . . . I'm a mother . . .*

"Have dinner with me."

"Tonight?"

"After you finish here," he said. "We need to talk."

"If she won't, I will," the nosy woman piped up. "The hotel can just kiss my ass."

There were a hundred reasons to say no and only one reason to say yes: because every single moment she was with him she felt like herself. Not a version of herself. Not a little piece of herself. Her 100 percent true self.

She said yes.

They locked eyes.

"I like you in that white jacket," he said, referring to her austere snowy-white baker's coat.

"It was Lizzie's idea. We figured why go sequin *à* sequin with all the other caterers."

"And the hair."

"The ballet bun?" She touched her hair. "That's Lizzie's idea too. The austere and professional look."

"It's sexy."

"I don't think so."

"Trust me," he said. "It's sexy as hell."

The nosy woman next to Hayley started twisting her long, dark hair into a topknot. They both pretended not to notice.

"I'm partial to hot pink myself." She tried for a deadpan delivery but couldn't manage to wipe the smile from her face.

"Not me," he said. "I like Scooby-Doo."

"You two are very disappointing," their one-woman audience said. "I expected better from a rocker."

She noticed that he seemed a little edgy, a little wired, but she chalked it up to stage fright.

Of course, there was always the possibility that the sight of her clad in crisply starched whites and bright red clogs was more than mortal man could handle in public.

"So we're on for later," he said.

"We're definitely on." It was going to require a lot of phone calls and probably a minor clash with both Fee and Jane when she got home, but she couldn't have said no to him if the fate of civilization depended on it.

They agreed to meet right there at the cake table after the show. The moment seemed to wrap itself around them, drawing them closer together, and for a moment Hayley thought he was going to take her in his arms and kiss her and really give the nosy woman something to talk about.

But he didn't. He touched her hand instead and then ducked out the side door.

"Why are you still standing here?" the nosy woman asked. "I'd follow him and jump his bones in the hallway."

Little did the nosy woman know that was exactly what Hayley was doing in her imagination right that second.

She gave what she hoped was an enigmatic smile and turned back to prepping the cakes for display.

She told herself that the nonkiss was a good thing. They had acted like responsible adults. Making out with a rock guitarist in the middle of a job venue wasn't exactly the best way to get your name out there, but the thought of wrapping herself around Finn Rafferty made her burn.

She remembered how he looked after his shower, all damp and rumpled and slightly embarrassed in that man's man kind of way. She remembered the way his skin smelled, the long gleaming expanses of muscled flesh . . . and it didn't hurt that he had already taken inventory of her cellulite and not run screaming back to the Hamptons.

Their sweat-slicked bodies sliding against each other. The way he trailed his tongue between her breasts, over her belly, between her legs. He had touched her in ways she had never been touched before. She had wanted to do things with him, to him, that she hadn't dreamed of until that moment.

Deep inside her thirty-eight-year-old-body lurked the soul of her seventeen-year-old self, who craved romance the way other girls craved chocolate. She had to keep her eye on that girl or she would get both of them in trouble.

Backstage

They were doing a stripped-down version of the tour show, tailored for the hotel showroom, which meant only four trucks filled with equipment instead of the fifteen they usually needed.

The run-through had gone well. Light machines, laser effects, the view screen that would accompany some of the old songs, all had worked the way they were supposed to. There had been a spot of trouble during the sound check but his people were on it.

Tommy, however, had been running on autopilot. Dress had been less than terrific even if nobody had the cojones to tell him so to his face. Usually everything in his life dropped away when he hit the stage and the spotlight found him, but not today.

"Is she here?" Tommy asked when Finn showed up backstage.

"She's here."

"That's all you're gonna give me?"

"That's all I have," Finn said. "She's here. The cakes are here."

"How does she look?"

"Professional."

"Good," he said. "I like that. It shows that she's serious."

"She's definitely serious," Finn said.

"How about the cakes?"

"They're great. You'd swear you were looking at the real deal."

"And the drums?"

"She's an artist, Tom. It shows."

"Why do I get the feeling you're not telling me everything?"

Finn said nothing. Not a good sign.

"Is Lizzie with her?"

"Lizzie stayed home. She's coming down with the flu."

"Damn," Tommy swore. "I wanted to meet her."

"You'll meet her," Finn said. "Just not tonight."

"Willow knows something's wrong. I think she's afraid I'm going to back out."

"Are you?"

"Not a chance in hell, but she might when she finds out about Hayley."

"You're better off she's not here tonight," Finn said.

Willow was smarter than people gave her credit for. She would know the story the second she looked into Hayley's eyes and all hell would break loose.

Anton, in his requisite black leather, joined them. "We're going with the three/four/

three high-energy intro and no intermission, right, boss?"

Tommy nodded. "Gotta get 'em on their feet."

But then getting the crowd on its feet had never been a problem for Tommy Stiles.

Last-minute prep work had reached fever pitch. Hotel staff raced around the ballroom at warp speed performing last-minute miracles while Hayley guarded the cakes and tried to stay out of their way.

"It's crazy today," one of the bartenders said as he joined her.

"Yes, it is."

He was young, gorgeous, and reeking with insincerity.

"I hear you're with the band."

"Not really," Hayley said, answering his smile with an insincere one of her own. "I know one of the members, that's all."

"That's known as being with the band, babe." He inched a little closer and lowered his voice. "I'm a singer too."

"Really," she said. "I bake cakes."

He glanced over at the amazing (if she did say so herself) display of virtuoso baking.

"Cool." A beat pause meant to convey interest. "Listen, I'm the best thing to come along in years. I almost made it through the first round of judging when *Idol* came to South Philly. I was only two songs away from showing that English fucker what I can do."

"Wow," she said. It was the best she could come up with.

"I could put the After Life back on the charts."

"I thought they were on the charts."

"Hell, no. They haven't been on the charts since 2003."

"Interesting."

He fished a CD jewel case from a secret pocket and handed it to her. "Pass it on to your boyfriend," he said in a conspiratorial whisper. "I've got what they need."

Clearly she was the only person who wasn't secretly hoping to be a rock star. The news that she had a connection to one of the After Life musicians spread faster than wildfire through the Pine Barrens during a drought. She had fielded CDs, 8-by-10 glossies, and résumés from just about every single member of the waitstaff, bar staff, and hotel kitchen.

She was starting to feel like a baker/talent agent.

During breaks in the madness she had managed to check in twice with Fiona. "*Ugly Betty* is still on," Fee had complained. "Don't call again until *Grey's Anatomy* is over." Thursday was Fee's night for television and she didn't suffer interruptions gladly. Hayley almost wished she could be there to see the fireworks if Jane showed up before ten p.m.

Lizzie got on the extension and begged for details. "They think I'm with the band," Hayley had said to her daughter's delighted laughter. "They saw me talking to Finn and jumped to conclusions. I'm now the most popular woman in the ballroom."

"Channel Three's covering the concert for the ten o'clock news. Make sure they know you're local."

Lizzie rattled off a list of things she absolutely, positively had to do in order to snag publicity for Goldy's Bakery and Hayley had laughed while she yes'd her daughter.

"You won't do any of this, will you?" Lizzie had asked.

"I'll do what I can, Lizzie." Mostly she hoped the cakes would do it for her.

"Grab the spotlight, Mom!" Lizzie ordered. "You'll never get a chance like this again!"

RAINBOWGIRL is online

RAINBOWGIRL: I'm really getting worried. Where r u?

RAINBOWGIRL: I checked Bahamas weather and there r no storms. Did u forget to go online?

RAINBOWGIRL: mom's gonna be on tv tonight. She got a big job doing the Tommy Stiles after party in a.c. this is gonna be great for business

RAINBOWGIRL: ok ur not there. I'll email you.

RAINBOWGIRL has disconnected

20

Two encores and five standing ovations later, the show was over and every man, woman, and child in South Jersey who had ever met, gone to school with, dated, or gotten drunk with Tommy Stiles somehow found his or her way backstage to greet their old friend. The hallway and dressing rooms were bursting with people who had been there for Tommy and the After Life from the beginning and they all had stories they wanted to share.

Some of those stories were about Finn. Every time he managed to get closer to the door somebody from his past jumped out and grabbed him by the arm, eager to share their memories of his parents.

They meant well. He knew that. He wanted their memories, their stories, but not now. Right now all he really wanted was to get to Hayley before anyone else did.

Tommy's mother, CeCe, had brought a group of friends up from her beachfront retirement village in Naples for the occasion. CeCe was a refurbished eighty-something redhead who relished her minor celebrity status as mother of a rock star. She also wasn't above feeding minor tidbits to the tabloids if the spirit moved her.

"Finney!" CeCe wrapped her birdlike arms around him and kissed the air in the vicinity of his armpit. "It's been too long!"

He made all the right noises. "Some crowd you brought with you." He gestured toward Tommy, who was surrounded by a mob of tanned, retired Floridians.

"I'm so proud of my Thomas," she said. "I feel sorry for children who never got the necessary encouragement from their parents."

Finn smiled and said nothing. He remembered the stories about CeCe's attempts to thwart Tommy's music career and push him toward adventures in life insurance.

"It was good to see you onstage," CeCe

was saying. "Your father would have been just as proud as I am."

He asked a few polite questions about life on Florida's Gulf Coast as he eased toward the door. Anton, who had been sipping a mineral water while he chatted up one of the backup singers, turned to make an escape but Finn was too quick for him.

"CeCe, you remember Anton, don't you?"

CeCe turned an assessing eye on the bald-headed drummer. "You've gained weight, Anton. You should go back on South Beach."

He would pay for this later but right now all he could think about was getting to Hayley.

Tommy was trying to extricate himself from the crowd. "We're missing the party, people," he announced. "Why don't we move this to the ballroom?"

Finn pushed his way through the crowd in the hallway, past the curious faces, the photographers, the hangers-on. He didn't have time to wait for an elevator. He took the fire stairs two at a time.

"Hey!" a security guard stopped him as he popped out on the ballroom level. "Where's the fire?"

He stopped while the guy checked out the all-access pass hanging from a cord around his neck.

"Good show," the security guard said.

"Thanks." He was already in motion.

The hotel staff had worked their magic and transformed the ballroom into a galaxy of black velvet sky and brilliant stars. Pale ivory candles glowed from every available surface. Music spilled out from hidden speakers and vied with the sounds of laughter and conversation. He couldn't get his bearings. Roaming bands of reporters carrying plates piled high with lobster and shrimp walked right past him without a glance.

First the swag, then the interview. They had their priorities.

Like her father, Hayley attracted a crowd. He felt an odd tugging in the vicinity of his heart as he caught sight of her standing near the cake table. Somebody with an eye for drama had situated baby spots aimed directly at the edible drum set and the shimmering gold and platinum record cakes. No sugary flowers. No tiers. No pastel swirls. There was nothing familiar about what she had created. The design owed nothing to anybody. It was new and fresh and totally hers.

She had earned this. She deserved all the good things that came from it. Whatever else happened, she would have this launching pad.

She hadn't noticed him yet. She was speaking to a reporter from one of the local television stations while a camera crew focused in on her phenomenal creations. Another camera crew waited its turn as the glitterati, always looking for the next big thing, gathered.

She looked young, eager, utterly professional. If she was nervous, it didn't show. Her laughter was natural, unforced. You would think she had been facing the cameras all her life.

Someone tugged at his pants leg and he looked down to see Gigi, Tommy's youngest, smiling up at him.

"I got ice cream," she said with a big grin. "Now I want cake."

"Everybody wants cake," he said, scooping her up in his arms. "Even grown-ups."

He glanced around and sure enough there was Margaux, Tommy's most recent ex-wife, striding toward them. Margaux worked as on-air talent for one of the bigger, more successful, cable news outlets. Mother and daughter both had curly black hair and big smiles but only Gigi had Tommy's blue-green eyes.

"Hello, Finn." Margaux kissed him on both cheeks and he returned the gesture. "Leave it to my girl to find the ice cream and cake."

He was on automatic pilot as they exchanged pleasantries. Margaux, of course, noticed immediately.

"So you weren't joking when you said you liked cake." She inclined her head in Hayley's direction. "She does great work, doesn't she?"

"Amazing," he said, trying to figure out how to get away without arousing Margaux's investigative reporter's instincts. "Listen, I—"

"Go," she said as he put Gigi down. "I promised LeeLee we'd have a chat."

The ballroom was quickly filling up with people. The famous, the infamous, and the in-between were making beelines for the carving stations and the bar. CeCe and her band of merrymakers were scouting out the best tables. LeeLee and Margaux were loading up their plates with shrimp while Zach and Winston, terminally teenaged, watched Gigi devour a dish of chocolate ice cream. Sherri, Tommy's first wife, was holding court at one of the bigger tables with her three daughters, two sons-in-law, and four grand-children.

Willow was conspicuously absent.

So was Tommy.

He might not have another chance.

The reporter from the Atlantic City affiliate was either a great actress or genuinely in-terested in the art of decorating cakes.

Not that it mattered. As far as Hayley was concerned, she could hold up Twinkies as the standard of baking nirvana as long as she gave Goldy's Bakery a plug on the eleven o'clock news.

"Cal Rivera from News Philly." Another re-porter took her place. "We're talking to Hayley Goldstein, owner and chief baker of Goldy's, a landmark shop in Lakeside, New Jersey." He turned to Hayley with a big I-sent-my-dentist-to-Maui smile. "So tell us, Hayley, how did you manage to turn cookies into a set of drums?"

She told the story again. She had told it so many times this evening that she could recite it in her sleep.

Cal Rivera nodded. She could see his mind leaping ahead to what he would say next.

The cameras zoomed in on the gold record cakes.

"These edible works of art represent just a few of the gold and platinum records won by Tommy Stiles and the After Life over the years."

She explained the process for him in quick, manageable sound bites of information, making sure to lavish praise on her friends and staff for helping her out. If she didn't, she would need one of Tommy Stiles's bodyguards to escort her home.

Cal Rivera looked over her left shoulder. His smile widened. "We've been joined by one of the After Life's band members."

She knew before she turned around.

Finn was standing about six feet away. He shook his head. "Finish your interview. I can wait."

Cal Rivera, however, had other ideas.

Finn did his best to turn the conversation back to Hayley's cakes but the reporter had a particular agenda in mind and there was no going back.

"Sorry," Finn said when the television crew moved on in search of other prey. "I didn't mean to interrupt."

"Rocker trumps baker," Hayley said. "I

don't blame them. I was out of things to say anyway. The next step was reciting my recipe for double-chocolate-chip cookies."

"You're the most popular woman in the place," he said, noting the huge stack of business cards on the table.

"I can't believe I ever thought about backing out on this. Thank God Lizzie kept me on track."

"You really thought about backing out?"

"Only every other second since we signed the contract. I thought you drove down to deliver Chinese food and some bad news. I figured it would go easier on my pride if I backed out instead of waiting to be fired."

"Take another look at those cakes," he ordered her, "then tell me who would back out of a deal with the baker."

Her cell vibrated against her hip. "Lizzie's phoned at least five times. I can finally tell her we might be getting some TV time."

"You're not going to answer it?"

She glanced at the phone. "She's texting. Texting means nonemergency. I'm not morally bound to respond to a text immediately."

"Another example of the baker's code?"

"Nope," she said, smiling up at him. "An example of the mother's code."

"Are you ready to go?"

"Not while there's still cake to be eaten."

"Your workday's over," he reminded her. "Union rules are in play. The hotel's waitstaff slices and serves. So how about we get something to eat."

"I'm starving, but Tommy Stiles is coming this way right now and if I don't at least get to see him up close so I can tell Michie if he's had a face lift or not, then she will absolutely never speak to me again as long as we live, which, I hope, will be a very long time."

She wanted him to laugh and he wished he could, but the adrenaline surge in his veins made it hard for him to think. What he wanted to do was grab her hand and make a run for it, but Tommy and Anton were just a few feet away.

This was a hell of a time to start praying but prayer was all he had left.

"Hayley!" Anton pulled her into a warm bear hug. "I heard the style editor from *People* talking about you."

"Don't tease me," she warned him. "My cakes are serious business."

"Expect a phone call tomorrow. She's going to include you in a round-up piece she's putting together for one of their special issues."

Great, Anton. Keep talking about cakes and magazines until I can get her away from here.

Too late. Tommy broke away from a star gone nova and stepped forward.

"Tommy Stiles," he said, extending his hand. "Great job."

Hayley extended her right hand. "Thanks," she said with a big smile. "I'm Hayley Goldstein."

"From Goldy's," Tommy said. His eyes never left hers. "Thanks for taking the job on such short notice. I appreciate it."

"I'm one of those people who thrive on pressure, which is a good thing since I'm the mother of a teenage girl."

"The charming and witty Lizzie." Tommy was almost beaming with pride. How could Hayley not see it? "Is she here?"

"She's home tonight. She might be coming down with the flu, or at least I thought it was the same flu her aunt Michie has, but Fee is with her tonight and it's looking like it's really just one of those twenty-four-hour things, which makes me very very grateful for flu shots." She started to laugh. "Too much information. Sorry! I'm always doing that."

"Not even close to enough information," Tommy said, laughing with her. "So who's Fee? Another child?"

"My aunt," Hayley said. "I lived with her when I was in high school."

They were completely easy and natural with each other. If Finn didn't know better, he would think they had known each other forever. One second Hayley had been giddy and starstruck and the next she was chatting away with Tommy like they were old friends.

Except they weren't old friends. He knew it. Tommy knew it. Only Hayley was in the dark.

"Sorry to interrupt but it's getting late. Hayley and I were going to go out and grab something to eat."

Tommy looked like he had forgotten Finn was standing there with them. "You're going out to eat when there are three carving stations, a chocolate fountain, and these amazing cakes?"

Hayley pointed toward her starched white uniform. "I'm the hired help. They frown on having us socialize with civilians."

"You're my guest," Tommy said, ignoring the look Finn shot him. "There won't be any problem."

"I really appreciate the invitation, Mr. Stiles—"

"Tommy."

She grinned at him. "Tommy, I really appreciate the invitation, but if I'm going to get more work from some of your famous friends, I don't want them to think I expect dinner and cocktails with the contract."

He wouldn't have thought it possible but Tommy looked prouder than ever. Tommy told her a story about his first job waiting tables at a diner in Rocky Hill. She told him about the time she accidentally baked a binky into a loaf of bread. They were two old friends exchanging war stories, completely unaware of the fact that everyone in the ballroom was watching them like they were game seven and it was the bottom of the ninth.

"Lee Irvin is waving at you, Tom," he said. "He probably wants to talk about the Chicago show."

"I've been monopolizing you." Hayley beamed a warm smile at Tommy. "It's time I took off."

"This was the best part of the night." Tommy's voice cracked with emotion but he covered it with a cross between a laugh and a cough.

"Dad." Topaz, the youngest of his three daughters by Sherri, popped up next to Tommy. "Lee is just about hyperventilating. If you don't talk to him in the next ten minutes, I think the poor man will need another triple bypass." She turned toward Finn. "Hey! I was wondering if I'd bump into you." And then to Hayley, she said, "Did you make those?" She pointed toward the cakes. "I have one of Dad's gold records in my bathroom and I swear I can't tell the difference. You're good!"

"Thanks," Hayley said with a smile. "You think you know what the things look like but except for the basics, I didn't have a clue. I had to Google gold records. The images weren't all that clear so I made a few lucky guesses."

"I Google prospective boyfriends," Topaz said with a self-deprecating laugh. "Then I go out with them anyway."

"I Googled my ex-husband last year," Hayley said. "My judgment was even worse than I thought."

"Oh, don't get me started. The last guy I—"

Finn looked at Hayley. "If we don't leave now, she'll tell you about every guy she ever dated and, believe me, there have been a lot of them. The trail of broken hearts goes from coast to coast."

Topaz pretended to punch him in the arm. "Hey, my father is standing right there, you fool."

"I'm not listening," Tommy said. "There are some things a father doesn't need to know."

Now they were really entering dangerous territory.

"This has been great," Hayley said to Tommy. "Thanks for giving me the opportunity."

He saw Tommy wrestle with what he wanted to say and what he knew he should say. "I think it's safe to assume there will be more work for you in the future."

"That's great!" Hayley beamed. "Call me. You have my card. Wait! That sounds terrible. I don't mean it like that. What I'm trying to say is Finn has my number—actually you have my number too, right on the contract." She started to laugh. "I really do have to learn when to shut up."

And then Tommy did the unexpected. He leaned forward and kissed her cheek. "Don't change," he said, his blue-green eyes suspiciously damp. "Don't change anything."

Finn looked across the room. Tommy's fiancée stood inside the entrance, looking like an Amazon warrior in search of a battle.

"Come on," he said, grabbing Hayley's hand. "We're out of here."

"What's wrong?" Topaz touched Tommy's arm with a gentle hand. "You look strange, Dad. Is everything okay?"

"I'm fine," he managed, fighting down the huge wave of emotion washing over him. "Just tired."

Hayley was everything Finn had said she was and more. She was his daughter. Any lingering doubts he might have harbored had vanished the second he looked into her eyes. His heart opened instantly to let her in.

He had another daughter. Another grandchild. He might have lived the rest of his life without that knowledge if Willow's lawyer hadn't stumbled onto the truth. He wanted to send the man a magnum of Cristal.

"You're probably starving," Topaz was saying. "Mom said you never eat enough before a performance. Why don't I make you a plate while you talk to Willow."

"Willow's not here."

"Oh yes, she is," Topaz said. "She's standing in the doorway and she doesn't seem too happy."

Willow looked like every man's dream. Long blond hair. Short black dress. Stiletto heels with straps that snaked up her ankles. Flawless face. Flawless body. Sometimes he thought he was the only one who could see through all of that perfection to her vulnerable heart.

"You know what?" Topaz said as Willow joined them. "I think I'd better go see what's happening at our table." She smiled at Willow, blew a kiss at Tommy, then ran for her life.

He reached for Willow but she slapped his hand away. "Who is she?" she demanded.

"What are you talking about?"

"The chick in the white coat Finn dragged away like she was on fire. The one you were falling all over. Who is she?"

Willow attracted attention simply by breathing. All she had to do was enter a room and every eye in the place focused in on her. Right now the entire ballroom was their audience.

"Her name is Hayley Goldstein," he said. "She made the cakes."

"Who is she really?"

"A baker from South Jersey." *And my daughter, but I can't tell you that here, Willow.* "Why don't we go someplace and talk?"

"No!" She stepped away from him. "She's the reason you haven't signed the prenup, isn't she?"

"Willow—"

"I'm not stupid, Thomas. I see what's been going on. You sent Finn and Anton down here last week to make sure she got the job, didn't you?"

He had lived most of his adult life in the public eye. He knew how to create a zone of privacy around the things that truly mattered. Willow, for all her fame, was still new to this.

"Yes," he said, "but it's not what you think."

"Brilliant. Really brilliant." Her face was red with anger. "You get to screw around and call it business. How could I have been so stupid?"

"I've never cheated on you, Willow." He was an anomaly in this world, in his profession. He had never cheated on any of the women he loved.

"I can't believe you'd do this to me." She gasped for air. "I mean, my God, Tommy, she's almost forty!"

She swayed slightly. He reached out to steady her. "You need to sit down, get some food into you."

She pulled away from him again. "Don't patronize me, Tommy. You've been giving me the runaround for weeks about the prenup. Even Sloan thinks something weird's going on."

"It's a family issue," he said, trying to inch her toward the door.

"Are you screwing her?"

The entire ballroom fell silent. They were the only show in town.

"Willow, let's step outside and talk in private."

"I don't have anything to hide," she said, even louder than before. "I'm not the one fucking the bakery girl."

"You need to calm down."

"Don't tell me to calm down! Tell me why you're fucking the bakery girl."

"It's not what you think. Her name is Hayley. She owns the bakery."

Willow pushed past the reporters, the photographers, the crowd of old friends who were hanging on every word.

"Like I care what the hell her name is. She's not even that pretty. Her boobs are too small. She seriously needs highlights. I can't believe you're cheating on me with that old—"

Sorry, Finn. When you have your own kids you'll understand.

"Shut up, Willow!" he roared. "You're talking about my daughter!"

21

"You're talking about my daughter!"

The man's voice rang out above the noise as the crowd from the ballroom spilled out into the hallway near where Finn and Hayley were waiting for the elevator to reach the fifth floor.

Bits and pieces of chatter exploded all around them like grenades.

Who is he talking about . . . Did you hear what Willow said . . . He's got another daughter?

The atmosphere seemed charged with some kind of crazed energy that made her instinctively wrap her arms across her chest and take a step back.

"Was that Tommy Stiles talking about his daughters?" she asked.

"I don't know," Finn said. "I wasn't paying attention."

"It sounded like he was fighting with somebody."

She threw the ring at him . . . hit him in the eye . . . He's screwing some cook . . .

"They're all looking at you," Hayley said as the crowd grew. "They must recognize you from the band."

He ignored her comment. "These elevators aren't moving. Let's take the stairs."

"I've been up for two days straight. I'm not doing five flights of stairs."

That's her . . . over there . . . that's who they're fighting about . . .

Wait a minute. They weren't looking at Finn at all. They were looking in her direction. She turned around to see who was standing behind her as an orange-haired photographer slid to a stop in front of her.

"The woman of the hour!" he bellowed. "So how does it feel?"

Finn stepped between them. "Ten feet back," he warned the guy. "Hotel rules."

"Fuck off," the photographer said. "This is between me and Daddy's little girl."

Daddy's little girl?

"I think you have the wrong woman," she said as evenly as possible.

The orange-haired guy was joined by a local TV reporter with crew in tow. "That's some secret you've been keeping," she said with cameras running. "We talked for ten minutes and you couldn't give me an exclusive?"

"I don't know what you're talking about."

"Come on. It's over. You can—"

Finn stepped in.

"No interviews," Finn said as the crowd around Hayley grew. "Ms. Goldstein has nothing to say."

"That's because Ms. Goldstein doesn't know what's going on." Hayley turned to Finn. "Help me out here."

She could barely hear over the wall of noise surrounding them. Photographers jostled other photographers. Reporters shoved microphones under her nose. People who had fawned over her cakes just a few minutes ago were looking at her with a mixture of pity and curiosity.

But the look in Finn's eyes scared her more than the chaos breaking out around them. He leaned down until his mouth brushed her ear.

"I'm so sorry, Hayley," Finn said. "I thought we'd have more time."

"Time for what? I don't know what you're talking about. I'm starting to feel like everyone in this hotel knows something I don't and—"

A hand grabbed her shoulder. She spun around and found herself eye to eye with Willow the supermodel.

Fury shot from every pore as she fixed Hayley with a deadly look. "Stay away from him." Willow made sure she had everyone's attention. "I'm only going to tell you once."

Hayley blinked in shock and looked toward Finn. "Are you sleeping with her?"

"No!" He looked genuinely shocked. "You've got to be kidding. She's Tommy's fiancée."

She turned back toward Willow. "You'd better tell me what you're talking about because I'm at a loss here."

Even red-faced and trembling with rage, the woman was still drop-dead gorgeous. "You know what I'm talking about. Stay away from Tommy!"

"Tommy Stiles? I just met him tonight for the first time."

"Don't lie to me. I know the whole story. I know how you got this job."

"I got this job because I'm good at what I do."

"I'll bet you are."

Hayley bristled with anger. "What's that supposed to mean?"

"What do you think it means?"

"I think it means you've got the wrong idea about something."

Tommy, his right eye squeezed shut and beginning to turn shades of purple, broke free from the crowd and put his arms around the angry young woman. "This isn't the time or place, Willow. Let it go."

"Let it go? I can't let it go. I saw you drooling all over her back there, then you give me that bullshit excuse that she's some long-lost relative. I want to know what's going on. I have the right to know."

"Long-lost relative?" Hayley repeated. "I'm with Willow. I want to know what's going on too."

Finn looked over at Tommy.

Tommy looked from Finn to Willow to Hayley, where his gaze lingered.

Those eyes, she thought as she stared back at him. *Lizzie has the same eyes.*

Why did that suddenly seem so important?

Willow shook Tommy's arm off her shoulder and faced Hayley. "He said you were his daughter."

"You said that?" Hayley asked Tommy. "Why would you say something like that?"

Lizzie's eyes . . . my eyes . . .

She turned to Finn, expecting to see a look of total disbelief on his face. What she saw instead was compassion and her stomach slid sideways.

"Tommy's name was on your original birth certificate."

Funny how you could think absolutely nothing at all. She had never really understood the expression *her mind went blank* because hers never really did. Her mind was always buzzing with snippets of conversation, myriad half-formed worries, and ideas for new cake designs. But this time her mind went totally empty. All she heard was the sound of her own heart beating frantically in fight-or-flight mode deep inside her chest.

Finn was speaking to her from a great distance. So was Tommy. She couldn't make sense out of either one of them. She couldn't make sense out of anything. Not the endless clicking of cameras. Not the shouted questions from the reporters. Not the soft chime from the elevator as the doors slid open.

"Excuse me." A hotel exec complete with clipboard and BlackBerry stepped out. "Don't block the doors, people."

A pair of young women in short, tight dresses the color of tequila sunrises breezed past them. A late-fiftyish woman with an all-access pass strung around her neck and a *Best of Tommy and the After Life* vinyl album clutched to her chest joined the parade, not realizing her idol was standing an arm's length away from her.

People saw what they wanted to see. They heard what they wanted to hear.

Sometimes reality was the most unreal thing of all.

Like the fact that the man they were all rushing to see was her father.

Tommy Stiles—the same guy whose music had formed the sound track to the lives of almost every American her age—was her father. She thought her brain was going to implode from the sheer ridiculousness of it all. The only thing more unbelievable than the thought of calling Tommy Stiles *Daddy* was the thought that the rocker and her mother had had sex.

No matter how hard she tried, she couldn't link the two of them together in her mind, not even if she had a bottle of champagne to help her.

"This is crazy," she said as the elevator emptied. "Somebody somewhere got it all very wrong. Trust me, there is no way that—"

And then she saw her.

Jane was leaning against the side railing. A tall, distinguished white-haired man had a proprietary arm about her shoulders. Jane's eyes were closed and in that instant Hayley saw her mother for the very first time.

She wasn't the Amazon warrior who faced down sharks and tsunamis with equal aplomb. She wasn't the professor with the sharp intellect and keen understanding or the fiercely independent woman who had made her way through the world following only her own star. She wasn't the woman who had battled cancer into submission twice.

The woman in the elevator was old and frail and tired. She leaned into the man standing with her as if she gained strength from his nearness. The thought of her mother gaining strength from any man was inconceivable. It rocked Hayley to the core.

"Jane." Her companion's voice was rich and mellow. "Your daughter is here."

Jane opened her eyes, straightened her shoulders, and exited the car with her companion by her side. She looked anxious and vulnerable and very human, and in that instant Hayley knew there was only one reason why her mother would set foot in a hotel in Atlantic City.

Her mother and Tommy Stiles . . . Tommy Stiles and her mother . . .

"Oh my God," Hayley said. "It's true!"

Willow looked from Hayley to Tommy then back again. "Holy shit," the model said as the family resemblance clicked into place. "It *is* true!"

The woman's face went dead white.

"Grab her!" Hayley shouted. "She's going to pass out."

Tommy caught her just before she hit the ground. "Call nine-one-one. She's pregnant."

Anton was already on it.

"Hayley." Jane stepped forward. "I didn't want you to find out this way."

"You had thirty-eight years to tell me, Mom. What in hell were you waiting for?"

Tommy's mother CeCe peered down at

poor Willow, who was struggling back to consciousness. "She doesn't eat, that's her problem. They eat a raisin, then go into the bathroom to throw up. God knows what she's doing to my grandbaby."

"Shut up, Ma," Tommy said. "Don't make things worse."

"Worse? You want worse? I'll give you worse. I bring my friends up from Naples and you can't even throw a decent after-party. An hour? How long is an hour? Sixty minutes! A baby's birthday party lasts longer than sixty minutes. I expected better, Tommy."

That's my grandmother, Hayley thought. This tiny, brassy woman, who was probably the same age as Jane, was her blood. Those beautiful girls named after gemstones, the two teenage boys with charm and attitude, that adorable curly-haired child were her siblings—they were all part of her family line. In a heartbeat she had gone from an only child to one of many.

CeCe's eagle-sharp eyes landed on Jane. "Who are you?" she asked, pointing a bejeweled forefinger in her direction.

"Jane Maitland. Who are you?"

"I'm Tom's mother."

Jane nodded a greeting. "I'm Hayley's mother."

CeCe tried to frown but her obvious Botox dependency made it hard. "Who is Hayley?"

"I am." Hayley stepped forward.

"But you're the caterer." CeCe clearly didn't think caterers should mingle with civilians.

Finn opened his mouth to say something but Tommy got there first.

"She's not the caterer, Ma, she's a baker. And yes, she's my daughter."

Hayley actually felt sorry for the woman as she sorted through the tangle of information. She looked at Tommy, then over at Jane, then at Hayley, then back at Jane.

"You're Harley's mother?"

Jane nodded. "I'm *Hay*ley's mother."

CeCe turned to Tommy. "You can't be her father. She's almost forty."

He actually looked proud, which made Hayley's heart do a funny little flip inside her chest. "I'm her father."

"That means you two—"

Poor CeCe. It was too much for the woman and she started to fall over like a sapling in a storm. Hayley dashed to her side and gathered the tiny woman into her arms.

"I've got her," Hayley said as she gently lowered her grandmother to the ground. "Anton, tell nine-one-one we've got another one."

"I'm on it," Anton said, flipping open his cell phone one more time.

"She's not made of very strong stock, is she?" Jane remarked as she looked straight down into CeCe's coiffure. "Although I'll grant that she's quite well groomed."

In Jane's world that wasn't necessarily a compliment.

"Stay with her," Hayley said, standing up. "I have to do something."

The press was arguing its case with the hotel's director of publicity. Finn was on his cell phone. Anton was checking up on the status of the emergency crew. Tommy and her mother were playing catch-up over the heads of his semiconscious fiancée and mother.

And she was about to make her escape.

Tommy was in a free fall. The situation was hurtling toward total disaster. They needed his cool eye, his legal skills, his loyalty.

But Hayley needed him more.

Finn saw her make her getaway.

"Go to hell," she said when he caught up with her on the staircase.

"We need to talk."

"Go talk to my mother. I don't want to hear anything you have to say."

She had the right to her feelings. He couldn't pretend to understand what was going on inside her right now. The only thing he knew for sure was that he wasn't going to leave her side.

She was crying full out when they finally hit the parking garage. Neither one acknowledged the fact that huge tears were running unchecked down her cheeks. By the time they found her borrowed minivan her tears had turned into sobs.

"I'll drive," he said, reaching for her keys.

"Like hell you will."

"You're in no shape to drive."

"Reach for the keys again, Rafferty, and I swear it'll be the last thing you do!"

This wasn't the time to back off.

"You're angry and you're hurt, and I wish I had told you about Tommy before it exploded in your face, but I didn't. I screwed this up, Hayley, and I'm sorry. You can be as mad as hell at me, but there's no way I'm letting you drive that car."

"You can't stop me," she said through her sobs.

"Yeah," he said, "I can."

He took a step forward.

She held her ground for a long moment, then threw the keys at him. They bounced off his chest and clattered to the ground.

She climbed into the passenger seat and curled up into a ball of misery.

He drove them out of the garage and toward the A.C. Expressway.

"Do you want to go home?" he asked as they waited at a traffic light.

She shook her head no.

They rode a few miles in silence punctuated by the occasional sob.

"Are you hungry?" he asked.

She gave him a *you must be kidding* look.

"We could go dancing."

Her eyes widened and he saw the faintest hint of a smile.

"Bowling?"

The sobbing eased into crying. "Not funny."

"A little funny," he said. "In a twisted kind of way."

"I lied before." Her crying slowed. "I could eat my way through Hershey, Pennsylvania."

He exited the highway so quickly the tires squealed.

"Where are we going?"

"To get you some chocolate."

"I was only kidding about Hershey," she said, wiping her eyes on her crisp white sleeve. "You could pull into a ShopRite. A pound or two of M&M's would do the trick."

"I can do better than that. How does a hot fudge sundae sound?"

"Better than Valium," she said, "but I can't go in like this. My nose looks like something Bozo the Clown glued on."

He peered at her in the darkened van. "Yeah, it's a little red."

"A little? I could substitute as a traffic light."

"You're going in for ice cream, not a photo shoot."

"Look at me." She gestured toward her rumpled white coat and bright red clogs. "I'm a freak."

"You look fine."

"I look like I should join the circus."

"You want me to order take-out?"

"Yes."

"Hot fudge sundae with vanilla ice cream?"

"Hot fudge with chocolate ice cream. I need reinforcements."

"You're not going to drive off and leave me stranded, are you?"

"Don't worry." Her smile was wry and weary. "Right now I'd stay here the rest of my life if I could, Rafferty."

Hayley waited until he disappeared into Friendly's then climbed into the driver's seat, turned the key, and roared out of the parking lot. The last thing she saw in her rearview mirror was the shocked look on his face as he burst through the front door in time to see her drive away without him.

It should have felt a lot better than it actually did.

By the time she had gone six blocks remorse overtook her and she retraced her steps back to the restaurant where she found him inside eating the biggest hot fudge sundae she had ever seen.

She grabbed a clean spoon from an empty table and sat down opposite him.

"I was going to leave you here," she said as she scooped up some of the hot fudge.

"I probably would have done the same thing." He pushed the bowl of ice cream, fudge, whipped cream, and nuts closer to her. "Except I wouldn't have come back."

"I didn't want your death on my con-science," she said, licking the spoon. "I had a vision of you walking along the side of the road and being abducted by a cross be-tween Freddy Krueger and Jason."

"Thanks for the thought," he said. "I was going to call for a limo."

"I keep forgetting you're rich," she said. "Must be nice to be able to snap your fin-gers and summon up a stretch with a full bar."

"You'll find out for yourself pretty soon."

"Don't say that." She scooped up more hot fudge, this time with a little ice cream on it. "Nothing's going to change."

"It's changing right now."

"What do you mean?"

He popped a huge spoonful of ice cream in his mouth. "Trust me on this: you're on the radar."

"And here I thought my cakes were going to be what put me there." Her laugh sounded just this side of bitter. "You should have warned me."

"I wanted to."

"So why didn't you?"

"Would you have believed me if I had?"

"Don't go all lawyer on me, Rafferty. I

asked you a simple question: why didn't you tell me?"

"We had no proof. We still have no proof, for that matter, but if Lizzie hadn't called when she did on Sunday I might have told you then."

"With Tommy's blessing."

"Without it."

She scooped up a spoonful of whipped cream. "Did you call my mother and tell her about this?"

"We didn't tell anyone."

"So if she didn't know what was going on, why did she come home early?"

"That's something you'll have to ask your mother."

She started to say something, then shook her head. "How much time do I have before it hits the gossip columns?"

He checked his watch and she laughed hollowly.

"That much?"

"Even less."

"Oh God." She rubbed her temples against the dull ache that was building. "I don't want Lizzie to hear about this on TV."

"It's almost eleven," he said. "It might have already hit the local news."

She polished off the rest of his hot fudge sundae in three bites. "I have to get home."

"Give me the keys."

"I'm not crying anymore," she pointed out. "I can drive."

"Then I'll ride shotgun."

"You don't have to do this. I'm fine."

"I'm the one who was abandoned in an ice cream shop in South Jersey. You think I'm letting you leave without me a second time?"

"I'm not worried about you, Rafferty. You could always call for that limo you told me about."

"Is that what you want me to do?"

Her life would be easier if she did, but she could see herself with this man. The glass seemed half full when he was around. The timing was wrong. The situation couldn't be more complicated, but if she pushed him away now they might not get a second chance.

"My track record isn't the greatest when it comes to men," she said. "Sometimes I think Lizzie's judgment is better than mine." She took a deep, steadying breath then plunged in. "So here's the thing: are you doing this for me or are you doing it for your boss?

Because if you're doing it for your boss, then maybe you really should phone for that limo because—" She stopped. "Okay. For once I'm going to stop talking before I say something I shouldn't."

Something like *Kiss me hard and long until I can't think any more about Tommy Stiles or my mother or how I'm going to tell Lizzie.*

He didn't say a word.

Neither did she.

It didn't seem to bother him, but it bothered her a lot.

"I don't think I can handle another one of our awkward silences tonight, Rafferty," she said after the waitress dropped their check on the table and dashed off.

Their eyes locked. Neither one looked away. They were more naked in that moment than they had been the other afternoon in her bed. More naked than if they had stripped down to the skin right there in Friendly's.

She slid the keys across the table toward him. "You drive."

"You're sure?"

She inhaled softly. "I'm sure."

It wasn't much, but they both knew it just might be everything.

22

"I guess I'd better check for messages," Hayley said when they settled back into the minivan.

"Seventeen voice mails," Finn said, glancing at the display on his phone. "Six texts."

"Eleven voice and fourteen texts," Hayley countered, "but then I have a teenage daughter with a keyboard fixation."

"They're keeping CeCe and Willow in the hospital overnight," he said, reciting a message from Anton. "Nothing serious. Just to be safe."

"They're keeping my mother too," Hayley said, listening to one of Fee's messages.

"Sounds like jet lag caught up with her. She had a dizzy spell in front of an EMT."

"So where do you want to go?"

"Hawaii," she said, "but I'll settle for the hospital."

While Finn placed some call backs, Hayley phoned home.

"You're famous," Fee said in lieu of hello. "You're on all the local stations."

"Oh God," Hayley groaned. "How bad was it?"

"Pretty bad," Fee said. "I wish you'd warned me. I would have brought my nitroglycerin with me. The thought of Jane and that rocker gave me angina."

"So you didn't know either."

"Not a clue. I never quite bought the sperm donor story but since there wasn't anyone on the horizon I let it go."

"Who's the guy she brought with her?"

"Happy Father's Day times two," Fee said with a dry laugh. "He's her fiancé."

"How's Lizzie taking all of this?"

"She was running a fever so she took her meds early. So far she's slept through everything but your mother's arrival and abrupt departure."

"I'm on my way to the hospital but I'll come right home after. If she wakes up, just stall her until I get there."

"I'd think twice if I were you. The street in front of the bakery is crawling with news crews. One of them banged on the door but I called Joe at the station house and he sent a car over to keep an eye out. Like it or not, you're famous, honey."

So far she didn't like it at all.

At the best of times, emergency rooms were chaos central. When you dropped a rock star, a supermodel, and their respective entourages into the mix, you were asking for trouble.

"Where the hell have you been?" Tommy barked when he first caught sight of Finn near the nurses' station. "You had your cell off."

"I was with Hayley," he said.

Tommy looked like he wanted to say something but thought better of it. He gestured instead toward the curtained cubicle behind him. "Willow won't talk to me. She says its over and she's going back to the city without me."

"She's upset," Finn said, stating the obvious. "Give her time to digest all the new information. She'll calm down."

Tommy glanced around. "Where is she?"

"Talking to her mother's friend."

"How is she taking it?"

"Pretty well, all things considered. She's mostly worried about Lizzie."

"You were right," Tommy said, looking suddenly very old and very tired. "This was one shitty idea. I should have listened to you from the jump."

"Who knew her mother would show up?"

"Or CeCe," Tommy said, dragging his hand through his hair. "What a fucking disaster."

"How is she?"

"She screams for Valium every time she realizes she has a thirty-eight-year-old granddaughter."

"She'll adjust."

"Don't bet on it. This is a major blow to her self-esteem."

Anton, nursing a cup of coffee, joined them. "Zach and Winston found a game room on the third floor. I think a career in medicine is starting to look good to them."

The entire extended Stiles clan had taken over the place. They were in the ER, the self-serve cafeteria, talking on cell phones in the hallways, the game room, playing cards in the lobby.

"What happened to our friends from the press?"

"Hospital security kicked their asses out," Anton said. "They screamed like bloody hell about their First Amendment rights, but the hospital hung tough. I was impressed."

"Speaking of security," Finn said, "how did Hayley's mother get into the suite without a pass?"

"I asked the old guy," Anton said. "Apparently, we need to hire on new staff." Jane and John had followed the minidressed models into the venue unnoticed.

"Hayley phoned home," Finn told his friends. "Her aunt said the street was lousy with news crews."

"She doesn't have a clue what she's up against," Tommy said, drumming his fingers against his thigh. "They'll eat her alive."

"She shouldn't go back there," Anton agreed. "Not until this blows over."

"She can't afford to check into a hotel," Finn reminded them. "Besides, she has a kid and a business. She's going back."

"She could close until this blows over,"

Tommy said. "We have plenty of room at the house."

"You've been rich too long, Tommy. She can't afford to shut the place down."

"She has help. Why can't they run the place for a couple of days?"

"Hayley isn't great at delegating."

"What does that mean?"

"When you get to know your daughter, you'll understand," Finn said.

"Talk to her," Tommy said. "She'll listen to you."

Maybe before this happened, Finn thought, but now he wasn't so sure.

"I think it's a wonderful idea," Jane said from her hospital bed. "Tom told us about his home. There would be plenty of room for all of us."

"You'd actually stay there?" Hayley asked, amazed. "You don't even know the man."

"We had a child together."

"A child you never told him about."

"A bad decision on my part," Jane said. "One I was hoping to correct."

"You wouldn't feel strange being there with him and his family?"

"Not at all," Jane said. "He's a lovely young man. He always was. I think it would be a good thing for us to bond as a family."

Hayley made a show of searching the room. "Where's the Kool-Aid?" she muttered. "It has to be here somewhere."

"John is in total agreement," Jane went on, ignoring Hayley's best theatrics. "He and Tom were talking about playing a round of golf together."

"Well, I hope you and John have a lovely visit." She had already heard their tale of love among the ruins. It would take her two or three lifetimes to adjust to Jane as part of a couple. It might take eternity to adjust to her as a married woman. In some ways it was a tougher adjustment than accepting Tommy Stiles as her biological father.

"We want you and Lizzie to join us."

"Not going to happen."

"I spoke with Fiona. She told me about the news vans out front. They won't be able to harass you at Tom's home."

"Thanks, but I can handle myself."

"And what about Lizzie? She's a child. Can you imagine the pressure they'll bring to bear against her just to get a morsel of news?"

"Lizzie has the flu. She'll be staying in the next few days anyway."

"You're an exceedingly stubborn woman," Jane observed with almost clinical detachment. "It's not your best character trait."

"Hiding the identity of your daughter's father for thirty-eight years isn't one of your better traits either, Mom."

"I explained my chain of logic. At that time, in that world, I believed it made perfect sense." The Women's Movement was just getting started when Jane found out she was pregnant with Hayley. Pregnancy without marriage didn't carry the same stigma it once had. It was a new world and she was a strong and independent woman blazing a trail into uncharted territory.

And then there was Tommy himself.

"You should have told him you were pregnant."

"I considered it," Jane said, "but ultimately I decided against doing so." Which explained why his name was on the original version of Hayley's birth certificate.

"Because he was twenty?"

"Yes," Jane said, "partly because he was so young and had his entire life ahead of him. Even I could see he was heading toward something wonderful. He needed the freedom to follow his path."

Hayley rolled her eyes. "How noble of you."

Jane bristled. "I meant it as an act of generosity."

"You meant it as a way to keep control for yourself."

"That's a very perceptive observation."

"You should hang out with us right-brainers more often, Mom. We might surprise you."

"You've never been anything but a surprise," Jane said. "And a delight."

"And a bit of a disappointment."

"A puzzlement, but never a disappointment."

"At least now I know why I'm the way I am. I have rock and roll in my veins, not academia."

Jane didn't laugh often but when she did, her daughter took it as a personal triumph. Hayley was one of the few people on the planet who could reduce her serious mother to helpless laughter and she enjoyed every second of it.

John popped his head around the curtain.

"Ladies, is everything all—"

Hayley watched as his lined and serious face split into a smile as wide as the Atlantic beyond the hospital windows. He locked gazes with Jane and the look of love in their eyes was so real, so intimate, Hayley had to look away.

"Clearly all is well," he said with a smile for Hayley. "I'll leave you to your conversation."

"I like him," Hayley said after he left. "I can see why you decided to come home early and show him off."

Jane's smile faded then reformed itself into a weaker facsimile of the original.

"What did I say?" Hayley prodded. "That is why you came back to the States early, isn't it?"

Given a choice, Jane would have kept her secret to the grave. But her daughter had asked her a direct question and in light of all that had happened and was still happening, only the truth would serve.

"No, it isn't," she said. "I came home because my cancer is back."

Her daughter flinched but said nothing. She had taught her well.

"I found out a few weeks after I met John.

It was, as you would imagine, a bitter discovery."

Hayley nodded but still said nothing. Her blue-green eyes were swimming with tears.

"I'm a scientist. I understand the importance of family histories, DNA testing, genetic counseling. I know all of that but I still willfully kept you from learning about half of your DNA."

"That's it?" Hayley sounded amazed. "All of this just so I can blame my cellulite on the Stiles side of the family."

"The implications extend far beyond cellulite."

She forced a smile. "I guess the humor gene comes from the Stiles side too."

"You're deliberately missing the point."

"I wish I could, Mom," Hayley admitted with the bluntness characteristic of all Maitland women. She took a deep, shuddery breath. "What's your prognosis?"

Jane's candor failed her and she looked down at her hands. "I'm almost eighty. This is all icing on a very wonderful, very old cake."

"A cake metaphor," Hayley said, clearly struggling with her emotions. "I like it."

She met her daughter's eyes and saw the beginning of forgiveness in them.

"I like it too," Jane said. "Very much."

Hayley hesitated for only a second before she fell into Jane's open arms and cried like her heart would break.

"You surprised me," Finn said as he rode back to Lakeside with Hayley in her borrowed minivan. "I didn't think you'd take Tommy up on his offer."

"I surprised myself," she admitted. "The last few hours everything has been a surprise to me."

"You made the right decision. A couple of days in the news cycle and then something else will come along to take its place."

"That sounds cynical."

"It's a cynical business. You have to learn how to protect what's important and let the rest go."

She checked her mirrors, then changed lanes. "I've never been very good at the letting-go part. Worriers never are."

"How are you holding up?"

She was silent for a moment. "It still seems pretty surreal to me. With all the drama around my mother, I haven't really had a chance to think much about Tommy."

"Willow kept him pretty busy at the hospital."

"I noticed." She shot him a sideways look. "Not to mention his mother."

Finn started to laugh. "CeCe doesn't like giving up center stage to anyone. She was seriously disappointed the doctors couldn't find anything wrong with her."

"My grandmother," Hayley said with a shake of her head. "The mind boggles."

"Did you have a chance to talk to the rest of the crowd?"

"Not really. Two of his exes chatted me up for a few minutes but the kids kept their distance."

"You don't sound very concerned."

"You sound disappointed. This isn't a fairy tale, Finn. Just because we share some DNA doesn't mean we're going to share our lives. My life is with Lizzie and Fee and the bakery. Nothing's going to change that."

"What about your ex?"

"What about him? This isn't any of his business."

"Lizzie is his business."

"What exactly are you trying to tell me?"

He wished he could take a step backward into last Sunday afternoon in her bed with the setting sun streaming through the windows and her naked body in his arms. Reality was definitely a bitch.

"Your ex-husband isn't exactly a great guy."

"Tell me something I don't know."

"Hayley, we ran some basic searches on you after Willow's lawyer first turned up the original birth certificate. The information about Michael Goldstein wasn't good."

"Wait a second. You investigated me?"

"It's a standard part of drawing up the prenup. As one of his potential heirs, the other side had run a search on you. We needed to do the same."

"I'm not too happy about that."

"Neither was I once I met you."

"How much do you know?"

"Basic stuff. Birth date. Schooling. Your Social. Credit rating."

She groaned.

He laughed. "Marriages. Divorces. Offspring."

"Shoe size?"

"Some things I want to find out on my own."

"You have me at a disadvantage, Rafferty."

"I'm sorry," he said. "Before we met it was just part of the job." He started rattling off his own vital stats starting with his birth date. By the time he reached the balance of his 401(k) she had thrown her hands up in surrender.

"Enough! We're even." She gave him a funny look. "Did you really say you were arrested when you were in college?"

"We were protesting the faculty's refusal to recognize rock as a viable music form. The charges were dropped." He grinned at her through the darkness. "I like to think it added to my street cred."

"Michael was arrested twice during our marriage," she said. "And the charges weren't dropped. That's one of the reasons why I divorced him."

He drove his point home a little harder. "The guy's bad news and he's going to become worse news when he finds out Lizzie is Tommy's granddaughter."

"Tommy's her grandfather, not an ATM. Michael's going to be very disappointed if he thinks there's some kind of financial reward in this for him."

"Be careful, that's all I'm saying." He told her about the time a distant relative tried to shake down Zach and Winston for start-up money. "The kids were a little younger than Lizzie. They actually fell for the guy's line about hospital bills and swiped Tommy's platinum AmEx card."

"That's a scary story," she admitted, "but—and no offense meant, those kids are my half brothers—we're talking about Lizzie here. She would never fall for a hard-luck story like that, not even from her father."

"Her life is about to change," he reminded her. "That could make her vulnerable."

"I think I know my daughter, Finn."

The conversation was over. He had done his best. Now all he could do was hope it was enough.

MKG329302 is online

MKG329302: r u there lizzie

MKG329302: emailed u 2X but no answer

MKG329302: ok

MKG329302 has disconnected

TO: rainbowgirl@goldysbakery.biz
FROM: mkg329302@stealthmail.biz
SUBJECT: u

Lizzie pls answer this email asap. I'm in bad trouble. They want the full amt. I swear I'll pay u back as soon as that annuity from gpa stan kicks in next month. Help me lizzie pls

23

Tommy bumped into Hayley on the third-floor landing early the next morning.

"Are you settled in?" he asked, trying to pretend this was a casual encounter when he had been stalking her door for over an hour.

"We're getting there," she said with a self-conscious laugh. "Rhoda and Fee thought the stairs were too steep so they're going to be spending the nights at Finn's place for the duration."

"Rhoda and Fee?"

"My dog and my aunt. They have very specific requirements. Poor Finn doesn't know what he's in for."

"He's a good man. They'll be fine. How about the rest of your crew?"

"Well, our cats are jockeying for position with your cats. Mr. G claimed one of the curtain rods in Lizzie's room. Lizzie—" She stopped. "We're getting there."

"She's not too happy about this, is she?"

"No, she isn't. It's a pretty big gulp of information to swallow."

"I think we both know how she's feeling."

"Fourteen is a dangerous age," she said. "A few years earlier, a few years later, it would be so much easier on her."

"Maybe she needs to talk to someone she isn't related to about this."

"I thought about that," Hayley said. "I don't believe counseling is necessarily the answer to everything life throws at you but this might be an exception."

"How about you?" Tommy asked. "How are you handling this new situation?"

"The truth? Everything's happening so fast that I haven't had time to process much of it."

"I'm a week ahead of you and I'm still trying to figure out why we didn't find you sooner."

"Jane made that decision for all of us."

He looked for signs of bitterness but to his surprise he saw none. "No point fighting a thirty-eight-year-old battle. We're better off moving forward."

Her eyes widened. "You really feel that way, don't you?"

"You sound surprised."

"Most men would be angry."

"Are you angry?" he countered.

"I was," she admitted, "but—" Another shrug. "Life is short. What's the point?"

"Lizzie will work this out," he said. "She won't stay angry with her grandmother forever."

"The thing is we don't have forever."

"Your mother is a vibrant woman. She'll be around a long time."

Hayley shook her head. "No, Tommy."

He listened as she told him about Jane's two previous battles with cancer.

"We thought she had it beat," Hayley said, "but it's back and this time the prognosis isn't good."

"I'm sorry," he said, trying to put a lifetime into the words. "For all of us."

He wanted to pull her into a hug, but in all the important ways they were still strangers to each other.

"I'm glad you decided to stay with us for a few days," he said as he walked her down the hall to the suite of rooms she was sharing with Lizzie. "If there's anything you need or want—"

She gave him a look that made him laugh. "Hello," she said. "Have you seen this place? You have an indoor pool! We're fine, Tommy, believe me."

"Lizzie doesn't seem very happy about the arrangement."

"Like I said, she's fourteen. I think she wanted to stay home with her friends and be the center of attention."

"This has been—" He stopped as emotion started to overtake him.

There was a deep well of kindness inside his oldest child. She waited patiently, eyes averted, while he pulled himself together. She had his smile and his eyes and so far she hadn't asked him for anything else. No hints about her circumstances. No veiled references to the ex-husband whose problems continued to dog her business. She talked about Lizzie, about her mother, about music and art and baking, but she never touched on the fact that he was rich and she wasn't.

There was also a certain wariness about

her that hurt him to see. He had the sense that she was always looking over her shoulder, ready to duck for cover.

"I'm glad you and Lizzie are part of my life."

She thanked him warmly, but she didn't echo his words.

He looked forward to the day when she would.

Welcome to Lakeside Community Bank—one-stop banking at its best
What can we do for you today?
To transfer money to another account, click here.

ACCOUNT ID: rainbowgirl
ACCOUNT OWNER: Elizabeth Goldstein
PASSWORD: ********
AMOUNT REQUESTED: 4000.00
TRANSFERRED TO: 82073***289393
ACCOUNT OWNER: Michael K. Goldstein
TRANSACTION CODE: 7

Hit return if correct
Transmission FAILED
Destination account INVALID

Is there anything else we can do for you today?
To log out, click here
You are now logged out
Have a nice day

Lizzie's room was on the other side of a beautifully decorated sunshine-yellow sitting room that Hayley shared with her. Not that Lizzie had spent any time in the sitting room yet. So far she had stayed closeted in her room, tapping away on her laptop. Hayley knocked softly on the door. "Hey, Lizzie," she said. "How are you feeling?"

She waited a moment, then poked her head inside. Lizzie was sitting in bed, propped up by a mountain of down-filled pillows. A schoolbook rested, wide open, on her lap. Her computer, lid closed for a change, sat on the nightstand. Its little green power light blinked rhythmically.

"I'm okay," Lizzie said, casting a quick glance toward her laptop, then back again at Hayley.

"No fever," Hayley said, "and you're not coughing or sneezing. I think you're good to go."

"Home?"

"I meant downstairs."

"I don't want to talk to her."

"Listen, honey, I know you're angry with Jane. I was too but what's the point? What's done is done. Why don't you come downstairs with me and get to know this brand-new family we seem to have found ourselves part of."

"Why?" Lizzie asked. "They hate us."

"They do not."

"His mother hates us."

Hayley sighed. "Okay, so maybe CeCe isn't all that thrilled but who cares? She lives in Florida. We don't have to see her again if we don't want to."

"You don't care that she's your grandmother?"

It was a good question. It deserved an honest answer. "Right now, this very minute?"

Lizzie nodded.

"No, I don't."

Lizzie giggled. "Really?"

"Have you seen that red hair?" Hayley rolled her eyes. "Whatever happened to aging gracefully?"

"He colors his hair too," Lizzie said. "Zach told me."

"I didn't know you talked to Zach."

Lizzie shrugged. "Zach and Winston rang

me on the house phone and asked if I wanted to go out to a movie but I said no."

"I don't care if they are your—" She stopped. "What are those boys to you anyway?"

"My uncles," Lizzie said, which set the two of them laughing.

"Okay," Hayley said. "I don't care if they are your uncles. You don't go anywhere with anybody without telling me first. Understand?"

Lizzie nodded. "Why did she do it? I mean, how could she not tell you that you had a real father?"

"Jane thought she was doing the right thing for everyone."

"But she lied. How could she think that was right?"

"I don't know," Hayley said. "People tell lies. They keep secrets. Life can be pretty messy at times."

"He must hate her."

"You mean Tommy?"

Lizzie nodded.

"Actually he doesn't. He says he's just glad he found us."

Lizzie pretended to stick her finger down her throat.

"I think he really means it," Hayley said,

feeling surprisingly protective. "He seems like a good man."

"You mean you like him?"

"Yes," she said. "There's a lot to like about him."

"Do you like him like a friend or like your father?"

"Friend," Hayley said. "I'm thirty-eight years old. I don't think I need a father at this point."

"I don't need a grandfather either."

She leaned forward and took Lizzie's hand in hers. "I have an idea," she said. "How about we both keep our options open when it comes to Tommy Stiles. We've only known him for a day. Let's give the guy a chance."

Lizzie didn't say yes, but she didn't say no either.

Hayley took it as encouragement.

RAINBOWGIRL is online
MKG329302 is online

MKG329302: r u there lizzie
RAINBOWGIRL: sorry mom came in i
    had to shut down
RAINBOWGIRL: i tried to transfer $ to yr

acct but it wouldn't go thru whats up w/that?

MKG329302: computer glitch my accts down for maintenance

MKG329302: ill need cash instead

RAINBOWGIRL: i can't get that much cash

MKG329302: go to the bank they'll give it to u

MKG329302: lizzie did I lose u?

RAINBOWGIRL: they don't have a branch here

MKG329302: where r u

RAINBOWGIRL: long island w mom

MKG329302: LI?

RAINBOWGIRL: u haven't seen the news

MKG329302: no

RAINBOWGIRL: it's kind of major google tommy stiles u'll see

MKG329302: I'll do it later—where on LI r u

RAINBOWGIRL: one of the hamptons, east I think

MKG329302: I'm in nyc we could meet

MKG329302: I'll rent a car

RAINBOWGIRL: ill email you later let me see what I can do

This session has ended

* * *

Zach and Winston were teaching Lizzie how to play Texas Hold 'Em in the front living room when Finn showed up early that evening.

"Hey, guys, Lizzie." Zach and Winston grunted at him. Lizzie gave him a smile. "Is your mother around?" he asked the girl.

"In the kitchen with Anton," she said. "They're cooking."

"The rest of the crowd? Are they back yet?" Tommy had rounded up Jane, John, Fiona, and CeCe that morning and taken them on a tour of the East End of Long Island. Willow, still under the weather, had opted to sleep in.

"They're on the deck," Zach said, "with a pitcher of martinis."

He shrugged out of his jacket and tossed it over the back of a very expensive chair. "Deal me in later, okay?"

The boys' enthusiasm was underwhelming. Nothing like an old guy to ruin a perfectly good evening.

When had he become the old guy anyway? He didn't feel old. Thirty-nine wasn't old these days, not by anyone's standards.

Lizzie, however, favored him with a smile

that was a wonderful combination of her mother, her grandfather, and her own unique self. There was something about her that touched him deeply and he didn't know why. He felt strangely protective of her and oddly vulnerable at the same time, a combination he had never experienced before.

"Great timing," Anton said as he walked into the kitchen. "We already did the heavy lifting."

"It smells incredible in here. What are you up to?"

"Our asses in work," Anton said with a wink for Hayley. "Hayley decided to make dinner for everyone tonight."

"Which meant Anton cooks and I bake," Hayley said with a laugh. "I wanted an excuse to work in this fabulous kitchen."

Finn glanced around at the great expanse of Charles Peacock–designed marble countertops, Jenn-Air ranges, Sub-Zero fridge, things he had seen every day over the years and never really noticed.

Hayley was bent over a white marble slab, rolling a small dark ball beneath the heel of her hand.

"Truffles," she said as he crossed the room to join her. "A little pre-dessert dessert."

He quickly nuzzled her hair, breathing in the sweet scent of sugar and shampoo.

"Go ahead and kiss her," Anton said with a fake scowl. "What happens in the kitchen stays in the kitchen."

"Just you wait until you find yourself in a real working kitchen, Anton," Hayley said. "You want to know what's going on in town? Step into my kitchen for five minutes and you'll know everyone's secrets by the time you leave."

"I'd like that," Anton said. "Is that an offer?"

"What the hell—?" Finn turned to look at his best friend.

"Down, boy," Anton scolded. "This is a business proposition, not personal."

Hayley, whose cheeks were flushed bright red, rolled her eyes. "Are you serious?" she asked Anton. "Would you really want to apprentice at Goldy's?"

"Tommy's talking about retiring after this summer. If it happens, damn right I would."

"If it happens and you still feel this way, you're on," Hayley said.

"I'm not completely worthless in the kitchen," Finn volunteered.

Hayley met his eyes. "I can vouch for that."

"It's getting hot in here. I think I'll step outside for a smoke." Anton hung his apron on the peg near the back door. "I'll knock before I come back."

"He thinks he's funny," Finn remarked.

"He is funny." Hayley pressed a quick kiss to the underside of his chin. "And talented, and kind, and a very good friend to you."

"You'd really hire him at the bakery?"

"In a heartbeat," she said. "Did you know he wants to open a restaurant when he gets off the road for good?"

"I figured he was moving in that direction but I didn't know he had anything concrete in mind."

"We could use a great little café in town. I hope he falls in love with Lakeside and decides to settle down."

"Did he tell you about his wife, Lyssa? She's not exactly the small-town type."

"Her loss," Hayley said. "Lakeside's a great town and Anton's a great guy."

"Put me to work," Finn said.

"You're kidding."

"I'm a quick learner."

She brushed her hands on her apron then took his hands in hers. "Too hot to work with chocolate. How about kneading the dough for pizza."

He was clumsy at first and self-conscious but she had an easygoing manner that made learning both fun and painless. She asked him questions about Tommy's daughters while they worked and he tried to paint a picture of the girls he had known and the women they had become.

"They're all gorgeous," Hayley observed as she showed him how to stretch the pizza dough. "Did you ever date any of them?"

"They're like sisters," he said, practically recoiling at the thought.

"Not even tempted?"

"They were too young when I moved in and by the time they were old enough, we had the sibling bond going."

He made her laugh as he described Gigi and then he made her frown when he told her about Zach and Winston and their current struggle getting through high school.

"My little brothers," she said with a shake of her head. "I feel like I'm going to wake up back in my own bed and this will all have been a dream."

"Lizzie might be a good influence on them," Finn said as he watched her slide the first pie onto a huge wooden paddle.

"If she ever comes out of her room."

"She's not only out of her room, she's in the living room playing poker with the boys."

"You're joking."

"Texas Hold 'Em. I think she's winning."

"You know them better than I do. Should I worry?"

"They're good kids. A little undisciplined but basically good."

"So I'll still worry but not quite as much."

"You know you're a lot like Tommy."

"Is that good or bad?"

"He's a worrier too."

"Really? He seems like a hang-loose kind of guy to me."

"That's what he wants you to think. When it comes to worrying about his kids, he could give you a run for your money."

"He's lucky he didn't know me in my teens. That lovely head of hair of his would be a whole lot grayer."

"Not if his stylist had anything to do with it."

"He colors his hair?"

"Welcome to show business, Goldstein. How many sun-bleached blond sixty-year-old men do you see walking around Lakeside?"

"You're in show business too," she said as she slid the pizza into the oven. "Do you color your hair?"

"I'm a lawyer. Lawyers are allowed to go gray. In fact it's encouraged."

"You were in show business the other night."

"The gray hairs are all mine," he said. "I earned them vetting prenups for Tom."

"I'm thinking maybe CeCe should lighten up on the color. I'm not sure that shade of red exists in nature."

"She's been a little tough on you," Finn admitted, "but she'll ease up as soon as she realizes you're not a threat."

"How could I be a threat to her?"

"Every woman in her boy's life is a potential threat to her crown. It's what keeps her young."

"This is one strange genetic soup I've got simmering," she said. "Life was a lot simpler when I thought my father was a test tube from Corning Glass."

He was still laughing when Anton rapped on the door. "I'm back," he called out. "Cease and desist or risk Page Six exposure."

Anton put Finn to work chopping onions for

a tomato sauce. Hayley moved on to peeling apples for a crisp. Tommy came in to get a pitcher of orange juice and got caught up refereeing a debate on the merits of Silpat over parchment. Fee, eyeing the tiled floor with distrust, poked her head in the doorway and called out, "We need OJ, rock star!" and they all laughed uproariously at the look on Tommy's face.

Next thing Finn knew, CeCe was critiquing Anton's knife skills, Jane was washing and drying salad greens, and John was waxing eloquent on the virtues of the vodka martini.

Zach and Winston wandered in from the living room to see what all the laughter was about and they were immediately put to work crushing tomatoes by hand. Lizzie sat quietly in the far corner of the room sipping orange juice while a pair of look-alike black cats vied for pride of place on her lap.

He wasn't the worrier. Hayley was. So why the feeling of dread that suddenly lodged itself in the pit of his stomach and wouldn't go away?

There was nothing wrong with the picture, nothing out of place. No reason to explain the sense that something terrible was right around the corner and he was the only one who knew it was coming.

"The only thing missing is the boardwalk," Hayley whispered as they ducked behind a sand dune a few hours later. The rest of the family was either asleep or trading war stories in the sunroom. This was their first chance to be alone all day. "Every teenager in South Jersey has an under-the-boardwalk story."

"I have a boardwalk story," he said.

"Do I want to hear it?"

"You tell me yours and I'll tell you mine."

"High school prom," she said as he unbuttoned her blouse and unhooked her bra. "Twenty-one years ago. We went to the . . . umm, yes . . . beach after the dance and I don't really like the water so . . . oh God, Finn, keep doing that . . . somebody brought a couple Thermoses of screwdrivers . . . the other nipple . . . oh yes . . . and I thought it was orange juice and . . ." She couldn't think much less talk with his teeth grazing her nipple.

She slid her hands under his sweater and ran her palms across his chest, rubbing his flat male nipples until they grew almost as hard as his erection.

"Finish your boardwalk story," he said as he unzipped her jeans and slipped his hand into her panties.

"I made out with my date until my lips were so swollen I couldn't talk."

She arched against him as he claimed her lips.

"We can do better than that." He slid two fingers inside her and she arched against him, clutching him tightly with her body. "You're wet," he said. "You'd taste sweet on my tongue."

He rolled her over onto her back and slid her jeans and panties down over her hips so he could prove it. She came against his mouth, hard and long. The silence made it even more exciting. He moved back up her body and slid his tongue into her mouth.

"Sweet," he said. "Very sweet."

"Your turn," she whispered, and he rolled onto his back. She unzipped his jeans, not an easy thing to do, then laughed softly at the sight of his huge erect penis. She cupped his length with her hands, gently rubbing the head over her lips, again and again, touching her tongue to the tiny bead of moisture, strange and familiar both. Slowly, cautiously, she began to take him into her mouth, cupping his balls with her hands, stroking, pressing, aware of nothing but the smell and size and feel of him, wanting nothing beyond that moment, the thrill of knowing she was the one who made him lose control and cry out her name in the still night air.

"You should have warned me," she said as they lay together waiting for their heartbeats to return to something close to normal.

He drew her closer and kissed her temple. "Warned you about what?"

She waved her hand in the air. "About this," she said. "The beach, that house, the way you live. I thought I knew what to expect, but I was wrong."

"The way I live? I have a cottage in Montauk, not a mansion like Tom."

"A cottage? That cottage is bigger than most four-bedroom Colonials where I come from."

He had stopped seeing his surroundings a long time ago. They were just part of the scenery. "Really?"

"Really." She cuddled closer. "If I'd realized you were one of them, I might not have let you seduce me."

He laughed softly. "Funny."

"When do you think I'll be able to go home?"

"You're not having a good time?"

"I'm having a fine time, but I need to get home."

"Another day or so should do it," he said. "Tommy gave two interviews this morning before he left on that sightseeing trip. They went a long way toward satisfying the media outlets. We should be able to start seeing each other without garnering too much publicity."

She didn't move an inch but she might as well have. He could feel the distance between them grow.

"I don't belong here."

"You're Tommy's daughter."

"I'm a single mother from New Jersey with a bakery to run and a daughter to raise. Being Tommy's daughter is an accident of biology. It doesn't change who and what I am. I wish—" She stopped and he heard her long intake of breath. "Forget I said anything. We should all have my problems, right?"

"What were you going to say?"

"I'm the glass-is-half-empty girl, remember? Pay no attention to me. This was wonderful, Finn."

"Was?"

"It *is* wonderful, but I feel like I woke up in the middle of some other woman's life."

"That's not necessarily a bad thing, is it?"

"If it were just one part of my life, I'd agree with you, but it's everything. I suddenly have a father I never knew existed and he's not a plumber or a professor, he's a rock star. My half sisters can't seem to get it through their heads that I'm not just the hired help. My half brothers taught my daughter how to play Texas Hold 'Em and God knows what else. My brand-new grandmother suggested I contact the *Extreme Makeover* people for an overhaul. And as if that's not enough, my mother's cancer is back. Every time I look at her holding hands with John I feel like crying, yet I've never seen her happier or more serene."

"She's in love," Finn said. "Love can do that to the best of us."

It seemed Hayley was just getting started. "And then there's you."

"I figured I was your one problem-free zone."

"You're not a problem."

He mimed a big sigh of relief. "You had me worried."

"I'm the problem. I've been on my own for a long time now. The one thing a lousy marriage does for a woman is teach her how to take care of herself. I'm the one Lizzie depends on and until she's in college and on her own, it's going to have to stay that way."

He felt like he had been body slammed. "So now I know where I stand."

"She's my daughter, Finn. I managed just fine without a father figure in my life, but Lizzie is different. She loves her dad even though the son of a—" She stopped and shook her head. "If her own father doesn't care enough to put her first, how can I expect any other man to step in and do it for him?"

No matter how hard he tried, he couldn't find the answer.

24

Hayley's cell phone vibrated at 4:32 Sunday morning and it wasn't good news.

"Trouble," Michie said. "The water heater blew."

"Blew as in exploded or blew as in broken."

"Broken," Michie said. "We have a major flood. The emergency plumber is here. He wants to talk to you."

Five minutes and two thousand dollars later Michie got back on the phone.

"Any more good news?" Hayley asked.

"A reporter tracked Ma down in Florida looking for dirt on you."

"Oh great. I can just imagine what Connie had to say."

"Actually she told him to fuck off."

Hayley's jaw dropped. "Is that a direct quote?"

"No," Michie admitted. "Ma told him to get lost but it's the same thing, isn't it?"

They talked a few minutes longer. Michie wanted all the details on Hayley's extended family and Hayley had to promise to deliver the goods the second she got home.

"So when will that be?" Michie asked.

"Tomorrow morning," she promised. "I guess we'll have to use Tommy's limo again to get us all back down to Lakeside."

"That poor driver must still be talking about loading three cat carriers, a parrot cage, and an eighty-pound dog into a hundred-thousand-dollar stretch."

"We might have to zap Fee with a tranquilizer dart to get her back to New Jersey. You wouldn't believe how fast she took to the good life."

"So how about you? Will you be opening a chain of Goldy's bakeries in the Hamptons?"

"Not a chance," Hayley said. "It's a whole other world out here, Michie. I might as well have Jersey Girl stamped on my forehead."

"If they're being snotty to you, I'll—"

"No, no! I didn't mean to give you the wrong idea. Everyone's been fine to me." Almost everyone, if you ignored Willow and CeCe and the chilly teenaged acceptance from Winston and Zach.

"Are you and the lawyer getting along?"

"We're getting along."

"That's all you're going to give me?"

"That's all I've got."

"What's his place like? Typical bachelor? Is poor Fee sleeping on some ratty beer-stained couch?"

"'Poor Fee' has her own guest suite," Hayley said. "Trust me, Michie, nothing is the way I thought it would be. It's like Tommy is a money machine and everyone who comes in contact with him catches the overflow."

"Lucky girl," Michie said. "Catch a few fifty-dollar bills for me while you're at it."

Hayley had the feeling she would be hearing a lot of comments like that once she got home.

"Hey," Michie said. "I was only kidding. But you are his daughter, right? He owes you something."

"He doesn't owe me anything," she snapped. "Up until a week ago we didn't even know the other existed. If you're looking for some kind of Cinderella ending, you're going to be very disappointed."

"I *am* disappointed. I was hoping at least you'd have a fling with the lawyer."

I wish it was just a fling, Michie. A fling would be a whole lot easier than this.

Flings were all about great sex without expectations. You didn't expect your fling to love your child the way you did or to be willing to put himself on the line for her.

That was the kind of commitment you expected from the man you loved, the man you wanted to build a future with.

The kind of man who didn't exist anywhere but in a single mother's fantasies.

"You don't have to do this," Finn said to Hayley's aunt as he stacked the breakfast plates in the dishwasher. "You've been a great guest."

"I want to do it," Fee said as she popped the extra pancakes into a storage container. "There is nothing sadder than a bachelor's empty freezer."

"No wonder Hayley thinks you hung the moon. You really did."

"I'll need a few things from the market."

"Give me a list," he said, "and I'll get right on it."

An hour later he was pushing a cart through the local grocery, plucking unfamiliar items like crushed tomatoes, anchovy paste, and extra-wide egg noodles from the shelves. He was trying to figure out how to tell a male eggplant from a female and why anyone would care, when his cell phone went off.

"Sorry to call on a Sunday morning but I'm at JFK waiting to board a plane to Antwerp and this will be my last chance for ten days." Charles Militano was one of the investigators they routinely used to run background checks on prospective employees at Stiles Enterprises.

"No problem, Charlie. What can I do for you?" The knot that had appeared last night in Finn's gut turned to solid ice.

"A call came in a few hours ago from one of my informants in Miami. Damn voice mail. I didn't get it until just now. Anyway, that asshole Goldstein has been shooting his mouth off, telling everyone who'll listen that he's about to come into big bucks. He said he was headed up your way to start collecting—he called it his 'inheritance.'"

"Any idea when he's coming up here?"

"Yesterday. Tomorrow. From what I heard, he could be there right now. It may or may not have anything to do with your client, but after seeing him on the news the last few days, I figured can't hurt to tell you what's going down, right?"

What the hell?

He flipped his cell phone shut and was standing in line at the checkout trying to figure out what to do with the disturbing information when he glanced toward the banking window near Customer Service, then looked again. Was that Zach standing there, counting a fistful of bills?

He watched, astonished, as Zach pushed his way through the exit then climbed behind the wheel of a Highlander Hybrid and drove away.

It wasn't any of his business if the kid drove to Montauk to do his Sunday banking but he filed it away in the *curiouser and curiouser* category just the same.

Fee was happily chopping onions when he dropped off the groceries, checked up on Rhoda, then headed to Tommy's house where he found Hayley pacing the driveway while she fielded cell phone calls from home.

She smiled when she saw him but he saw the tension in her eyes. She covered the mouthpiece. "First the water heater, now the furnace. I go away for a day or two and everything falls apart."

"I'll be inside," he said, touching her hand. "We need to talk when you're done."

"The last time you said that I found out Tommy was my father."

"Nothing like that," he said. He wished he could be more comforting but he had the feeling everything to do with her ex-husband carried risk with it.

Tommy's place seemed unnaturally quiet. Jane, John, and CeCe were watching one of the Sunday morning news shows in the media room. Zach, Winston, and Lizzie hadn't come down for breakfast yet according to Anton, who had happily taken charge of kitchen duties on the cook's day off.

"Where are Tommy and Willow?"

"Jilly's daughter had the baby. They drove in to Ronkonkoma to see her."

Willow had been holding herself apart from the newest additions to Tommy's extended family and in a way Finn didn't blame her. Willow was young, pregnant, and insecure. Having to share her much-married fiancé with another old lover, a new daughter, and a granddaughter would be enough to shake the confidence of even a more secure woman.

"Make yourself useful," Anton said. "Slice and toast the bagels before CeCe slices and toasts my ass."

"I'm starting to feel like a line cook at Denny's."

"You're not good enough to be a line cook at Denny's."

They bantered back and forth, but Finn's mind was elsewhere and it showed.

"Jesus," Anton said with a shake of his head. "What did that bagel ever do to you?"

Finn looked down at the mangled baked good on the cutting board. "I'll admit it's not my best work."

"Put the knife down," Anton ordered. "Maybe you'd better stick to plating." He pulled a platter of smoked salmon from the fridge and placed it on the counter. "You and Hayley have a fight?"

He shook his head. "Nothing like that."

"Your houseguests giving you agita?"

"Fee's filling my freezer with home-cooked meals and Rhoda has fallen in love with me."

"So what's the problem?"

"There isn't one. At least not yet." He gave Anton the condensed version of his conversation with Charles. "It might not amount to anything. The guy's a player. He probably has a hundred scams going and this is just one of them."

"Maybe," Anton said, "but he doesn't have a hundred ex-wives with a rock star father."

"I thought of that."

"Did you tell Hayley?"

"I'm going to as soon as she comes in."

"Can't hurt," Anton said. "The good news is this place is like a fortress. Nobody's getting in."

The bad news was Lizzie had gotten out.

"Lizzie's not in her room," Hayley said to Jane as they carried two enormous salad bowls out to the crowd waiting on the deck. "Have you seen her today?"

"Early this morning," Jane said. "She came down in her bathrobe for some toast and juice."

"Did she say anything to you?"

"No. I'm not certain she even knew I was in the room."

"She has seemed distracted the last few days," Hayley said.

"As are we all." Jane laughed softly as Hayley slid open the French doors leading out onto the deck. "This house is very lovely and very distracting."

"I think she might still be running a fever."

John rose when he saw Jane and Hayley. He was at Jane's side in an instant. "Sit down and enjoy this beautiful afternoon," he said, taking the salad bowl from her. "I'll help Hayley."

He followed her back into the kitchen.

"Anton and Finn pretty much have everything under control out there," Hayley said. "All that's left is the pitcher of lemonade and the ciabatta."

"I want to thank you," he said.

"Thank me? I haven't done anything."

"The kindness you showed your mother in difficult circumstances has not gone unnoticed or unappreciated."

"One of the advantages of getting older," she said with an embarrassed laugh. "Your perspective shifts."

"This is not a small thing," John said. "Another woman might have held Jane to greater accountability."

"I might not have been so mellow if—" She couldn't bring herself to finish the sentence.

"I know," John said, placing a gentle hand on her shoulder. "Her illness casts a giant shadow."

"I hope Lizzie comes around soon," Hayley said as she handed the platter of warm bread to John.

"I'm sorry Lizzie chose not to be with us today. It's our last full day together here and when I saw her leave—"

Hayley felt like she had been jolted with a cattle prod. "You saw her leave?"

"About thirty minutes ago," he said. "She left with your brothers."

"They're kids," Tommy said, trying to put a lighthearted spin on the situation. "The boys are showing off."

"She's fourteen," Hayley snapped. "She has no business riding around with two strangers."

"They're not strangers," Jane offered. "They're her uncles."

"John saw them leave almost two hours ago. How long can you drive up and down Montauk Highway?"

"I seem to remember you and Michael spending a lot of time riding around in his Trans Am," her aunt Fee observed. "It might be a family trait."

"That isn't helpful," Jane said to her sister.

"I'm trying to remind my niece that minor rebellions are normal for teenage girls."

"You should call the police," Hayley said to Tommy.

"You're jumping to conclusions," Tommy said. "Fee is right. The boys took off last week. Finn helped me bring them back from Great Neck. They probably did it again and Lizzie went along for the ride."

"This doesn't make me feel better either," Hayley said. "First they teach her how to play poker. Now—"

"They're good kids." Anton placed a fresh pot of coffee on the outdoor table. "You don't have to worry, Hayley."

"She's my daughter. She's fourteen and she's out there somewhere with two teenage boys we don't really know. Yes, I do have to worry."

She pushed back her chair and stormed back to the kitchen. What was wrong with all of them? Tommy and Jane were Lizzie's grandparents. Fee was her great-aunt. They should be almost as worried as she was about Lizzie. They weren't stupid people. Why couldn't they see that this was serious?

She wanted Finn. He would understand. He had driven back to his place to get Rhoda. How long did it take to drive to Montauk and back? If there was something to worry about, he would tell her. He hadn't minced words earlier when he told her about the phone call from the private investigator. He wouldn't mince words about Lizzie either.

"Idiot," she said out loud. He always had his cell phone with him. She had his number programmed in hers. She dashed upstairs to get her phone.

Finn answered on the first ring.

"I don't like it," he said after she explained the situation. "I saw Zach at the supermarket near my house this morning. He was getting money from the seven-day banking center."

"I don't understand. What does that have to do with Lizzie?"

"I'm not sure," he admitted, "but I don't have a good feeling about this."

Ten minutes later he pulled into the driveway and for the first time since she discovered Lizzie was missing, Hayley felt like they were doing something to find her.

Finn had Tommy call the local police.

"Nothing," Tommy said after he hung up. "No accidents. No reports."

The relief was palpable.

"Maybe it really is nothing," Hayley said. How many teenagers could resist that bouquet of cars in the driveway?

"You need to check her computer," Finn said.

"I can't do that."

"E-mails, browsing history, whatever you can find."

"That's an invasion of her privacy. I would never do that."

"I read your diary when you were in sixth grade," Jane said. "I was afraid you were taking drugs."

"You did what?" Hayley spun around toward her mother. "I didn't know that."

"You weren't supposed to know it," Jane said. "Fortunately I had nothing to worry about."

"Thomas made my life a living hell," CeCe said. "Now don't be shocked but this"—she patted her coiffure—"isn't my natural color. I was entirely gray by the time I turned forty. He and Jack—" She turned toward Hayley. "That's Finn's father. He and Jack used to cut school and head into Manhattan to hang out with other musicians. God knows what they did when they got there. I needed Valium to get through his teen years."

"I eavesdropped on you and Michael when you first started dating," Fiona admitted. "I knew he was bad news. I should have followed my instincts and kept you two apart."

"Parents do what they have to do to keep their kids safe," Tommy said. "It's a dangerous world. The old rules don't apply."

"I concur," John said. "My late wife and I had many difficulties with our oldest daughter. For what it's worth, now is the time to take charge."

"I'm not a parent," Finn said, "but I know which side I'd come down on."

Her daughter's safety or her daughter's trust. At that moment she was willing to forfeit the latter for the former.

"I can't do it," she said to Finn. "You do it."

Finn looked at her but she refused to meet his eyes. He wasn't part of the Goldstein girls' permanent landscape so he was the perfect candidate for the job. Lizzie's anger would fade right along with his memory.

He followed Hayley upstairs to Lizzie's room.

"A teenager who hangs up her clothes," he said, trying to keep things light. "Wow."

"She doesn't get it from me," Hayley said.

"The shower curtain. I remember."

There had been something between them. Something real. The possibility of something lasting.

Damn.

Lizzie's laptop was open on the center of the bed. The AC cord snaked across the pale ivory spread. He followed the trail to the wall outlet a few feet away.

So this was parenthood, he thought as he pressed the power button. Feeling like a low-life bastard for a very high-minded reason.

Resuming Windows . . .

"Okay . . . there's her e-mail client . . . AuntieEm?"

"My sister-in-law Michelle."

"GoldCoastConnie."

"My former mother-in-law."

Friends. Teachers. Spam.

"MKG329302."

"Her father."

He scanned the folder of e-mails. Lizzie's

heart was right there on display in every single one of them. She loved her father and the son of a bitch had been using that to his best advantage.

He searched Word folders and Notepad files, and checked her browsing history.

"Does she have an account at Lakeside Bank?"

Hayley blanched. "Her college fund."

He hated to ask the next question. "Does she have access to it?"

"Yes."

"Go through her files and e-mails," he said. "Take the computer downstairs and print out everything that might be pertinent."

"You're scaring me."

"I don't think she's in physical danger."

"But—?"

"I think she's been making withdrawals from the account," he said, wishing he didn't have to tell her his suspicion.

He could see the thousand different scenarios, each one worse than the other, as they flew through her mind.

"I think she's been giving the money to her father."

"Not even Michael could be that big a bastard."

"I saw Zach at the bank this morning. He was making a withdrawal. I have a gut feeling it's connected somehow."

"Zach? How could he figure in this?"

"Another suspicion," he said.

"What aren't you telling me, Finn?"

"Nothing. I—"

The house intercom crackled to life. "Better get down here," Tommy said through a hail of static. "The boys are back and Lizzie isn't with them."

They raced downstairs and found Tommy, incandescent with rage, and two extremely uncomfortable teenage boys in the study.

"Tell her," Tommy commanded the second Hayley and Finn burst into the room.

Zach shot him a look. "But—"

"Everything," Tommy said. "Every last thing you told me."

Hayley felt like she had stepped into the eye of a category 5 hurricane. Zach and Winston finished their story and before she could fight down her fear Finn stepped in and took charge with Tommy not far behind.

"What's the name of the café where you left her?" Finn asked as he grabbed for his car keys.

"Kelley's," Winston said.

"That's in Quogue," Tommy said to Hayley. "Off Montauk Highway, west of here."

It might as well have been an island off Sumatra for all she knew of Long Island geography.

Finn hesitated then drew her into a quick embrace. "We're going to find her and bring her home," he said. "Keep your cell on."

"I'm going with you."

"No chance in hell."

"She's my daughter."

"You need to stay here in case she phones."

"She has my cell number. She'd use that."

"I'll go with you," Tommy said.

"Not a good idea," Finn said. "You don't exactly have a low profile, Tom."

When Tommy Stiles walked into a room, everyone noticed. Finn's biggest advantage was anonymity.

"You can't stop me from going," Hayley challenged him. "I'll take one of Tommy's cars and follow you."

"Is that what you really want?" Finn shot back. "Do you really want Lizzie to see her mother and father going at it right in front of her and everyone else in that café?"

"No, but—"

"Think about it. He's in trouble. You read those e-mails. Who the hell knows what he's not telling her? He's set himself up as a victim in her eyes and she'd do anything to help him. She knows how you feel about him. Whose side do you think she'd take if it hit the fan?"

The truth really did hurt. A lot more than she would have expected.

"You shouldn't go alone," she said as the fight began to drain out of her.

"He's not." Anton loomed in the doorway. "Never hurts to have backup."

She almost cried with relief. "I don't care about the money," she said as bile seared the back of her throat. "I don't care about Michael. Just get her away from him." She struggled hard to keep from crying. "Just bring her back."

"You know the odds, don't you?" Anton had never been one to sugarcoat the truth.

"I don't give a damn about the odds," Finn said, adjusting the windshield wipers.

"They dropped her off over an hour ago. She's probably gone off with her father by now."

"Maybe," Finn said. "Maybe not. From what Zach said, she was going to meet him somewhere between two and three. He doesn't strike me as a real punctual kind of guy."

"People can get real punctual when there's money involved."

He clued Anton in on the information Charles had given him earlier that morning. Hard to believe that was less than five hours ago. It felt like a lifetime.

"He's connected?" Anton asked.

"Seems like."

"Not good."

"Tell me about it."

"If he has that crowd after him, he's desperate."

"Yeah," Finn said. "Desperate enough to strip his kid's bank account."

"It could get ugly."

As far as Finn could see, it already had.

The rain let up and Hayley escaped the house for the relative solitude of the terraced deck. The endless offers of food and drink and company were meant to comfort her but they made her feel more of an outsider than ever.

"Give me ten minutes," he said as they reached the entrance to Kelley's. "If I'm not out, come in and get me."

Kelley's was lit more like a bar than a coffee shop. The lighting was dim, the ambience close to nonexistent. It smelled of coffee, bacon, and rain-soaked sweaters.

The cashier looked up as he approached. "All we got is the counter," she said. "Five percent surcharge on take-out, ten-minute wait for a booth. What'll it be?"

"I'm meeting someone. Can I take a look around?"

"Knock yourself out."

The crowd was standard Long Island diner. An old married couple sipped coffee while they read the *New York Times*. A younger couple nibbled from the same bagel as they basked in a definite postcoital glow. A handful of families pretended they were having a good time while their kids flung pancakes across the room like Frisbees.

No sign of Lizzie. No sign of Goldstein.

Come on . . . come on . . . you've gotta be here, Lizzie . . .

And then he saw her. Second booth from the back. He recognized Michael Goldstein from the photos Hayley had printed off Lizzie's computer. Goldstein was leaning forward, reaching across the table toward his daughter. A thick white envelope rested in the space between them. Lizzie's head was down. Her shiny blond hair spilled over her young shoulders. He was pretty sure she was crying. The bright, funny, self-confident girl he had met at Goldy's less than two weeks ago was nowhere in sight.

He could almost hear the adrenaline rush moving through his bloodstream as he walked slowly up the aisle. He glanced to the right and then to the left. Casual. Unconcerned. Just a guy looking to hook up with his friends on a rainy Sunday afternoon. His heart pounded so hard he could barely hear the old rock music blaring from speakers overhead.

He reached their table. Goldstein's voice was low, urgent. He caught the note of pleading and it made him want to drive his fist into the man's face. He let his eyes linger on the guy for a second then drift casually toward—

"Lizzie!"

"Mr. Rafferty?" He saw the shock of surprise rocket through her body. "How did— what are you doing here?" Her eyes were computer. Goldstein was leaning forward, reaching across the table toward his daughter. A thick white envelope rested in the space between them. Lizzie's head was down. Her shiny blond hair spilled over her young shoulders. He was pretty sure she was crying. The bright, funny, self-confident girl he had met at Goldy's less than two weeks ago was nowhere in sight.

He could almost hear the adrenaline rush moving through his bloodstream as he walked slowly up the aisle. He glanced to the right and then to the left. Casual. Unconcerned. Just a guy looking to hook up with his friends on a rainy Sunday afternoon. His heart pounded so hard he could barely hear the old rock music blaring from speakers overhead.

He reached their table. Goldstein's voice was low, urgent. He caught the note of pleading and it made him want to drive his fist into the man's face. He let his eyes linger on the guy for a second then drift casually toward—

"Lizzie!"

"Mr. Rafferty?" He saw the shock of surprise rocket through her body. "How did— what are you doing here?" Her eyes were

"Give me ten minutes," he said as they reached the entrance to Kelley's. "If I'm not out, come in and get me."

Kelley's was lit more like a bar than a coffee shop. The lighting was dim, the ambience close to nonexistent. It smelled of coffee, bacon, and rain-soaked sweaters.

The cashier looked up as he approached. "All we got is the counter," she said. "Five percent surcharge on take-out, ten-minute wait for a booth. What'll it be?"

"I'm meeting someone. Can I take a look around?"

"Knock yourself out."

The crowd was standard Long Island diner. An old married couple sipped coffee while they read the *New York Times*. A younger couple nibbled from the same bagel as they basked in a definite postcoital glow. A handful of families pretended they were having a good time while their kids flung pancakes across the room like Frisbees.

No sign of Lizzie. No sign of Goldstein.

Come on . . . come on . . . you've gotta be here, Lizzie . . .

And then he saw her. Second booth from the back. He recognized Michael Goldstein from the photos Hayley had printed off Lizzie's red from crying and a trio of crumpled paper napkins littered the tabletop.

"I live out here, remember? This is one of my favorite places."

Did she buy it? He wasn't sure. He wouldn't have, but then he was pushing forty. Lizzie might be scary smart but she was still only fourteen. The advantage was his, but it wouldn't last long. He had to act now.

He waited for her to introduce him to her father but she looked down at her hands instead. Any lingering doubts he might have had about the situation vanished.

He turned to Michael and extended his right hand. "Finn Rafferty."

Goldstein looked up and met his eyes. Recognition charged the air between them.

He knows. The realization had barely registered on Finn when Goldstein grabbed the envelope and took off for the door.

"Daddy!" Lizzie's voice rang out. "Wait!"

"Hey!" The cashier stepped out from behind the register. "Where the hell do you think you're going?"

Goldstein careened off a waitress carrying a tray of juice glasses. She yelped a curse. The tumblers shot into the air then crashed to the floor, shattering into a mess of broken glass and sticky orange liquid.

Finn skidded across the puddle of juice and fell to one knee. The crack of bone against tile sent shock waves through his body. He would hurt like hell when this was over.

Goldstein was halfway out the door. Lizzie darted around Finn in pursuit of her father. Finn regained his footing and tore after them. The street was rain-soaked and eerily still. Goldstein was headed for the silver Camry Finn had noticed before.

"Dad! Stop!" Lizzie's voice pierced the stillness. "Wait for me!"

The son of a bitch was fast.

Too fast.

Those seconds back there had cost him.

Anton rounded the corner. Goldstein was maybe twenty feet away from the silver Camry with the angry-looking dark-haired woman. Anton stepped in front of Lizzie. The girl cried out and tried to push past him but he was a human brick wall.

At the sound of his daughter's cry Goldstein missed a step. The envelope flew out of his hands, lifted on the wind, and settled in a puddle a few feet away.

Goldstein darted to the left.

Finn angled right.

The two men collided with the force of a pair of locomotives at full throttle, then slammed to the ground.

"Fuck off, you son of a bitch!" Goldstein reared back and landed a sucker punch to Finn's jaw.

"No!" he yelled as Anton moved into view. "Lizzie . . ." *Get her out of here . . . she doesn't need to see this . . .* Like it or not, that bastard was her father and this moment would stick with her for the rest of her life.

Goldstein was on his feet again. The dark-haired woman in the silver Camry was out of the car and screaming, "Michael! We're gonna miss the plane!"

Finn grabbed for the man's ankle and brought him down hard. White-hot rage burned away what was left of rational thought. He wanted to slam the son of a bitch into the concrete, drive his fist into that unlined face until he felt the crunch of bone beneath his hand.

He had the bastard cornered. He could almost taste triumph. He saw the fear in Goldstein's eyes. He could smell it. He had the guy exactly where he wanted him and he had a free shot coming.

Time, motive, and opportunity. He had them all.

By anyone's reckoning, Goldstein was fair game.

But he was also Lizzie's father and that changed everything.

"What's wrong?" Goldstein asked. "Lose your nerve?"

Finn leaned in close so nobody but Goldstein could hear. "If it was just the two of us, you wouldn't get up again for a long time. Drop the money, get in the car, and get the fuck out of here and I won't let your daughter see what a coward you are. I'll let her figure it out for herself."

They locked eyes. The guy was calculating his odds and they didn't include his daughter.

"Try me," Finn said in a casual tone of voice. "I'm also Tommy's lawyer. Go after Lizzie or her mother for money or anything else again and so fucking help me, I'll make sure your life gets worse in ways even you can't imagine. It's up to you."

Hayley would never forget the sight of her daughter walking up the rainswept driveway flanked by Finn and Anton. She walked straight and tall, the way Hayley had always told her to, but nothing could erase the sadness in her beautiful blue-green eyes.

Lizzie had tried to help her father when he claimed he needed it most. Hayley prayed this experience would open her eyes but not harden her heart. It was a lesson Hayley had taken a long time to learn.

"She's fine," Finn said as Lizzie fell into her arms.

"Michael?" she asked.

"On his way to Bermuda with a woman named Gayle."

She reached up and touched his jaw.

"It's nothing," Finn said. "I'll tell you later."

She had questions, a thousand of them, but this wasn't the time. She had had a lifetime of Michael's problems. The divorce had marked the end of their marriage but it had taken until this moment to mark the end of her guilt.

All the time she had spent worrying about how to protect her daughter from the world and its dangers and it was Lizzie's father who posed the greatest risk. She wished there was some way she could step back in time and make different, better choices, a way she could protect Lizzie from the pain she was feeling, but it was like unringing a bell. This wasn't the kind of pain a mother could kiss away. Pretty words wouldn't make it better. Only time could do that.

Suddenly she and Lizzie and Finn were surrounded by people. Tommy. Zach and Winston. Willow and Jane and John and Fee and CeCe. Even Tommy's stylist Jilly and her husband joined the group.

Nobody seemed to notice that it was raining or that Rhoda was doing a mud dance on their clothes.

They were her family.

And this was a homecoming.

Jane and CeCe quickly assessed the situation.

"Upstairs," CeCe commanded, draping a stick-thin arm across Lizzie's shoulders. "We need to get you cleaned up."

"Your grandmother's right," Jane said. "Let's get you out of those wet clothes."

Lizzie didn't protest. Actually she seemed to melt into the flurry of female nurturing as Jane and Cece swept her upstairs. A dose of grandmotherly attention, no matter how untraditional, might be exactly what Lizzie needed right now.

"I'm going to call the station," Finn said, "and let the cops know Lizzie's back where she belongs."

"Tell me everything," Hayley said to Anton after Finn left the room. "And don't leave anything out."

"Stay another night," Tommy urged as Finn carried their bags out to his Rover two days later. "It's a long drive."

"Lizzie needs to get back to school," Hayley said, torn between her desire to be in her own house and a surprising desire to stay here with her family. "And I've been away from the bakery long enough."

"You've done a great job with her," Tommy said. "She tried to help a drowning man. It's hard to fault her for that."

"I know," Hayley said, "but I can't help wishing she had come to me before she stripped her college fund."

Tommy waved a hand. "She doesn't have to worry about college. You know I'll take care of everything."

"And you know how I feel about that," Hayley said. "She needs to know she can do this herself, that she can trust her own judgment again." She wanted Lizzie to have a strong sense of who she was and an equally strong belief in her ability to take care of herself.

Lizzie had never been under any illusions about her father. She knew she couldn't change Michael Goldstein. All she had hoped to do was keep him safe. The fact that he planned to take her money and blow it on a trip to Bermuda had been a terribly bitter pill for Lizzie and while their new extended family had rallied around the girl, only Hayley truly understood how the betrayal made her feel.

She and Lizzie had stayed up that first night and continued the conversation that had started—was it really less than two weeks ago?—at the Olive Garden. They talked about family, about mothers and daughters, about fathers and the kind of pain only love in great measure can heal. She needed to rethink the way she relied on her daughter to keep the bakery running. Lizzie was a brilliant and beautiful young woman. The world was going to come knocking on her door any day now and she wanted Lizzie to feel free to pursue her future wherever it led without guilt or worry.

Who would have thought Michael

Goldstein would be the one who taught her the importance of letting go?

"You probably won't believe me," Tommy said, "but I'm going to miss you two very much."

"I'm going to miss you too," she said, surprising herself once again. "I always liked your music but I think I like the man even more."

He hesitated, then wrapped her in a bear hug that embarrassed and delighted both of them.

"Come down for dinner sometime," she said. "I guarantee the desserts will be worth the trip."

She wasn't sure if his eyes were wet with tears or if it was a trick of the lighting. She intended to blame the lighting for the telltale dampness in hers.

Even CeCe seemed sorry to see them go.

"Look how skinny you are," CeCe said. "You work too hard. You should take a vacation."

"I'm fine, CeCe," she said, trying very hard not to roll her eyes. "I have my mother's metabolism."

No point explaining to the Social Queen of Naples, Florida, that not everyone could afford to take a vacation. Or wanted to for that matter. She had missed the controlled chaos of Goldy's and she definitely missed her friends.

"I hope you don't mind if John, Fee, and I stay on a few more days," Jane said. "I'm going to speak with the directors of the Oceanographic Institute in Montauk and see about mounting an exhibit to run concurrent with a series of lectures on the current state of Great South Bay. That will give you a chance to settle back in before we descend on you en masse."

She knew her mother was enjoying every second of her stay at Tommy's wonderful beachfront mansion. The proximity to the ocean was incentive enough to linger, but Hayley had the feeling the seven-hundred-thread-count sheets on the guest beds didn't hurt.

"We don't have phones in the bathrooms," she reminded her mother with a laugh. "I don't want you to be disappointed."

"We'll be fine," John said, placing a warm hand on her shoulder. "It's being with family that counts."

She had already said good-bye to Willow, who was upstairs napping, and to Anton, who went off to have supper with his wife and kids a little while ago. Next week he planned to drive down to Lakeside and take a look at the possibilities available to him if Tommy's retirement plans panned out.

Anton had told her the whole ugly story while Finn was making his phone call to the police department. Lizzie had seen her father land a cowardly, vicious shot to Finn's jaw but she had also seen Finn turn away from a chance to even the score because it was the right thing to do. He had put Lizzie's needs before his own. He had allowed compassion to win out over satisfying his own ego. Not even Lizzie's father had been willing to do that.

And it scared her right down to the bone.

She had meant every word she'd said on the beach the other night. She owed Lizzie the very best life she could give to her, the very best of the world. Up until Finn she had believed that giving her daughter the best meant going it alone until Lizzie was on her own. It was one thing to risk your own heart when you fell in love with the wrong man. It was something else again to risk your daughter's heart as well.

But what if you met a man and fell suddenly, hopelessly in love and he wasn't the wrong man at all? What if he was honorable and kind and smart and funny and sexy and gorgeous and blind to the fact that your thighs were a day-care center for cellulite? What if he had shown more respect for your daughter today than her father had shown her in more years than you cared to count?

What if . . . ?

Conversation slowed down a few miles west of Riverhead. By the time they hit the Southern State en route toward Brooklyn and the Verrazano, it was dead.

Okay, so it wasn't easy to be heard over the racket made by three hissing cats, a snoring dog, and a talkative parrot, but the acoustics were pretty good in the roomy Escalade. They could have managed.

Finn told himself it was because Lizzie was asleep in the backseat, safely buckled in between Rhoda and Mr. G. He told himself they were being considerate of the girl. He had never been big on self-deception but he was willing to make an exception this time. It beat facing the truth.

"We should've picked up some Chinese food before we left," he said.

"That's okay," she murmured, not turning away from the fascinating view of Staten Island whizzing past her window. "I'll make Lizzie some eggs."

It was hard not to think about the last time he made this drive with his heart on his sleeve. He had had a million reasons why he shouldn't make that crazy drive down to Lakeside to see her and only one reason why he should: because there was nowhere else on earth he would rather be.

Something had clicked into place this afternoon, the last piece of the puzzle they called love. He got it. Really got it. It was more than great sex, great conversation, great laughs. It went deeper, all the way to the place inside your heart that you hid from the world, the place whose existence a man didn't always admit even to himself.

He loved her. He loved her daughter. He loved the man he was with them, the man he could be if they let him.

A new lover shouldn't know all the things he knew about her. He had believed the balance between them would level out once she learned that Tommy was her father and they could move beyond the past, but he had been wrong. There were other obstacles, ones that couldn't be overcome so easily. Michael Goldstein had hurt her. Not physically, but his selfish choices had left scars behind that might never go away.

He was in so far over his head that he couldn't see daylight. The only thing he knew for sure was that he loved her and wanted to build a future with her and with her daughter.

But he didn't know how to win her wary heart.

Lizzie woke up a few miles from home. She yawned, then laughed softly as Rhoda started licking her chin.

"Good timing," Hayley said, taking the laughter as a good sign. "We'll be home in a couple of minutes."

"I'm hungry. We should have brought home Chinese."

"Since when are you such a big fan of Chinese food?"

"I was thinking about the shrimp from that place near Finn."

She was surprised Finn didn't say anything about Lizzie's request but then he hadn't said a word for quite a few miles. Neither one of them had. The easy banter, the connection between them, had vanished somewhere between East Hampton and the turnpike. Silence was all that remained.

"The press is gone," Finn observed as he pulled the Escalade into the alleyway behind her Buick. "That's good news."

"Looks like it rained down here too," Hayley said. "That probably helped scare them off."

Lizzie shot her a look that could have curdled milk. Hayley ignored her.

Rhoda burst from the SUV like a gunshot. Finn helped Lizzie get Mr. G's cage out of the car while Hayley unlocked the back door to the bakery.

"Pets first," Finn said, "then I'll get your bags."

Rhoda bounded into the house ahead of everyone. Hayley and Lizzie maneuvered Mr. G and his cage up the narrow staircase while Finn unloaded three very angry cats and their carriers, then went back for the bags.

Five minutes later Rhoda was asleep on the sofa, the cats were claiming their litter boxes, Mr. G was exploring his domain, and Lizzie was in her room setting up her laptop.

Finn stood looking up at her from the bottom of the staircase.

She looked down at him from the landing.

They might as well have been on different planets.

She took a deep breath. It was now or never.

"Finn, why don't you—"

"I love you." He hadn't meant to say it but damn it, there it was just the same.

For a second she forgot to breathe. "What did you say?"

"I love you." He raised his hand and held it palm out. "You don't have to say anything. In fact, I don't want you to say anything. It's too soon. We're too new to each other. You have a daughter. I know all the reasons why we need to take this slow. That's fine. I'm okay with it. But I want you to know that I love you and I'm going to keep on loving you through more Chinese take-out dinners, more family squabbles, more weekends with CeCe, more Tommy Stiles Farewell Tours, more old wives and new wives, more babies, more muddy dogs and angry cats, two upcoming weddings, and at least fifty birthdays and Christmases and christenings and family reunions, and one day, in the middle of all that living, you'll wake up and realize you love me too."

She couldn't think. She couldn't talk. She couldn't move. He loved her. He wanted to spend his life with her and Lizzie and the cats and the dog and the parrot and the bakery and the huge extended family and everything that came with it. All the things she had prayed for her entire life but never thought she would be lucky enough to find were hers for the asking if she could just find her voice.

Finn wasn't sure how long he waited for her to say something. Five years, maybe ten. Sometimes silence was an answer in itself. It was time to call it a day.

"Okay," he said, turning toward the door. "I'm going. I'll give you a call."

"Mom!" Lizzie's voice rang out from the top of the stairs. "Say something!"

"Do you like scrambled eggs?"

Finn stopped in his tracks, heart thudding hard against his ribs. "With chives?"

"I was thinking scallions."

"Fresh coffee?"

"With cream."

"So you're asking me to stay for supper?"

She took a deep breath, then plunged into this uncharted ocean called love. "*We're* asking you to stay."

He saw Lizzie, smiling broadly, a few feet behind her mother and suddenly he knew everything would be all right.

Scrambled eggs today. *I love you* tomorrow.

It was only a matter of time.

Epilogue

East Hampton—Fifteen Months Later

"Mom!" Lizzie burst into the sun-splashed solarium like a late-summer hurricane. "They're threatening to start the ceremony without you."

"Look at this!" Hayley crouched down and fiddled with a sugary blossom with the tip of her palette knife. "The gladioli are off center. I . . . just . . . need to—"

"Mom!" Lizzie's voice rose an octave. "I'm not kidding! You have to stop now!"

"You're right. I'm obsessing. I know I'm obsessing. It's just that it's a lot easier to worry about the cake instead of whether Aunt Fee found her glasses or if Lou from the dry cleaners will hit CeCe up for a fiver to hold her seat at the reception." She looked over at her daughter and her heart rose up into her throat. "Oh, honey!" she breathed, the cake temporarily forgotten. "You're beautiful!"

Willow had spent months picking out just the right gowns for each of the attendants and she had done a spectacular job. Each dress was different and was meant to represent the personality of the woman wearing it. Hayley had worried that Willow's fashionista tendencies would lead to some odd choices but once again she had underestimated her. Lizzie's dress was a sunny lemon-yellow silk confection that suited the sixteen-year-old's good nature and her rapidly growing maturity. Lizzie had always been a very pretty girl but suddenly Hayley could see the beautiful young woman she was becoming.

Lizzie looked almost unbearably pleased as she twirled in front of Hayley. "Tracy said it makes me look eighteen."

"Eighteen?" She pretended to shiver. "Time moves fast enough, honey. Don't push it along any faster."

Lizzie, of course, gave her the same blank look Hayley had given her own mother years ago during a similar conversation and she knew the day would come when Lizzie's daughter delivered a variation on the theme.

But time really did move faster with every passing year. Wasn't it just yesterday when she had carried Lizzie everywhere in her Snugli? Once upon a time her worries had revolved around the transition to solid food and when to send the binky into permanent exile. Next year her baby would be heading off to college.

"Gladioli," she muttered, in an attempt to stem the flow of tears threatening her mascara. "Nobody in her right mind would pick gladioli... What was I thinking... Daisies... peonies... anything but gladioli." They were too tall, too fragile, they would fall over long before the cake-cutting ceremony. They weren't what a sane cake decorator would choose for the most important project of her life.

Lizzie reached out and grabbed for the palette knife but Hayley was too fast for her.

"Mom, you really have to let it go. The cake is amazing. If you keep messing around with it, you'll ruin it."

"Hello," Hayley said. "Have we met? Your mother's a worrier." She stepped back again and examined the towering pyramid of vibrantly tinted sugar-paste flowers with a critical eye. Letting go had never come easily for her, whether it was a child, a cake, or a way of life. "I don't know about the ribbons. I think I should have triple braided them near the bottom." Nobody on the East Coast did a triple braid. She would have knocked this assignment right out of the park.

"Too late now," a familiar voice declared. "It's showtime."

Tommy, resplendent in Armani, was standing in the doorway. Jane, fragile but still a force to be reckoned with, was at his side. She wore a vintage dress from the 1950s that reminded Hayley of something Katharine Hepburn might have worn if Hepburn had been an eighty-something professor of oceanography who once upon a time had a fling with a rock star.

"She's a perfectionist," Tommy said to the mother of his first child. "She must get that from you."

"And she's running late," Jane said with a chuckle in her voice. "I know she gets that from you."

Tommy looked over at Hayley. "Did you forget there's going to be a wedding on the beach in twenty minutes?"

"So I've heard," Hayley said as a wave of love for those two very different people washed over her. "I'm almost finished here."

"The cake is perfect," Jane said. "Don't touch a thing!"

"That's what I told her," Lizzie said. "It's her best ever but she's worried about the gladioli."

Hayley cocked her head. "Anybody want to take credit for the worry gene?" She grinned at the theatrical silence. "Somehow I didn't think so."

She finally put down her palette knife.

"That's my girl," Tommy said. "Now let's get this show on the road."

"Wait until you see the baby," Jane said with an indulgent smile as she reached up and smoothed a lock of Hayley's hair. "Willow dressed her in that little outfit you knitted for her."

Tommy beamed with fatherly pride. "She looks like a princess, doesn't she?"

"Amanda *is* a princess," Hayley said. "She's the only munchkin I know of who has a Maserati and driver."

"Your father likes to spoil his children," Jane observed. "There's nothing wrong with that."

Hayley and Lizzie exchanged amused looks. This from a woman who lived the life of the mind. Times were definitely changing.

"Where's John?" Hayley asked. Her mother and stepfather had rarely been seen apart since their wedding over a year ago.

"Waiting down on the beach with Finn and Anton and the guests."

"Good luck finding him in that crowd from Lakeside." Tommy shook his head in bemusement. "Didn't anyone stay home to mind the town?"

"I warned you." Hayley put down her palette knife. "You can't stand up in a pizzeria and invite everyone to a wedding and expect them not to show up."

Especially not if you were a rock star with a mansion in the Hamptons, a private jet, and a yacht that slept twelve.

Funny how quickly those things had stopped mattering to her. The fancy house, the cars, the shock of seeing a superstar rummaging in her fridge for a can of soda—in the blink of an eye it had all faded away until she saw only the man with the same blue-green eyes she saw in her mirror every morning.

Her father.

She had lived for thirty-eight years without him, but now that he was part of her life, she couldn't quite remember how she had managed.

Everything Finn had said about him was true. Tommy Stiles was one of the good guys. If she let him, he would shower both her and Lizzie with everything their hearts desired. An updated kitchen for Goldy's, a separate shop for the cake-decorating side of the business, an Ivy League education for Lizzie. Fancy cars, designer clothes, all the trappings of celebrity with none of the work. Saying no wasn't always easy, especially when it came to Lizzie and all the things she wanted for her future. But she still believed that hard work and talent mattered and she knew that her father believed it too.

All of her protests, however, hadn't been enough to dissuade Tommy from surprising her with the most spectacular thirty-ninth birthday gift on the planet when he bought out Michael's share of Goldy's Bakery and presented Hayley with papers declaring her sole owner.

"For all the birthdays I missed through the years," he had said over her protests.

"But I can't . . . I don't want—"

"I know," he said, "and I respect that. What you do with Goldy's is up to you. All I did was help get Michael Goldstein out of the picture."

Tommy's openhearted generosity had freed her from financial responsibility to her ex-husband and made it possible for her to plow a percentage of the growing profits into expanding the operation. Without the endless worry about what Michael would do next to undermine Goldy's, she had discovered a sense of joy in her work that she hadn't imagined possible and that joy was quickly translating into a new level of success.

Her tenderhearted daughter had derived great comfort from the fact that her father was financially solvent. Hayley, who was considerably less tenderhearted when it came to her ex-husband, derived comfort from the fact that at least for the moment he was living in the Bahamas and out of their lives. She still worried about what he would do when the money ran out but for now she was able to keep her anxiety to a reasonable level, a goal she hadn't attained since high school.

Not surprisingly, the publicity about her connection to Tommy had bumped up business at Goldy's. To her delight, most of the new customers quickly became regulars. Being Tommy Stiles's daughter had caught the public's attention, but nobody would pay thousands of dollars for an elaborate cake if the baker couldn't deliver the goods.

Six months ago *InStyle* featured her in a four-page spread about up-and-coming cake decorators. The phone rang off the hook for weeks after the issue hit the stands. Being named "Best in the Northeast" last month by the Food Network didn't hurt either. The phone was still ringing thanks to that one.

While the tabloids embraced her as the latest member of the Stiles clan, her siblings hadn't been too sure about the working-class single mother from South Jersey and, to be honest, she hadn't been overly impressed with the spoiled rich kids from East Hampton. Over time she developed a cordial relationship with her half sisters and half brothers, a warm one with their children, and an amused friendship with her grandmother CeCe.

To everyone's surprise but Hayley's, Willow had become a good friend. She enjoyed helping the new mother decode baby

Amanda's signals and watching as Willow gained confidence in her new role. She had the feeling this marriage would be the one that finally lasted.

Despite their misgivings about Hayley, the extended Stiles clan had welcomed Lizzie into their circle immediately and without reservation. At a time when her daughter needed it most, these strangers who happened to be family opened their hearts to the girl and Hayley would be forever grateful. Family could break your heart but they could also heal your soul and that was exactly what they had done for Lizzie.

Lizzie had a tough time dealing with her father's treachery but she was a Maitland woman, which meant she was strong and smart and resilient and those attributes rose to the top like heavy cream. Hayley was proud of Lizzie for coming to terms with the way things were with Michael and accepting the fact that they were unlikely to change.

"We'd better make our way down to the beach," Jane said to Lizzie. "I walk a little slower these days."

Lizzie smiled at her grandmother and Hayley felt a burst of joy deep inside her heart. Thank God their estrangement had been short-lived. Their time with Jane was growing short and she wanted Lizzie to treasure every moment.

"Looks like it's just the two of us," Tommy said as Lizzie and Jane left the room.

"Seems like," Hayley said over the huge lump that had suddenly lodged in her throat. The moment had finally arrived.

"You look beautiful," he said.

"Like a forty-year-old princess?" she teased.

"Like yourself," he said. "Which is even better."

She watched as he shot his cuffs twice then tugged at the hem of his perfectly tailored jacket.

"You're not nervous, are you, Tommy? I mean, this isn't your first time."

So that was what a sheepish grin looked like. "I'm always nervous. There's something about walking your daughter down the aisle that shakes a man to his core no matter how many times he's done it."

"And here I was counting on you for a little wedding-day advice."

They locked eyes and started to laugh.

"You might want to rethink that, honey. I've made my share of mistakes."

"I know," she said. "And most of them were on the cover of *People* magazine."

"At least I don't have to keep a scrapbook. The tabloids do it for me." He considered her for a long moment. "How about you?"

"Everything's perfect," she said, "and it's freaking me out. I keep waiting for something to go wrong and nothing has. That's not normal." At least not for her.

"Perfect is good," he said.

"On a cake," she said. "In real life, it makes me nervous."

"Do you love him?" Leave it to Tommy to cut right through to the heart of it.

Her breath caught in her throat. "So much it hurts."

Tommy gave her one of those smiles that had launched a thousand magazine covers. "And I know he loves you."

She had put Finn through his paces and he had proved his love every single time. Another guy might have thrown up his hands and walked out, but not Finn. Whether it was cheering Lizzie's soccer team, pitching in at the bakery, or making love, he was the best partner she could ever ask for.

"Yes," she said, matching his smile with one of her own. "He loves me."

Every time she raised the bar Finn met the challenge with compassion, understanding, and just enough of a rocker's edge to keep things interesting. But old habits were hard to break and she was still having trouble believing that silver linings didn't always hide big, dark clouds.

"So what's the problem?" her father demanded. "The man is giving up the Hamptons to live in Lakeside. If that isn't love, I don't know what is."

She couldn't argue the point. They had it all: love and friendship and great sex and in a handful of minutes they were going to say their vows in front of everyone who mattered to them and become a real live family.

So why was she still waiting for the other shoe to drop?

Finn had teased her that an entire warehouse of shoes could drop and she would still find something else to worry about. She had laughed at his joke but a small secret part of her wouldn't have minded the fall of at least one sandal, just to prove this was still her life. She thought of it as the worrier's equivalent of a good-luck charm.

The weather was beautiful. The paparazzi hadn't found them. Michael was far away in the Bahamas. Lizzie loved Finn almost as much as Hayley did. Jane was still with them. CeCe and Fee had given one another a wide berth. Her siblings were there to celebrate with her and so far Lou hadn't tried to extort parking fees from any of the guests.

Things were as close to perfect as any bride could wish.

Too perfect, she thought as Tommy took her arm and they made their way down the beach to where the wedding party was gathered together, bathed in the glow of the setting sun. Perfect wasn't normal. She and Michael had had a perfect wedding and see how that had ended up.

A couple of raindrops. A short-lived family argument. A seagull with great aim. Something, *anything*, to take the edge off and turn fate's attention away from her happily-ever-after ending and onto something less important, like world peace or global warming.

Tommy's cousin Bobby, a priest from South Jersey, smiled at her as she and Tommy approached the temporary altar some fifty feet from the water's edge. Anton,

Finn's best man, smiled at her too. Lizzie and Jane and John and Willow and Aunt Fee all beamed at her. Everywhere she looked she saw familiar faces with big happy smiles aimed in her direction.

But where was Finn?

She scanned all of those familiar faces, looked right, looked left, and just as she was about to look for a runaway groom in a row-boat, the crowd parted and she saw Finn, barefoot and in a tux, next to a mountain of shoes.

Manolo sandals. Crocs. Flip-flops. A pair of bowling shoes. Wingtips. Sneakers with candy-striped laces. Penny loafers. Dominatrix boots she would have a few questions about later on. Tommy's platforms from the '70s. A tiny pair of Amanda's Mary Janes.

A mountain of Madagascar vanilla beans couldn't have made her happier.

"I did the calculations," Finn said, "and the way I see it, these should get us through to our golden anniversary."

She started to laugh. "*You* did the calculations?" Finn had many talents but math wasn't among them.

He winked at Lizzie, who was laughing

too. "Okay, so maybe I had a little help but the research is sound."

The beach, the altar, family and friends, everything and everybody faded away until nothing remained but the incredibly silly, incredibly wonderful mountain of shoes and the man she loved.

She did the only logical thing she could do under the circumstances: she thrust her bouquet into his hands, gathered up her skirts, then took off toward the water with Finn and the entire guest list on her heels.

She stopped at the water's edge and glanced at Finn over her shoulder. "That will never get us to our fiftieth."

Lizzie opened her mouth to protest but Finn played along. "Are you sure?"

"Positive," she said as she slipped off her shoes, "but I know what will!"

Willow shrieked, "Those are Manolos!" as Hayley spun the shoes overhead by their slender ivory straps, then sent them sailing out into the ocean. They landed with a pricey splash, then disappeared beneath the waves, taking the last of her worries with them.

Ten minutes later Father Bobby said the words everyone had been waiting to hear.

"Fifty years," she whispered to Finn as their friends and family cheered. "How does that sound?"

He looked at Lizzie and winked, then swept Hayley into his arms.

"Like a good start," her husband said.